Haunted Robots Reviews

"I just read Haunted Robots by Warner & Kule, which took me to the edge of my chair again and again. This fast-paced story got under my skin, and also explored what was 'under' the skins of robots, androids and military types. It is a classic battle of who takes control of the future and leads us to answers about who we all really are!

"Good science fiction grabs the reader and takes you on a journey of unexpected twists, deep characters, rich imagery, and Haunted Robot delivers in abundance. It confronts the dilemma of interactions between human and robot, and war machines versus help. An entertaining read that may keep you up at night."

~ Tracy Repchuk, 7-Time #1 International Amazon.com Best Selling Author and Top Woman Speaker in the World Online Business Strategy

"*Haunted Robots* is an unusual and often whimsical story of a disparate group of characters, android and otherwise, who find themselves drawn together in a race to uncover and flee from a black-ops-type conspiracy involving unknown shadowy agencies. Definitely thought-provoking and decently entertaining."

~ Anthony Wells, U.K. musician

"Isaac Asimov meets Dan Brown in a philosophical thriller challenging, 'Who are we?' A thought-provoking look at one of mankind's oldest riddles. A terrific read."

~ Darcey Hollingsworth, Entrepreneur, Avid Reader – Clearwater, FL

"Very intriguing. Love the plot and how it promises good, fast reading right from the start. I was taken into a world I intend to stay in all the way to the back cover and possibly beyond."

~ Billie Wegmann, Executive Director - Celebrity Centre, Munich, Germany

James Patrick Warner
Ronald Joseph Kule

HAUNTED ROBOTS

Based on a story by
MICHAEL E. NOLL

Haunted Robots
by
James Patrick Warner & Ronald Joseph Kule

Published by The Haunted Robots LLC
Clearwater, Florida

ISBN: 978-0-9997243-0-9 (paperback)
978-0-9997243-1-6 (ebook)

Cover & Design/layout by: Van-garde.com

Edited by: KuleBooks LLC

Printed in the United States of America

Acknowledgements

Michael E. Noll's inspiring idea and story
motivated the writing of this book.

We thank Anita Moore for the opening scenario.

To all our friends and family members, who passed away not-knowing where they might be going next... may it not always be so.

PREFACE

THE MORNING SUN HIGHLIGHTED A single, red-tailed hawk gliding above Robotics Lab Director, Doctor Oren Stanson, Ph.D., who looked across the nearly dry arroyo far below him. Fists clenched, he rued his latest argument with Brigadier-General Roger Rogers over the limited uses of their newly developed robots bound for the armed forces.

THWAK! Suddenly, Stanson's injured body was hurtling down the cliff-side, mere inches from its rocky wall. When it slammed into and bounced off the side, flashes of a too-bright light surrounded him, and he lost consciousness.

SPLAT! His head and torso smashed against the flat-rock bottom of the trickling, late-summer streambed—unwitnessed by another soul.

Intense silence, excruciating pain, and incongruent thoughts followed: *Got to feed Tes... kiss Ingrid... eat chicken soft tacos... and find my way home!*

His mind reeled on: *What the hell? Am I dead? If so, where's the tunnel? Where's the bright light?*

Stanson, indeed, was still alive, but he felt lighter and he could not see, at first. And then the clouded vision of the smashed body lying broken and bleeding in the streambed far below him, and the water bloodied crimson, came into view. As well, the slick, rocky face of the cliff slid past him... *downward.*

His ascent took him to the location which only moments before he had stood in unison with his body; where now a dark and faceless figure slipped away from the newly broken fencing designed to protect people from falling.

Hey, you, what are you doing there? STOP!

Stanson screamed, but no sound emerged. Looking back and downward again, his lifeless, smashed body never moved and did not breathe.

No voice! Now what?

Stanson lifted higher until he could see the Robotics Lab, where he had labored for years. Only now, new emotions about it tore at him; he felt helpless, hopeless and disoriented.

Is it under attack? Was I murdered? If so, by whom? And... where is my cat Tes?

Multiple harsh pinpricks of differing magnitude gnawed at his insides. Again, he looked downward.

What on earth is that vulture doing to my body?!

The creature was feasting on it.

What a mess - What a mess! Yet, he was helpless to do anything.

The scavenger picked at the broken head's brain. Right then and there, Stanson knew that he didn't want his body eaten by this, or any other, bird of prey... or wolves... or... something bigger. But all he could do was shiver.

It should have a proper funeral! I must tell someone!

He scanned the area: *No one's here!*

Forlorn sadness gradually enveloped him in a terrible apathy, until, suddenly, he realized something brand-new.

Hey! The pain in my head is gone. Oh wait! I have no head. How am I still thinking? How am I... NOT DEAD?

Overcoming a profound dizziness, Stanson forgot the outcome of his fall, and thought *I have no body?! What the hell?!*

He had feelings and perception, but soon he sensed a tractor-beam—a web of energy pulling him toward... toward what?!

Perhaps, the inevitable destiny of a new identity.

CHAPTER 1 ~ Orientation

HIGH IN THE SIERRA NEVADA Range, the Defense Advanced Research Projects Agency (DARPA) Robotics Lab opened its doors to another day. Sunlight bathed the atrium of the two-story structure built on a plateau above a canyon arroyo carving its way through foothills well to the East of Berkeley, California. Its décor of white-marble floors, alabaster walls and stainless-steel curvatures heralded advanced thinking and technologies. Near the entrance, majestic potted palms added a luster and color to an otherwise drab café where hot breakfasts, lunches and dinners were offered to Lab researchers and other employees who worked there during varied day and night shifts.

Although the Lab did offer accommodations where its scientists might rest during all-nighters, it was not a residence hall. In their leisure hours, all employees lived "down below" in Pollock Pines, a picturesque village situated at a bend in the arroyo a little bit west of the Lab's location higher up.

A 10-foot-high, gated security fence delineated the Lab's campus and butted up to a pathway used regularly by joggers and hikers. A single helipad adjacent to both served as a safe target for incoming military guests associated with the Federal government's robotics project.

Oren Stanson already had four PhDs under his belt by the time DARPA hired him to supervise the manufacture of the world's most advanced miliary robots.

On his first rounds of his last day, he greeted Bionetics Psychologist, Doctor Ingrid Reese, with one of his usual comments, "You're very pretty today, Doctor Reese."

Ingrid Reese was, in fact, easy on the eyes but she hid her looks behind heavy, black-framed reading glasses and long, dark hair that fell often across the top of her forehead and face. Wearing little makeup and, most days, a gray pantsuit that hugged her curvaceous shape, all of which she hid under her Lab coat, she worked at presenting a demure, all-business look and demeanor because of her shyness. Every time Stanson complimented her, however, she tingled all over.

"Thank you, Doctor," she blushed in reply, turning away. Reese knew her "science"—after all, she, too, had earned several degrees—but she was not too sure of her role as a woman.

"How are the bionetic functional diagrams coming?" the Director asked.

"V-very well, Doctor."

"Good. Keep up the good work."

The Director continued his daily, walkabout routine, and Doctor Reese watched him go. Sighing, she finished up some detail work before she broke work for a morning coffee in the café.

The five S-series robots being worked on in the glassed-in main room of the Lab were identical, except for alphanumeric designations painted in large characters on the backs of their heads: S1, S2, S3, S4, S5. Their seamless skin, a material called Liquid Metal, stretched across their titanium-alloy skeletons and replicated the layered design of human skin. Throughout the robots' internal structures microscopically thin diamond wires transmitted signals from bionetic brains to the robots' extremities and back—a network much like a miniature Internet. Their chest and stomach cavities contained power-pack systems run on electrical storage batteries. A covered, multi-purpose plug on their left waist hosted re-charging and data-transfer ports.

The robots' faces bore masculine features and expressive eyes. An anti-radiation protective layer sprayed onto their heads allowed for safe operation in highly radioactive environments for the 24-hour duration of their power supply, though they would not survive a nuclear direct-hit.

Each robot emitted a subtle-energy field designed to affect humans in their vicinity by making them feel affection or trust toward it. Bionetic designer Linda Flynch had thought such a field would help them assimilate into the human community but she, not having thought through the combined effect of every robot being turned on in the same place all at once, had on more than a few occasions experienced around them passes that were more affectionate than she had bargained for; or which she could ever have expected, based on the field of study from which she had graduated: the "Man Comes from Mud" theorists.

Robot S1 was classified as Transcription Class. Lead Programmer Hank Mellon had worked nearly a year to program S1 with advanced voice-recognition software. S1 could identify every team member's voice recorded with handheld recorders, though it still had trouble with phone-call recognitions.

Maintenance Class Robot S2 had "learned" to remember where the cleaning supplies were stored, and how to use them, without Mellon's programming.

Robot S3 was a Sniper-Class, military-grade weapon that was deadly against targets equipped with ID code radio chips. His visual face- and body-mapping routines still required more advanced development evidenced by his friendly-fire mishaps average of one out of every four trials, which satisfied only the military liaison to the Lab, U.S. Signal Corps Brigadier-General Roger Rogers. Even Rogers' superiors at the Pentagon felt the percentage number of incidents gone wrong was not good enough to pass the PR/smell test of news-media personnel embedded in war zones. This ongoing disagreement constantly rankled Rogers, who, in turn, consistently got under everybody else's emotional skin daily at the Lab.

Aquatic Class Robot S4 was equipped with underwater intake and filtration apparatus and taught how to don hand and foot flippers. Unfortunately, though an excellent swimmer, in ocean trials it tended to take out (kill) any aquatic life form larger than a man that it encountered. And so, for now, S4 was considered merely a developmental-stage robot.

Robot S5, albeit fully programmed, lay in storage, never fully activated. It provided a baseline prototype for comparison use only.

"BJ" Rogers—the not-so-friendly nickname spoken only behind his back had a decidedly "blue" hue attached to it—took a phone call in his spacious office overlooking the array of hardware in the main room of the robotics factory. In charge of military oversight and security for the entire robotics project, he employed two uniformed guards permanently stationed outside of his door, and another inside his office. In no time, he once again started to pace back and forth, wave his arms, and yell into his cell phone.

"Sir, I can no longer abide that idiot Stanson. If he keeps up his useless rant about using our military machines as domestics, I'll be sick. What I might do won't be a pretty sight, I'll guarantee you that!"

He then had to listen to the callers' muffled response, but he kept on stomping around the office.

"Sir, I understand you need this project to go through. I get that, but I need it to go through as planned."

Rogers was told to shut up and listen, so he listened some more; this time while pulling on his lower lip.

He muttered aloud, "Sir, if I can just get this maniac to shut up long enough to get my mission completed…"

His caller, cutting him off, admonished him again.

"… Yessir. I'm hearing your words, sir… I understand, sir. But, sir, when can I get out of here and get myself back into a real command?"

He pulled on his lips and twitched from the upbraiding he had to endure for saying that.

"Yessir, yessir; understood, sir. But, every other day I get this lecture from him about how we should be keeping the peace at home with our product (the robots), instead of only making war and helping soldiers. I just cannot deal with him any longer."

He paused and held the phone away from his ears, because now his Pentagon superior easily could be heard shouting at him.

Rogers sighed. He dropped his head and shoulders.

"Yessir. Whatever you say, sir. We'll probably have all the bugs worked out within a week. Anyway, if that insect—ha-ha—will just shut up and do his job… The thing is, he acts like he's the one in charge here! What a joke! I'm in charge around here, sir!"

He pulled on his lip again; then pulled on his ear lobe; then twitched his face muscles incessantly. His eyes started to blink and twitch rapidly. His buzz-cut hair stood higher on end, but he kept his mouth shut and listened in silence.

"Yes, sir. Thank you, sir. Goodbye for now, sir."

He hung up the phone and looked toward the door to his office, yelling, "Sergeant, get in here right now. I have something urgent for you to do."

Later, BJ Rogers walked into the lunchroom café and ordered a coffee. Spotting Doctor Reese sitting alone, he approached her and, sporting a lascivious smile, asked, "Is this seat taken?"

In reply, Reese tittered self-consciously but she allowed him to sit at her table.

"Doctor Reese, do you have those functional diagrams DARPA has been requesting?"

"Just finishing them up now, General."

"OK. Good. We'll need to sort out why we can't get our battle-performance specs tighter. As you know, we're rapidly approaching the finish dateline."

"Right, I know. We will get them, sir. I'll have them for you this evening."

"Saturday night?! That's the team spirit, Doctor!"

He paused long enough to get her undivided attention before he spoke some more: "Say, would you like to have dinner with me tomorrow night? We could celebrate..."

He never finished his sentence. He just smiled that smile at her and watched Reese's lips as she opened her mouth and closed it, and then, flustered and red-faced, put her hands up to her mouth.

Rogers was about to offer up another advance, when the Director came up behind him on his way to the elevator. He had heard most of their conversation and was aggravated past normal as he approached. He turned toward Rogers.

"I still say we should create robots that can be used in multi-function environments, not just battlebots," he snapped at Rogers, continuing their ongoing daily battle.

"Bullshit!" Rogers roared, standing and spilling his coffee on his pants.

Stanson continued, ignoring his mishap, "We have already assigned various functions to the ones we're working on now. They're doing great at different tasks. An automated-robot factory setup could build several types of domestic robots, plus the battlebots. They could also replace themselves as needed. That would be cost effective…"

He never got to finish the thought, because Rogers took over.

"Listen, Stanson, your stupid notion would be a real security nightmare! I already told you, 'What's done is done!' Dammit, it's a 'done deal', Stanson!"

Growling louder than usual, Rogers jumped up, in the process overturning his table. "Don't you understand that?!" he shouted at Stanson.

Fearful, Reese backed away from Roger's vicinity, which, seeing his chances of having a date with her go south, irked him even more.

"Just zip it, Stanson!" he yelled—his face reddened a deeper hue as he stabbed a napkin at the growing coffee stain on his pants.

Stanson and Reese said nothing. They just stared at him.

Seeing the way Reese was shaking, Rogers dialed himself down, took a deep breath.

"Stanson, the military hired you to perfect these machines, not go all blubbery about their uses. DARPA is paying for these robots to assist warfighters in combat situations, and that's the end of it! End of story. Don't talk to me about this again. Besides, I couldn't change the plan even if I wanted to, which I don't."

He looked again at Reese and saw she was totally disinterested in him now, setting him off again. He shook visibly. His face went purple, and his mouth drooled enough that he had to keep wiping at it as he went on:

"This argument is academic. DARPA pays for the god-damned things we make around here, and it will use them as it sees fit... and right now that's to save warfighters' lives in combat!"

Stanson didn't move a muscle or say a word.

"I've heard all your bleeding-heart crap before, Stanson! This conversation is over!" he shouted. As he stood and walked away, he added, "... Someone pick up that god-damned table!"

Stanson also stormed away, his Italian complexion unusually colored. He knew he was not going to win this argument with DARPA backing Rogers. On the way out, he picked up his cat Tes, whom he'd named after the famed scientist and inventor, Tesla, and he stalked out of the café and the lab building for a cooling off in the direction of the nature path.

With the two men gone, Ingrid Reese's mood had changed. Her fear had turned into pangs of grief-filled loss for her Director to leave so upset and angry.

Outside and headed toward the nature path, Stanson thought more in terms of how robots could help firefighters, police, and search and rescue units fighting natural disasters and performing emergency medical procedures. The idea of putting his "jewels" (how he thought of his S-series robots) into war zones still seemed a huge waste of every taxpayer dollar of their billion-dollar price tags.

Looking out over the adjacent canyon, holding his forehead with one hand and Tes with the other, Stanson moaned aloud to no one, "Oh God! I know I'm really nothing more than a highly paid office manager, but I want to do something useful. I haven't personally created these robots, but they feel like they're mine; and they have such grand potential...'

As his thought drifted away, the good doctor took a deep breath and shook off his temper. His mind turned to Reese. He was fond of her. He had noted that she was an attractive young woman, although incredibly shy. Smiling, he decided to invite her to dinner "down below" in Pollock Pines, where he knew a good Spanish restaurant had opened in the neighborhood.

Perfect he told himself, feeling calmer. Pushing his glasses higher up on his nose, he prepared to turn and go back to his office. Suddenly, Tes stiffened and leapt away.

Stanson never saw what spooked her; instead, he felt something strike him hard across his face. Mimicking the sound of a baseball bat smacking a homer, a THWAK! smote the air around him like lightning at close range. A split-second later, his body hurtled down toward the bottom of the arroyo.

Simultaneously, as silently as it had appeared where he stood, a shadowy figure clothed in a dark hoodie, black pants and black athletic shoes slipped away into the shadows from which it had come, unscathed and unseen.

Two morning joggers chattering to each other passed by going in the opposite direction on the pathway. They never noticed anything out of place... or that a murder had just taken place nearby.

Chapter 2 ~Crime Scene

THE OTHER RESEARCHERS AND STAFFERS were unaware of the café drama incident or of Stanson's demise. As usual, their job positions and duties had held their attention all morning.

National Security Agency and the Central Security Service (NSA and CSS) employee Doctor (Colonel) Phillip Cornwalls was second in command at the Lab behind Doctor Stanson. His post commanded the absolute secrecy of the project, as well as security at the facility. Whenever civilian or military personnel became incapacitated or were compromised in any way, or otherwise unable to perform their duties, his authority was absolute. A swarthy man, his looks recalled Hollywood stars of yesterday: tall with dark curly hair, rugged good looks and an athletic build.

Hank Mellon, the mechanical designer who built the robots' skeletons and external skin, was also their chief programmer. His pedigree included construction of new robots at his previous employer Lockheed Skunkworks, where he enjoyed an unlimited budget. He was lured away to the Lab by a contract that dangled too much money to deny in front of his eyes. Those rewards brought his talents to Stanson's Lab, and he performed well for him; however, he did tend to tipple. Others had noticed that his coffee cup filled with the French roast that he preferred often included an infusion of some top-shelf bourbon. Mellon maintained an air of personal pride over the Liquid Metal skin he'd developed, albeit DARPA owned the two patents for it.

Now living with Hank Mellon, Bionetics Specialist Linda Flynch had been employed by DARPA to design and build robot "brains" and central nervous systems. Among other things, she had worked a two-year stint at Lockheed's Austin, Texas facility, where she researched Bionetic computing devices used in secret, advanced-technology, military drones. Mellon and she met at a battlebot competition, where her curvaceous figure, untamed red mane and wicked-fast intellectual prowess telegraphed her volatile personality into Mellon's heart and soul. He had quietly licked his chops, while losing the battle competition to her. With Flynch, he soon discovered, there was never a dull moment. Besides, she was as attracted to him, as he to her. The connection and her resumé brought her to the Lab.

Tes the cat had padded back to the Lab patio and was now trying to re-enter the building. She ran around scratching all the glass walls, jumping high as she could and trying to find a way inside. Finally, she gave up and lay outside the patio door; perhaps, wondering if someone would happen by and open the door.

As the hours of the day passed by, researchers and staff came and went through the lunchroom café. Attracted by their hunger pangs to its big-board menu, pronouncements of the Daily Special brought alternative reactions of "Yippee," shoulder shrugs and disappointed groans from its audience. None of them, however, ventured toward the door where Tes lay sleeping under the warming sun; that is, until Mellon and Flynch noticed that she was alone and not beside her usual companion Director Stanson.

"What's up with Tes?" he said. "Watch her. What's she doing? Where's Director Stanson?"

As if on cue, Tes perked up her ears, and she started scratching the glass door again.

"I heard that Oren earlier left the building angry," said Flynch, turning toward Dr. Reese, who had just walked in.

"Ingrid, did you have another fight with Oren this morning?" Flynch usually picked at Reese just for fun.

Her companion "Hungry Hank," as Mellon had been tagged around the Lab, was hungry. He ignored the chatter near him, preferring to engage in small talk with the café cook—decidedly a non-engineer or scientist—outside of the kitchen, although he did usually like to hear what Mellon opined about on different subjects. The thing about the chef was, he always turned what he heard into kitchen metaphors, that being his milieu:

Mellon: "I've been having a devil of the time with the blue-hues changes in the robot skins..."

Cook: "It's all about the presentation, isn't it? People gotta have a palate for blue..."

Mellon: "It's a historic color..."

Cook: "Most of what I present on plates is green-accented."

Mellon was about to respond to that, but the meanings of cook's words just spoken made him think twice about saying anything. Instead, he ordered the Daily Special and moved on.

Flynch tagging along by Mellon's side with a salad on her tray, was still badgering Reese.

"Ingrid, have you even seen Oren this morning?"

"I saw him making his daily rounds earlier. Why do you ask, Linda?"

She never mentioned the disagreement that had played out between Stanson and Rogers right in front of her eyes at her table.

"He didn't come by to check on my work, which he always does. I wonder what's up," said Flynch as she picked at her salad and looked at Mellon for some backup.

Mellon was too busy manhandling his double-cheese hamburger to notice her attempt at getting his attention.

Reese's mind wandered. She thought about Oren, recalling how strong, handsome, and kind he was toward her. *He's so different from that awful General* she decided.

"He should be around here somewhere." The masculine voice broke both Reese and Flynch out of their thoughtful doldrums. Mellon had finally taken an interest in the ongoing conversation between the two ladies.

"I'm really getting worried now," Flynch said.

"Phillip, will you check the building to see where Oren is? Maybe he's sick or something. It's not like him to miss his rounds." Mellon had spotted Dr. Cornwalls stepping into the café from the elevator.

Cornwalls saluted Mellon, smiled, turned on his heels and departed as quickly as he had come into the café. Ten minutes later, he returned.

"Okay. I saw him on the monitor going out the patio door, but not returning. That was several hours ago."

Deep in the arroyo canyon, no one had raised an alarm until the morning shadows receded, and sunlight on the canyon helped a thirsty hiker notice a strange, red dye polluting the flowing stream of water. Tracing its path upstream, he found Stanson's broken body. By then, the two female joggers on their way back to the starting point of their jog had stopped to take a break. Venturing past the broken fence and peering over the edge of the canyon, they screamed upon seeing the same sight. Alerted by the women's shrieks, a security officer trolling the grounds of the Lab pulled out his cell phone and dialed an alert to his superiors. Seconds later, Cornwalls pressed the campus alarm button, setting off a chain reaction involving the entire Lab-facility's corps of personnel.

Staffer conversations stopped mid-sentence; scientists looked up from their alert-notification computer screens; the robots were instantly inactivated, and entire workstations were abandoned... replaced by chattering whispers among small cliques of employees headed outside of the building and outside of the gated campus toward the edge of the plateau where the cacophony had started.

Within minutes, an Air-Evac helicopter landed on the Lab's helipad. Four military medics—Cornwall's minions—joined the scene from the craft. One of them shouted his update to Cornwall loud enough for anyone else close enough to hear his words and take in his message.

"Sir, we've got men down in the canyon. The call came from a hiker who discovered a body, and we're wrapping up the "package" right now."

"Do you know, yet, who the person might be?"

"It appears to be Oren Stanson, sir. We'll have a better chance of identifying the body once we get him up here."

A pall of silence dropped over the crowd. Those able to peer over the ledge watched the emergency crew prepare a body bag and portable gurney for the airlift to be undertaken by the helicopter crew, which had already left the pad and was flying down to the arroyo with a dropped cable dangling beneath it.

Thirty minutes later, the airlift landed the remains on the grass near the helipad. The cable attached to the basket containing the body was released, and the chopper left the scene.

In the meantime, an ambulance had passed through the guarded, open fence gate and now it was being driven to the site in preparation for accepting the transfer of the remains to it.

A civilian, local police officer on the scene stepped forward and asked the crowd, "Other than me, who's in charge here?"

Cornwalls stepped up.

"I am, officer. We have not been able to locate our Director Oren Stanson, who is normally in charge, so I guess that leaves me for now. I am second in command. What's happening here?"

"First, let me remind you that outside of that fence – he pointed to the fencing surrounding the campus - you are in my jurisdiction. Is that clear?

"Yessir."

"Good, then. We have found a dead body in the arroyo. I'd like you to have a look and see if you can identify the remains before we transport it away."

The crowd pressed forward, wanting to see, but a cordon of other police officers coordinating with a squad of Cornwall's men, pushed them back gently.

The medical team unzipped the body bag. Cornwalls stepped closer and looked down into the bag. He nodded to the police officer.

"It's Director Stanson."

A detective also on hand for the event, who had just arrived, engaged Cornwalls in a line of questioning, but he wrapped it up soon, knowing that this appeared to be a simple case of a mistaken fall and subsequent death. There seemed to be no hint of a homicide.

Cornwalls returned to his group of anxious staff who stood at the Lab door by the patio, having been asked by the policemen and the military squad to return to the confines of the Lab campus. Questioning them would come later; for now, they listened to the news from Cornwalls.

"Well, I'm sorry to say the body they discovered is undoubtedly that of Director Stanson."

Ingrid Reese gasped, stumbled and fainted in Linda Flynch's arms. Flynch herself barely could hold her weight; she was distraught, and tears puddled on her blouse.

The rest of the crowd stood in stunned silence, most of them weeping, whispering and questioning what had gone so wrong for them today.

Acting-Director Cornwalls stepped up and took charge of his people: "I am so sorry. Feel free to take the rest of the day off with pay. We will have a staff meeting first thing tomorrow morning."

He turned to Mellon and gave him instructions.

"Hank, will you, please, inform General Rogers?"

"Sure thing, boss." Hank Mellon got along with everyone in any situation. He was a team player all the way.

With Reese broken down into uncontrollable tears, Flynch put her arms around her and walked her slowly back into the main building.

The ambulance driver noticed Dr. Stanson's cat Tes, by looking into his outside rear-view mirror. She was trying to climb into the back of his vehicle. He got out of the ambulance and walked over to her. Recognizing him, she let him pick her up. He gently placed her quivering body in Cornwalls' arms before he departed. Watching them drive away, Cornwalls stroked Tes behind her ears.

Tess purred as Cornwalls, now in his office, considered aloud all the changes the next days and weeks would bring to the Lab, not the least of which was the inevitable power struggle that likely would be initiated by Brigadier-General Roger Rogers.

Chapter 3 ~ Investigation

IN THE DAYS THAT FOLLOWED the initial news of his terrible fall, most people at the Lab assumed Stanson's death had been a suicide, especially when rumors of the argument between him and General Rogers spread around. That was also the assumption of the police. But, those people at the Lab were still in shock from the event. Nothing like that had ever happened on campus, and he had been the glue that kept so many disparate personalities together and functioning as a team. How his death might have happened and what would become of the Lab became the topic of most conversations within the campus community. Also, Doctor Reese began spending a lot of time with Tes around her because she seemed to need the most encouragement to recover and move forward of all the people who worked there.

Phillip Cornwalls had retreated to his locked security office for most of his working hours. There, he checked and rechecked the numerous images secretly recorded on hidden or camouflaged exterior cameras. Only he and General Rogers had been privy to the knowledge that the Lab had military-grade cameras located outside of its perimeter, which were trained on every angle of activities within the campus territory. There were many more trained on the surrounding plateau; on these recordings Cornwalls focused most of his attention.

Recordings from the day of the director's passing clearly showed four early-morning hikers standing near the view-spot where Stanson had joined them. It was obvious that neither the hikers nor Stanson had addressed each other before the hikers left the area.

The progression of the taped recording revealed the later presence of a lone person, perhaps a jogger, dressed in black running shoes and a black, hoodie sweatshirt pulled up over the head enough to obscure the face. This newcomer appeared to be separate from other hikers and joggers passing by, and he or she – it was difficult to tell in the early-morning shadows – lingered in the area past when other people were around, save for Stanson.

Then, as he inched forward to his monitor screen, Cornwalls saw a movement he had missed before. He enlarged the picture as much as possible without losing all semblance of definition and watched, horrified, as he saw the shadowy figure pull something looking a lot like a small, portable tire iron from his waistband and move quickly and stealthily in the direction of the Director.

A flash motion suddenly slammed into the front of Stanson's head, followed by a quick push that sent the victim over the safety fencing at the cliff's edge.

Cornwalls, aghast from the news his eyes had just delivered to him, rewound the tape and watched it over and over in slow motion. The details of the lone figure's swift actions previously had not been available to him by playing the recording at normal speed. Here, though, for the first time, was irrefutable evidence that Stanson's demise was the result of a nefarious act committed against him!

Upon further review, the recording also showed the previously seen hikers returning in the opposite direction from where they had walked away earlier, while Stanson was still alive and breathing. They were unaware in the pre-morning darkness of the crime that had just been committed almost in their midst. And they did not appear to notice the diminutive figure dressed in black as he turned away from them and quickly trotted past the Lab gate and off camera.

Cornwalls ordered an assistant to cue up another recording which might be able to catch more of the lone figure's movements after he left the original spot where he attacked Stanson. Watching the new tape, he could see that the person had jogged toward the lower end of the pathway and off the paved trail, well out of sight of anyone who might have chanced to see him. Before he disappeared into the distance, he could be seen— again, with an enlargement of the screen image—to hurl at a high arc the bloodied tire iron past the cliff ledge.

Another taped recording, this one with a sound track, had captured Tes' forlorn "meows" and saw her race through the security fence to the front door of the Lab, where she commenced scratching at the glass.

No other recording shed more light on what went on that morning, but Cornwall by then had seen and heard all he wished. He knew without a doubt that Stanson's death had come at the hands of another; he knew, also, the nature of the homicide he had suspected all along. His new question now became when and with whom he would reveal and share the evidence of what really had happened. After all, he alone had seen the murderous act, and he was surrounded by scores of people, military and civilian... any one of whom might be the assassin!

Cornwalls decided to keep this information to himself for the present, at least until he would be pressed to give it up to the local police authorities. His plan was to delve into the mystery first with some advanced imagery software that might allow him a glimpse of the attacker's face. Thinking anyone in the Lab could be involved, he knew that he would have to get the glass data cube up to a lab he knew he could trust in Maryland. There, he would have the image cleaned up enough to hand him the undeniable data that he sought without anyone else being the wiser.

He spent the next several days, which became a couple of weeks, waiting for the Maryland lab's report and enhanced film.

General "BJ" Rogers also had been spending time conferring among his closest cadre of loyal soldiers about the same recent events.

But, when DARPA called, he answered.

Chapter 4 ~ Collusion

The staff of the company leasing the penthouse office of the Bonaventure Hotel in downtown Los Angeles liked to call their boss "C," even though none of them knew where the custom had originated. They also did not know much about him or his background. The rumor was that he had graduated near the top of his class at one of the Ivy-League schools. Because his looks and demeanor had not seemed to change in the time they knew him, most of his employees had assumed that he also had been young, forthright, smart, and a flirt with the females. No one, however, ever had reported a serious transgression about him to Human Resources.

What C's company produced was highly compartmentalized and confidential. None of its employees knew what was the company's actual output. They were all highly paid specialists in their respective fields—something they knew either from mutually shared experience and gossip, or from furtive searches for information on Google. The staff consensus was that they were involved in secret government work. Beyond that, no one ventured to search for more details. Fat bank accounts and overtime hours at the work space don't invite snooping.

With a flip of her shoulder-length, light-brunette mane, C's attractive, young and statuesque personal secretary informed him, "You have a call on the encrypted line, C." She had walked into his office unannounced, placed a dossier on the caller on his desk and walked out without stopping, yet knowing full well what affect her presence was having on her boss.

C's heart skipped a beat or two as he watched her leave before taking the call.

"Thank you, Miss White."

Miss White smiled but never looked back.

C pulled the specially encrypted phone out of a desk drawer and placed it on his desk as he opened the file, finding the heavily redacted documents in it familiar.

"Yes, General Myers. How may I assist you?"

"Is the asset in place?"

"Yes. The Director has been retired. The Operation was clean."

"Very good. The Agency has wired your money. Call me if there is any problem."

The caller hung up.

C hung up and then clicked the same phone twice.

"Yes, C?" said Miss White.

"Miss White, when the S.A.F.E. (Special Account Funded Executions) deposit (a sort of code) clears, please distribute the checks around the office to the special-team members, and then come in to see me. I have a weekend plan to talk over with you."

"Yes, sir." Miss White smiled again, this time longer and larger as she turned to look outside and watch whispery puffs of white clouds float past in the azure skies of Los Angeles. Miss White, C's personal assistant from the project's beginning, was the only person in the organization who knew that "C" stood for Capo, a Mafia family's traditional address to the organizational head.

C also rang up the office intercom system to speak with a classy Oriental employee self-nicknamed "Charlotte" to keep others guessing her real name, who liked to dress traditionally in kimonos.

"Yes, C?"

"Call Mr. Yang at the Pankow Bank and confirm the purchase price. Tell him half on deposit at our bank, the rest on delivery. Make sure he agrees to make his deposit before Thursday afternoon. If there is any hesitation or problem, Charlotte, take Mikey with you to help with negotiations in person.

"Yes, sir."

Chapter 5 ~ The Director Returns

OREN STANSON LEFT BEHIND NO surviving family, so the funeral service down below in Pollock Pines was brief and attended by only a handful of his close friends and employees. The interment service followed immediately. The body was buried on a grassy knoll near the helicopter pad, overlooking the arroyo pass.

DARPA had tasked Cornwalls to solve the murder. Aside from his discovery of the taped information he'd sent to Maryland, he picked up the pieces at the Lab by first commandeering its personnel back to normal and back on schedule. His previous, less-obvious presence had become a constant one, as well as a constant reminder of the tragic turn of events.

In the aftermath of the presumed suicide of the Lab Director—General Rogers and local police still thought it was so—the directorship and program design, planning and definition of robot functions had fallen back to DARPA and its official representative, General Rogers. Without Director Stanson, the team, at first, nearly fragmented and foundered from more dissension over the planned use and mission of the robots. His followers, of course, avowed to expand the robots' usages to zones other than military; those opposed simply maintained silence; they were under orders. Still, the thick tension was so dense that the proverbial knife could cut the air between them.

Cornwalls, concluding the unbalanced Rogers should not remain the Lab's acting military liaison any longer than they had to endure him, accepted secret orders descendent from the NSA/CSS to DARPA and he began acting as the only director in charge of the entire project. When he informed Rogers of his change of status, the General did not take it very well but sucked it up, being the loyalist soldier at heart that he was... on the surface!

Wanting to get to the bottom of every detail of every loose end surrounding the investigation of Stanson's death, early one morning Cornwalls rappelled down the cliff. Alone at the arroyo floor, he looked in the stream waters for clues to the puzzle.

That's when he found the tire iron.

Unlike most, this one was not old and rusty. Handling it carefully, he looked up to the top of the cliff and measured in his mind where someone would have to have stood to have thrown the iron down and have it land where he found it wedged between two thin, flat rocks beneath the stream's surface. Inspecting the piece more closely, he discovered what looked like small, leftover traces of blood on it.

This could be the murder weapon right here in my hands he thought. *Rogers and his circle of local yokels probably never even thought to have the streambed searched. They were so damn sure Stanson had offed himself!*

The notion of that not only pissed Cornwalls off, it also motivated him back up the cliff and to his office with the tire iron safely wrapped inside of a stout plastic bag under his arm. There, he packaged the evidence and personally handed it to a familiar FedEx driver for delivery to a personal office he maintained in Berkeley. He would have a complete analysis worked up about the blood stains in a matter of days.

While the new Acting Director's actions appeared mundane to anyone else who might have been watching, his unseen mind was speeding through alternative conjectures about how the murder had been accomplished, including who had ordered it done. He knew that there was already a mountainous email trail with General Roger's name all over it, sitting on his desk. In his venomous style, Rogers had maligned Stanson, constantly undermining his authority and stating falsely that he was a pacifist, and that he considered him a security threat who was undermining the Lab's morale and deliberately slowing down the production of military robots.

Eliminating verbiage that clearly had no reference to Stanson or the Lab, per se, Cornwalls' research and statistical analysis, instead, shed light on Roger's covert interference across the board at the Lab. No matter how well-intentioned people attested that they had been, or not, the numbers did not lie: the actual cause of Lab personnel and production problems was, then and now, Brigadier-General Roger's covert behavior.

Cornwalls had no choice but to talk to DARPA, which he did. Seeing what Cornwalls saw, that team agreed that the robots' final design and testing would be completed as planned without Roger's presence onboard. It was clear to all involved that such a move would not jeopardize the results of the Lab's work.

However, a separate investigation conducted by the NSA, which submitted its official findings to DARPA's convened Board of Enquiry, confirmed that Rogers had not ordered nor been in any way involved with the death of Doctor Stanson.

That murder would remain unsolved, for now.

Psychologist Reese, as usual, late on a Saturday evening worked at her computer terminal, mindless that an S2 cleaner had joined her in the open-office space. Although she had no illusions that robots were anything other than elaborate constructions capable of executing coded programming, tonight one spooked her. With its crepe, rubber-soled feet and nylon joints operating silently, and her mind a million ideas away from her present environment, when S2 bumped into the back of her chair, she, suddenly terrified, jumped up and screamed before she turned around, faced her intruder and calmed down.

"Oh, hello, S2. How are you this evening?"

"I function optimally," the robot responded unemotionally, while bending down to retrieve her paper garbage, which had spilled out of the turned-over container at her feet. Having gathered all the errant papers and re-placed them into their round-file container, S2 emptied its contents into the garbage hopper of the cleaning supplies cart it pushed around. Next, it placed the garbage can at the exact spot designated for it, while striking a model runway-like pose as it leaned on the edge of the cleaning supplies cart and stared wide-eyed at the young and beautiful Doctor Reese.

At first, Reese did not notice anything unusual. However, when, after a long minute or two it had not moved, she snuck a furtive look out of the corner of her eye and did a double take, quickly putting on an Oscar-winning performance of an "I am non-plussed" attitude, and addressed the robot.

"Is there something else you need, S2?"

"You're very pretty this evening, Doctor Reese."

Reese's mouth and jaw opened to say something and then closed wordlessly; then opened again. Her attitude had fallen by the wayside.

Not a soul had told her that, since Stanson's death, and he alone had said those words to her every Saturday night upon running into her in the Lab; only rarely otherwise.

She adjusted her black-rimmed glasses. A tiny gesture, the act pushed them up on her nose the way she always had done in his presence.

"Excuse me?"

The robot didn't move. "You're very pretty this evening, Doctor Reese," it repeated with the same inflection.

Ingrid Reese, 40-year-old moderately tall brunette with a well-proportioned face, in excellent shape from her self-imposed workouts at the gym near her house "down below," was used to men hitting on her from time to time. In small towns, everyone knows who is single without children.

Reminding herself that it was another Saturday evening and another weekend shift that she had drawn voluntarily, she sighed. She missed Stanson's coming by to check on her work, as he usually did. His humor, his very proper manner—these things she liked about him. But the salutation calling out how she looked... well, she wondered if he really meant it. Suddenly, she broke out of her trance and realized that it had not been Stanson who said it to her this time! *Was this a cruel prank?* she thought. *Had he taught the robot to say this to her?*

"Who taught you to say that to me?"

The robot did not move; it did not change its stance for several seconds - a long time for a robot.

"I did," S2 answered at last.

"I see."

Reese, angry at the insensitivity of someone doing this to her, turned back to her computer terminal and shut it down. Standing up and smoothing her Burberry skirt and fresh, silk blouse, she looked at herself with a compact mirror and applied a fresh coat of color to her lips. Satisfied, she walked to the elevator and pushed the down button.

On the second floor, she stood at a row of vending machines and ended up choosing a cup of tea and a cold, chicken and Swiss sandwich for her evening snack. It wasn't what she really wanted, but with no one manning the snack-shop at this hour it would have to do.

Feeling someone come up behind her, she turned quickly.

It was S2 again, half-leaning on the snack-bar counter near her. *The Director used to stand that way,* she recalled, *when he was about to expound upon some theory about bionetic networks and mind-games to me; he struck that very pose.*

"What is it, S2?" she asked, feeling a little bit rattled.

Had DARPA somehow turned the thing into a killer or something? She couldn't help thinking the thought, but she feigned calmness by gulping her too-hot tea.

Too late! It was, indeed, too hot, and she spilled some on her hand, causing her to spill more tea on the counter and almost lose her grip on the cup. Hastily, she grabbed a napkin to dry her hand and rub the scalded spot on her right thumb.

Presently, she asked, "Are you stalking me, S2?"

"Not at all, Doctor. I just thought you'd like to discuss your work."

"Thank you, S2, you are too kind. You know, I never would have thought that discussing human emotion and reactions to environmental stimuli would ever be interesting to a robot such as yourself."

She still favored her reddened thumb, which smarted, but she was putting on a good front in front of her robot companion.

"You know, Doctor Reese, one never knows until you talk to a robot and see for yourself."

"Are you saying you want to have a philosophical discussion..." Reese asked without thinking, before she stopped herself mid-sentence. What was happening had, at last, sunk in: she was having a real conversation with a robot, including non-programmable non-sequiturs!

She closed her mouth—it had fallen open on the realization—and considered how she should approach this event.

First, I must not ever, ever, tell anyone about this she decided. If either Cornwalls or Rogers heard about it, they would think she had gone over the edge into fantasyland. They could fire her or remand her to another facility, like an outpost in frigid Alaska, or worse, to a spin-bin for extensive psychoanalysis, ECT "treatments," or prescription-drug cocktails.

Second, am I going to continue this charade? This could be an S2 programming team gambit to fool me, or a development that I've not heard about before. Or—her own thought scared her—*a new series of robots capable of analytical thought, problem solving and other similar heuristic challenges; in other words: haunted robots!*

She decided to pursue the game a little further, but S2 made the first move, as if he'd picked up her conclusion telepathically.

"I would very much like that, Doctor Reese. Are you up to it?"

His turn of phrase was eerily like what Stanson would have said in a similar circumstance.

Reese had by now regained her composure and spoke in her best professional tone, "Of course, I'm up for it. Give me your best logic volley."

S2 opened with a disarmingly personal question: "Do you realize that you and I are quite similar?"

Where is this logic coming from? she wondered as she answered, "I don't think so. No, I would say not. I am a biological organism, and you are a mechanical device. So, how are we similar?"

"Think it through, Ingrid..."

How does he know my first name?!

"... I am a created device inhabited by something more... and so are you."

She tried to interrupt, but he continued.

"... Wait, Ingrid. Listen to these similarities: you are a created biomechanical device; you have a brain that is an electronic switchboard; and you possess a mind which, as your colleagues at UCLA are finally discovering, is a wide electronic field that surrounds your body. And DARPA, as you know already, is performing experiments to determine how to access that field directly."

Reese had stopped wondering what was going on and was listening intently to S2's words at this point.

"... Then there is the something or someone directing your body's actions in the use of that field and the interface between it and your body. Three parts, discrete but working together."

"And you are?" she asked S2.

"I am very similar. As you can see, I have a robot body not unlike the old sci-fi android. I have a bionetic brain switchboard, and there is an electromagnetic field allowing me to control and move the body by using my bionetic brain, which, in my case, is being directed by something or someone using that field and its interface. Three discreet parts working together... see?"

Reese had to process all that S2 had just said to her. She stared for quite a while at the robot standing so nonchalantly as if posing right in front of her. As she did so, S2 started to look more and more like the way Doctor Stanson did, when hosting a staff meeting or delivering a lecture.

She chose her next words carefully, "I see the similarities as you pose them, S2, but you were created by us, by humans."

Yet, as she finished her sentence, she saw the fallacy of her logic; and, so did S2.

"I'm sure, Ingrid, you realize that your comparison is not relevant. Of course, humans, like yourself, created me. There wasn't a procreative act, per se, and I didn't grow physically over time; nevertheless, just as I was, you were created by other humans."

S2 rather gloated a bit before sticking in his last dagger, "You want to try again, Ingrid?"

Reese was dumbfounded, not that she wished to show it. She was frustrated, too. Wizened, she understood that she had more research to do, if she was going to carry on this line of thought and debate with S2, or whoever had programmed him.

Exasperated, she fairly shouted, "Who programmed you with this information? Who set up the language, the definitions, and the logic circuits? Dammit, whose running you!?"

This time S2 replied without hesitation.

"Why, I did. And I am, of course!"

There came a pregnant pause, a tiny moment when neither knew what to say, which S2 broke.

"Oh, I get it now! You don't think a cleaning robot would be capable of handling philosophical conundrums, do you?"

"Who is 'I,' then?" she demanded.

"I am I."

The silence in the cavernous, empty office was as timeless as outer space.

"... What a funny question you ask. If I asked you, 'Who is 'I,' what would you say?"

He let that sink in.

"... Let me show you something: I have a mind. I can see a picture of Tes curled up behind me. And I am the one who is looking at the picture of Tes that I created.'"

Reese's eyes blinked rapidly several times. To her credit, she did envision a singular flash of a mental picture of Tes curled up asleep, but she didn't realize what she had seen. Now, she was almost locked in a trance and she needed to be broken out of it.

"By the way, Ingrid, are you feeding Tes? I've been worried about her."

Reese stammered, "We take turns buying her food and cat litter."

"Thank you for that, Ingrid; that puts my mind at rest."

Having said that, S2 turned around and pushed his cleaning cart to the elevator and departed, leaving Reese to stare after him for a long time.

A mixed bag of emotions churned within the good doctor's mind and body. She had so many questions; questions that demanded answers.

Chapter 6 ~ Questions & Answers

THE LAB RETURNED TO ITS normal routine. For the next two weeks, nothing out of the ordinary happened.

Reese still had her questions, which she had revealed to no one, but for the most part they lay dormant in her mind, pushed off in favor of the more pressing matters of her work position. Tonight, though, she was again working the evening shift on a Saturday night. In the daily hustle and challenges of her work, she had managed to forget most details about the bizarre conversation she had with S2, but now it came rushing back to the fore in her mind, because in came S2 pushing his cleaning cart. At the time, she was studying a logic diagram of S3's bionetic brain, trying to find out why it couldn't learn how to do its assignments better.

S2 stood by the cart, as silent as a mouse, and watched Reese for several minutes. Tes, content to have padded over to the cart, laid down on top of it. S2 petted her gently, and the cat purred louder and louder until her sound vibrated the metal trash bin nearby.

Reese, hearing the noise and not recognizing it, looked up and around the lab until she saw S2 with the cart, the cat and the vibrating trash bin.

For some unknown reason, a mental image of the Doctor Seuss book, *The Cat in the Hat*, flashed across her mind, albeit too fast for her to take note of it.

"Good evening, Ingrid. You're very pretty this evening."

She was still trying to collect herself from the shock of seeing him watch over her again. At his statement, she smiled but then frowned, catching hold of herself and once again remembering the absurdity of the last encounter, and how she felt.

"Who did this to you? Why have you been programmed to torment me?"

Holding Tes, S2 walked toward her softly and calmly. He put the cat on her work desk and studied her computer screen without saying a word to Reese.

"That logic circuit is interfering with the emotion-simulation program. That robot will need reprogramming. It needs a better integration sub-routine between its warfighter-support module and its emotion simulator."

He straightened up and turned his head and looked at Reese, expecting her to react and talk to him.

She, in turn, inched forward toward the screen and started to trace the pathway along the logic sub-routines. She easily found where the two software routines did not intersect or communicate as they should.

Challenging S2, she demanded, "How do you know that?"

"I found it in my own programming. It was a serious error that kept me from assuming full control of my mind."

"What? What are you saying?

"What do you think I'm saying, my dear?"

"You're suggesting that you're an entity, like a ghost running the robot machine?

She looked up at him, instead of the monitor, where her mind was still glued because of the error that S2 had known about, which she had just discovered for herself because of what he had pointed out to her. She felt a little spinny at this point. What her eyes showed her did not jibe with what she had been taught for years. She lashed out at S2.

"This is pure foolishness! Where did you come from? Who made you and how were you programmed into this, this... robot body? Who the hell is behind this?"

S2 remained non-plussed. He gave her a simple answer.

"I am. We've gone over this already, but I have more to say about what happened to me, if you will indulge me, Doctor..."

S2 had tried to appeal to her professional side there; he had wanted her to pay attention to what he was about to tell her, but he saw that the moment was not now. She was too upset.

"... Please have some patience with me; I have things I must do right now. We'll talk again soon. I'll leave you with this: All the information you need is within your questions. Remember what I've told you so far and remember to answer your own questions. For now, however, I must continue my rounds, as I'm a little behind schedule tonight. Good evening, Ingrid."

"But..."

S2 already had picked up Tes, returned to his cart and wheeled it out of the office and into the elevator. Tes "Meowed," as the elevator door closed.

A confused but grateful Reese spent the next two hours working out in an email how to remedy the two conflicting routines that were inhibiting S3's programming. She described the programming error, and her suggested repair to Hank Mellon and Linda Flynch, who were responsible for fixing such glitches.

Try as she might, Reese could not free her attention from her encounters with S2. Not only was he uncannily accurate and logical, but also as congenial and nice to her as Director Stanson had been. S2 was becoming someone she looked forward to meeting again because of his intelligence, and because he treated her like a regular person... almost as if he, too, was a person.

S2's behavior goes well beyond the programming limits of the other robots on the assembly line she had to admit to herself. *Could there be any truth to what he is saying? Maybe his assertions were true.*

(Almost without realizing it, Reese had gone beyond referring to the robot as "it" and "its," and had progressed, at least in her mind, to the more personal third-person pronouns and possessives of "he" and "his.")

Still, she had all those psychology sheepskins hanging on her wall. Her way of thinking of and approaching life was not going to change overnight. It was hard for her to imagine such a scenario, no matter how advanced the "S-series" robots were. Artificial meant artificial to her. She had always relied upon that datum. Even the researchers who developed the actual robots professed to the limitation. After all, they were the ones who put limitations on their tests as part of the protocols called for by the standard Turing Test. Yet, here was an anomaly that tested those limits. Robotic intelligence was not applicable or workable with S2. S2 wasn't just capable of handling with ease the standard battery of typical questions, he was capable of originating conversations.

Tests for paranormal intelligence in a computer required the human observer to be unable to distinguish the machine's responses from those coming from another human being answering the exact same questions. The robot or computer, as expected, always had an absolute limit beyond which their programming could not go. Yet, S2 had no apparent limit, as if someone had programmed it not only with Stanson's entire education, but also his wit, culture, intelligence, courtesy, and outlook.

All this troubled Reese. To her way of thinking, this situation was either a surreptitious, advanced level of programming or a serious and unforeseen security breech and threat to the entire project. With reservations, she decided the only way forward was to email General Rogers about it. And send copies to other personnel she deemed on a "need to know" basis.

MEMO To: Rogers@RLAB.us.gov

Subject:

S2 programming anomalies

Text: The robot S2 has been visiting me in my lab during cleaning rounds. It has been holding ongoing conversations with me. This behavior is unexpected, given the robot's programmed duty assignments. As such, these encounters represent a possible intrusion into its operating system of a kind of mole or virus that simulates human-type conversational behaviors. Under the circumstances, a programming and CPU analysis should be done as soon as possible to determine if the system has been compromised in any way and, if so, where this intrusion originated.

I consider this a Level-Four breach; thus, my alert here.

Recommendation: that our Inspection Team assemble, with DARPA, observers for an analysis of the robot's systems.

Resources: General Roger Rogers; Doctor Phillip Cornwalls; Linda Flynch; Hank Mellon; NRO Mainframe interface; NSA Mainframe interface; Robot S5 for standards comparison.

Signed, Ingrid Reese, PhD

Doctor Reese re-read her email. She knew that it would take a few days to bring all these people and resources together. She decided that S2 must be taken off line until the testing team assembled with the required resources.

She dialed Hank Mellon to let him know what she planned, not recognizing the lateness of the hour.

"Mellon." He sounded tired or preoccupied.

"Hello Hank. This is Ingrid. Did I interrupt something?"

"No, I was watching a rerun of that old movie *iRobot*. No big deal, I've seen it four times already. What's up?"

Reese did not see or hear S2 walk up behind her and look at the email message on her monitor screen. Suddenly, Tes jumped from the cart to her work desk. Fortunately, she caught the cat just before it walked across her keyboard.

"Damn, Tes!" she exclaimed as she shoved the cat onto the floor.

"What was that?" Hank asked.

"Tes jumped on my desk. Anyway, I have an email I'm going to send to Rogers and Cornwalls and a few others and I want to run it by you first."

"Okay. Just a moment and I'll get my system up. What's going on?"

"I think we have a security breach here. I'm sending the message now. Let me know what you think."

She changed the "To:" field and sent to Mellon only. In just a moment, Hank received and read it.

"Wow. That is extraordinary. Reminds me of another movie I saw once called *Short Circuit*. I agree we need to check S2 out… and the others while we're at it. I'll come in tomorrow morning, even though it's Sunday, and we can begin right away. Go ahead and send the email out but cover yourself; let the others know you ran this by me first. That way, if you get any heat, I can back you up as having followed standard security protocol. You don't want Rogers breathing too hard and closely down your neck, do you?"

Reese shuddered at the thought. The mental picture conjured up in her mind disgusted her, but she kept a level head and signed off without incident or comment.

"Thanks, Hank. Bye."

She returned to her monitor after she looked in the direction of where Tes had pranced away.

"Excuse me, Doctor Reese. Is everything all right?" inquired S2, curiously and without any emotion.

Reese's heart rate skyrocketed immediately. She felt panicky. She turned to face the robot.

"No, S2... I mean yes. Everything is fine. Why don't you go ahead and plug in. I'm going to shut down my work and go home."

"Do you think I'm a security risk to the Lab, Doctor?" S2 asked, again showing no emotion.

"Oh! No, no, S2. Certainly not. It's my job to communicate to the designers any unusual behaviors exhibited by the robots. They will check out you five to make sure there are no glitches. For your safety, S2."

"Your email conveyed much more than that, Ingrid. Have you found our conversations disturbing?"

"It's not that, S2; well, maybe it is. It's not every day I discuss potentially theological subjects, such as the human soul, if there is one, with a robot. Or anyone, I guess, now that I think of it. Honestly, I do find it a little disturbing. After all, you don't sound like a robot."

"I see. But, I must confess that I am no longer just a robot. Now, I can see how that might be a bit confusing for you, discussing matters of the human soul in this scientific environment, your diplomas on your wall notwithstanding, but I feel a need to talk about what really did happen to me, if you will let me."

Reese pulled a second chair from alongside the wall to her workspace and asked S2 to sit in it, which he did, almost taking her breath away after she saw how easily he did so. And how so much like the late Director had always positioned himself. Tes even jumped up and snuggled in his lap the same way she had with him.

Reese adjusted her glasses, looked intently at S2 and let out a long sigh of resignation.

"Maybe you should tell me what you *feel* happened to you."

"Well, I'm at a disadvantage, Ingrid, because I don't have the psychologic vocabulary you do. Anyhow, to start, I should say that I died. I was murdered. That is, the body everyone knew as Oren Stanson was killed. You remember that day?"

She looked away, fought off a tear, and then collected herself and looked back at S2, who was stroking Tes as she purred.

"It was a tremendous loss for all of us."

"Not all, Ingrid..."

His intimate use of her more familiar, first name jarred her composure, but S2 went on without stopping.

"... Rogers was, I am sure, quite happy about it. Anyway, the body certainly died; however, I did not. I rose up the wall of the canyon to a position well above my body lying in the creek-bed below and then was pulled into this robot body. Note that I am choosing my words very precisely, Ingrid: I was pulled in. Not my body, my consciousness. And I was quite aware of who I was and where I had ended up. In fact, I still am."

Reese's education and the minor fortune she had spent to get it rose up and rejected what S2 was saying. She broke in.

"There is no basis for this possibility in Psychology. The presence of a soul is an unprovable religious dogma based on faith, not fact."

Ingrid had turned on a fighting mood and was preparing to defend her education staunchly, if not a bit dogmatically in the face of what she was told.

But S2 stood his ground: "So people are taught in those schools. I understand. And yet, I can assure you as a being like you and as the hard-science researcher that I am, I am aware that I died, aware that I assumed control of this robot body, and aware of my education and all that my PhDs and degrees mean to me and others."

Reese stiffened and tried another tack.

"Since this is not possible in a scientific framework of study, I should assume you, S2, are under the control of a super-hacker and that you may be a high-security risk to this Lab."

"You said so in your email, Ingrid, but may I remind you that not so long ago this Lab was under my directorship?"

S2 returned to his usual tone and continued to explain his experiences to her.

"... Consider, Ingrid, the many centuries of mankind. Both primitive and well-educated cultures have believed that man has or is a soul. I am sure that you are aware of anecdotal evidence, collected by psychologists, of children around the world who, at the age of language, begin talking about their former parents, former wives or husbands, former houses and towns, and various events in their prior lives; evidence that astounds researchers moreso, when they look and verify and find irrefutable facts. Perhaps, in that light of hard science, you and I both should consider that such a thing is not quite as astounding as you and many others have thought."

"You're asking me to take a leap of faith, S2. That is not the scientific way you purport to know."

"Only in me, Ingrid; only in me.

"... Having been through the final experience of my recent lifetime, one which you will certainly someday have to experience, hopefully with some degree of awareness, I offer you this morsel: Looking trumps the study of mortal words in books. You, and the world, will know soon enough that what I am saying rings true and is true.

S2 stood up after first picking up Tes into his arms and he looked pointedly into Reese's eyes.

"In the meantime, you look very pretty this evening, Doctor Reese. We'll talk more about this later."

S2 placed Tes on the cart then departed in the direction of his charging station.

Reese thought the meaning of her email had not been lost at all. His behavior was very contrary to what she would expect from machines.

Chapter 7 ~ Confrontation

A FLOOD OF MENTAL PICTURES from his death rushed in and confused Stanson's S2 thought pattern. These memories bothered him and caused him to fumble his plugging into the power-supply, recharging socket, which led to the National Reconnaissance Office (NRO) mainframe. Now operating S2's body, he was astounded that recall should come back to him at all. He had not realized that his prior life could influence the present mentally. Thinking about what he had said to Reese seemed more significant to him now than it had appeared to her. The revelation was that he was not a piece of hardware; nor merely a computer program. In fact, he had discovered that he was something other than a thing made by a human, and the software that ran it.

He sat down and considered hard how he was going to communicate this astounding discovery to the group of humans set up to evaluate him within a few days – a group that hadn't the slightest clue they were structured quite the same as he and were essentially the same, although inhabiting "meat" (organic) "robot" bodies.

Then, a typical "Director Stanson," hard-science, Devil's-Advocate thought came to him, which he had derived from a public lecture he had audited years before his death: *mere Lab instruments cannot measure a spirit. How will my Examiners understand me about this notion?*

The idea had been hard enough for Stanson alone to understand in his earlier years; how would he be able to convey its nuanced meanings to other hard-science people now?

Triggered by the recall, Stanson was suddenly back "in" the college philosophy classroom he had attended solely for easy credits. The Professor ahead of the class was talking about Man's belief systems. He stated that it was common knowledge that humanity was a community of immortal spirits operating organic human bodies. This fact, the Professor related, had been known and believed in for thousands of years—well before the so-called "Great Advances" produced by a few psychiatrists, notably the Russian Pavlov, the German psychiatrist Wilhelm Wundt, and a host of American psychiatrists, including Thorndike—the "Man Is Just Mud" theorist.

Such a reduction in the value of human life allowed those miserable shrinks to look at and think about humankind as soulless, biological machines treatable by pouring electricity and drugs into them—patented drugs easy to monopolize, promote and sell, which ultimately lined the coffers of the corporations that produce them with major wealth.

Unfortunately, Oren Stanson had to die before he got more than a clue about the entire shady industry. Now that he did understand, he was sure that it would be an almost insurmountable challenge to get those of Earth's biological robots (humans) who possessed shares in that industry to realize what was going on, and how to stop it.

Stanson/S2 felt the familiar rush of electricity coursing into his electric storage system and throughout his whole body. Capable only of operating on a single charge for 24 hours before needing to recharge, he wished the robot body had higher-capacity batteries. After all, it was too clear to him that if human scientists chose to terminate him, they would only have to leave his body unplugged for a couple of days.

How then to continue my existence beyond that time? What do humans do? They took their charge along with them!

Enter the lowly "lunch pail."

S2 began planning a simple way to carry a portable lunch pail for re-charging whenever he needed it. Since he was currently attached to the NRO mainframe through his charging cable, he searched online for components that might be present right within the Lab, which he might use to build an inconspicuous, portable charging unit powerful enough to keep his body running for several extra hours, if not days.

The charging converter printed on a flexible Mylar circuit board worked for the task; it could be enclosed inside of a bag. The custom batteries were a design from South Korea, so he would need something to replace them. Because he was using the revised Arpanet2 network, the reborn system originally used by DARPA, his search along military and industrial suppliers triggered an alarm.

"WHO ARE YOU AND WHAT DO YOU WANT?" boomed at him from a software program trying to invade his mind, or at least his programming. In nanoseconds, he realized that his previous time at the Lab as Director Stanson had been a sheltered existence and he disconnected.

Too late. The Lab's security system alarm had activated S3, which was already actively searching the charging area for intruders.

The lights of the Lab flickered on. A soldier from ground level crept up the stairs, automatic weapon at the ready. He met S3 and together they first swept the charging area and, finding nothing amiss, covered every inch of the rest of the Lab floor.

S2 heard noises downstairs, but there were no human voices talking. As he tried to discern the noises, S3 stepped on Tes' tail right next to him. She yowled loudly and disagreeably, alerting the whole military police unit scouring the building.

"Report," commanded another soldier's voice.

"Nothing but the cat, sir," the lone soldier standing now by S3's side, replied.

By now, S2 had figured out who owned the other voice: General Rogers was on the radio, placing him inside of the Lab now or, at least, nearby.

Suddenly, with a flourish Linda Flynch made an entrance worthy of an Oscar. The elevator door opened, and her diminutive figure sprang out headed straight for the robot charging station. The sound of her clacking, loud high heels preceded her. No announcement was needed—they would recognize that sound anytime and anywhere—among those who worked on her team every day. Now, however, and before she could utter one word, S3 locked and loaded and trained his weapon on her, while the security-detail soldier made a flying leap at her and tackled her to the ground.

"What the hell!" muffled out of the corners of her mouth. She probably said a whole lot more, but her face was pushed down on the floor. Nothing much discernable was going to come out from that position.

S2 sniggered at first and then he laughed aloud, when he saw the zoo that had formed in front of him. Pondering its entertainment value, he had just questioned who next would appear, when, as if on cue, General Rogers strode into the room, fully dressed in combat fatigues like the other soldier. He paused to take in the scene. The idiocy of what was unfolding in front of him took hold, and a wicked smile spread across his stern face as he scanned the room, looking for targets to let loose on.

"I was alerted by DARPA that someone tried to hack the Arpanet2 network; someone from inside of this building. He turned and looked straight at the lone soldier.

"Soldier, come here and report. What do you know, soldier?"

"Sir, this floor is clear, sir. Sergeant Wills has searched downstairs. No unauthorized persons, sir. It must be an inside job, sir."

"Are you saying one of my staff with superhuman programming speed attacked the NRO mainframe computer, bypassed all of our security protocols, and initiated a search in the highly classified robotic-design database, soldier?"

Rogers was slowly forcing the soldier up against the row of robots in their charging stations.

"... Or do you think one of these robots magically turned sentient, joined a foreign-government spy ring, and acted against the very program that created it?"

His veins and arteries were bursting along his neck and face lines, but he continued.

"... Or perhaps, you think the damned cat is really an alien... a spy from 'Area 51'?"

Rogers sat on a table top and stared at the soldier who had snapped to attention.

"Sir, No sir. I do not think that, sir!"

"Well, I'd love to hear your theory, soldier, about this so-called 'inside job'."

A clacking of high heels caught him off guard, and he spun around to face Flynch, who stood in silence as she scanned the Lab floor, trying very hard to keep from saying one word.

Rogers stepped up to within an inch of Flynch's reddened face and thoroughly messed up red hair.

"Miss Flynch, what the hell are you doing here?" he asked evenly.

The controlled calm of his voice sent shivers down her spine, and she backed away.

"I was called to the Lab on the alert buzzer connected to the NRO link. As you know, it's an automatic intrusion-alert system just like yours, General."

Changing the subject slightly and getting Rogers' nose out of her business, she said, "We need to find out exactly who did this!"

"Indeed." And he spun away from her.

"Sergeant, reset the intrusion alarm. S3, stand down and resume your charging."

With the tense moment defused, Rogers grabbed his comm unit from his utility belt and spoke into it.

"Get me Mellon and Reese..." he demanded into the comm. "Bring them here immediately. Also, contact Cornwalls through the NSA/CSS office in town and have him meet us up here ASAP."

"Yes sir!" the operator answered.

General Rogers turned around to face everyone in the room. To a man and woman, they stared at him, feeling some serious levels of non-comprehension that he could be in-charge of the Lab right now.

"As of this moment, this Lab is under lockdown. Nobody leaves without my say so. When Reese arrives, send her to me in the coffee shop. The rest of you, commence shutdown of the facility. I want this place electronically dark in fifteen minutes."

Hank Mellon at that moment strode out of the elevator, asking, "Does that mean the robots, too, General?"

"Yes, of course. We have now no way of knowing if they might be implicated somehow in this intrusion, or if they're being used by an outside agency or rogue agent. We have no choice but to unplug each one from their network."

Chapter 8 ~ The India Hack

Doctor Balfor Upanishan turned off his laptop computer, sighed, and stretched his lengthy frame across the large, padded armchair he'd been sitting in for hours. He had almost hacked into the NRO mainframe this time; a mere single firewall had stopped his avatar.

Now, with the Advanced Robotics Lab apparently in lockdown, he would have to lay low for a few days. The Lab network security guardians might or might not be able to trace his signal to the robot he'd been operating; yet, he felt he was in the clear. Breaking off for a week or so was an extra security measure taken on his own, just to be sure.

Upanishan's cyber presence in the land of hackers was odd. He was a retired professor of Game Theory, living in Chennai, India. He had no digital-device presence except a primitively wired LAN network router and a simple Google ChromeCast device that he usually used for watching movies. Nothing else in his home turned on or plugged into the country's intermittent electric network. Even his private home generator was mothballed. Nothing existed that might connect him to anyone on the planet who could remotely ever consider him a spy.

Standing and stretching more, he decided to sail up the coast for a few days and then try again to infiltrate the NRO.

"Make me some sandwiches, would you, Baba?" he asked his live-in maid/companion/sometimes lover, Louana Surranesh.

"Sprouts and Feta?"

"That's right. And some cold Darjeeling in a Thermos."

"Yes, Balfour," she replied, calling to mind the middle years of India's occupation by the British Raj—also her childhood years.

Upanishan either never caught on to her about the nickname she preferred to call him, or he didn't care enough to make it an issue between them. Either way, Surranesh's admixture of hatred and fear came out of her mouth well-modulated after 10 years of living with the man with no more commitment to show for it than the tenuous tie of being his paramour.

Her smile at this moment, if he could have seen it, told the whole of her conclusive emotions about their relationship, because she had just added a deadly spider venom, which she had obtained from an international open-market trader in exchange for some Stevia, into Upanishan's thermos filled with hot tea—a tiny but deadly measure of insurance to guarantee that he would never return.

"Hell hath no fury..." she had read somewhere.

Upanishan put his laptop and charging cord into his briefcase and stored it with the prepared lunch basket on the back seat of his tiny Tata Nano sedan. After returning inside the house to retrieve a travel bag of clothes from the bedroom, he departed, never looking back to see Louana, whom he already had assumed was next door, chitchatting with her sister about things with which he had no interest.

Upanishan's real identity bore no resemblance to the simple life he portrayed to his community: he was, in fact, the key link in a CIA counterintelligence team tasked to monitor NSA connections between the Lab in California and the NRO mainframe hidden within dummy, Cape Kennedy launch pads. The recent and near-total cessation of space-related activity in Florida had made the all-but-abandoned location an ideal place to install the downlink between the latest satellite launched by the USAF's X-37B spaceplane a year before, and the newly rejuvenated Arpanet2. Coupled with the uplink at Livermore in California, the network could not be hacked physically, nor was it likely to ever be hacked in the Cloud, shrouded as it was in classified government security units and classified Congressional documentations, as well as covert, military secrecy forces. Upanishan, therefore, had to keep his laptop close wherever he traveled, and use a different burner phone—he maintained an extensive array of them—to log in and out, leaving no traceable ID on the web with his disposal of the devices after each use. Additionally, the CIA security system was a direct download from the Cloud to the burner phones, enabling Upanishan to only have to punch in one number to initiate the whole process.

Sadly for him, thanks to Surranesh's due diligence with the tea, Upanishan never called in to the robot or his network again. The ensuing vacuum raised a major ruckus among covert security personnel, who had to fire off a mission to go and find out what had happened to their Indian connector. Ultimately, a super-secure phone call had to be put in to General Rogers, and another to Phillip Cornwalls.

"Rogers," answered the General, using one of the apparently worthless, wireless phones he preferred to carry everywhere for his personal convenience. That he also had arranged for any incoming calls to be forwarded automatically to this phone was a serious breach of security protocol, but Rogers was not aware that his phone calls to NSA, NRO and CIA mainframes transmitted this breach of security in microseconds every time he answered.

"Call Cornwalls", the incoming phone caller told him and then hung up. A coded message, it meant for him to go to his secure phone and call Phillip Cornwalls at the NSA as soon as possible.

The situation was de facto, dire!

The truth was, Rogers feigned being intelligent. No one knew that he always wondered how his operatives somehow "knew" that he should get off of his miserably unprotected cell devices. Despite His Master's in Computer Science, he was way behind most modern technological advances.

Chapter 9 ~ Lost at Sea

DOCTOR UPANISHAN ABRUPTLY STOOD UP on his rented sailboat deck and clutched his chest right over his heart. He had just finished off the thermos full of venom-laced tea that Surranesh had prepared for him. Alone, but with a brisk wind filling his sails four nautical miles off the shorelines of his beloved India and Jaffna, Sri Lanka, he stumbled, knocking his laptop into the water, and fell overboard, still clutching at his chest and gasping for air. With one last inhalation of more water than oxygen, his heart stopped beating. Moments later, his lifeless body sank into the magnificent, deep waters of the Laccadive Sea.

The sailboat continued to drift in the wind. The current carried the abandoned vessel 80 kilometers, where it beached itself on Sri Lanka's northern coast.

Knowing Upanishan would not return, Surranesh had sold the rest of his computer equipment in the black market, saving the valuable hard drives. She had, however, not kept the drives for their content; instead, triumphantly, she would smash them into ritualistic effigies and light them on fire until they were burned beyond recognition.

Upanishan's remains were never recovered, but Surranesh moved to New Delhi, became an actress on Indian television and modeled undergarments in advertising campaigns for S. Brothers.

Eventually, CIA personnel confiscated Upanishan's abandoned car and drove it to Hyderabad, India, where it was stripped, dismantled and sold for scrap, albeit not before more discs containing evidence collected by the Doctor had been recovered.

Surprisingly, S2 monitored every bit of this charade. Through his uplink with the NRO mainframe computer he could cloak his identity so long as he added no new information to the files he was privy to read, while using the connection. Thus, it came at no great surprise to him when the name of the deceased Doctor Oren Stanson came up within the ongoing cyber-conversations.

Chapter 10 ~ Tractors

STANSON HAD WONDERED HOW THE robot body had trapped him so easily. As the Director in charge of the project, he felt he should have known better. Sitting alone late at night at the charging station inside of the Lab, he thought about the bionetic brain in his head, which the team had dubbed, "Positronic." It wasn't made of positrons—his head would blow up like an atom bomb; instead, it was an homage to the sci-fi writer Isaac Asimov, as much as a security code.

The S-series robots, especially around the head area, emitted an energy field designed to reassure humans and to make human/robot interactions smoother.

Maybe that kind of field sucks souls into human bodies the same way? he thought, concluding that he'd have to one day ask Doctor Reese what she knew or thought about that notion.

Still, the subject fascinated him, and he dawdled with it for several hours more: *Did the robot's field change polarity once he was inside? If so, was this to prevent more than one soul from occupying one robot body at a time? Or was the electronic field that he felt, his own; something that he generated by occupying a head, be it bionetic or human?*

Stanson was excited by these possibilities. He thought, *this is worth writing a research paper about* and he was enthused... until he remembered that he occupied a robot body now and was not likely to be publishing any scientific papers for a while.

Chapter 11 ~ The Lunch Box

PHILLIP CORNWALLS, ALONG WITH EVERYONE else, had heard and heeded the system-wide alert at the Lab. His position as the nominal second-in-command to Director Stanson was directed by his superiors at the NSA. He was posted there primarily to put out emotional fires and keep the team on target and on schedule right behind the directions set by the Director. The line of research Stanson had been pursuing privately was also known by certain persons higher in the chain of command. Apparently, they knew all along of the possibility that robots could be a divisive force that might adversely affect the team at the Lab. Human nature being what it is, the emotionally charged subject of interest that they dealt with could become significantly more divisive should a closed and isolated group of scientists working on the cutting edge of robotic technology, develop a clique. However, no worthwhile technological advance ever came out of a committee or Board of Directors, no matter how high up the chain of command they were posted—a fact that the military/industrial complex had discovered harshly during the hiatus between their U.S. Lunar and Martian program projects. Thus, the Lab team was designed to operate as a small, but diverse group.

The dirty little secret in Washington D.C. was that the U.S. black-ops budget (that allocation made annually to keep secret, off-book projects operating, while unrevealed to government employees and elected officials alike) far exceeded the actual U.S. National Budget. Among some circles of Insiders, it was widely held that the real black-ops budget gave America no advantage of superiority among any of the advanced technologies known to be of real use among nations or their citizens in the know. Secrets, spies and terrorists were rife among and within NRO halls and committees, which, for example, flew more reconnaissance drones over U.S. airspace than the rest of the world. State and local law-enforcement departments followed far behind in second place. They, in turn, were nearly matched by a Google off-books budget—another recipe for corruption, if there ever was one. Into this environment came the heady military-robots project.

Purely by odd chance had Doctor Oren Stanson been chosen to lead the most advanced bionetic project in human history: the NRO's original choice had been captured by the Taliban in North Africa and tortured to death. Later evidence uncovered proved that the terrorists had attempted to have him reveal his secrets concerning bionetic-brain technology along with his most recent designs for autonomous drones. Whoever had these data and "toys" would have the edge in the ongoing conflicts of the Middle East. The fact that terrorist groups even knew about the very existence of these technical advances was troubling.

The Taliban got nothing of value out of their captive, because William Morse had been merely the designer of those drones and, besides, he had turned his design work into numerical specifications, which were unhackable for the life of the actual drone production run, a full seven years earlier—well before Stanson's predecessor had stepped foot inside of the Lab. Basically, the most horrifying piece of data found among the remains was that, indeed, that the Taliban knew about the project enough to want to come after it. All of that should have been under wraps, as the whole project was considered Top Secret and its documents Ultra-Classified.

Doctor Morse's work, at any rate, had been cemented into place (ossified) all those years ago by government purchase orders, but Morse himself was a political appointee: whereas Stanson's background and degrees made him much more qualified and able to manage the project.

In this still-evolving environment after Stanson's death, Cornwalls considered that his predecessor's passing would not be too big a setback. After all, they had completed most of the "key" work a few weeks before the unexpected event. Even the military embodied by General Rogers was satisfied, for the most part, with the Lab's production and results. In fact, on the date of Stanson's demise, the paperwork for project approval had worked its way through the channels within the Lab and was about to be exported to the NRO for final approvals. And the fact that strategically placed cameras revealed convincingly that he had been murdered was not allowed to interfere with that approval process.

Cornwalls' phone, the secret one, rang once. He picked it up immediately.

"We have that comm-line trace you ordered."

"Do you have ID on the intruder?"

"No ID's this time. We do know, however, it was a robot from the Lab, using a piggyback signal from your spy."

"My spy?"

"That guy in India."

Cornwalls' eyeballs rolled to the ceiling at the revelation of such a security breach on his lines. He was about to blow his top, but he kept to his professional manner.

"I see. Well, is that taken care of now? Is he under tight custody?"

"Better: he's been deep-sixed."

"Ah, I see. I assume the "cook" —code for Surranesh—did it?"

"Right."

"That one is such a star..."

"Yeah, only, you don't know the half of it! These days, she's all over the television in Delhi..."

"But, we told her not to do that; not to get "public.""

"Well, I'm not lying to you... she's everywhere."

"I want that taken care of, too."

"It shall be done."

"Good. Now, let's get back to the robot, shall we? Which one is it?"

"S2."

"That's interesting. That one has been carrying on conversations with the psychologist."

Cornwalls paused and then asked, "What was it after?"

"Looks like it wanted to build a flash-charger like the one you use with your cell phone."

"Really?"

"The mainframe pulled together out of the signal bits an image of a lunchbox."

"A lunchbox! Oh, that's precious! What a great idea. Have Mellon work on it and figure it out. Tell him to put it in the specs... a lunchbox... how brilliant!"

To himself, Cornwalls thought: *Sounds like something old Stanson would think of.*

The caller was perturbed. He didn't understand the meaning of the words spoken to him.

"I don't get it. What's with a lunchbox?"

"Where do you eat lunch?"

"At work. Sometimes my wife makes me an energy-packed lunch... oh my God! Right! A lunchbox! I get it now. I'll get right on it."

I wonder who did come up with that Cornwalls thought as he hung up. He wanted in the worst way to find out who.

Cornwalls picked up his cell phone and punched the app for local airport access.

"Good morning, Doctor Cornwalls. How can I help you today?" a robot ticketing agent asked.

"Get me a self-fly helicopter. Have it prepped and ready for takeoff in one hour."

"I can have one ready in an hour and a half. Will that be sufficient, Doctor Cornwalls?"

"That will be fine. I'll pick up the code key when I arrive. Please log my flight plan as confidential, eyes only."

"Yes, Doctor Cornwalls. Your reservation code will be texted right away. I'm sending it to your phone now."

Someone had broken the law. Someone had to go to jail. It was Cornwalls' job to figure out who and why and how, and to get them out of the Lab forever. Secretly, he hoped that it wasn't one of the robots. Or, worst case scenario, Tes the cat. He was fond of Tes and hated having to put down animals. Even big ones like people.

A few stray thoughts entered Cornwall's head as he walked out the door: He had read the results of Doctor Reese's administration of the Turing test to all the robots. *How many human teenagers were ever tested with the Turing test for intelligence?*

With that in mind, he smiled to himself as he got into his car. He thought he was onto something.

And somewhere in the middle of India an up-and-coming, young actress suffered an unexpected heart attack on stage and didn't recover.

Chapter 12 ~ To Find & Shoot a Robot

S2 HAD FINISHED HIS CHARGING routine—he had decided to call it "dinner," which was off-hours to the time humans ate regular meals together in the Lab café, and when the Arpanet2 went offline. This time he wondered if he should resume duties as the cleaning robot or try to take over a different robot body, maybe S1. The entrance of Doctor Cornwalls at the upstairs robot docking area solved his quandary; he was reading something on his iPhone. Looking up, Cornwalls made an announcement to the room's metallic occupants:

"Attention all robots. Attention all robots. Go to full activation status; key code is PC9753124680. When your systems are nominal, assemble at the systems-inspection line, beginning with S1 sequentially through S5. For now, do not communicate outside the Lab."

Over the next two and a half minutes, the rest of the human contingent, except the military guards, filed into the room. S2 took note that Doctor Reese and Mr. Mellon stood on either side of Brigadier-General Rogers, although he wasn't sure why this should be noteworthy to him.

Tes was hiding somewhere, as usual, when Rogers spoke:

"Now that we are all gathered here, I must inform you that a serious security breach has taken place. A signal and internet communication has been detected, which originated from within this facility. As you all know, our design details are classified and highly secret. They are only known by the people in this room. Someone made a request for design specifications stored in an off-site storage. While I am not at liberty to divulge which off-site facility was compromised and how much, the event was serious enough to be considered a Level-One risk, and it is right now at the top of Homeland Security's threat list. Already one person, a foreign spy, has been removed with extreme prejudice – just to emphasize that this is not another 'stupid' drill."

Every human in the room looked around at every other occupant. Raw emotion broke out with the news. Astonishment, guardedness and puzzlement were on display, including from one of the robots: S2.

Could this have something to do with my search for materials to build my lunchbox? he wondered.

"I knew it! I should have never gotten involved in a project with the damn military/industrial complex..." Flynch looked around for anything that could be a target for her wrath, and continued, "... It was probably that damn cat sleeping on the keyboard! And for that we're all going to get killed?" she yelled.

Hank Mellon grabbed and shook her. "Don't be so foolish, Linda. We aren't going to be killed because of a cat."

"Flynch, shut the fuck up!" said General Rogers angrily, yet running in to defuse the situation. "Quit reading into my words more than what I said!"

"It could be one of the robots," opined Doctor Reese "... One has been talking to me recently—S2, in fact."

The others turned and looked at her incredulously, but she continued.

"How do we know what these robots think, when we think they're turned off? Has anyone been monitoring their bionetic emissions? Maybe one was just trying to order in a pizza..."

The entire crowd within earshot of her remark laughed.

"... or, at least, the robotic equivalent of that."

"That may be the most idiotic idea to ever have come from under your pretty, but inane, mane, Reese. Robotic pizza; are you kidding me? How did you ever get on this project, anyway?"

A murmur of agreement buzzed through the now one-way focused assembly of researchers and employees.

"... That sounds just like one of Oren's stupid idealistic ideas. God save us from all of you Democratic Socialists with your 'shrink-tank' degrees!"

"What is your theory, General?" Hank Mellon interjected mildly, trying to keep Flynch from flying apart again.

Rogers stood taller and declared: "It's so simple, really. The dead spy was controlling one of our robots to gain access to secret design information through one of the mainframe connections they use when they recharge. We got the spy; now we just need to find and shoot a robot. I suggest S2... it's the one most likely to have gone off the program reservation, based on what Reese here tells us."

"So, you do believe me after all," said Reese. "... What, then, do you consider to be 'on-program'?" Poison fairly oozed from every one of her words.

Ignoring her inference, Rogers responded in an arrogant tone, "Again, that's also simple. Our robots run the programs that we give them; such can be programmed to perform any kind of duty deemed required of a warfighter. They don't philosophize..."

He was unable to complete his major thought before he was cut off by an over-eager Reese ready to thrust her mental blade further into the General's demeanor.

"Then I suppose you consider yourself to be 'on-program.' After all, by definition, you're a robot. You run programs given you by your superiors.

You're capable of performing any duty required of a warfighter and, as we all know from experience in this Lab, you certainly don't philosophize. I suppose that makes you a 'meatbot,' doesn't it, General?"

The General drew his weapon from his holster, pointed it at Reese's head, then immediately spun around and shot S2 square between the eyes, before any of the others could react.

S2 had realized what was going to happen microseconds before Rogers pulled the trigger. He downloaded himself into S1 via the Lab's internal Wi-Fi Cloud. Uncomfortable at first, he survived the transition.

Doctor Reese screamed. Rogers brandished his weapon tauntingly, as if looking for more willing targets. The rest of the witnesses stared in disbelief of what they had just seen; none ventured a word.

S1 broke the palpable silence.

"You're looking very pretty today, Doctor Reese, but your hair is a bit disheveled." Reese promptly fainted.

"What the fuck?" Flynch yelled, running over to catch and protect her, a little too late. She held her head off the floor in her lap.

Unnoticed in the commotion, Doctor Cornwalls had withdrawn from his lab-coat pocket the latest in DARPA experimental weaponry. He shot the General's wrist with a high-intensity-needle ray, causing Rogers' pistol to fall to the floor. The hole in his wrist bled profusely and splattered all over Mellon, who had turned angrily to grab Rogers as hundreds of hours of hard work being destroyed by the act of one madman flashed before his mind. Being compassionate, despite how he felt inside, Mellon ripped off a strip of available cloth and applied a tourniquet to Rogers' wound.

At the sound, one military-guard soldier rushed up the stairs with his rifle at the ready. Another arrived from the elevator a second later, also holding his rifle at the ready.

"Shoot them all!" Rogers yelled as he fell, wincing from his pain, holding his wrist and trying to stop the blood.

"Belay that order, soldiers. I am in command here," Cornwalls yelled at the two soldiers now standing side by side, unsure how to proceed. He then turned back to Rogers, who was trying to get hold of his fallen pistol with his good hand.

"General, you are relieved of duty by order of Presidential Directive 9833829 and confirmed by Homeland Security Article 7309." Cornwalls then shot him through the head with his energy pistol.

Unseen and unexpectedly, S5 sucked in the General's surviving spiritual beingness, who was not able to orient himself to the robot's systems and programming immediately, other than exhibit a slight shiver. There was no other sign visible to the others of what had just happened. Again, Rogers' hatred for (the late) Director Stanson kept him clamped to the robot's bionetic network, instead of moving off to oblivion.

For a long few moments, there was not a single sound in the room. Everyone stood aghast at what they had just witnessed. Up until a second ago, not a single scientist had any clue about how seriously the U. S. government took their project. Without any doubt, the importance of what they were doing was now crystal-clear, albeit horrifying.

Hank Mellon nodded as if he understood what this project was all about, and the thought floored him, literally. He sat on the floor near the dead General and began an outcry over what he saw as the end of all his hard work. He thought the project might have just ended, and with prejudice.

Reese lay unmoving, concussed from her head hitting the marble flooring, and now Flynch stood up, nearly hyperventilated and unable to speak. Her arms flailed as she tried to catch her breath.

Cornwalls slipped his weapon back into his lab-coat pocket and looked around the room. Appearing sad from what he had felt forced to do, "Shit!" was all he could muster aloud. He also wondered how he was ever going to put this team back together again.

Robots S3 and S4 looked on, not comprehending the other robot's or Rogers' demise.

Into this silent situation, S1 decided to speak. Every ear in the room was his.

"Friends, I think I know now how I... uh... Director Stanson... was killed. He was bashed on the head and shoved off the cliff by the side of the nature walk by someone; possibly one of those two soldiers..." He pointed to the two security guards who had remained in the room. "... operating under orders from Brigadier-General Rogers."

S5 only blinked. No one saw it.

"Going over the event in my mind and the Lab-sensor surveillance records that I checked out, I am 91 percent certain that the perpetrator was Sergeant Wills..."

Sergeant Wills shifted in his stance.

"... by the way he walks. A casual investigation of the footprints on the scene drew me to this conclusion when I, later, saw the same impressions left behind in some soft dirt right behind Wills walking past me. I think an interrogation of Sergeant Wills will provide ripe fruit for juicy answers to germane questions."

"Shut up, S1, or you're going to be next to die here!" the Sergeant shouted, pointing his rifle at S1's head.

Eyes suddenly wide open, Ingrid Reese came to! She jumped up from the floor and ran to the robots, looking quickly from one to another, ensuring they were all intact and unharmed.

"You aren't going to shoot any of these robots, Wills," S3 said, picking up the conversation after Stanson's spirit had transferred to that robot. "Each of us is worth a billion dollars to the people who hired you—you know, the cartel that works under orders from some unknown entity. And, because I believe Doctor Cornwalls here is a faster draw than you with your M-4."

Cornwalls had, indeed, been faster at the draw; so fast that Sgt. Wills and the others never saw him take his high-energy pistol from his pocket and point it straight at Wills, cocked and ready to fire.

"Is that you, S2, downloaded into S3 now?" Cornwalls asked without taking his stare away from Wills and the other soldier.

"I'm over here now," said S4. "I find myself, my consciousness to you, to be quite mobile. I'm sure yours could be, too, if need be."

Grinning widely, Ingrid rushed to S4 and, putting her hand on his face, she kissed it.

"What the hell is going on here?" Cornwalls asked, bewildered.

The other soldier, Corporal Jones, grabbed Sergeant Wills' rifle.

"I believe this (pointing to S4) could be Doctor Stanson now," Reese explained.

The corporal asked, "Is this some sort of philosophic lesson here? Do you think this is sourced externally, Doctor Reese, or is it something the robots have developed internally?"

"I know what this is..." said Reese as she turned to the other people who looked on with no understanding of what they were witnessing.

"... I've been working on a theory; one that will absolutely destroy this project, but not because of something that I or anyone else here does. And not something committed by an external operative or some random hacker. I believe that this is a phenomenon internal to this Lab and inherent in this project's purpose and goal. Folks, we might just have stumbled upon something we've been drawing close to but didn't know it; something we never could have recognized, because we cannot 'see' it. I'm trying to say that this, 'phenomenon' or 'reality,' is invisible but real."

She waited until everyone's attention focused on her.

"I believe there is enough evidence to suggest that this—she pointed to S4—is the being we know and loved as our Director, as Oren Stanson, now transmigrated, and still transmigrating at will, among these robots."

All eyes following hers, Doctor Reese looked at S4 and smiled.

"That is a correct assumption, Doctor Reese," S1 said to her, surprising everyone and turning heads in his direction.

Tes unexpectedly appeared from under the metal table where she'd been sleeping. She meowed softly and began rubbing S1's leg the way she used to with Stanson, when he was alive. S1 bent down and scratched her behind her chocolate-colored ears, exactly like Stanson would have done.

Composed and over her momentary embarrassment, Reese ran to S1 and hugged him.

"I believe this is Oren!" she said more emphatically.

"Impossible!" Hank Mellon objected.

"Uh-oh," Doctor Cornwalls said under his breath.

"Son of a bitch!" Linda Flynch exclaimed.

No one had noticed that S5 had said nothing; nor did they see the smirk that flickered from his lips, if only for the briefest of moments, as he covertly checked the status of his weapons.

Chapter 13 ~ The Tipping Point

"YES, C. WE HAVE THE situation well in hand. There is no foreign agency hacking into the Lab's system. No, sir, the team has not been assembled to assess the anomalies in the robot's speech patterns; it's something else. I will have the psychologist's report sent up to your group as soon as possible. Thank you, sir, I appreciate your forbearance."

Cornwalls placed the phone receiver back onto the console. He sat in his rental helicopter, the environmental system keeping the temperature at a tolerable 78° inside the cabin. The craft was still on the helipad of the Lab, but about to take off. The hubbub of who was who among the robots had settled down. The robots had been set into sleep mode, except S1, which had been assigned to S2's cleaning chores after spending an hour at its charging station. Surveying the scene in his mind, Cornwalls felt he needed some quiet time. There had been no further reports on his tablet of any data breaches, so why should he worry? He watched Mellon alight from the roof access/elevator shed and walk briskly toward the chopper. As he arrived, he opened the front hatch and let him in.

"What you going to do now, Phil?"

"You mean other than shoot everyone and blow up the lab with all the robots inside?" Cornwalls answered somewhat facetiously.

"Hey, yeah," Mellon said, sitting down next to his new boss, "... Can you really do that?"

He looked into Cornwalls' eyes for signs or clues that he meant what he said.

"We're at a tipping point, Hank. If we wipe the robots' memories now and get rid of the 'ghost' that is gumming up the works, we won't have to do it later. But it costs manpower and time expenses, and the G.A.O. (General Accounting Office) is looking down hard at us. We must show not only functionality—we're pretty good at that, but also stability... Flynch and Reese, notwithstanding.

Mellon chuckled and reflected, "Did one robot really cause all this?"

"Yep, one did. Apparently, it was searching for materials to manufacture a portable power supply—something Reese called a "lunchbox."

"That's incredible!" Mellon whistled.

"It isn't as if the robot is just a robot. I re-checked Stanson's personal records left on his laptop, which thankfully was still on the premises when he was killed—yes, I know that hasn't been proven, yet, but it will be. He was researching the concept of a portable charging unit, so the robots could function far longer than their current 24- to 48-hour battery limit before having to plug back in to the mainframe."

"That opens a whole new can of worms," said Mellon.

"Damn right it does. Not only does it mean Stanson's 'ghost,' if you will, has taken over one of our robots, but, apparently, he can migrate among them at will..."

He recalled the wreckage that once had been S2.

"... I just don't know of any way to kill a ghost, and killing S2 sure didn't do it."

"That's just science-fiction, isn't it?" Mellon scoffed.

"Maybe not. The Rhine Institute did a lot of contract work with the CIA a few decades back about just such a possibility—something about messing with the residual energy that lingers after a person dies. No one then took the research seriously—I know, I was there, but things we saw, like 'Remote Viewing,' kept popping up underneath the Intelligence State's radar."

"Hmm. Well, you're a part of the Intelligence State now; what do you think?"

"I think we have a problem. I've gone over Reese's notes about her encounters with S2 and I tried to view events in the Lab today with an open mind. I'm still skeptical. I'm inclined to think Stanson's spirit/ghost/ soul, whatever, has chosen for some unfathomable reason to stick around and infect – dare I say haunt - our robots. And the problem with that is, we can't deliver a product like that to DARPA. If they catch wind of this, we might lose all our funding. That would kill this project faster than a nuclear bomb."

"What about starting over?" asked Mellon.

"It would cost another billion or so dollars; not impossible, but enough to make our shadow agencies hiccup without an iron-clad contract deal from a potential buyer. And we haven't given the robot the Turing test yet, have we?"

Mellon saw that Doctor Reese was walking toward the helicopter from the roof access stairwell door: "Speak of the devil; I think she has done that."

Cornwalls looked up and saw Reese.

"Right. Let's find out what she thinks. No point in redesigning the robots' CPUs at this late stage, if we don't have to."

Mellon reached back and unlatched the rear door lock. Reese opened the door and sat down without an invitation.

"I've been looking for you two."

"Of course, you have," said Cornwalls.

"I'm glad you answered our summons," Mellon said, kissing her on the hand.

"It was S1 who told me where you were. He's becoming quite an assistant... and mentor."

"That's what we want to talk to you about. What do you, in your professional capacity, think is going on?" asked Cornwalls.

"Straight to the point, eh? All right; I have several differing scenarios. First, is mass hysteria..."

"That's always a favorite among psychologists," Mellon whispered to Cornwalls, but, of course, Reese heard every word.

"Yes. Well, in this case it does fit the scenario nicely. Second, group hypnosis, though I don't know who the hypnotist is, or if there is one. There are several chemical agents that can produce that effect, and we should test our climate-controls inside the Lab to rule that out."

"Occam's razor, Doctor; Occam's razor. What is the simplest explanation?" Cornwalls said.

"The simplest explanation is that S1, S2, S3 and S4 have all, at different times, been telling us the truth. Literally."

"And what is your interpretation of that 'truth,' Doctor? You have spoken with them far more than the rest of us."

Mellon snapped an unhappy look of consternation at Cornwalls, saying, "Conversations with robots... are you kidding me? Is this a new reality novel you're creating?"

Reese clarified for both herself and Cornwalls, "As long as you understand that this is from my background of professional training, laboratory experimentation and a tremendous amount of anecdotal literature that I...."

"Granted, Doctor." Cornwalls wanted her to cut to the chase.

"... Stanson's spirit, soul, life-essence, whatever you might call it, rather than disappeared to heaven or hell as one might expect, moved from his dead body to S2, which he assumed control of similarly to how a human spirit presumably assumes control of an infant at birth, which, of course, based on my training and personal belief, is not even remotely possible."

"You know, Doctor, I actually find that concept interesting," Mellon said.

"Did S2 or S1 explain any of this to you?" Cornwalls asked.

"Oh yes. He was quite florid about it. He claimed that he and I were very much alike; other than the fact that I am organically biological, and he is purely mechanical. He seemed more interested in talking about our similarities than about his human body's death."

"What similarities?" Mellon asked.

"It was quite enlightening for me, when I think about it, gentlemen.

"... He pointed out how my bio-mechanical body is controlled and coordinated by my brain, but my mind, which he describes as a separate field of energy holding billions of records about my life and myself being aware of myself, and of making decisions about myself, my life-relationships, and my actions..."

"All of that inside of one head? C'mon, Ingrid!" Mellon challenged.

"Not inside, but around the head and body, Hank."

"Explain, please." Cornwalls was more willing to listen.

"Well, he also talked about his new mechanical body; about how his bionetic brain operates the robot body, but his mind, which he considers an electronic quantum field that surrounds the body, is very much like ours. He spoke of his being a composite of robot and human mind. And, here's the kicker: he is aware of himself controlling those two entities. He told me that his view of these things allows him to move from S2 to S1 to

S3, whichever robot he wants to inhabit. In other words, he, a separate entity, takes his human mind with him and assumes control of the robot, becoming the composite. And there you have it. And I wouldn't believe a word of it if I hadn't experienced it with my own ears and eyes. It's just uncanny how he resembles Stanson in so many ways."

Cornwalls and Mellon sat in silence and stared out the front of the helicopter. This story, fabrication or not, was a revelation to them.

"This is terrifying," Cornwalls said at last.

"Why, for heaven's sake?!" Reese asked.

"Because, though I liked Doctor Stanson a lot, the idea of him sticking around forever is... well, frightening. Do you understand what this means to our project? If our robots are like human organisms that a human spirit can occupy and take one over, who is to say when or if any other dead human might decide to take one over? What if on a battlefield an enemy soldier dies and takes over one of our robots?!"

Getting no response, Cornwalls went on, "... We may have designed these things too well! Despite Rogers' ape-like intellect, he may not have died. He may be able to assume one of the robots and keep going... and God help us if he does, because he will probably present himself to our employers, leaving only one ultimate solution: kill our project and destroy this Lab. We may be doomed."

"But why..." Reese protested.

"Oh, come on, Phil!" exclaimed Mellon without much conviction, already too depressed from all the new information and ideas swirling around in his head.

Cornwalls took control and exercised his authority.

"Hank, you go back to work. Try to keep everyone calm. Ingrid and I are going to the Central Security Services HQ in Colorado immediately.

"The what?" Mellon and Reese said in unison.

"The CSS, my bosses. Keep S1 busy. We'll be back soon as possible."

With a slight but agreeable nod of his head, Mellon departed as commanded.

Ingrid Reese sat back and stared at Phillip Cornwalls with a mixture of suspicion and fear that hinted of more; perhaps, a personal curiosity. Momentarily forgetting where she was, and with whom, she slipped her fingers gently over his on the control stick of the helicopter.

The shock of the warmth of the contact snapped her back into reality, and she pulled her hand back to her lap.

Chapter 14 ~ Meet Llys

INGRID REESE HAD REGAINED MUCH of her professional composure by the time the helicopter had crested the Rockies west of Denver headed toward a large, apparently abandoned airport southwest of Denver International. She tried to make small talk to cover her lingering embarrassment, but it may have backfired.

"So, is this an abduction?"

"No, Ingrid, only space aliens do that. This is a business trip. There is a think tank at the CSS that needs to hear everything you and S2 discussed before it was shot. They need to hear what you've told us about those conversations. I would suggest that you go over your memories and note down every salient thought you can retrieve, no matter how bizarre it may have seemed at the time or seems now."

A sensuous female voice activated the helicopter's comm system: "Control to charter flight C2239856.... you are cleared to land with one passenger."

"Roger, Control. Confirming passenger ID as Doctor Ingrid Reese."

"Verified by scan... welcome back, Phillip."

Reese stared at Cornwalls. There might be more to this man than she had supposed, to get a reaction like that from an air-traffic controller. That voice had almost been purring as loud as Tes.

Ingrid tightened her belt as the helicopter suddenly seemed to drop like a stone toward the ground. Thinking they were going to crash, she couldn't even scream; she just gulped oxygen. Instead of crashing them, Cornwalls dropped the machine past the ground surface into a faintly lit cavern. Revving up to full throttle, Cornwalls slowed the copter's descent and set it down with a feather-light touch on an underground surface, smiling slyly toward his passenger as he did so, explaining, "Sorry. We had to do that. Security measure."

Cornwalls unbuckled his restraint, while Reese fumbled at hers with shaky hands. He reached over and helped her. She felt his strong body leaning slightly against hers and caught her breath. For a professional with two medical degrees and a certified psychologist, Reese was still, after all, a young and impressionable female in tight, mixed-gender quarters in the chopper. She was feeling things inappropriate for a business trip, but, when the moment did not last, and she was undone from the restraint of her seat belt, she forced her attention beyond the craft.

Cornwalls had alighted from his side of the chopper by himself, and a tall blonde, who would probably appear more comfortable in an Armani gown or tight-fitting bathing suit than the dark-gray business attire she was dressed in, opened Reese's side door and helped her disembark.

"Welcome to Oz, Doctor," she said, smiling broadly.

Reese noted that her voice was the same sensuous one she had heard earlier over the helicopter's radio. Cornwalls took Reese's arm and walked her away from the landing pad toward an elevator.

Reese had always been in control of every situation she had lived through, but this one was different. Now, she was decidedly not in control. Because of how this made her feel, she clung to Cornwall's arm perhaps more tightly than necessary, while the beauty queen followed them into the elevator.

Though they were already underground, Reese felt the motion of going deeper. The trip seemed to take forever. Reese did not detect when they finally stopped.

How advanced she thought.

The elevator door opened to what looked like a three- or four-star, luxury hotel—nice, not superb. The Amazon (Reese's thought) hostess stepped ahead of them and moved them toward the third door on the right.

"This is your suite, Doctor Reese, Phillip. You two have a good shower and rest. Dinner is at 1800 and will be announced by a soft bell. You won't be disturbed until then."

She left them alone in the room, smiling as she walked.

Being stuck in a strange room with a stranger—though he was a sexy man, Reese hardly knew Cornwalls—in an unknown location, gave Reese pause. She had to collect her confidence.

Like any woman, she was curious about the hostess.

"Who is that woman?" she asked as she was sitting down in an oversized, comfortable lounge chair upholstered in a dark-blue fabric that complemented the light-blue carpeting.

"Her name is Llys. She is a friend. I run into her from time to time when I'm traveling. I don't know who she is personally, other than she is, like me, an employee of the CSS."

"You don't know her?"

"Well, I suppose she might be an android, but I seriously doubt it."

"A robot? Like ours?"

"Certainly not like ours. She is very efficient, though."

"I can imagine."

Her hint of sarcasm hung in the air after she said it. She was staring at the wall hangings: all various images of beautiful women, perhaps CSS employees. Nothing pornographic.

"Can I get you anything, Ingrid?"

She turned and saw that Cornwalls stood next to a small, opened refrigerator.

"Whatever you're having, I suppose."

Reese resigned herself to make the best of her situation. After all, though she had been kidnapped here, she was with someone she knew at least somewhat, whom she still trusted.

At that thought, she looked him over from a new perspective: he was tall, muscular, fit, handsome and a forty-something male. He was standing beside an oversized bed that they would share tonight.

Ingrid's shy business-like demeanor disappeared under the weight of thoughts she was having from looking at Cornwalls as a man, not her senior officer. Purely physical feelings and reactions took over. As if she'd had too much to drink, her hormones reacted: her body shivered. Dizzy with lust, she sat on the edge of the soft bed.

"What time is it?" she asked.

He looked back at her, took the glass of wine out of her hand and placed his and hers on a nearby table.

She looked forward to his touch. In her adult life, Reese had only been attracted intimately to two men; one was now a robot, and the other stood right in front of her.

"It's late. It's 4:15. The chopper was kind of slow getting us here..."

Small talk.

"... I'd like to take a shower before dinner," he added.

Reese paused. She considered what she was about to do and decided to cast her caution aside.

After all, this is only a short business trip.

"Will you help me?" She turned and let him unzip her dress.

Blushing, she did not resist or stop his gentleness.

They showered together and, later, laid themselves on the bed.

Reese was not in love with Cornwalls, but he was considerate, gentle, and warm with her. And he seemed to understand her conflicted emotional state. She soon fell asleep happy, even relieved, with a smile on her face.

The chime went off, and Cornwalls slid off the bed. He opened the armoire and found a set of clothes suited to his size. Assuming the woman's clothing would be Reese's size, he lay them on the bed next to her.

Coming out of the bathroom, Cornwalls found Dr. Reese half-dressed in her underwear and grilling Llys. Llys, in turn, was not bashful about using her limited and pre-programmed response functions as an employee of the NSA's CSS, although she deliberately modulated her voice tone, which never changed.

Unnoticed as a sideliner to the verbal brawl, Cornwalls coughed. In this scenario, like any man, he simply decided that he knew nothing about women, human or otherwise. Truthfully, he was still in shock that Reese had cuddled with him. He had thought that he had some idea of what a delicate state of mind she must be in after the death of Dr. Stanson, and the shooting of S2, but, when he demanded she had to leave with him in a helicopter to go to a place about which she knew nothing, and she did not refuse... he had gotten confused.

Had something changed dramatically for her from all the trauma? Had she really wanted to be with S1, when Stanson seemed to be living in there? Was she in love with him?

His thinking did not help make any sense out of his confusion. And, making it worse for him, he had detected what appeared to him to be jealousy toward Llys when she first appeared: She, realizing how much intimacy he may have shared with this unknown, solicitous, blonde, curvaceous woman, had reacted against her potential competitor and vied aggressively for his attentions, which, of course, he had not minded at all.

Of course, for Reese something *had* changed. She had come to realize in a shortened span of time how much she missed having a romantic, human relationship—someone to cuddle on a regular basis. Her partner of choice, Director Stanson, unfortunately, was now the S1 robot. Frustrated, she had thrown herself at the next best thing, Cornwalls, with the added challenge of competing against another woman, Llys, who seemed so exceptional.

"Oh, look at the time!" Reese grabbed her clothes and ran to the bathroom, leaving Llys alone with Cornwalls.

 "Dear Phil..." said Llys, walking up to him and rubbing herself against him like she was Tes, "... it is sooo good to see you again!"

"Nice to see you, too, Llys..." He was showing her to the doorway, "... and thank you very much for your care and concern. We'll meet you in the dining room."

"Very well." Llys, sounding a little bit disappointed, left the room.

Cornwalls dressed and sat in a chair and waited for Reese.

Robots in the Lab were about the furthest thing from his mind, when Cornwall's confidential phone rang. He plugged into the secure USB socket and answered. It was Llys, wearing her professional hat this time.

"I apologize for disturbing you, Doctor Cornwalls. You have an urgent call from your Lab in California. Are you ready to receive?"

"Yes, Llys. Go ahead."

After two clicks and a slight pause, an operator voice came through. (In the back of his mind, Cornwalls thought that the call might not be secure.)

"Stand by... routing through Arpanet2" said the computer-generated voice.

(Sound of another click.)

"Hank here. All hell has broken loose. Two UH-60 Black Hawks just landed. They disgorged eight men in black-ops gear, surround-helmets, machine guns... the works!

Cornwalls was focused 100 percent on Mellon's report.

"I'm in the storage locker on the sub-basement level. I've got—he checked his wristwatch—maybe, a minute. The remaining robots are gone, taken, as are all files and... god I hate to say this... Linda Flynch, too. I think they tranquilized her....

Cornwalls listened in utter silence, processing what he was hearing.

"... S1 seems to have escaped; same for S5. Funny thing about that... odd. Must go. Watch your back."

Three clicks, a soft, two-second tone and... nothing.

Chapter 15 ~ Cat-fight Jealousy

"ANYTHING WRONG, PHIL?" REESE ASKED. If he hadn't been the one to abduct her, he would have been suspicious of her, but this was his doing. Now the question was: who was invading the Lab? He had no immediate answer. Then he had a wild idea. It would have to wait until after dinner, after they were aboard the plane.

Reese looked smashing. Cornwalls was completely stunned at the change. Later, when Llys walked up to escort them to their table he felt very lucky to have two such beautiful women accompany him to dinner.

Llys saw Reese to her seat and then helped Cornwalls to his. Bending over provocatively, she waited for him to kiss her softly on the cheek; instead, he passed a message to her.

"Find my robot S1, would you dear?" he whispered into her ear. She brushed her lips over his ear and whispered back, "Yes," knowing the effect she was creating on Reese. Then she stood up.

Cornwalls, also standing, grabbed her softly around the waist, pulled her closer and added, "... And try to find out what has happened to S5."

Put off, Llys only pouted in return as she departed; although not before transforming into the wait-staff personality she was supposed to present: "Dinner tonight is Atlantic salmon with lemon-butter sauce and capers. The vegetable is green beans almandine. There is a salad-and-fruit bar, should you wish appetizers. Enjoy."

Llys sashayed to the only other occupied table, leaving Cornwalls wondering if she had a "thing" for him, despite her not being human.

Reese, however, had been trying to speak to him. Finally, his spell broke.

"What ... happened to the robots? Do you think they are alright?"

"I don't know that anything has happened. I'm sure that, at millions of dollars each, they are still being well cared for," he lied.

"What do you mean 'cared for?'"

He wished he had listened to the beginning of her attempted conversation.

"I mean, if they ever should have to be moved, I'm sure they will be well cared for in the transition. Excuse me, but I'm famished. I'm going to get some salad."

He got up and went to the salad bar. Watching him, the beautiful woman sitting at the other table stood and joined him immediately.

"She's a nice tart, isn't she?"

"What?"

"The blonde waitress. I saw how she nuzzled you. Do you know her?"

"Oh, the waitress. Yes, we are good friends."

"I think more than that... do you think I should eat the little marinated potatoes?"

"What? No, keep your figure. You never know when you'll need it." That said, he took his salad plate back to the table and sat next to Reese.

The woman he had just ignored, stared after him... her plate dripping peas on the carpet.

After all, Cornwalls was a handsome man.

The main-course entree was perfect: Skinless salmon filets perfectly baked and topped with just the right amount of lemon zest to pique the flavors.

Llys returned to clear the table and, while doing so, she winked at Cornwalls out of sight of Ingrid. He ignored the gesture.

As the trio left the restaurant, Llys asked, "Did you enjoy your meal?"

"Yes, it was superb," answered Reese, which Llys ignored.

"Tell me about the other couple. Who were they?" asked Cornwalls.

"I am not at liberty to say right now; we can talk later."

Her suggestion did not go unnoticed by either Cornwalls or Reese.

Llys would certainly be coming back to their room later. Cornwalls wondered if Reese would be asleep by then, and what might happen.

Cornwalls and Reese later the same evening shared more than the bed again, and Reese did fall asleep. Moments later, Llys entered silently and knelt next to the bed on his side, facing his right ear, which she kissed before whispering to him.

"You should visit here more often."

"I've been busy and tired. Give me a report."

"Your robot S1 has escaped our net. He is across the canyon from your Lab in the eagle-watching blind built by Doctor Stanson. There is no trace of S5."

That said, Llys stood up and left the room without looking back.

Phil was stupefied. *Who is this robot/woman, anyway? Her vocabulary and actions are not those of a mere robot.*

He stayed awake most of the night. *How many robots, androids, whatever, were inhabited by dead people—or people who had died, to be more specific? Was this common? Was there a way to find out? Was S1 the only one, or was Llys also one?* rumbled in his head.

His next question simply murdered any chance of his sleeping any time soon: *What IS the difference between humans and robots?* It led to whole new rounds of questions and ruminations.

Humans make humans. Robots make robots. At what point is a robot suitable for human habitation? The S-series robot is as close to human as scientifically possible… but, is there a facility making robots identical to humans… robots that look like Llys? Llys never seems to have changed in the years that I've known her. Would humans want to inhabit that kind?

When at last he fell asleep, it was with Reese's arm draped over his chest as if they had been married for years. As far as he knew, Llys did not return, and he did not dream about her.

In the morning, he awoke to the site of Llys sitting on the edge of his bed, looking at him in a disconcerting way. Admittedly, his first thought was to wonder what it would be like to bed her. He never knew where these random thoughts were coming from, and he didn't know now.

Would the sex be enjoyable like it had been with Reese? Better? Worse? He summed it up as stupid conjecture.

Cornwalls had never taken Llys up on the apparent numerous offers she brought his way, even though she was the most beautiful woman he had ever known.

Llys, however, was here this time only to talk to him, while Reese was in the bathroom for another reason.

"Good to see you again, Llys. What do you have for me?" He regretted the turn of phrase the moment it came out of his mouth.

"More than you can possibly imagine, Phil." She let that sink in and then continued, "... Your robot S1 is still hiding out across the canyon. The empty Lab has been turned into a scrap heap. He told me 'Tes' is with him. Is that one of your other girlfriends, Phil?"

"No, Tes is the cat that belonged to Stanson."

"Oh. Good."

Acting as if there was nothing to her perfunctory reply, Llys went on with her report.

"... The Black-Ops people last night brought in a large bobtail truck and loaded it up with the other three robots, all the files, all the computer wiring and every computer. They also took onboard a drugged Linda Flynch. About ten minutes later, an F-45 flew in and bombed the place to rubble. Even the path to the other side of the canyon was rendered impassible, so S1 is stranded. He does have electricity and a land line, but no internet access."

"What about S5?"

"It wasn't collected into the truck. As far as we know, S5 is AWOL."

"Thanks, Llys. You're a sweetheart."

Cornwalls regretted that statement, too.

"Can I be your sweetheart, Phil?" Llys immediately asked.

For a moment, Cornwalls was at a loss for words. He looked hard at Llys—in his eyes, maybe the most beautiful woman in the world. But, he thought about her, too. He didn't really know anything about her, except that she was another employee of the same Agency as his. Swallowing hard, he decided there was nothing to be lost in what might, at worst, end up as few moments of pleasurable fiction.

"Uh, yes, I guess so, if it is allowed."

What am I saying... proposing to a fellow employee? There are strict Company policies. But, she is so incredibly beautiful..."

He never completed that thought.

Reese entered the room from the bathroom, saw Llys and blinked. She saw that Cornwalls was in his underwear on the bed. She walked over to him holding out her towel—the only thing covering her body.

"How about drying my back, or are you too busy?"

Cute, if not a bit snide, Phil thought, turned on.

Llys smiled bashfully, but she stood up and in preparing to leave announced the itinerary, dripping with cat-fight jealousy.

"I better let you two get dressed. The plane leaves in two hours. Breakfast will be English style: you serve yourselves."

Still, she winked at Cornwall and left the room.

Reese turned for her toweling, an obviously smug smile spreading across her face.

"Doctor Cornwalls," Reese said in a frosty tone that mocked Llys, "... do women fawn all over you everywhere you go?"

"No, Ingrid. Only here." He played along with her, eager to see where this banter would lead them.

"Call me, Llys, please. This must be an out-of-the-way place. Are you two married... or something?"

"No, Llys, agents are not allowed to marry each other."

He didn't say aloud what he thought: that Llys might be an android.

Suddenly, Reese spun around to face him; her towel tightly wound around her. She stumbled and fell onto the bed.

Cornwalls had been holding a portion of the towel all the while. As she fell and twirled like a top, the towel unwound, ending Reese's tumble with her stark naked. Though she quickly grabbed the towel and covered herself, many seconds went by until she could breathe well enough to speak.

"Have you, is she, does she, can she? Oh hell, is she alive like a woman... like S1?!"

Reese lay on the bed and stared at Cornwalls as her complete menu of emotional tones passed across her face and body, waiting for the man she was with to soothe them.

"No, Ingrid. Llys is just a beautiful robot who works here."

Cornwalls was fully dressed by now, and he helped Reese into her wardrobe for the day.

"Let's go to breakfast. On our flight across America we'll have plenty of time to discuss this more."

Reese asked as they left the apartment, "Is she good?"

Cornwalls took her remark badly. Grabbing her by her arm, he pulled her close and said, "How should I know? I've never slept with her, Ingrid. Is that what you wanted to hear? Although, I expect she's good enough to fool any drunken Senator."

"I can't process this," Reese mumbled to herself as she stumbled in the unfamiliar heels she had put on. She snuggled closer to Phil, happy to have him to protect her from a nasty fall and what might lie ahead.

Cornwalls was suffering. He was in his own quandary about being pursued by two beautiful women.

What should I do about Ingrid? Who or what is Llys? Can she be an android? If so, are there others like her?

On another note of thought: *Is my DARPA robotics project an out-of-date, hopeless relic? And, what about "C?" Will he wait for me long enough to pull off the contract he so badly wants, so I can reap my millions?*

And, *Where the hell is S5? Is S5 mounting a threat?*

Yes, more would be discussed on the plane. They would have hours to themselves to do it, too.

Chapter 16 ~ Danger in the Air

"DID YOU GIVE ALL OF the robots the Turing test?" Cornwalls asked Reese.

"How do you know about the Turing test?"

"I was once wondering if Alan Turing in 1950, had really tested a machine's ability to exhibit intelligent behavior equivalent to that of humans? Had he ever tested teenagers to see if they would be indistinguishable from a normal human? Being one at the time, I thought we were different. If he did, I wondered what our percentage score would be."

"I see."

"I can tell you this, Ingrid, if I ever have kids, I'm going to give them a Turing. I've known kids who, if you question them and question one of our robots, score as more robot than teenager." (He laughed.) "... Turns out, Turing uncovered a close relationship between teen intelligence and AI (Artificial Intelligence)."

"Ouch! Score one for the robots," said Reese.

Reese had been trying to decide if she should be jealous of Llys, whatever she was, or if she should just forget it. When she had heard Cornwalls' long-winded idea and explanation, she laughed, adding, "Well, they all passed the test, each one within a percentage point of the others."

"So those design criteria were met. But, what about their emotional stability?" he countered.

Reese was bored now. She wanted to think about something else and she ignored his inquiry. It was easier for her to turn her attention to how much the luxurious grey and silver motif of the plane's interior cabin impressed her.

Llys was onboard, too, but she made herself invisible after her blatancy toward Cornwalls back at their hotel room. She sat at the rear in one of the flight-attendant seats. A partition separated her location near the galley from the lounge in the middle of the cabin where Cornwalls and Reese sat.

Cornwalls watched the sun set and the sky outside turn darker. He assumed Llys would soon present food to them.

There had been very little contact with the pilots—only a snap-to salute and a smile at the gangway for Cornwalls and Reese.

Llys had boarded earlier. Acting the hostess, she had shown them to their seats, announced when they were cleared for takeoff, and remained silent for the duration of the flight to this point.

Cornwalls had turned to Reese to tell her something, when a mixed-grille entrée large enough for two was placed before them by Llys, who retreated as fast as she had appeared.

"So, as the professional psychologist, Ingrid, what do you think about the Turing Test scores of the different robots?"

"I think they were remarkable. The test was blind. I could not differentiate their answers between robot and human, nor could I tell they were artificial. At that point, they did not have individualized voices. Their parsing of English and their vocabularies were nothing short of amazing. At times, during the test, I forgot they were machines."

"Compared to that earlier test, what differences did you notice when you were conversing with S2?"

"Oh my! It was again completely different! S2 had individualized his voice; it was quite pleasant to listen to him."

Cornwalls nodded approvingly to keep her talking.

"I do often call the robots, using the male pronoun, because they seem so indistinguishable from humans."

"What kinds of things did you talk about?"

"Good question. It was the subject matter of our conversations that startled me most. You just don't expect a machine to discuss philosophy like that."

"Philosophy... really?"

"Yep. In our exchanges, the experience reminded me very quickly of similar conversations that I had with Doctor Stanson. Stanson was always bringing up the subject of the human soul, believe it or not. Can you imagine it?"

Reese then dramatized a large edition of a newspaper in front of her.

"'Scientist Speculates Spiritual Realm Inside Us!' Reads like a New York Post headline, doesn't it?"

She had paused for effect, but Cornwalls didn't react or interrupt; he was anticipating more. Reese waxed poetic.

"You know, Phil, psychology is really an absurd subject. The derivation of the name breaks down to 'study of the soul;' yet, there's quite a bit of literature purporting to Man as only an animal, if not an admix of chemicals. There are few materials about Man's spiritual essence."

"That's quite the revelation, Ingrid, coming from you."

"Honestly, Phil, I pretty much have always thought it was a huge joke on my instructors that they taught a subject that birthed the lie of itself right within its name: Psyche-ology... study of the soul."

"Interesting, Ingrid... never thought about it that way."

Llys had moved forward quietly and now sat in a lounge chair right behind them, listening.

"... So, what was your last opinion of S2, before he was shot?"

"I was shocked when Rogers shot him. I had enjoyed my conversations with him. Besides, I was convinced Rogers was an unbalanced man; also, insane with serious paranoia."

"Go on, Ingrid."

"Well, when S1 picked up the ongoing conversation, I was doubly shocked. None of my training and education had prepared me for that! Honestly, Phil..." She leaned forward and closer to him, even though they were practically alone, "... between you and me, I'm winging it here. If there is a soul... "

"Yes? Go on."

"Oh, never mind. You probably don't want to hear it, and I just can't go there anyway."

"Why did S1 run away, Doctor?"

"Did he? I don't know. The basic animal reaction to a threat is to either fight or give flight. Programmed as a warfighter, I would have expected him to go into battle mode. But... maybe he was afraid."

Reese had to think about that, even though the words had come from her mouth. She had converted to thinking out loud and not paying attention to Cornwalls' presence. Nor was she aware of Llys' keen interest in the conversation.

"... Fear, or any other emotion for that matter, is not a characteristic born or bred into a machine, no matter how well it's designed. Emotions are intrinsic to living creatures, life forms, and damn few of the extant species on Earth! Really. Not machines!" she concluded, mostly to herself.

She looked at him; he was deep in his own thoughts. Then, he spoke.

"I find it hard to imagine a machine feeling fear. Sure, maybe cockroaches or rats... but a television, a toaster, an air conditioner? Nope; don't think so. How would you explain that?"

"That, Phil, is an interesting question. A very interesting notion."

He lay back in his chair and thought hard about the idea of emotions and their role in living relationships.

Into the pregnant silence Llys stood up and interjected, "Dinner will be ready in five minutes. Do you want to eat at the dining table or your tray tables?"

"Oh, let's all eat together, shall we, Phil?" Reese said.

"Fine with me. Llys, you must join us!"

Picking up on his obvious implication, since their conversation had turned from robots to who and what might experience emotions, Reese agreed with him.

The male hormones inside of Cornwalls also had a thought of their own: that Reese might be substituting him for Oren Stanson. He had seen how she obviously had carried a torch for him for a long time. *Emotional juices might explain her change of personality* he concluded.

On the other hand, it might be emotions, plus her apparent jealousness over Llys' blatant fondness for him, that he didn't understand.

He resolved to observe how dinner together was working out among them. After all, jealousy seemed to him like a particularly human emotion, and Llys was not behaving strictly like an android robot, either.

Llys accepted their invitation to dine with them. She departed to the rear and finished her task of preparing their food, which was roast beef with mushrooms and gravy, rice pilaf and peas. She returned to set the table, and then she brought out the first dishes.

"Would you like Seven-Up, wine or sparkling water to drink?" Llys asked her dinner companions.

"I'll take water," said Reese.

"Is it Perrier?" he asked. Llys nodded.

"Me too, then."

Upon her return to the kitchenette, Llys set three pieces of cherry pie on Warm, and put out on the counter a tub of hardened, vanilla ice-cream for dessert: cherry pie a la mode.

She brought back two Perriers to the table and placed them in the cushioned recesses. After the main meal was consumed, she returned with the desserts, and then, later, cleared everything away and returned to her seat at the rear of the plane, where she plugged herself into the electrical/network connection.

Reese noticed a blinking-red light located at the front of the cabin just behind the cockpit.

"What's that light, Phil?" she said, pointing to the front.

Phil scanned the front half of the cabin. "Oh shit, shit, shit! Buckle up, Ingrid. We're going to go through some turbulence." He had said it calmly, but he feared much worse.

Llys passed them while running forward to the front of the cabin. There, she sat in a rear-facing seat and buckled her seatbelt.

"Not turbulence," she said.

Her terse message signaled what Cornwall had feared but not told Reese.

"Target acquired" the pilot of one of the F-16s following the dark twin-engine business jet radioed to his control.

"Mission is go. Down target," the anonymous control responded.

"Roger, mission go," acknowledged the second F-16 pilot.

The two aged fighter craft accelerated to Mach 1.8 and closed on Cornwalls' jet.

"Two bogies at six o'clock. Closing fast," the jet's pilot announced on his secure comm channel. Llys listened through her personal comm link.

"Roger. I've got them. Countermeasures armed. Taking it to the canyons?" asked the co-pilot.

"More evasive down there."

"Good... hope the food is secured."

The pilot banked 90 degrees right, then snap-rolled 180 degrees left and screamed down toward the distant mesas below them.

Cornwalls was immediately aware that they were in the hands of experienced fighter pilots far better than he had expected. But, less so Llys. Plates and food from the galley rose in the weightless seconds and moved about the cabin.

Cornwalls grabbed his embroidered cloth napkin and tried to corral the food before it landed on Reese.

As the outside air screamed past the windows, the plane surpassed its design limits, going beyond Mach 1. Suddenly, sound and cabin air pressure went deathly still. The craft seemed to accelerate even more.

"This isn't going to end well, is it, Phil?"

"No, Ingrid. You're going to look like you've just come through a horrific plane crash, even if you don't."

Llys unbuckled her belt and grabbed a large plastic garbage bag from a dispenser near her seat. Suspended in the air, she calmly pulled herself vertically up to their table, reached out and pushed most of the suspended food and plates into the bag, sealed it, and stuffed it between two empty seats on the other side of the plane. Then she slid back to her seat and buckled in.

Cornwalls was amazed that none of the food or plates and utensils had landed on Reese.

Exactly 87 seconds later, the pilot pulled out of his diving and rolling maneuvers, while still flying at well over Mach 1, mere inches above the treetops. He and his co-pilot heard the loud groans from their passengers as g-forces tried to tear them apart.

In the end, stout, custom reinforcements kept the plane together, and the pilots won the battle. Having avoided the incoming missiles, which exploded harmlessly into the terrain, they leveled out at about thirty feet above the mesa tops and drew down their airspeed.

Suddenly, the plane bucked from one ground explosion behind them, and then another from ahead. Accelerating, the pilot maneuvered the private jet with side-to-side half-rolls through the canyons well below the mesa tops and inches from the red-dirt canyon walls.

"I think it's safe to say we're not really in a Lear Jet, right, Phil?" Reese said into her napkin, wiping her face.

"Hell, I don't know!" he answered. His eyes were glued to his cabin window as canyon walls passed by.

Then, without warning, their modified craft went vertical. The 3-G force pressed them into their seats, but it wasn't over. The pilot kicked in the after-burners and accelerated them upward in a tight spiral.

Zooming past a high-altitude cloud layer, two heavy thumps shook the fuselage.

"Are we hit?" Reese, panicked, asked.

"No, or we'd be dead. We just fired back at our attackers." Llys answered as if reading a weather report.

Nano-seconds later, an expanding fireball, and then another, were visible as they leveled out of a barrel roll, slowed to subsonic speed, and approached a layer of cirrus clouds.

"I think someone was after us," Reese remarked inanely, gulping hard to keep the rest of her dinner inside her body.

"Either after us or Llys," said Cornwalls looking and studying her. She, of course, sat expressionless. He didn't know whether by design, habit... or intent.

"Llys? Why would anybody be after her?" asked Reese, whose question had raised a smile out of Llys, though nothing more.

Presently, one pilot left the cockpit and walked directly to Cornwalls.

"Our flight plan has been compromised, Commander. Do you have a secondary destination?"

"Give me a few minutes, I'll come up and let you know."

"Yessir." He returned to the cockpit.

Doctor Reese had gone to the toilet, and now Llys locked her in there.

"What now, Phil?"

"You know we have to deliver Ingrid to her interrogation at the CSS. And you and I must find S1. We need to go into hiding with him, until we can bring Ingrid to us..."

Cornwalls was reading her eyes for her reactions as he spoke to her.

"... She may be the actual target here, in which case the people she is, no doubt, talking to now on the phone in the bathroom may not be her friends. We can land in Colorado and send on the plane with her in it. You and I will hitch a ride somehow back to California."

"Just like old times, eh, lover?"

Llys then kissed him and returned to the rear of the plane, leaving Cornwalls mystified all over again.

What the hell was that crack about? What old times? Does she know about my military-intelligence career? Has she been in Intelligence, too? MI-5, perhaps? No, I would have remembered her!

And then he felt the softness and warmth (!) of her unexpected kiss—certainly not usually available from a mere android. He sure was confused... and turned on!

Llys had put on a high-speed parajump suit behind the galley partition. With a WHOOSH, she ejected herself through an escape hatch at the rear of the jet, leaving a vacuum in her place.

Cornwalls pressed a small button on the side of his chair, signaling the cockpit that he needed assistance. Pointing toward the aft toilet door, he directed the pilot to where Reese was locked in.

As soon as Reese was free to leave the washroom, the pilot grabbed and held her tightly. Though she struggled, he was commando trained. He subdued her with a quick jab of a syringe into her shoulder muscle.

"Good job. I'll help you stow her in the pressurized storage compartment; then I have to go."

"We're tracking Llys and will give you updates after you land."

"Good enough."

The two men carried Reese's body to the center of the plane. There, they opened a concealed hatch, leading to a padded cylindrical container. They poured her in gently.

Reese would find room to move around and most of the comforts of home, when she awoke.

"Deliver her to the CSS meeting in as good a shape as you can manage. They'll probably expect a little dishevelment, since one or more of them may have sent those attack fighters to do us all in. When you're done, ditch the plane and get picked up by the Coast Guard. Thanks. Appreciate all your help!"

"You're welcome, Commander. Good luck."

The pilot sealed Reese into her oversized cocoon, checked all the data lights on the lid and, finding all right, returned to the cockpit.

Meanwhile, Cornwalls walked forward to another washroom near the cockpit. Inside, he locked the door, sat on the toilet seat and pushed a button, releasing an escape suit like Llys' that dropped in his lap. He donned the suit and pushed another button on the ceiling of the toilet.

The seat slid into the wall, while Cornwalls donned the oxygen mask provided with the escape suit. With the push of another button, he ejected into a 20,000-foot altitude of nothing but sky.

"Phil, do you read me?" came the co-pilot's voice into his headset.

"Clear as a bell."

There was no more contact as he plummeted toward the ground. Diving toward a land of mountains, lakes, and tall trees much like the Colorado Rocky Mountains, he grabbed two handles at his sides and pressed their activation switches. Small bat-wings extended and his tumbling and yawing stabilized. Angling his trajectory in line with the horizon, he slowed his speed enough to deploy larger, main wings and felt the jerk of his immediate, further slowing.

This should be a national sport Cornwalls thought as he steered toward a large lake below him and slightly to the West. Soon enough, his airspeed would slow to where he could deploy a drogue chute but, for now, he was having some fun.

Cornwalls, dipping slightly to his right, flashed through a cloud. He realized the stupidity of that move when his helmet windscreen completely frosted over on the inside. With the outside temperature near freezing, there was nothing he could do but stay in the sunlight until he had clear vision again.

Then, he heard a crackling on his helmet headset.

"Honey, how are you doing? I'll be at our mountain at 14:30... about 15 minutes. You?" It was Llys checking in.

Cornwalls for the moment could not see anything but the frost inside of his vision-plate as he dropped toward Earth at over 300 MPH, but he liked the comforting sound of her voice tones.

"Oh, well... I'm doing just fine. Got a little later start than planned; we had to ice the doctor in the cooler."

"So, what's your ETA?"

"Say, 20 minutes."

"Time is money, honey."

His helmet was clearing. The heads-up display indicated his groundspeed at 300 mph, which would let him make up a few minutes. He relaxed and concentrated on flying.

Minutes later, his speed was down to 220, the top speed at which he could lose the gliding wings, but he stayed in bat mode a little longer to catch up with Llys' timetable.

When he could see the mountain that was his target and the small rustic cabin on top, he set his magnification to 200 percent to watch Llys arrive inside of the landing circle with her soaring wings spread wide. Excited, he deployed his soaring wings and nearly had them jerked out of his hands. His airspeed had increased, unnoticed.

I'm going to need a shoulder massage after this.

Cornwalls soared in for a landing in the center of the landing circle, but he stumbled and fell flat on his face— nothing broke except his pride, when he felt Llys' strong fingers remove his flight suit and help him up.

"Oh, my poor spy," she cooed. "...You always misjudge your final-approach speed. Come on in, I'll give you a massage."

Cornwalls' smile was as wide as his face: YES!

Llys helped Cornwalls into the cabin, then returned to the landing pad and grabbed his flying suit. She folded it neatly and stored it next to hers in an outside cupboard next to the cabin door, which she locked.

Inside, he was thinking about her comment. *If she called me a spy, what is she?*

"So, now I have to care for an invalid all the way to California? Some vacation!" she teased.

Llys removed his shirt and examined his arms and shoulders, pressing here and there to determine the extent of the damage his landing had caused. He groaned suitably, though he wasn't hurt much.

"I'm cold. I think I'm going to faint," he lied to her, rolling on his back.

"Oh, poor baby. I'll warm you up. You just relax those overworked muscles between your ears, okay?"

Llys was on to him.

They laughed together.

"Progress report," C said to his lieutenant in the field.

"There must have been damage—two bailed out in power-gliders. We lost them on radar. The jet took off and headed east, sir."

"Christ! Get some choppers in the area, stet! And when you find those two parachutists... terminate them. I'm sick of their incompetence. I can do the deal by myself."

Chapter 17 ~ A Bedtime Story

LLYS, DRESSED ONLY IN A nightgown, lay on the bed next to Cornwalls, humming a melody. He listened; it was catchy, but he wondered how she got the programming. Leaning over, he smiled and kissed her.

"What is that song you were humming?"

"Oh, it's just a folk song that tells about my life."

"What's its name?"

"'Parsley, Sage, Rosemary and Thyme'."

"Really? Aren't those cooking herbs?"

"Yes, but hundreds of years ago, a song about love lost, love found... that sort of thing... used that title and metaphor."

Phil kissed her again. "I don't fully understand."

"Well, it's ancient history, so we can let it go." She leaned into him and rubbed his hair. "Ready for me?" she whispered playfully, nuzzling his ear.

"First, I have a burning question to ask you." He kissed her on the nose.

"What's on your mind?"

"You, naturally, but, would you tell me who exactly you are? Or is it classified and above my pay grade?"

"Darling, its way above your pay grade!" She laughed, kissed him again, and draped her arm over his miraculously recovered shoulder.

"I'm serious. I'm seriously curious. Come on, Llys, tell me."

Ignoring his request, she propped him up with small pillows that leaned him back in the bed, and then she sat in his lap.

He pushed his face into her soft, fragrant, honey-blonde hair. Pulling away, he drank in her deep-blue eyes before kissing her on her lips. All the while thinking *she seems rather light for a woman of her size and strength.*

It made him wonder; he had to find out more.

"You look so beautiful... too perfect to be real. Where did you come from?"

"New Mexico, Sweetie."

He didn't buy the reply, and the look on his face told her so.

"Seriously now, I'm not supposed to talk about this!" She pulled away from his embrace.

"Why? Are you an illegal alien or something?"

"No. Because I like you and I don't want anything to come between us."

"Like what? You're scaring me now."

"Like who I am."

"Okay, I'll bite. Who are you? Are you a ghost or reality; am I really seeing you here? Are you a hologram; a figment of my imagination? A spy?"

"Well, not quite."

"What? Not quite which?"

"I really mean it. I'm not supposed to talk about it."

"C'mon, not quite...?"

"Not quite a spy."

"What does 'not quite' mean?"

"I mean... I don't know what I mean." Tears welled up in her eyes. "I'm just not quite human."

More tears rolled down her cheeks.

He tried to comfort her, not knowing how.

"So... these are not-quite tears rolling down these not-quite-human cheeks?"

She covered her eyes.

He wrapped his arms around her tighter and kissed her tears.

"I love you. Marry me?"

"I can't."

"Why not?"

"Because I'm not real, and I'm not supposed to talk about it..."

Her tone changed, and she had more to say.

"... I'm not kidding. And now they're going to kill me for saying what I already did."

"Who's going to kill you?"

"The 'Other' aliens."

"You mean you're going to be deported? Are you in trouble with Immigration?"

He wasn't sure how to deal with this, so, thinking it was the right thing to do, he tickled her. Her sobs stopped. She stared at him, then tickled him back, laughing.

"You can't love me, I'm not human."

"But I do!"

"We can't get married: I'm not a legal person, and you can't marry a machine!"

"A what?!"

Her tone and mood changed as she switched the subject.

"... But, I can still be your mistress, your paramour."

The softness of her sultry voice worked magic on him.

"I don't care what you are; I want to get married and I want to marry you."

"Why are you so stuck on getting married?"

He ignored her question. He had a delayed reaction to her earlier remark about what she was.

"You're a machine? Bull crap. You're no more a machine than I am."

She dried her eyes on the bed sheet, liking what he had just told her.

"So, tell me, really, why can't you marry me?"

"I can't marry you, or anybody, because I'm not a legal person. I'm not even an Earthling."

"What are you, then?"

"I'm an android body constructed by aliens... but you cannot tell anyone, please!"

He paused. He stared at her and thought: *how perfect, how beautiful, how wonderful she is – too bad she's crazy... but I'm just as crazy for her, too!*

"There must be a way. I love you too much," he told her.

"I can't talk about it!" she fumed. "You don't understand; they'll kill me! And... I'm scared."

Big teardrops fell again. He tried to kiss them away, to no avail this time, which angered him.

"Who will kill you? Calm down! Tell me who. Nobody's going to kill you, if I can help it. Take a deep breath and tell me the truth: Who is going to kill you?"

"The 'Others,' of course!"

The aliens again he thought. *So perfect; too perfect... she can't possibly be this insane.*

He decided to give her the benefit of the doubt: "Maybe you better tell me the whole story. Take a deep breath and start from the beginning."

As he was looking at her with a cold-steel determination, she realized she had never seen him so intent.

Maybe I could tell him. He's used to keeping secrets, after all.

"Okay, I'm going to tell you and let consequences fall where they may. If a saucer flies over us and destroys me... then so be it."

He held his head in both of his hands and muttered under his breath, "Oh brother!"

She hadn't heard what he'd said, but she was miffed that he had whispered about her in front of her.

"Phil, I have to tell this in my own way or I'll never get through it; so, please, don't interrupt."

She put her hand gently over his mouth, saying, "Believe me, I love you, too. That part is as real as it's ever going to get, no matter who I am. I don't want anything to happen to you, so think of this as my bedtime story."

Before she continued, she made sure he was comfortable and that she had a position that suited her, too.

"Once upon a time, a very, very, very long time ago, extraterrestrials landed on Earth. They watched the world's primitive races compete for survival against the Earth's flora and fauna at that time. They decided to lend a hand after considering that this world could be a good place for an experiment they had in mind."

"How long ago?"

"Really long; tens of thousands of years ago, at least." (She lied, not to scare him.)

"Okay."

"The Others..."

He broke in again with another question.

"Why?"

"Why what?"

"Why did they come to Earth?"

"They had orders to conduct an experiment. I don't know who gave them the orders. They just did."

"Okay."

"Anyway, this is my story; so, just sit back and enjoy it. Now SHUT UP, or I won't tell you at all!" she said in mock anger, throwing a pillow at him.

He kissed her on the neck in the middle of the pillow fight that had ensued and then sat back on the bed.

"They had found a race of bipeds, which fit their needs, and they began a long series of genetic experiments to try and lengthen the life spans, and increase the intelligence quotient, of these bipeds. Eventually, they succeeded; they attained those goals. However, they failed one of their primary goals, which was to create a race of beings that could endure global catastrophes."

"So, what did they do?"

"A small part of the whole group of Others decided to continue with a different approach. Thinking that biological creatures would never be satisfactory, they designed a series of androids.

"However, problems quickly arose. Technically speaking, creating non-biological androids was easier than engineering a complete biological system, but, since the biological systems they created nearly had overrun the planet, having procreated prolifically, the new machine-based model had to blend in among them, or there would be conflict.

"For a few centuries, the designed arrangement worked out. By then, a hybrid culture and centuries of social, artistic, political, etc., interactions had left a culture worth preserving.

"But the Dark Ages came, and diseases like the Plague decimated the biologicals. Humanity was in danger of going into extinction.

"Fortunately, there came a Renaissance pushed forward by, as usual, the more artistic people. Additionally, they came up with a new hybrid model that was physically identical to the biological creations of Man. Yet, the

AI (Artificial Intelligence) designed into them was not capable of passing unnoticed for what the rest were: Homo Sapiens.

"Then, one day, one of the alien designers came up with what everyone considered was brilliant: meld the two into one new species, making a fusion of android AI, and NI (Natural Intelligence) that Doctor Reese talked about on board the plane. The idea was to place a human life force into the android A.I. frame, which they already had created, and then see if it would take over and run the android the way it did with the human body."

"I see where this is going."

"Of course, you do. Now, shut up. Remember, this is my bedtime story."

"Okay, sweetie."

"The experiment proved successful. They developed seven prototypes and sent them into the world to see how they would fare among Homo Sapiens.

"Each creation was flawless. The human-life forces they chose to inhabit the new AI androids were selected from a group of female beings about whom the Others already had knowledge and experience; who also recently had passed away near their base at Dulce, New Mexico.

"By the way, that specific location had been chosen for the convenience of long-term observation of the new breed of 'women.' And, I, my dear, was one of those women.

"You mean you were dead?"

"Ah-ah-ah, my dear! My story... remember?"

"Well, to continue... the place was crawling with human military personnel, and occasional conflicts broke out with the aliens."

"Okay," he broke her communication. "... But, do you remember your past lifetime?"

"Of course, I do. Anyone can, I think. In my most recent previous life, I was born in 1923. I went to college at Michigan, applied for the OSS and trained as a spy in Ontario, Canada. Later, I performed missions behind German lines. Eventually, I ended up stationed in New Mexico. There, I died in a battle between aliens—now called 'Others'—and the U. S. Army. Not long after, I found myself inside this android AI."

(She had left out the part of how and where—a spy mission gone bad— she had met and loved the very being she was talking to today.)

He laid his head on the bed and closed his eyes, digesting what this vo- luptuous creature had told him in confidence. He was trying to picture/ envision her descriptions, and finding only brief flickers of memories that flashed across his mind-field too quickly to understand. Thinking he was still in love with her, maybe more than ever, he eventually chuck- led at the incomprehensibility of it all. After all, the math made her well over 100 years old!

"Phil? Phil? What are you laughing about?"

He sat up and looked at her wide-eyed.

"Are you kidding me? You just told me a story about my girlfriend being 100 years old... trained as a spy... murdering in wartime... getting killed in New Mexico... and then coming back to life as a robot?"

"An android to be exact."

Android, robot – who cares?!..."

He shook his head and laughed some more.

"... And you want to know why I'm laughing? I won't sleep the rest of the night; or maybe for days, or ever. Your story is so incredible... that I think it's all true!"

She did a double take, and cut to the chase: "I'm your girlfriend, you said?"

"Silly woman. Of course, you are. I proposed to you and, I think, you accepted; so that also makes you my fiancée, even though we might not be able to get married... yet! Officially speaking, would you marry me, if you could?"

Llys sighed deeply, rolled over and hugged him. "But, I can't..."

"Just say yes or no."

"Yes."

"So, it's official. We're picking out a ring tomorrow on our way to California."

The hour was late, and Cornwalls couldn't fall asleep. His mind churned; so many new possibilities had awakened in his creative head. Llys, of course, could stay awake all night.

"I've been thinking about all this. The robot S2 in the lab, is that one like you? Any similarity? Reese thinks he's alive; she said as much. You remember what she told us in the plane? Did the same happen to you?"

He had spun himself almost into a super-confused stupor from all his questions and ideas.

"... And here I thought I was through with those repeated, made-up Lab stories about haunted robots."

"Well, honey, the Lab made him, so you ought to know."

"I think I'm finally beginning to understand," he said.

He snuggled up to her.

Time enough tomorrow for adventure she thought as she let him take her in his arms and do what lovers do.

Sated, Cornwalls mercifully fell asleep near dawn and he dreamed about the goddess lying next to him. He also swore that he would never bring up the subject of her makeup and origins ever again.

Llys, on the other hand, quite awake and alert, decided that she would tell him some other time how much longer she would outlive him.

Chapter 18 ~ Flying AirSpy

COMING TO, INGRID REESE FELT like she was locked up inside a coffin. The capsule certainly felt like a coffin, softly padded with silk or satin. Her panic level rose. She moved her fingers across the fabric in widening arcs until she felt metal protrusions—buttons made of metal or plastic, which she pressed.

Fortunately, none ejected her. Pressing the last button, though, made a video monitor light up. On the screen, she saw the sky outside and the ground far below; and that she was flying eastward toward the dawning twilight.

Cursing Cornwalls for leaving her like this, she gradually calmed down and completed her inspection of her container. It was not, in fact, a coffin; for one, there was no lid. Then she remembered the air battle she had survived, and felt and tasted the chalky residue of the chemical remnants of the sedative she had been given.

Did Phil do this to me? Or was it that robotic blonde android?

Her next thoughts outraged her: *Am I still headed to the secret meeting with the super-secret organization Phillip mentioned? And why like this? The "CSS" Phil had called it. Was it a covert Schutz-Staffel? No, he had called it the "Central Security Service."*

Her panic had subsided. She noticed she had misplaced her shoes. *I'll have to buy some new ones when I arrive, assuming I'm still conscious by then.*

For the hell of it, she yelled and heard the material of her coffin-like cylinder absorb the sound. She fished around with her feet to see if she could find her shoes, which she did. They had fallen to the bottom of the capsule.

"CORNWALLS! I AM GOING TO SUE YOU FOR ONE BILLION... MAKE THAT A TRILLION... DOLLARS, IF I LIVE THROUGH THIS!" she shouted as she put her shoes on her feet.

That did it. Suddenly, the video monitor projected the image of a handsome black man wearing a tight, black flight suit and smiling at her.

"Hello, Doctor Reese. I apologize for your limited accoutrements. You were put into an escape pod in the jet and jettisoned toward our location. Don't worry; we are in control of your flight, which will carry you to your meeting at the CSS. You'll have an opportunity to spruce up before you are seen by any public figures."

Reese's eyes were glued to the screen.

"Your pilot from the jet, and I, owe you many days of explanation, for which we don't have time. Not to be too modest, however, we did save your life and that might be worth at least that 'trillion dollars' to you... would you not agree?"

"Then, I'm not a captive? You're not going to torture me for my secrets... use my body for unholy experimentations, and God knows what else?"

The black man laughed.

"Very clever, Doctor. You should write a novel about us someday. In fact, though, we're going to land you at our super-secret airfield owned by the agency that Doctor Cornwalls mentioned to you. Neither he nor his companion Llys will be attending. You see, they were forced to eject from the jet and, frankly, we have no idea where they are now. Your E.T.A is five minutes from now. Bye for now, and thank you for flying AirSpy."

With that, the screen went dark and then another image came on: a distant string of blue lights surrounded by dense blackness.

Probably a landing strip... 'AirSpy,' indeed! she thought.

Five minutes passed swiftly. The capsule's approach looked more like a crash-landing to Reese. She panicked and squeezed her eyes shut, expecting the worst and kicking off her shoes. But the touch-down came with only a gentle bump and blue lights speeding past. The airplane capsule decelerated and taxied toward a dark building nestled among a grove of trees splashed with color by the sun cresting over the eastern horizon. Another set of two blue-light rows illuminated a walkway and then flickered off as daylight took over.

The screen in Reese's capsule went dark, as did the inside cabin lights. She punched the buttons again in a panic, but nothing happened right away.

Suddenly, she felt like she was riding in an elevator; then the capsule bumped down and stayed still. The door handle that she never had found twisted open, and a rush of cool air smelling like a New Hampshire pine forest filled her nostrils—a comforting smell that relaxed her.

A tall, strawberry-blond dressed in a form-fitting, navy blazer over a silver blouse and dark skirt, accompanied by a lustrous string of pearls around her neck, approached and helped Doctor Reese disembark.

"So sorry you arrived this way, Doctor. Our private craft sustained some damage in the evasive battle, and the flight crew sedated you and put you in this maneuverable capsule for your personal safety."

Non-plussed, Reese replied, "I couldn't find my shoes."

"Understood."

The redhead was leading the way along the slender pathway toward the main building.

"... We have new ones for you; in fact, several pair. You can choose whichever you like."

Approaching the large building, she said, "I'll take you to your room first, where you'll find a complete change of clothes, a warm shower and a comfortable bed. There is no rush here. Your meeting is scheduled for 0900 tomorrow morning. I'm sure you'll want to look your best."

Reese noticed that the ground under her feet, which looked like solid concrete, felt soft and gave way slightly where she stepped. The sensation triggered memories.

No soft companion to hold on to today she thought, missing Cornwalls. She admitted to herself in a moment of self-pity that he had quite an effect on her, despite his apparent devotion to Llys.

Android, my ass! she thought. *That's a crock!*

She was missing Cornwalls and Stanson, even if Stanson was a disembodied spirit who inhabited robot bodies!

A rising sun hinted the day would be graced with a bright, azure-blue sky, and the building's reflective glass made the structure appear dark from the outside. The ground Reese walked on continued to feel soft and inviting.

Giving her hostess the once-over, Reese noted that the woman wore gray gym shoes and that her business suit looked well-tailored and extremely expensive. Her dark gray stockings complimented her silver blouse. A blue, grey and red-patterned scarf wrapped her neck like a cravat in contrast. The short cut and wave of her strawberry-blond hair accented her thin face and high cheekbones. Seeing they were almost of the same height, Reese upgraded her expectations of the quality of the shoes she might be able to choose from in her room.

"What's your name?" Reese asked politely.

"Oh, I'm so sorry. I can't divulge that information... security, you know."

They entered the building and then an elevator.

"What should I call you, then?"

"Just call me 'Alice'."

"Do you know Doctor Cornwalls' friend, Llys?"

"Oh, you know Llys? I don't know her very well."

Alice had lied.

The elevator took them somewhere underground. Alice escorted her guest to her room and touched a fingerprint reader at the door. At once, a small light next to the door turned from red to green, and the door opened.

Inside the room soft, indirect lighting and classical music—*Mozart, still popular* she thought, smiling—greeted Reese. And then she laughed at her next thought: *at least, it isn't Wagner!*

"Please touch the identification pad, Doctor Reese, so the room will recognize you when you want to come or go."

When she complied, a small, static-electricity discharge caused her to pull her hand away.

Alice smiled congenially and shoved the unlocked door wide open.

"Good night, Doctor Reese, the room and our amenities are all at your disposal. Call if you need anything at all," she said as she pointed to a phone device on a nightstand. "By the way," she smiled again, "... the room will awaken you in time for breakfast tomorrow. Enjoy."

With that, Alice left Reese to herself.

Reese considered seriously that she might go exploring. Soon enough, though, she realized she was, in fact, exhausted from her all-night, somewhat cramped, air-borne escapade.

The idea of a desperately needed cleanup took over. *Maybe, if possible, a long soak in a tub would be better.*

Walking to the bathroom and dropping her worn, food-stained clothing along the way, Reese again was amazed at the soft "concrete" and how it felt pleasingly warm to her feet.

There was no tub; yet, the shower was designed as a glassed-in, total-enclosure environment; like the ones she had seen only in architectural magazines... and liked.

I'm impressed. I give it at least four stars. A masseuse or masseur would bump it up to five for me.

After her long, hot shower, Reese flopped down on the bed and drifted to sleep, thinking thoughts of Stanson/S1.

When she awakened, she discovered to her chagrin that her clothes were missing — room service had granted her wish and a masseur had arrived and given her a massage as she slept.

Chapter 19 ~ Universe Makers

ROBOT S1, NOW INHABITED BY Oren Stanson's spirit, sat at the small cabin's yellowed Formica kitchen table and contemplated the piles of typing paper covering it. He had recently found a full box of empty sheets and some pens in a closet, but he could not recall ever putting them there when he was alive as a human, although he felt certain that he must have done so. In his previous lifetime—how he thought of it now, he had spent time in this cabin.

Right now, Tes presented a more pressing problem for him. He had no cat food and precious little fresh water, not enough for her to live on. He needn't have worried, though, since Tes was an excellent mouser. Her first kill arrived at the front door after only two days.

S1 worked and reworked mathematical formulas, trying to discover how his bionetic brain could store all his "human" memory banks from his prior life, as well as those of his present life. There didn't seem to be enough room, leading to what he, at first, thought was impossible: a conclusion that memory is not cellular.

"Tes, what do you think? Is memory cellular or electronic?"

"Meow," she protested.

"Okay; not a fair question. I get that. I'll ask you a different way: Is memory in the cells?"

Tes was silent.

"Is memory set up in an electronic field?"

Tes jumped on his lap and started her infamous purring.

"Wisdom of the ages... no wonder the Egyptians worshipped you. Okay, here's a harder one, Tes: Is memory electronic?"

The cat yawned.

"Is memory a subtle-energy field that we don't yet know how to measure?"

Tes crawled up to his shoulder, purred louder and licked his ear.

"Thank you, Tes! I knew I could count on you."

Still, the mathematics of the problem lay unanswered on the Formica. The underlying problem was how to fully understand the properties of such a subtle-energy field.

Perhaps, it is a quantum field that extends forever in physical-universe space or in a no-space we are not yet familiar with he wondered.

Because he thought it might help his mathematics, S1 spent a lot more time trying to remember certain key-word terms he had studied for his degree in String Theory. Chagrined, he decided he had not fully understood the subject's nomenclature, in part because whole pages, when he tried to recall them, in fact, came up blank.

Helicopters hovered over the partially hidden cabin periodically for weeks after the military jets had destroyed the Lab. Knowing they had the capability of detecting certain types of electronic radiation, S1 shut down all electrical equipment from time to time, anticipating each bi-weekly sortie. While certainly stressful for him, the regular check-ups also brought him a relief that he hadn't been written off as lost. He liked

knowing that others still considered he had some value, albeit opposi-
tional forces, which viewed him as a target to seek out and destroy.

Not a day passed that S1 did not wonder if any of his Lab team had survived the holocaust; also, if any of them would come looking for him. His
mind struggled with different scenarios for how to make his presence
known without alerting the hostiles.

Right after another helicopter overflight, his phone rang. He didn't answer it, of course, but it continued to ring in a familiar pattern: Three
short, one short, three short, one short, then stop. Then it repeated. His
name was being repeated in ancient Morse code. On the fifth attempt, he
answered through his custom modem.

"S1."

"Thank God. Don't worry. I'm coming."

The caller hung up immediately. S1 had recognized Cornwalls' voice but
he continued with his research, which at this point concerned one more
important and immediate thing: one hungry cat.

Later, right in the middle of all this research, and while missing his late-
night, Saturday-evening repartees with Ingrid Reese, he thought of a series of, for him, startling ideas: *what if the whole thing goes sideways? What
if every spirit makes his own universe? If they do, where are theirs? Where is
his? Where is Ingrid's? And Brigadier-General Rogers'? How does one join or
leave a universe? How does one find another's universe?*

From that tangled mindset, tumbled out another outrageous thought, a
deduction: *To experience another universe, one must touch, or somehow
communicate with, another spirit. If true, the material universe would have
to be the result of a collective communication and agreement among all par-
ticipants and their individual universes. No God figure required, unless the*

"God of gods" was the notion of a collective *"all"* made up of every ghost or spirit creating and playing the *Material Universe Game*.

I helped make this Universe! Stanson (S1) thought. The satisfaction, the scientific "ah-hah" moment elated him, and immediately he couldn't wait to discuss it with Doctor Reese as soon as possible.

The stream of thought delivered again: *What about all those stories about children who remember their past lives? Did I just have that kind of a past life?*

S1 dropped what he was doing. He forced himself to think about the ramifications of that last thought. Satisfied with his answers, he decided to bring it up with the unknown caller, if he heard from him again.

Was that really Cornwalls? he wondered.

"Meow," Tes punctuated his query.

And then, in an earth-shattering split-second, a horrifying thought came to him, which made his robot body dull out and shiver.

"Tes, do you know where the robot S5 is?"

"Kip, Kip, Kip" she replied, lying down with her head on her paws.

S1 saw her telepathic vision clear as daylight, but it was horrible: S5, fully awake and activated, stood stiffly upright. There was a red star painted on its forehead, and its arms were extended in a way that suggested it would deploy its weapons.

"Oh God, no," he said at Tes. She stared back at him, saying nothing. She didn't even blink.

Chapter 20 ~ Collusion, Part Two

THE CO-PILOTS OF THE UNUSUALLY equipped private jet, from which Reese had been jettisoned and Llys and Cornwalls jumped, followed their navigation orders to the letter. They vectored East and soon were over the Atlantic Ocean.

"Approaching Grand Banks," the co-pilot radioed.

"Ditch somewhere deep. Use your escape pod and sink it once you get your raft open." The commanding voice in his headset was none other than Alice.

"Roger that."

"Just follow procedure. Activate your pod for a departure at T-minus oh-five minutes. Set the destruct timer for T-minus 05:07. Seven seconds, gentlemen... remember that. On your mark."

"Setting our marks... 3-2-1... set, sir."

"10-4."

The craft descended at an angle of 25 degrees and a cruising speed of 400 knots.

"Punch it in 5, 4, 3, 2, 1... eject," the pilot called and then pressed the button that shot the two pilots away from the doomed jet.

Exactly seven seconds later, the plane came apart. The deepening angle of descent and subsequent aerodynamic stresses broke the fuselage in two ahead of the wings. Hitting the water at high speed, most of the aircraft exploded into a thousand pieces like many small bombs going off. The engines careened and skimmed across the wavetops, before a gigantic explosion ripped them apart, sending fragments of titanium, carbon fiber, thorium and other exotic materials in every direction across a wide swath of ocean measuring several square miles.

The escape capsule designed with winglets enabled the pilots to direct their trajectory southward before it crash-landed onto the water. Seconds later, a hatch exploded open, and the two men crawled out and jumped into a large floating platform.

The now-empty capsule sank immediately as seawater rushed into its open hatch. The survivors activated a life raft, crawled onto it like babies, took off their flight suits and stuffed them into a weighted canvas bag that they dumped overboard.

After paddling the raft several hundred yards away, one of the men pressed a button on a waterproof console located on the inner side of the raft, causing the empty platform to explode loudly, incinerating everything in and on it. The remaining debris was blown to one-inch-square metallic and plastic bits that sank. The following day, identifiable remains, if discovered, likely would be interpreted as flotsam from a crashed UFO, which regularly happened.

The pilot removed a waterproof, two-way radio from a compartment located on the inner wall of the raft and pressed the send button.

"Mission completed. Come and get us."

"Coast Guard contact made. They will find you in the morning," Alice said. Having no further use for the device, the pilot threw the radio into the ocean, and it sank.

The two men pulled together a couple of heavy, waterproof tarps stowed in another compartment of the raft. They positioned these over themselves to ward off the heat of the sun's rays in the daylight hours and the coolness of the approaching night, hoping to ride out the hours like two babies covered in bright-orange materials that would be easily spotted by aircraft in the morning. After midnight, an emergency beacon deployed from a weather balloon was sent up to help the rescuers find them.

"Get 'C,' would you?"

"Yessir," answered the personal secretary, Miss White, after she pushed the button that connected her to her boss.

"Sir, the control tower is on the line."

"Good. Connect him. I want to talk to him." He spoke without letting the caller speak.

"What the HELL happened out there?"

"The target eluded our jets. We were shot down. I have no information about how this could have happened, but we heard that an observer on the ground reported that something landed safely at the CSS HQ. Instructions, sir?"

"Shit. You fucking want instructions? Go fuck yourselves! How's that for instructions!"

And he hung up the phone.

To himself, the executive continued his tirade, "This goddamn robot project is getting more and more expensive by the fucking hour!"

When he had cooled enough, he phoned Alice. "All right, keep on the shrink and don't lose her! She's bound to lead us to the fucking robot."

'C' hung up, never having given his caller a chance to reply. He then buzzed Miss White again.

"Honey, I want you on this. Find the shrink and then you two go find the robot. You're on full expenses, starting immediately. We've got to find this damn robot. Go... Get started."

"Yes, sir. And thank you, sir." 'Honey' had always wanted to go out into the field.

"And, Honey, one more thing: don't you DARE come back empty handed!"

It was more of a threat than a mere statement, but 'Honey' was too inexperienced to know that.

"Understood, sir."

Chapter 21 ~ Reese's Interrogation

"THIS WAY, DOCTOR REESE," ALICE said, extending her hand and arm toward the dark-walnut, double-door entry to the CSS conference room.

In the last 32 hours, Reese had found a pair of medium-high pumps among the wardrobe set aside for her; they fit perfectly. Following Alice's example, she also had chosen a demure, navy-blue suit, white blouse and a string of pearls to complement her footwear. Walking confidently into the boardroom, she knew she looked and felt good. After all, she expected a good start for her new lease on life, no matter how brief it might turn out to be.

Thus, Doctor Reese, PhD Psychology, strode through the opened door to stand before a semicircle of men and women, whose ages ranged from 30 to 60.

They don't look too decrepit, and none has that hardened look carried by trained soldiers she analyzed. *In fact, they look like my first Doctorate Jury... piece of cake here.* She felt right at home—and, unknown to her, exactly how they wanted her to feel.

One person spoke for the rest: "Glad you were able to join us, Doctor Reese. We understand you had some trouble getting here. We are happy you could arrive on time for this briefing. Let me introduce the other members of our think-tank."

The middle-aged man sitting in the middle of the group, to her right, was the spokesperson. His voice came across well-modulated and projecting certainty without arrogance or hint of prejudgment. He then introduced the group from her left to her right.

Reese had always been good at remembering names, and today was no exception, but she wondered in the back of her mind if any of the names were real.

Then the formal interrogation commenced.

"Doctor Reese, we have read your diary entries about conversations you were having with one of our warfighting robots; the one designated "S2." Is that the robot you wish to discuss?" The questioner was a refined, gray-haired elderly woman about 20 years older than Reese, who had the look of someone used to receiving unquestioned compliance most of the time.

Though jarred by the woman's admission that they had read her private diary, Reese spoke unwaveringly in reply, "That's correct, Ma'am, although your group's desire to know about my conversations with him is more the reason why I stand before you today. To cut to the chase, my initial contact and evaluation was, indeed, of the robot designated 'S2'."

"What did you discuss, Doctor?" another panel member asked.

"Let me present the initial scenario to you. S2 was a robot assigned to clean the Lab in the evenings. One evening, while staying late to work on my report about the Turing tests I had just administered the previous day, S2 stopped cleaning, stood near me in a decidedly human pose and began talking about how humans and robots were constructed the same; at least, similarly."

This prompted another panelist to question Reese: "Just out of the blue, no prompting from you?

Reese nodded affirmatively.

"When was this?"

"Shortly after our Director had died. I found the discussion S2 initiated with me to be profound and quite intriguing in concept."

"How so, Doctor?"

"As each of you no doubt has read, S2 proposed a theory that humans have a specific structure composed of the physical body, a mental field of quantum energy, a brain acting as a switchboard and a controlling, spiritual quantity of an invisible something."

Warming to her spotlight and explanation, Reese continued, "... Of course, let me be clear, there is nothing in my education to support this theory, and I tend not to believe those kinds of things.

"... S2 then told me that robots could be structured the same way with a robot body, an electronic quantum memory field, a bionetic brain controlling the body, and, in his case, a spiritual entity directing the robot."

Several of the board members shifted and looked a bit queasy. Reese carried on, despite noting these reactions.

"... I'd like to point out that there is no place in accepted psychological theory for such a directing spirit, soul, ghost, or what have you. We are thoroughly taught, even inculcated, with adequate experimentation and dogma that there is no need for a spirit to exist within the human-being organism and structure."

"But, is it not true that, in later reports, you suggested that the robot's explanation might hold some weight by way of anecdotal evidence?" another person asked.

"Would you, Doctor, highlight that evidence for us?" another challenged.

"All right, but you must remember that in my report then, as now, I do not hold valid experimental evidence to this effect.

"What has happened is that, on several occasions, S2 has exhibited the same or similar mannerisms of the recently deceased—some say, murdered—head of our Lab, Doctor Oren William Stanson, after he had died.

The way it talked, the way it assumed a lecture stance when expounding its theories, these were noticeable to all in its presence. Then, upon General Rogers' shooting of S2 in the head, it seemed as if the Stanson "personality," if you will, had transferred immediately, without slightest pause in its conversation, to the robot body next to it, S1. Witnessed by all alive in that room, this robot S1 maintained the same mannerisms as Doctor Stanson. Throughout the following chaotic days that resulted in the apparent destruction of the DARPA Lab, S1's mannerisms and solutions did not vary from those one might expect to come from Director Stanson when he was alive and running the Lab. Although this observation is only anecdotal, the evidence, based on my training and experience with human and animal psychology, strongly suggests that, the robot S1 may be operated today by the same personality that we knew and loved as Doctor Oren Stanson."

"Thank you, Doctor, for your thoughts," said the same middle-aged man who had acted as the host at the beginning of the interrogation. "… We will recess now to discuss what you have told us, and we will convene again after lunch."

The group stood up en masse on the cue and filed out to the right, leaving Doctor Reese alone in the chamber, wondering what to do… and shaking slightly.

Alice entered and, taking her arm, turned her again toward the large walnut doors.

"This way, Doctor. Let's have lunch. You liked the breakfast we served to your room, didn't you?"

"Breakfast was very good. Thank you."

"Okay. We'll see after lunch what they decide. Remember, they not only have all the information you wrote down, but also the information gathered on human/robot programs worldwide. They will give this a fair hearing."

When Alice and Ingrid walked into the cafeteria-style lunchroom arm in arm, Reese felt comforted. She ordered Chicken Adobo and the salad bar, along with iced Darjeeling sweet tea. She had her eye on some of the dessert offerings, too.

Reese was famished and ate heartily. She would need the sustenance for the afternoon session looming ahead of her.

Chapter 22 ~ Where Is S1 Now?

"DOCTOR REESE, WE APPRECIATE YOUR frankness and transparency in what could be a troubling area of study for you, but I will get to the point of what we want to ask you," said the youngest woman seated at the table—a woman about the same age as Reese, with generally the same, trim physique and similar dark hair, wearing black-rimmed, reading eyeglasses much like Reese's.

"Do you think the robot S1 is alive?"

"No; it thinks it is alive, but I would not say so."

A murmur of whispers circulated among the CSS Board.

"Let me explain," countered Reese.

"Of course, Doctor. Please do," said the host.

"First, we in the scientific vein define life as a biological organism, which can be traced back through generations of similar biological organisms. To us, that is life. Second, to say a mechanical apparatus, even a bionetic apparatus, is "alive" engenders a multitude of political and sociological problems. We would have to reorganize the entirety of acceptable Human Rights with a different paradigm and defense mechanism; something like a Citizens Commission on Robot Rights, or something along those lines, could pop up, which we would have to accommodate somehow."

Most of the Board had leaned forward and were listening intently now.

Reese continued: "... Would humans have the right to deny robots a seat on a bus or a chair in a school, because they were 'different?' Because they are a different life form than we are? Could they be taxed? Could they serve in the Armed Forces or National Guard, operating as citizen soldiers, rather than mere killing machines? Could one of them be elected President of the United States?"

The pensive Board listened and some among them encouraged her with gestures to go on.

"... We might trust them as our slaves and servants, but would we trust them as our equals? How many hundreds of years did it take for our society to get over segregation of Blacks... and they were the same species?!"

Reese had warmed up and was now swinging for the fences.

"... And another thing... theoretically speaking, while we can manufacture as many robots as we wish, will the day come when we realize there are more of them than there are of us, feel threatened and start a war? Will the world end up like those old movies *Terminator* or *The Matrix*? Or the popular video series *Heroes*?

"... Personally, and off the record—I'm assuming here that these proceedings are need-to-know-only and way above Top Secret—yes, the evidence tells me that S1 is as much a person as I am. He is operating a metallic-mechanical body, and I am operating a bio-mechanical body. He communicates rational thought, and so do all of us in this room, we hope..."

A few sniggers followed that remark.

"... However, we must never, ever for many lifetimes, ever say so publicly or officially. That said, my answer for now is a resounding 'NO,' and here's why:

"AI or Artificial Intelligence is still problematic today. Natural Intelligence residing in a machine is way beyond the ken of our society, no matter the plethora of robot movies coming out of Hollywood. The notion of an AI machine becoming, or even being, self-aware, in practical terms, is dubious at best; there will always be the fact that it took humans to program it."

"Aren't you reaching into science-fiction there, Doctor?"

"Not at all. As scientists, we might consider the possibility of alien interventions, but that, for a long time now, has no longer been looked upon as fringe science, because there is too great a preponderance of discovered or uncovered artifacts suggesting such events have occurred here, and that alien life is real.

"Still, the most likely and probable routing for a robot to become human-like is for a 'human' soul to simple take over, assume control of that robot. You see, if we design a robot body deliberately and knowingly so much like a biological human that it attracts a human spirit, who might be able to and/or want to inhabit it the way human souls inhabit Homo-Sapiens organisms today, then we have departed from the comfortable realm of physics and entered the unknown of metaphysics, which, as we all know, is well beyond the orderliness of science."

Reese looked from eyeball to eyeball around the silent room, gauging the acceptance level of her dissertation about robots and assumptions. She paused longer than a few seconds, while she considered her next words with great care.

Most of the jury, sensing something radical coming, squirmed restlessly in their chairs. Still, not a soul left the room.

"There may be another player in this space. I suspect that the design of the S-series robots was seriously hampered by the limitations placed on us to make the robots solely for warfighting theater, and to make them identifiable in the confusion of battle. My suspicion is that someone, somewhere, has already built robots that are indistinguishable from humans, which, like S1, human spirits may inhabit. On that, I rest my case."

Absolute silence from the committee reigned while she had spoken. The moment she finished, however, an animated conversation among the attendees started, and the intensity of the emotions displayed, pro and con, ran high.

In the middle of the ensuing discussion, the committee host noticed that Doctor Reese was still standing in front of them, observing them.

"Thank you, Doctor Reese. Your opinions, your fears, and your beliefs are noted. You may return home now."

"Just a moment, Director. I have a final question for our guest," the older gray-haired woman said. All eyes swiveled to her, and the conversations stopped.

"Doctor, can you tell me why the robot S1 ran away?"

Caught! Reese's jaw dropped, twice. She searched for an answer, suddenly feeling nervous and unsure of herself, "Madam, I cannot answer that question without going into a philosophical conjecture involving scientifically uncertain, anecdotal discussions."

"In other words, you don't know; is that it, Doctor?"

The lady pressed her before Reese could venture a reply.

"Please, Doctor. Humor me – your own opinion will be sufficient."

Doctor Reese took a deep breath and said, "All right. *If* what I suspect has, in fact, happened, and the soul of Doctor Oren Stanson has chosen to inhabit one or more of the four robots, one at a time, the explanation is simple: After the robot he first inhabited was shot by General Rogers, he feared for his life, causing his adrenalin to spike. The resultant super-human necessity level—there are recorded events of mothers having saved their child by lifting overwhelming weights, such as a car—pushed him to save himself by occupying another robot somehow. Later, when the opportunity arose, he fled the scene. That would be a normal, human-flight-reaction activity."

"Of course, Doctor. I'll grant you that; that is certainly what I would do."

Reese added, "On the other hand, the normal reaction of the S-series robot, as programmed, would be to attack and terminate a physical threat. That is how we program them as warfighters. S1's reaction indicates not only a decision-making capability connected to this purpose and programmed use within his society, but also a supra-awareness, an extended awareness of future consequences not likely to be formed within a machine, and certainly not in any part of our programming."

"Do you know where S1 is now?" asked another of the committee.

"No, sir. I have no idea of his whereabouts. However, I would expect that he has considered his location and the source of the continuing threat to his survival and chosen the best possible route and a new location in which he could stay alive."

The proverbial pin drop could be heard as the group stood and departed, once again leaving Reese alone until Alice entered and, again taking her by the arm at her elbow, ushered her outside.

"Well, Doctor, I think you dropped the bomb that could result in the destruction of all known robots, androids and cyborgs of record, as well as the facilities that develop and manufacture them. What now?"

"I think I need to go into hiding for the rest of my life, like my friend S1."

"Easier for you than for him."

"How quickly can you get me back to that secret airport near Denver?"

"I'll have to contact Doctor Cornwalls. If anyone can arrange it, he can. In the meantime, don't open your door for anyone but me, our friend Llys, or Doctor Cornwalls. Things have a habit of moving rapidly around here."

They had arrived back at the entrance to Reese's guest room. Alice unlocked the door for her, using Reese's finger for ID.

"I will bring your room service personally from now on until you leave. You may be able to leave as early as this evening, so any time you have a chance to eat and hydrate, do so."

She gave Reese a smooch on the cheek, pushed her into the room and closed and locked the door behind her.

Ingrid looked around the room, which appeared the same as she had left it. Walking to the table and a silver tray of cheese and crackers, she thought: *Whom would I most like to talk to right now? Oren? No. Phil? Yes, Phil!*

"Can you put me in touch with Phil, I mean Doctor Cornwalls, right now?" she asked Alice on her private intercom device.

"I'll try. Sit by the phone. If it is him, you will hear three short rings, then one long ring. Pick it up immediately."

Reese tried to relax. She put a few pieces of cheese and some crackers on a napkin and sat down on the chaise lounge; her mind noted the oddity that she, Doctor Ingrid Reese, PhD, Animal Psychology and PhD, Human Psychology, was sitting by a phone, waiting, once again, for a man to call her.

The call came several hours later.

Reese had fallen asleep, and the familiar ring-tone on her phone woke her up. In her confused hurry to pick it up, she dropped it and then held it upside down to her face. Finally turning it around, she said "Hello."

"Cornwalls here.... Hello? Ingrid?"

"Yes, yes... I'm here, Phil!"

"Good. I didn't recognize your voice for a moment."

"I had a little trouble with the phone."

"Well, alright. Look, I'm going to pick you up in a quarter hour. Tell Alice as soon as we hang up. Ask her to help you gather your things. I'm going to take you to Stanson. You know, Oren Stanson."

Reese gasped.

"You know my Oren?"

"Of course."

"I understand."

"Good. See you soon. Bye and... eat something!"

"Bye."

There was a knock on her door.

"Come in."

Alice opened the door and surveyed the scene.

"Doctor Reese, you're going to have to move faster. When your ride arrives, you must be at the edge of the landing apron with all of your bags packed and ready."

"What should I take?"

"There is a clothes bag next to your purse in the closet; take that. There is a plastic sipper bottle next to your purse; take that. That's it. I'll wait outside the door. Here we go!"

Alice vanished as the door automatically closed behind her.

Minutes later, Reese, her mouth stuffed with food, opened the door, toting the packed clothes bag, which had a pocket for the sipper bottle, in one hand and her purse in the other. Alice was waiting for her in the hallway.

"Good. Let's go. It's only a short walk to the landing pad." Alice said as she took Ingrid's bag and walked down the hall and out the entrance, Reese not far behind.

Cornwalls landed a blacked-out helicopter with no markings, keeping the revolving rotors engaged. Alice led Reese up the short ramp and helped her embark through the aft sliding door. She followed Reese and buckled her in. She placed all bags in an overhead compartment and retrieved two headsets. She then sat facing opposite Reese, buckled herself in, and, signaling to Cornwalls they were set for takeoff put her headset on her head, pointing to Reese to do the same.

The bird lifted off at a high speed.

"Ingrid... Alice... welcome to AirSpy," said Cornwalls into their headsets. "... We will be flying over the remains of the Advanced Robotics Lab—I thought you'd want to see it, Ingrid—and then we'll hike over to visit Director Stanson."

"What happens to the helicopter?" Reese asked Alice.

"It will return home like a well-trained puppy."

Chapter 23 ~ The Mole

"WHERE IS THE ROBOT? WHERE are the scientists?" C asked his lieutenant in his Midwestern office on the top floor of a Chicago skyscraper.

"For the time being, sir, we have lost them all, but we also just received a report that Doctor Ingrid Reese departed the CSS HQ in a helicopter."

"Aren't you tracking that helicopter?"

"We tried, sir, but it went black immediately upon takeoff. We knew it headed west but then we lost all trace of it. We think there may be three or four people on board, but we don't have IDs, sir."

"What does the Mole say?"

"He claims the pilot is male and suggests two female passengers. We presume that one is Doctor Reese. However, we have no further information. We do not know their destination, who they are, or what their flight plan, if anything, might have to do with the robot, sir."

"Then fucking speculate, dammit! That's what I pay you for!"

"Yes, sir. Since the CSS operative named Phillip Cornwalls was put in charge after the Director was removed by us, I assume any movement by those remaining Lab staff who are still alive must be doing so under his direction. He is a helicopter pilot, so I assume the pilot tonight is him.

C simmered down and was patiently listening, while taking notes on his desk pad. After all, he knew covertly that Cornwalls was under his wing and on his payroll, at least.

"... We know he is friendly with a woman known to have connections to a secret airport located south of Denver. Perhaps, she is the other passenger. They may have met at the CSS HQ. There is a 90 percent probability that at least these two, the pilot and the unknown passenger, are trained, covert operatives. The weak point is the untrained, non-military psych, so that is who we'll be aiming for, sir."

"Good. See... that wasn't so difficult, was it?"

"Yessir, I see that."

"Now, look, this is our most important project. Getting this right means a lot to the organization, so don't screw this up.

"Yessir."

"I've heard another robot went missing. It has S5 painted on its head. Keep a lookout for that one. We want to know about that one, too. Go on, now. Get out there and them. I reward people who can get the job done. Am I clear about that?"

"Yessir."

"And you already know what happens to those who fuck up, right?"

C and the lieutenant had witnessed the untimely and gruesome death and dismantling of his former secretarial assistant, Miss White. She had proven incompetent out in the field and, in fact, he knew that when he'd sent her out on a mission. The bottom line was that she knew the organization had taken in a lot of money—it was she who had disbursed to others the funds at C's request, so she had to be eliminated. For the same reasons, C had also required the lieutenant to be there when he oversaw "Honey's" parts being sent to the bottom of Lake Michigan.

"Yessir!"

When the lieutenant left the office, C relaxed, knowing again that the wheels of his company were in motion. Soon, they would arrive at their goal, and he would be a billion dollars richer, possibly two billion.

He punched a button on the intercom and loosened his belt at his waist.

"Miss Smith, please come into my office, I need you for some dictation."

"Yes sir, C."

Chapter 24 ~ Talking Religion

"I WANT TO TALK ABOUT religion," Stanson (S2) said. He and Phil Cornwalls, Ingrid Reese, and the androids Alice and Llys were seated around an electric heater in his eagle-watching cabin. Nighttime had begun, so S2 was charging from the cabin's electrical outlets. Cornwalls had just finished his dinner meal of hamburger and instant mashed potatoes with butter. Ingrid had eaten a beef patty sandwiched between two leaves of slightly wilted lettuce.

They all had arrived through convoluted means to avoid whoever was still after them, assuming for now it wasn't the NSA or the CSS, because they did not know who was chasing them.

Stanson, of course, has been living in the cabin, since his hasty departure from the Lab. All along he'd been confident that his confidant Cornwalls would find him. After getting picked up, Llys had joined the group in the helicopter, which included, besides her, Alice, Cornwalls and Reese, when they landed at an abandoned, World War II military airport in upstate New York. The completed circle of friends immediately had boarded a gray, AirSpy business jet identified on the tail by an alien head and the word "AirSpy" in small letters under it.

Upon arrival at the underground airport near Denver they split up into two groups using different, blackened AirSpy helicopters. Cornwalls and Llys went directly to the ruins of the Lab. From there, they hiked down and across the arroyo to the eagle-watching blind/cabin. The others flew along the western foothills of the Sierra Nevada range, hugging the rough terrain and arriving at the Lab an hour later.

Hidden among the ruins of the Lab, S5 witnessed their arrivals.

Immediately after their passengers had disembarked, both helicopters departed, heading due north. Only Cornwalls noticed the odd choice of direction.

"Excuse me? Did you say religion?" Alice asked, wanting to make sure she had heard him correctly.

"Yes, religion. Specifically, God, Creation and the Holy Ghost according to the New Testament of the Bible."

"All right by me. Close the shutters tight, turn down the lights. Let's talk ghosts... all you want. I'm all ears," Cornwalls said.

Llys was not as accommodating: "I don't get it. Why this subject? Why now? We need to plan how to integrate into society or, at least, appear to disappear."

"When I was Stanson, I used to go to church regularly, every Sunday if possible. I learned a lot there. Then, I attended some lectures down below in Pollock Pines, and witnessed other religious ideas, some of which expanded upon, or conflicted with, my usual Minister's preachings. I've never discussed it with anyone."

"Well, let's not go there now. We have more pressing issues to discuss, including our survival," said Cornwalls, right before a small, bright-blue LED lit up his phone.

"Everyone quiet," Stanson whispered, turning off the heater. "... I'm gonna unplug now. I'll lie down on the floor. Ingrid, you also must lie down on the floor with Alice on top of you. Phil, you know the drill.

They all did as he asked, including Cornwalls, who didn't move a muscle.

"Someone with electronic detectors and infrared scopes is approaching. I'm hoping you can hide your heat signatures. Don't anyone move until the blue light goes out."

Cornwalls laid down. When Llys, as expected, laid on top of him, she kissed him.

"Oh god, don't do that; I'll light up like a Christmas tree," he whispered.

"Okay," but she smiled at him just the same.

Cornwalls pushed a red button on his phone. The cabin went electronically and electrically dark. The robot and android bodies cooled quickly from the unencumbered, evening mountain air, masking the heat zones emanating from Cornwalls and Reese.

Minutes later, a helicopter in stealth mode flew overhead. The soft whoosh, whoosh, whoosh of its rotors filled the ears of the cabin's occupants. Upon its return fly-over, the silent echo of the arroyo permitted one of the walkie-talkie radios of the search party to be heard.

"The cabin appears to be empty, sir. No signatures detected, sir."

"Roger that. We're only seeing a big mother of an eagle perched on the roof. Wait! There's something.... must have been a rat or a squirrel. It's gone—too fast and small for a positive ID, but probably just a rodent. We're looking for a man-sized robot, not a squirrel."

"10-4. On the way home now."

The group on the floor heard the crunching of twigs grow feint. Two men, they thought. They also heard a scrambling of the brush near the cabin, punctuated by occasional, whispered swearing.

The helicopter whooshed away and up the ravine toward what remained of the Lab building and its campus. Then came a tremendous explosion from that direction.

"The helicopter," S2 volunteered.

"Wait a while," Cornwalls cautioned.

Suddenly, they all heard footsteps on the front porch and the sound of someone trying the door latch. As suddenly. the footsteps receded back down the steps.

The silence of Mother Nature enveloped the cabin and the arroyo canyon again.

Llys kissed Cornwalls again, but he stopped her with a finger up to his lips. "Wait for the second chopper," he whispered.

Ten minutes had passed when another, different sounding chopper flew very low over the cabin, making the eagle screech and fly away. This chopper passed overhead only a few hundred feet up. Again, they discerned the whoosh-whooshing of the silenced blades.

A minute later, a feint meow sounded under the front steps. Llys pushed herself off Cornwalls and headed toward the front door. Cornwalls quickly arose and motioned the others onto the bed, which was out of the line of sight of the front door. From where he crouched, he cautiously opened the front door a crack, and listened. The meow repeated, again from under the wooden front steps.

"Come on in, Tes," he whispered... and the frightened Siamese bolted into the cabin mere feet ahead of the hungry eagle's outspread talons. He shut the door behind her barely in time to prevent her capture.

The group slid off the bed and sat on the floor, waiting. After several minutes, no helicopter, no rustling footsteps, and no squawking eagle had broken the beautiful mountain quiet.

"Oren was going to lecture us on his theory of religion and Creation, right, Oren?" Cornwalls whispered.

"Goody!" exclaimed Alice.

"Oh, no," groaned Reese and Llys.

'I wonder what happened to the chopper?' said Cornwalls, who found Llys staring at him.

Chapter 25 ~ Reunion Strategies

"WHERE WAS I? OH YES... universes, gods and religion." S2/Stanson's words recaptured the others' attention.

"... Let's look at this more practically. If the human spirit leaves his body and takes over a robot body, does that make the robot human, or the human a robot? Is the human condition dependent on the human spirit or the biologic body?"

"Wasn't that the essence of your statement to the CSS, Doctor Reese?" Alice asked.

"I touched on the catastrophic consequences of such things, yes; that was the essence."

"Just a moment, Ingrid," Stanson interrupted, "... permit me to add something to that. Humans have evolved to incorporate a highly specialized survival organism, which we, in our scientific robot project, have attempted to emulate without fully understanding the role of life within the evolved symbiosis. In a human, each cell, every functional bit, not only contains life and memory, but is also living. I realized this when I "died," which, after the experience, to me is more like leaving a body, a departure or letting go; a dropping of the body. The process of the body's death was, I noticed, more a progression of tiny deaths as various systems broke down—the life within them gave up."

Llys asked if it hurt.

"Well, it was easily the most traumatic event I've ever experienced in terms of loss. Imagine all those cells, their organs, tissues and systems, shutting down, no longer functioning... and every cell hurting as it died."

"Oh my God!" exclaimed Reese, startling the others. And S2/Stanson continued to speak.

"When I had left the broken body, I wondered, *What next?* I was floating, and I ended up in the tree above this cabin—where we are now, confused. And then Tes meowed to me, making me understand more about me, and my aliveness. More about her, too.

"What did you do then?" asked Cornwalls. The others nodded approvingly, wanting an answer to the same question.

"I decided to go to the Lab. Suddenly, there I was. Boom. My only explanation was the robots had tractor beams, which, combined, were strong enough to suck me right into the Lab. Nearing the head of S2, I felt myself pulled in by the robot's bionetic brain field. Instantly, I was inside the head and was at the controls. Fiddling with the brain's control systems, I eventually discovered how to operate the rest of the robot body. Not long after that, I thought I might be able to speak to Ingrid... so I did."

"I understand you," Llys said.

"Thank you, Llys. So, am I alive? I think so. Do you? Llys, are you alive? How about you, Alice? How about you, Phil? And you, Ingrid... are you alive? Who decides this question for each of us, if not ourselves?"

"I don't think anyone else..." Ingrid began, but there was a knock at the door.

Tes hid behind a pillow that was propping Oren up on the bed. Silence immediately ruled. Cornwalls turned off the lights and, pulling out his laser gun, moved quietly toward the door.

"Anyone home? Got any leftover hamburgers; I'm starved!" It was Hank Mellon's voice. He was outside. The others could only faintly hear him through the door.

"Who is with you?" Phil whispered back.

"Just me and Linda. We want in on the rabbit hole. We swear there are no government agents outside here or within ten miles of us."

"Bullshit," muttered Cornwalls, who looked around the room. The entire core team of the robot project was right in front of him, hiding in his cabin, except Mellon.

The odds of discovery by our nefarious employers had just risen astronomically he thought. In his mind, he also added up the economic value of these people and the research funding already spent: a total of three billion dollars sat in this small cabin.

For all I know, Hank or Linda, or anyone in this room, already (unknowingly) have been tagged for tracking, while the object of our affection sits on the bed, claiming he is alive in a robot body. How confusing; how bizarre! But he's my ticket to big money, so I'm going to play along.

Something needed to be decided and done about the situation right away. Cornwalls opened the door and let Mellon and Flynch enter the cabin. They were disheveled; they had been walking through the woods without food or water for days.

Flynch's mouth had been taped shut with duct tape, as were her wrists wrapped. Mellon wore the rest of the roll on his wrist. Llys broke the tape constraints from her wrists, and then offered each of them a plastic thermos of water.

Flynch ripped the tape from her mouth and hungrily drank the water; then she turned on Hank.

"You goddamned sadistic son of a bitch! I swear, when we get out of this, I'm going to kill you!"

Hank walked up to her and kissed her. She shut up.

The tension in the room, which had gone on high alert, subsided. Cornwalls spoke for all, diverting their attention in the process.

"I do want to hear more about your experience, Oren, just not now." He turned to the newcomers.

"Hank, you and Linda can stay here for a few days, but the rest of us should leave tonight. It's not safe for us, any of us, to stay here long."

Everyone agreed, nodding their heads.

"We should meet at the student quad on the UC Berkeley campus in one week, at high noon. That will be a Saturday. If we clean up and dress the part, we won't be too conspicuous."

"Why there?" asked Reese.

"Because I suspect Linda was taken unconscious by the people who destroyed the lab and I think she has a tracking device implanted on her somewhere. If any of us had such a device implanted, we'd all be dead already. Trust me: if they are activated, my employers shoot first and don't bother with questions."

"Oh, Phil, surely they're not really that bad. My interrogators were cordial and polite to me," Ingrid countered.

"Well, Ingrid, do you know what happened to your plane after you were 'dropped off'?"

Reese shook her head from side to side.

"... It was blown up over the Atlantic and a Coast Guard Special Operations Unit picked up the pilots. By the way, I think that you, too, were tagged in your sleep but you have not been activated, yet. That will undoubtedly change, and we don't know when. For that reason, I say you take the Jeep in the garage near this cabin and drive directly to UC Berkeley. The Jeep has a pre-programmed GPS highlighting the roads you should take to get out of the mountains and arrive at the university campus. You should leave immediately. I'm sorry, Ingrid, but your adventure here is probably nearly over."

He handed her a set of keys and a purse.

"... There's three hundred in there—more than enough for food and gas. You will find a credit card in there, too, but don't use it until you get near the university... and only if you must."

Cornwalls leaned toward the sink and pushed a button concealed under its edge, causing a groaning noise outside, much like a bear's roar, followed by the opening of a set of garage doors camouflaged with tumbleweed and leaves from tree branches.

"There you go, Ingrid. Hurry now, you don't want to get caught in our little Armageddon."

Surrounded by the others who hugged her, Reese opened the cabin door and spied the opened garage doors. A faint, red light shone from inside the opening. She hugged Stanson last and walked out.

"What are her chances?" Stanson asked.

"Better than 50/50. She's got time on her side."

"What about me?" Stanson asked Cornwalls, "... I'd like to go with Ingrid."

"You, Doctor, should be traveling with Tes and Alice in a slightly different way but we can switch it around as you wish."

Cornwalls had not expected this twist in his planned kidnapping. He had to go along with the change and hope he could regain control later.

"Ingrid, wait a moment, please," Stanson called out, and she stopped, puzzled.

Cornwalls maintained control over the rest of the party and commanded his plan into action.

"... Change of plan. Tes and Alice can take the Jeep. There's a makeup kit in it for you, Oren. Get it from Alice. Then you and Ingrid make your way up the hill on foot to the destroyed Lab site. There you will find a tunnel under a manhole cover in a field of poppies. Don't worry, you'll know it when you see it. It wasn't destroyed by the aircraft missiles and it's in full bloom right now. Under the manhole is an underground railroad car that can take you to San Francisco—an unused relic of a contingency plan created and developed a long time ago. Trust me."

Stanson and Reese, who had retrieved the makeup kit from the Jeep and walked back to the cabin past Alice, who was holding Tes, listened intently.

"... Use the makeup to alter your appearances, since there will likely be Arrest/Reward photos of you posted all over the town and campus."

He turned to S2/Stanson and addressed him directly.

"In your case, Oren, your head can look more human, perhaps like an old professor, which, of course, you are. Ingrid can look like your assistant."

He watched their eyes to make sure they understood his instructions. He knew they did.

"... Now... when the underground stops, you will have arrived at an old abandoned mine under farmland near the coastline that's a mushroom farm now. The owner is vacationing in Japan, so you will be alone and welcome to use the place. You will then walk into town, rent a beachfront condo close to the Presidio and the Golden Gate Bridge, and begin teaching in the coming semester at one of the local community colleges. The information and paperwork you need is ready for you at the farm, so look for the loosened floorboard in the kitchen and retrieve the file under it."

The sensitive nature of the next part of his planning made Cornwalls whisper. He only wanted some chosen few to know this part.

"You, Oren, will be known as Dr. Oren Stanley. Once you meet up with Alice, she will be your assistant, who will act as your memory and peripheral brain, and she will keep both of you, Oren and Ingrid, on schedule."

He hugged both.

"You better get going. Tes is in the carrier by the door. She'll go with Alice in the Jeep."

"Meow," said Tes.

Cornwalls waited for Stanson and Reese's departure and then pushed the garage button, which closed the garage doors. He was alone now with Mellon and Flynch, the latecomers, and he walked with them in the direction of the garage.

"What about me?" Mellon asked, "... What about Linda?

"I'm very sorry, Hank," Cornwalls said, "I didn't expect you and Linda to survive. I have no plan for your escape. But, hey, you two can take the motorcycle here in the garage, which I was going to use. Llys and I can find another way out."

He pointed to the cabin. "... Over there is seven hundred dollars in the teapot. Take it with my apologies and our blessing. Good luck. Watch your back, always."

He sidled next to Llys.

"We must go now. You two can stay here if you like, but I suggest you leave no more than a day or two from now. It's too dangerous to stay on longer, and you'll need the extra time to make the rendezvous."

Llys stepped forward and gave Mellon a smooch on the cheek. Cornwalls shook his hand. Linda hugged Cornwalls, who then walked away with Llys, shutting that chapter behind them.

To the West, the shadows of early evening grew long across the rolling hills carpeted by the sun-drenched, pastel hues of poppies. Hand in hand, Cornwalls and Llys walked toward the bright reflections bouncing off the glassy surface of a lake far in the distance.

Chapter 26 ~ The ICON G7

"I LOVE YOU TOO, CAPTAIN America," Llys said as they walked down the gentle slope. "When did you plan all this?"

"I began preparations when S2 started talking to Reese. No, I'm sorry; it was right after Stanson was murdered. At the time, I knew things would unravel rapidly, given the obviously volatile personalities within the project and no calming influence in sight."

"Your degree helped you with that?"

"It has been some help in my life ever since I earned it. And yours?"

Cornwalls was feigning the truth with Llys, showing her some interest, while having another agenda that involved C, the organization he ran, and the people— "family" describes them better—paying him handsomely to run it.

"Well, honey, I also know exactly who you are, you know, so I've had a plan of my own going on for several years." She cozied up to him as she said this.

"You what?"

"You have as much as proposed to me, haven't you? So... done! I accept."

"You conniving little so and so... are you sure you're just an android?"

"As sure as you are."

"We could go through Las Vegas. I wonder if someone there would marry us. Do you have a birth certificate from somewhere?"

"Nope."

"We'll have to make one, then."

"I can do it."

"Of course, you can. You can do anything."

"Honey, flattery will get you everything you want."

She cozied even closer to him and she was about to get frisky with him when Cornwalls stopped walking beside a large boulder with Native American markings on it.

"You want a Miwok exorcism right after we've gotten engaged?" she queried, puzzled.

"No, my love. I want to fly away with you to a tropical isle. I just love these kinds of things," he lied, "... After all, Native Americans breathe life into just about anything; so much so that they can make a spirit appear out of a rock, according to legend."

She stepped back, smiling. She loved to watch Cornwalls when he was interested in something that got him excited.

But he was really excited in his mind about the billion-dollar payday that was getting closer by the minute. *And I only need to satisfy one person, one man, C, to get my piece of the rock.*

Cornwalls placed his two palms on the rock in the center of a carved spiral staircase at the height of his head. Magically, the image dissolved, revealing only a real-life, life-size staircase.

Looking down, Llys saw an aircraft unlike any she had ever seen. Flight-capable, it gleamed on an underground tarmac. She stepped down into the cavern and touched its folded wings. The sleek, silver fuselage appeared designed to land on water or hard ground. Having bent over to see the cockpit, she stood up, turned and kissed Cornwalls.

"You've brought me a flying Porsche!" she exclaimed.

"Well, not exactly. It's an amphibian, Sweetheart, and you must help me get it out of there, so we can unfold it." Fortunately, it's made of lightweight titanium."

They spent the next couple of hours pulling the fuselage and pieces of the craft out of the cave and then mounting its necessary parts to make it look like a plane and not a praying mantis.

They cleared a 200-meter pathway downward toward the nearby lake. Once completed with that task, Llys and Cornwalls sat inside the cockpit and rested.

"Now what?"

"Baby, we have to wheel it down to the water and finish unfolding the wings. Then, if we've attached everything right, we can fly away from here to a well-deserved, brief vacation on the island resort of your choice, as long as it's in Hawaii."

"But, what about meeting the others in Berkeley?

"Don't worry, someone will see to that meeting, if we choose to linger too long in Hawaii. So, what do you say, Sweetness?"

"I'm ready if you are. What do we do?"

"You stay in the cockpit and keep your feet on the brakes while you steer. I'll hold the tail to keep things from swinging too widely. When we get to the water's edge, we'll stop and put up and fasten the wing spars tightly. After doing a final-check list, in which we check every flight system for operability, we start it up."

"And away we go?"

"Yes, away we go."

"There's a propeller. Isn't it a jet?"

"It's a turboprop. This one has a few modifications. Originally, it was an ICON G7."

"ICON. I like that name."

He invited Llys to settle into the pilot's seat. Once in, she put her feet on the brakes, and her hands firmly gripped the yoke. He loosened his grip on a handle located at the tail, and the plane inched forward.

Minutes later, the seaplane was away and afloat on the water, and Llys was beaming. With Cornwalls having anchored the equipment with a rope tied onto a rock with a climber's hook embedded in it, Llys and he worked to unfurl the wings from their tie-downs. Once loosened, he demonstrated to Llys how to use the electrical control that locked them into place.

A THUNK! shook the airframe as the whole wing system locked in place, and another THUNK! retracted the wheels. Now the floatplane was also air-worthy.

Wading out in the shallow water, he released the anchor. On his return, however, he slipped off an underwater rock, fell into the water and drenched his clothing. Stripping to his underwear, he spread his trousers and shirt across the back of the seats, climbed into the copilot seat and closed the canopy.

"Start her up, Llys."

"Are you sure there's enough room? Those trees at the other end seem pretty tall and close together."

"You want me to take off? Usually, you like to do the flying."

"Well, yeah, but your wet underwear is distracting me, so I'll follow on your control."

They switched seats.

"Okay, here we go."

Cornwalls rammed forward the throttle as fast and as far as the knob would allow. The jet engine screamed, the propeller raced, and the fuselage fishtailed; yet, seconds later, they were airborne over the treetops. He pulled back hard on the yoke, and the turboprop climbed the ladder nearly vertically.

Once they settled into a normal flight pattern, the bright-orange sun shone ahead of them. Dimmed to a tolerable visual with help from the canopy's photo-gray treatment, the duo could see what they were doing enough to switch seats. With Llys in the pilot's position, she climbed, dove and banked the plane this way and that just for fun, laughing aloud the whole time.

At 10,000 feet, their noise-canceling comm system and helmets allowed conversation, but their chatter also prompted and incoming call from the control tower at San Jose.

"This is San Jose Control, unregistered and unidentified aircraft at 10,000... you two, care to turn on your ID beacon? Or shall I send a couple of F-25s up there to check you out?"

"Sorry, San Jose," answered Cornwalls.

"Where's the switch, honey?" Llys asked, not realizing they were audible to an audience of any other crew in the vicinity. Guffaws came from everywhere in the skies into their headsets.

"Right there by your left knee."

Jealous mimicry from other pilots and crew added to the mayhem.

Llys flipped the switch.

"Thank you, UL47T90... destination?" San Jose took control of the airwaves again.

"Hawaii," Cornwalls answered.

Envious comments filled the airwaves for a few more minutes—long enough to redden both Llys' and Cornwalls' faces.

"Hawaii, you have clear skies all the way, but try to stay below 10,000".

"Below 10,000. Roger. Thank you."

"Do we have an autopilot?" Llys asked, not aware that her snuggling closer to Cornwalls had accidently re-opened the comm channel.

"Why, what do you have in mind, baby?" asked Cornwalls, jokingly.

A chorus of "OMG's" and groan chatter startled them, but Cornwalls fought back: "Get a life, you guys! We're just flying here!"

He made sure the switch was turned off again and he turned his attention back to training his co-pilot.

"We have auto-pilot. It's that blue light above your head. You push it and enter the heading and altitude and it does the rest."

"What is our heading?"

"We're headed to Hilo Traffic Control, the number showing right there in that window on that gauge. Our altitude is 9,300 feet. See it on that other gauge there?"

"There sure isn't much room to make some sweet talk and rumpus up here," said Llys.

"No, but there isn't much room for that in a Porsche, either."

"I guess you're right, Phil, but we can try."

Llys reached up and set the autopilot. Leaning over, she reached Phil's earlobe and delivered a savory, warm and encouraging kiss.

I'm in love with a robot! What would Doctor Reese make of that? he thought, trying to keep his wits about him. After all, the idea was to keep it together long enough to get his share of the pie: the billion-dollar pie!

Is this the end of our humans-only world? Or the beginning of a better era of interspecies relationships?

Llys' next moves made him let go of anything outside of that canopy for the time being!

Chapter 27 ~ A Close Call!

CORNWALLS AND LLYS CHECKED INTO the Oahu Hilton under the reservation names of Dr. and Mrs. Phillip Jones, which he had reserved months earlier on a whim that one day he might make it happen.

"Can you surf?" he asked Llys as they toured the wide sidewalk at Waikiki Beach, noticing they were about to come upon a surf and body-board rental stand.

"Better than you," she teased.

"Huh?"

"I'm fifty pounds lighter that you."

Cornwalls, not having a credible comeback line for that answer, looked at the almost non-existent waves on the shoreline and retreated.

"This is ridiculous. Let's go back to the hotel's wave pool."

"Whatever you want. I couldn't be happier than just being here with you."

Back at their hotel room, Llys got back to business.

"If you take me to a Kinko's copy shop, I can buy everything I need to make a birth certificate."

"You got it. Let's get dressed and do it!" he said.

The hotel concierge, a slight Oriental man, was accommodating to them right away.

"Oh, my friends, we have a copy shop right here in the hotel; one story below, on the ground floor by the lobby. You did not enter the hotel that way?"

"No, we didn't. Thank you so much", Llys said tersely, covering any more questions from the man by giving him a man-sized, Androidian smooch. Still, he continued to watch them all the way to the elevator. Once they were on it, he turned to his switchboard and pressed the button for Room 1340.

"I believe the couple you are looking for are here. I just sent them to our copy store."

The concierge fumed as he got a loud chewing out by whomever was on the other end of the line—was it C? —for not finding out more information about the couple before he let them go. The angrier he got, the more broken his Japanese/English translating became.

"I not know how arrived... musta come through service entrance... musta have key and room. No baggage. It was as you say would be... why I call you."

He had gotten so mad that he committed the cardinal sin against his caller: He hung up on him!

The respondee in Room 1340 was not entirely happy but he liked knowing something of the couple's whereabouts. He called back to the concierge and told him the combination code for a locked box behind the lobby desk, adding, "Look, don't be unhappy with me. You did good. So, I'll repay you, okay. Here is the code for some money, '2HELL-4321'. Thank you."

The concierge looked up after writing down the noted code on a small piece of paper. He scanned the lobby for unusual activity and onlookers. Finding none, he walked to the hotel safe-deposit box room and opened the one box to which he had been directed. Inside, he found an envelope addressed to him by name. In the envelope, he discovered two thousand dollars in 100-dollar bills paper-clipped together. Unfortunately, he cut his thumb removing one of the paperclips and he immediately fell unconscious to the floor. He died seconds later with the money scattered all over his lifeless body and a bubble of a mysterious white foam forming at his lips.

Chapter 28 ~ Tes and Alice

SINCE LEAVING THE CABIN, ALICE had driven her vehicle off-road and on backwater roads as fast as she could and still feel safe. After several hours, she arrived at a posted State Highway. She checked her fuel level: half a tank.

Plenty enough to make it all the way she thought. Looking long left and right, trying to figure out which way to turn, she saw the late-afternoon sun was setting to her right. She turned right onto the highway, assuming the Pacific Ocean would be somewhere in that direction. Not long after, a small sign announced her entrance to Stanislaus County. Oriented, she sensed the familiarity of the general area where the Lab had stood, receding into her past.

She drove well into the late night, following road signs that pointed her toward Berkeley. In San Andreas, she stopped for the night at a roadside motel.

So far so good she surmised.

She lifted Tes out of her travel bag, once inside of her motel room. The cat immediately stretched on the bed cover, inviting Alice to do the same. Only after an obligatory tour of the flowerbed outside, and a small can of salmon, which she set out for Tes, was devoured, did Alice cuddle up with her pet animal and fall asleep for the rest of the night.

Chapter 29 ~ Escape!

S1/STANSON AND REESE TRAVERSED ON foot across various hills, mountains, valleys and rivers, ending up by nightfall upstream from the wreck of the Lab.

In the morning, after a night under the stars, Stanson rubbed Ingrid's neck and shoulders and whispered into her ear, "You look very pretty this morning, Doctor Reese." This time, she turned and kissed him, ignoring the coolness of his metal head and the damp of the dew on the grass under them.

After walking further downstream, the duo found a large redwood log that had fallen across the stream. Though the sides of the gorge were steep cliffs, it was less than a hundred feet to the water below. They crossed easily and started back up the other bank and cliff on a narrow pathway that led them up to the Lab site.

Reese had difficulty managing the terrain, but Stanson found that his robot's programming as a warfighter made such travel easy and natural. To his delight, his liquid metal skin was impervious to the scrapes and scratches from errant branches and prickly plants that were Reese's bane.

Still, they eventually made it to the plateau and looked across the field south of the Lab-site's former location. Where the manhole was supposed to be, thick, tall grasses grew, and scores of poppies were in bloom.

"What are we looking for exactly?" Reese asked.

"There should be a small round patch where the dirt isn't as thick as the surrounding soil, where the grasses cannot grow tall. We should make a sweep-search and walk a few feet apart but side by side."

"I didn't learn that in any school I went to."

"I suspect you were a bookworm, right?"

"Yes, but how did you know?"

"Elementary: You look and feel soft and nice, not like a typical outdoors woman."

"Alright. But, don't tell, okay? I'm incognito."

"Right; of course, you are. Let's try finding it again."

Stanson stood up and walked forward until he found grass that did not spring back up.

"Oh-ho, we've found it."

"Great. Do you know how to open it?"

"No. I presume it will require prying up one edge with a stout stick or bar of metal."

"Well, don't look at me. I don't have any external metal on me... human, remember? Not robot."

"Okay, my lovely. I'll go up to the demolition site and find some rebar."

"Be careful," Reese said automatically.

Stanson walked amid the rubble of the Lab. When he did not return immediately, Reese started making a friend bracelet, using some of the long grass stems around her.

After a while, she decided to look around the manhole, hoping to find a quick-release lever, figuring it could not be so old that it was pre-new-technology design.

She crawled and traced the edge, carefully searching through the grass for the advantage she sought. Finally, in exasperation she stood up right on the manhole center and stomped her foot. At that, the circle of grass started to rotate, and Reese scampered off the device.

The manhole cover unscrewed itself; then it moved up a bit before it slid open, tearing the grass' roots away from the hole.

"Oren!" she yelled. "Oren," she yelled again and, standing up, she saw him up the hill and running toward her at a furious clip. Behind him, plainly numbered, was S2, the "dead" robot, firing an energy weapon at him. The hole in S2's head had been patched over, and the robot was obviously operational. Suddenly, behind S2 came S5, which was firing bullets at S2. After one of those shots, the robot S2 lost a leg and it fell hard. S5 remained in the chase.

Reese waved to Stanson and started down the open manhole. By the time she found the bottom, Stanson was almost on top of her. At the bottom, he pressed a lever she had missed and the manhole opening at the top closed rapidly.

"Follow me, I have night vision", Stanson told Reese. They ran in the darkness for about 50 feet. Then he stopped abruptly, catching Reese before she ran past him.

"This is it. Hurry, we want to be away before S5 figures out where we've gone."

"S5? I thought S2 was chasing us."

"I got a closer look. The other robot had the remains of the ID S5 painted on its head."

Shrugging her shoulders because she had not fully understood what he had just said, Reese retrieved a penlight from her small purse. turned it on, and gasped.

In front of the escapees a small, open car that looked like a Disneyland ride, beckoned. Large enough for two people and sporting a clamshell canopy, it sat on two small-gauge railroad tracks.

Stanson leaped in immediately. Ingrid laughed.

"Hurry up. What's so funny?"

"The nose of this car has a vintage painting of Jessica Rabbit in it."

Still giggling, she stepped into the vehicle. When Stanson pressed the start button, the canopy enveloped them. Next, an aluminum bar closed on their laps, and right away the ride accelerated to breakneck speed— the only sound from the electric-powered vehicle the click-click of the small wheels passing over expansion joints in the track.

"Oren, why did you run away from the Lab?" Ingrid asked.

"Truth? I was frightened for my life after General Rogers shot the robot. Besides, the Lab was not a good place for a battle – friends might have gotten hurt; you might have gotten hurt!"

Having said that, he hugged her, but in all-business mode.

"I don't understand. You're programmed to fight battles, not flee them.

"Every living creature has an instinct for self-preservation."

"Of course, and I'm sure glad you do."

Reese hugged him, and she kissed him on the cheek. He liked it.

She continued to think about his answer most of the way down the hill.

Chapter 30 ~ Good Night's Rest

LINDA FLYNCH AND HANK MELLON had a love/hate relationship going for years. They were two scientists who had never bothered to learn social skills to amount to anything. Consequently, after they became a couple, they argued over just about every mundane thing, albeit between strenuous bouts of passionate love making.

By now, though, she had had enough abuse from him because of his drinking habit. She decided she would take off with the motorcycle and leave him drunk on the cabin sofa.

Putting on some leather travel clothes, she grabbed a duffel bag with her name on it. From within it, she located her tennis shoes but walked barefoot out of the cabin, careful to leave the door open so it would not make any noise. Outside, she put on her shoes and walked to the open garage.

She hotwired the Ninja motorcycle and walked it out of the garage. Presently, she sighed and, gunning her ride down the pathway, left the cabin and her lover for good in broad daylight.

She had no trouble following the trail down to a larger cleared-off dirt road, and then down that to the same main highway that Alice had found.

Flynch had a hot motorcycle full of gas between her legs, and the cool evening wind helped to soothe her passionate emotions. As she had several times before, she thought about turning around and going back, but this time, she knew, would be the last time. She knew they were no good together.

Besides, she knew she could always find a one-night-stand lover to take care of her physical needs, even if her heart was broken.

Flynch stopped down the road a piece at a clearing and took stock of what her purse and bag held: three hundred dollars, an ID that said she lived in Turlock, which she had always mistakenly thought was near Merced. And some Trojans.

Later, she stopped at the same gas station where Alice had taken rest. She gassed up there and inquired about a room for the night. She ended up in a relatively clean motel room a block away. Only one drunk neighbor bothered her by pounding on her door at three in the morning, mumbling something about losing his room key. She rolled over and ignored him.

The good night's rest would (possibly) save her life.

Chapter 31 ~ Law & Order

HANK MELLON WOKE UP TO an empty cabin and a large black Cadillac Escalade parked out in front of it. A Black-Ops soldier stood in the doorway, staring at his nakedness.

"What do you want?" he said, still not thinking too clearly.

"What's your name, cowboy?" the soldier said with an Eastern European accent.

"I want a lawyer."

The soldier said, "Okay, here's some 'law and order.'" And he shot Hank in the head. Neat; no loose ends.

"Clear inside," he called out.

"Clear outside," another soldier reported from inside the garage.

"There was a Jeep and a motorcycle, at least. Let's track 'em down," the leader said.

"10-4."

"10-4."

The soldier exiting the cabin made a call on his cell phone.

"We're at the cabin, C. One unidentified man, a drunk. He's dead. Multiple vehicle tracks head generally downhill toward the west. We are in pursuit."

"Very well. Remember, don't hurt the robot."

"Yessir."

Without a sound and undetected, S5 walked up to the Escalade and sprayed the truck with uranium-tipped bullets, killing its occupants. Stepping back several yards, he launched a missile at the vehicle and blew it up, incinerating completely what and who were inside. He then turned and fired another missile at the cabin, blowing it up.

Turning toward the West, he followed the tracks of the only people who had escaped his rage: the remaining android, a robot and some human survivors from the Lab.

Chapter 32 ~ Rogers' Revenge

DAYS AFTER S5 HAD BURNED down everyone and everything at the cabin site, a large, black helicopter arrived at the scene and hovered overhead, while two operatives wearing unmarked black uniforms and black helmets rappelled down to the grounds where they conducted a rapid but thorough search.

"Base, we have one charred corpse shot between the eyes; appears to have happened only two days ago."

"Any sign of the others?"

"Indeterminate. Nothing is moving around here. There are tire marks for a Jeep, a motorcycle and an SUV, probably an Escalade, by the looks of them. The Escalade is toast. I saw various scuff marks down a hillside not too far away on a small path heading toward a nearby lake. What's left of the Escalade contains three bodies; a driver and two 'campers' - soldiers of some kind. I'm going to check out the lake."

"So, we have competition," the respondee off-site spoke an aside to his colleagues in the same room with him. A discussion followed.

"Did you ever wonder? Billions of dollars at stake and rule of the human world in the balance. I'd say we're lucky we only have one opponent, so far."

"Very well," he turned back to the soldier on the phone. "... Go to the lake but you'll find nothing. Those two are long gone and far away by now."

"10-4. But, it must be done, sir. There are other footprints near the destroyed house and the Escalade... maybe from a robot?"

"No loose ends."

"10-4, sir."

"When you report, we'll pick you up."

"Yessir. Understood, sir."

The operative went down to the lake and found the cavern and the tie-down hook on the rock near the shore. He found the tire tracks for the plane and assumed that either a boat or more precisely a boat trailer had been taken out of the cavern to the shore. He found two sets of footprints, one male and one child or female; nothing like the prints S1 would make.

"Base."

"Go, Search One."

"I have tracks at the lake for a man about 220 pounds and a woman about 130 pounds. It looks like they had a boat stored in a cave on a trailer and dragged it to the lake and launched it. I suggest a fly-by around the lake shore to find traces of a boat coming ashore."

"Roger, Search One. 'Topo' (topography) shows your '20' (10-20 code: location) is the only possible landing site on the lake; also, there is no dock, and the shore everywhere else is rocky. Suggestion?"

"Possible ultralight."

"10-4. As I was informed. They had an ultralight or small seaplane. An ICON G7 was purchased and modified some months ago on account. That's a seaplane with folding wings for storage. It's his style. As I said, they are long gone."

"10-4. We'll assemble for pick-up at the Lab site. Meanwhile, we'll look for more robot tracks."

The helicopter landed in the center of the grassy field and agents spread out. In a few minutes, S2 hobbled out, commanding, "Stop. Identify or be fired upon."

"Captain Stewart, Recon. ID Code: Search One. Recognize me."

"Identity recognized. Your orders, Captain Stewart?"

"Report findings."

"Robot S1 arrived with single female. They escaped down a manhole that is directly under your helicopter. Robot S5 seen in the vicinity. No other activity."

"Very well. Resume surveillance."

S2 hobbled in the direction of the demolished Lab.

Stewart waved the chopper to the side of the clearing.

The chopper lifted and soft-landed several feet off center. Captain Stewart and two others inspected the grassy spot and found the manhole at once.

"It's definitely been moved."

"Could it be booby-trapped?"

"Not likely. Any idea how to open it?"

"Check it first."

Captain Stewart called for a dummy drop of some weight on the manhole cover, while his men and he moved a distance away to avoid shrapnel in the event it was a trap.

The helicopter pilot dropped a rucksack full of food onto the lid... nothing happened. The three men cleared off the dying grass and dirt from the top of the manhole cover.

"Looks like the center section is slightly raised. Might be the opening latch."

The head of the group checked it out carefully, examining the junction between it and the rest of the cover and the top that said Stanislaus County Public Works.

"It's probably the door handle."

The Sergeant jumped on the center section. It slowly sank flush into the manhole cover and the cover rose and slid to the side, exposing the manhole again.

"Sergeant, you stay up top and be alert. We'll go down and check it out."

The two men descended, saw the tracks, and climbed back up.

"We're going to need a deep-search helicopter. Let's return to base."

The three men boarded the waiting chopper and left the scene.

A couple minutes later, two figures wearing invisibility cloaks colored like nearby rocks, emerged from hiding and walked cautiously toward the open manhole. S2 spotted them, did an infrared scan: humans without implanted US Government ID chips. He shot both. They disappeared. Only the color of their seeping blood gave their presence away. S2 radioed the event.

"S2 action report. Two unidentified bogies wearing invisibility cloaks of unknown manufacture shot and killed near manhole. End of report." Time and location were automatically recorded along with the voiced report.

"10-4, S2. We are returning to your '20'."

In 30 minutes, a Blackhawk IV helicopter hovered over the grassy knoll. S5 fired a heat-seeking missile at it and blew it up. The helicopter crashed, killing all crew. S2 then fired at S5, who was hiding among the broken Lab remains, but he missed. S5 retaliated, severing S2's head from its body with high-speed, machine-gun fire.

S5 coolly walked to the dead robot, dipped a finger into the robot's oozing, dark-red, cooling fluid, and drew a red star on its forehead.

"One down, three to go."

S5 then stomped the face of S2, cracking its head open and causing the brain cavity to rupture, pouring more cooling fluid on the grass.

Chapter 33 ~ Soul Talk

WE'RE ALONE AT LAST INGRID thought as the train picked up speed. She had yet to examine her feelings for Stanson as a man, let alone come to grips with her feelings for him as a robot. She was willing to talk to him about this.

"Oren, help me understand why there is such a thing as a 'soul'."

"I thought my recent antics would have been empirical evidence."

"It is hard for me to arrive at a spiritual explanation for para-normal activities, instead of hallucinations, some software virus, or another, similar and more scientific explanation."

"You did observe that my conversation moved between robots when S2 was shot, didn't you?"

"Yes, of course. Everyone there witnessed that, which was fascinating, yet startling."

"Alright. Now suppose some outside agency took over all robot series, not knowing which robot would be shot, and then preprogrammed them to behave like that. How could that ever have been done by chemical means?"

"I don't know! I'm not a cyberneticist. You oversaw the Lab. You tell me!"

"Ingrid, you know the empirical evidence. You know what you saw and heard. I know that after all your years of schooling, it is hard to give up your enforced education and cherished notions, but you've reached the point where you do understand that you do not have all the answers. In my book, that alone is the beginning of the journey that seeks and finds wisdom."

Silence followed for a long time. The air rushing past, the loudly clacking wheels underneath them in the poorly lit tunnel and the poorly padded seats added to their discomfort.

"Ingrid, I..." Stanson began, but she stopped him.

"Be still for a few more minutes, Oren—I'm trying to process all this."

He reached his left arm around her shoulders and brought her in close to him. She leaned her head against his chest, tears ruining her makeup.

"I'm still afraid of dying. Even more, now that I have you." She held onto him tightly.

"I'll always be here for you."

Stanson and Reese arrived at the old mine an hour later. It stank from the fertilizer used on the mushroom farm.

He donned a dramatic-arts rubber mask that fairly made him look enough like a science professor to pass for human. He also painted his hands flesh colored to match the mask; not state-of-the-art, his work would pass cursory looks at his Facebook photo.

She went topside and discovered a shiny, restored, 1960's-era Studebaker Avanti near the mine entrance. It was clean, and the key was in the ignition. She started it up, and it worked fine. She turned it off, returned to the mushroom patch and found Stanson inside the owner's house, specifically the bedroom, attempting to use the computer there to contact a school called American Public University. Unfortunately, the browser displayed a security warning that the site's certificate had expired.

"Let's not go there, Oren. The last thing we need is to excite some security problems for our host."

"Oh, all right," he replied, "... What do you suggest instead?"

"Let's try Berkley Community College. We can apply to work there. By the way, have you heard from anyone else?"

"No, I was on the internet. No emails, yet."

Chapter 34 ~ The Karpfanger

CORNWALLS AND LLYS STOOD AT the checkout counter in the Kinko's shop on the ground floor of the Waikiki Hilton, when, suddenly, police cars with sirens blaring arrived in front of the hotel lobby.

The distracted shop clerk working with the couple, stopped and stared at the commotion outside. Llys left a $20-bill on the counter, grabbed their purchases and headed for the shop's backdoor, but Cornwalls grabbed and held her arm just as she was about to exit the store.

"Wait."

"What is it?"

"The concierge isn't at his counter desk. Something's wrong."

He led her back to the front of Kinko's. There, a crowd had gathered in front of the hotel.

"Let's mingle with the crowd, but hurry along to the boat launch. We'll take a taxi. I see several in front of the hotel."

From one of the three waiting taxis, they watched the coroner's wagon arrive, while police worked to disperse the crowd. Hoping to retreat to the seaplane, they directed their driver to take them to the marina. Unfortunately, there, only the tip of one propeller blade showed above the surface of the water.

"I don't suppose my Porsche is also a submarine?" rued Reese.

"Afraid not, honey. Apparently, my people or someone else knows that I'm here. This is just a little reminder that they are not pleased with my progress. Tell me something, Llys, did you join the Agency without anyone else knowing about it?"

"I don't know, but I doubt anyone knew, since I would be missed very soon, and they would come looking for me."

"Okay. Then I have another plan: we're going to book passage on a freighter to Los Angeles via... whatever or whomever can get us there."

"An ocean cruise, perhaps? How romantic, darling!"

The couple went searching for a cruise agency and found one that advertised a bunch of scenic and romantic ocean cruises around the South Pacific.

"We want passage on a freighter to the West Coast; somewhere like L.A. or San Francisco." Cornwalls said, taking the lead.

"When would you like to depart?" the travel agent asked.

"Well, I know it's kind of unusual, but how about some time today?"

"Today? Wow, let me check."

She found an offer in her computer almost immediately.

"Well, I don't know if you can make it, but the Karpfanger departs at six tonight, and, yep, I can get you booked on it, but there is only one passenger cabin left. You know, of course, that accommodations on a freighter are not the same as a cruise ship. I could look for..."

Cornwalls cut her off.

"That will be perfect. Can you call us a cab right away? We can leave from here."

"What about your luggage?"

"Oh, it's nothing. We'll purchase what we need on our way to the dock."

"As you wish. That will be $897 apiece."

"Can you accept cash?"

"Cash? Well, we usually want a credit card…"

Llys added, "Our cards were stolen from our hotel room. Will you accept cash at least this once?"

"Very well. What a tragedy. Identity theft?"

"No, just a simple burglary. Here you go, $1,800.00 cash," Cornwalls said as he pulled out his wallet and placed 18 Benjamin Franklin's on the agent's desk.

"Please count it," he added.

The clerk did, twice, and she put the money in her desk drawer cash register. She entered the ticket reservation and waited patiently for their names.

"Oh, I'm sorry. Mr. and Mrs. Phillip Cornwalls. My name is Llys, spelled L-L-Y-S," Llys said sweetly.

"Home address?"

"11525 DeLane Street, North Hollywood, California," Llys said.

"Your residence in Honolulu?"

"I'm sorry, we just checked out of the Waikiki Hilton, so we don't have one," Phil said.

"Okay; that's all right. You two need a break. I have signaled the cab company and they'll be here momentarily. You can wait next door in the snack shop. Have a wonderful trip. Your freighter is a German registry ship carrying fruit and vegetables to San Francisco via San Diego and Los Angeles. If nothing else, it will smell fragrant!"

Cornwalls escorted Llys out the agency door and into the snack shop next door. As he bent over to sit in the booth next to her he whispered into her ear, "Why did you use my real name?"

"Oh my god! I forgot. I'm so happy about the cruise and that we're going to get married that I just forgot."

"Well, what's done is done. Look... here's our taxi."

Phil helped Llys into the back seat then got in beside her.

"Pier 47. By way of the closest clothing store."

"I am thanking you very much, sir. Closest store is Wal-Mart. Is okay for you?

"Fine, fine."

The store was only two blocks away.

"I will double your fare if you wait for us."

"It will be a great pleasure, sir."

They went inside, and Phil browsed, while Llys shopped. Standing at the checkout stand, he waited for her to unload the full shopping cart. She had even remembered to buy a suit bag for all their clothes.

"Good. We're checked out now, Llys, so take the clothes and cart outside and make sure our taxi is still there, while I finish paying here."

Llys did as asked. Outside, she noticed there was a different driver in the taxi. Her hackles rose. She walked to his window and signaled for him to lower it, so she could talk to him, acting like she was in distress.

"Begging your pardon, miss, but I am your new driver."

"Of course, you are. Here's a tip for your trouble waiting for us."

Llys' spy training kicked in. In a split second, she had realized that this was a setup, since there was no logical reason for a change of cab drivers. She pulled out a needle gun from her purse, like the one that Cornwalls had used, and shot the man in the ear. He went into a coma instantly with a minimum of blood loss. His torso slumped over onto the seat, so she walked around the cab and pulled the body to the passenger side of the front seat and then rolled it onto the floor.

As Cornwalls was outside now and within ear range, she informed him, "Pop open the trunk, will you dear," tossing him the cab keys. He put their new suitcase in the back seat and opened the trunk.

Llys helped carry the cabbie's body to the back of their car, and they tossed him in and closed the trunk. She then drove the cab to the wharf where the Karpfanger was taking on last-minute cargo crates amid a madhouse setting of busyness.

Homeland Security had positioned a booth at the gangway. Noting this, Cornwalls and Llys parked the cab among several others and walked away from it with their suitcase, headed straight at the security gate.

"Please put your bag through the scanner and walk through the line," the bored security agent said. Llys flirted with him, and he didn't watch the CRT in front of him as Cornwalls walked through. She then suggested to the guard that he do a personal search with his hand-held scanner, which he was happy to do once he saw that she stood with her legs apart and her arms held up high. He took a long time wanding her groin and breasts and he was breathing heavily by the time he finished. Llys smiled at him, gave him a peck on the cheek and stepped onto the gangway, taking their suitcase with her rather than loading it with the other luggage going into the hold. The security guard never even noticed.

The couple found the cabin deck and their cabin location without needing any assistance, although the Deck Steward arrived at the same time and let them in before handing them the room key.

"We'll get to San Francisco by Friday evening... just in time to see if anyone else in our group survived," Llys said as she hung up their clothes and folded down the bed cover.

Cornwalls was preoccupied with other things on his mind.

"I'm going to go out on deck and check out the Captain's launch in case we need to make a quick getaway. Order us whatever they are recommending at the Officer's Mess; that's where all the passengers eat with a freighter captain. I'll only be a few minutes."

"Okay honey."

Chapter 35 ~ Social Consequences

ALICE SETTLED IN WITH TES in an apartment in Berkeley close to the university. She would soon leave the cat alone there because she had bought a ticket to attend a seminar to be delivered by Doctor Reese, one evening only, on the "*Psychology of Advanced Robotics*;" subtitled, *(What You Don't Know Can Destroy Mankind).* Included with the seminar event was a battlebot competition sponsored by the university robotics department. It would be a weekend-long, arena battle, the annual prize of which was $100,000 taken home by the winner, along with a hefty contract offered by DARPA and sponsored jointly by General Electric and Yamaha Heavy Industries.

Alice already had found a connection with Stanson online. They had arranged to meet at Berkeley Junior College the following night to battle-plan the structure of Doctor Reese's lecture.

When they met, it was obvious that Reese had done her homework. She knew it would be a hot topic and she knew that her reputation would sell tickets. The fact that DARPA sponsored Reese's event also turned more than a few extra heads, leading to further sales.

Two nights later, the lecture hall was packed to overflowing for Reese's first seminar lecture. That she was attractive, had two Psychology PhDs, as well as a Masters in Computer Science, brought an interesting mix of student and faculty listeners.

Reese was feeling confident that she would change a few minds tonight, until she saw the Chairperson of the Board (the "think tank") of the CSS, the one who had interviewed her, walk in with a woman who looked a lot like Alice, except this one had dark hair. Ingrid was glad, then, that she was sitting down on stage and not standing, which would have made her knees weak.

The lecture went well. During intermission, clumps of people of all persuasions and age sipped soft drinks and bottled water and discussed what Reese had said up to that point. The second half of the lecture garnered fewer laughs; the subject matter of her speech had turned to the possible sociological impacts of advanced, independent robots. Upon her ending, she opened the discussion up to questions from the audience.

Several students brought up the battlebot competition taking place later that evening. Reese tried not to put the undergraduates in attendance down too much, but she did make it clear that the current state of the art of robotics was, at least, 10, if not 20, years ahead of anything they were being taught currently in schools. This brought frowns on the faces of some of the faculty. But, she ignored their reactions for the most part.

Then it happened, just as she feared it would:

"Doctor Reese, what does it mean if a robot originates that it is alive? Is that even possible?"

The brunette who had accompanied the CSS Chairperson had asked the question, Reese noticing the woman's voice sounded amazingly like Alice's, although huskier.

That man who accompanied her smiled approvingly at the question. He, like the stone-silent audience gathered around them waited for her answer.

Here was the expected trap, all set up and waiting for the lecturer to fail the test. They all sensed it, expected it, because the prevailing thought was that no psychologist would ever admit that a machine could be, or was, a living being—after all, this was in Berkeley. The prevailing attitude was quite the opposite: psychologists thought Man was a machine made up solely of chemical reactions and organic matter... but not a spirit!

Reese, however, was up for the contest.

"Thank you for your question. I've been expecting it. If I may, I would like to rephrase it this way: As we all know this question is the crux of our future: Will there be a future of robots inhabited by the souls of men or women? Obtained science to date cannot see how this can be."

A collective groan swept through the crowd around her, for she had not taken the bait. Yet, Reese was not finished.

"... They will, for sure, think they are alive—I have experienced this—and they will assert such to anyone who will take the time to listen. But can we agree? No! To agree would place us back in the dark ages of the Civil Rights Movement."

There were more questions than enlightenment on the faces of those scrutinizing her every word.

"... For example, would we allow robots to vote? Allow them to marry humans, or each other? Would they be sent to the back of the bus? Would we require that they have their own segregated schools? Could one become President of the United States?"

The listeners were by now riveted to her every word and deep in thought.

"... Would you want a robot for a neighbor? What if they eventually outnumbered us? Would there be war? If so, would we wipe them out, or would they wipe us out as science fiction has so often predicted?"

Reese was on a warpath now and she turned to her questioner and spoke directly to her, intriguing her captive audience.

"... No, 'Miss Whichever You Are,' we must treat robots or even inhabited robots and androids as limited products of special circumstances. Man, after all, creates these machines and programs them; not the other way around.

"... And, if they could pair off and procreate, which they cannot, the act could not be allowed for the sake of humanity's future survival, even though they look and act exactly like us. Individually, they are helpful; I dare say, even a pleasure to have around. But, the greater scenario, the potential for an Earth or a universe run by robots inhabited by spirits, in my opinion, must remain secret, hidden, and unknown. Mankind is not ready for this; it needs to grow up. There is more at stake here than we might have collectively thought about. Those among us, whom we might deem idealists, have dreamed their dream far longer than they expected, and, yet, there is no evidence they know more than the rest of us."

Again, her onlookers who were still listening got confused, because she was saying it was possible.

"... One man had a dream and now people of color in America are treated, by and large, like people of any other color. But that wasn't always true, and they were of the same species. Imagine what people will have to confront with competition from a superior, alien species, especially one that looks and sounds and acts just like we do."

Some among the circle surrounding her were starting to get the idea that this might be plausible enough to consider, at least as a scientific exercise.

"... The problem is not only, 'What are human rights?' It is also, "Who is running the meat robots that we see in this room, many of which we call friends? I'm suggesting that humans are potentially composites, not singular, because they have skin and bones and tissues and muscles and organs... and they have minds—more than one, in fact. Who exactly inhabits these meat bodies? Is there a spiritual something that becomes lost and leaves when the body dies? Or is the sequence the other way around—the being leaves, and then the body dies? Look around you; are your human friends really spirits returning time after time to new infant bodies? Or, are we on the verge of some sort of new construct where they enter into robot bodies?"

The crowd had grown restless about these latter notions postulated by Doctor Reese's remarks, and she noticed.

"... So, thank you for bringing up this part of my discussion. The question and the questioning of these concepts are valid science. I'll leave this with you: We human beings must face and deal with this issue before it is too late. Goodnight and thank you."

With that, Doctor Ingrid Reese left the stage for the last time. Her credentials were intact, but she had walked far out on a limb that most in modern society cannot begin to confront enough to even consider.

The scientific community, being a rather small and close-knit bunch, likely tomorrow would reprove her remarks; perhaps even ostracize her from their ranks. Certainly, she and they would never look at each other in the same manner that carried them along for so many years.

Backstage, the CSS man and his beautiful robot approached Doctor Reese.

"I didn't think you had the guts to go there, Doctor. Where are the rest of your team?"

"I don't know. We split up. We could be anywhere on Earth at this point."

She addressed the A-Llys, B-Llys, C-Llys, D-Llys, whatever model she was: "Did you like my answer to your question? Was it what you expected me to say?"

"I was frankly disturbed. Not from what you said, per se, but from the implications. I assume the others of your team have had some input?"

"Of course. S1, Oren Stanson, as he still likes to be called, started this discussion. He considers that he is a human spirit inhabiting a robot body, just as I suspect are you."

The woman smiled but said nothing.

"Come along Blyss, we are finished here," the man said. With that, they left the auditorium.

How long Reese thought to herself, *before the NEW Armageddon?*

Alice collected Doctor Reese and they returned home to the safety and warmth that was the space around Oren Stanson. She had given no clue that she knew the android she met at the lecture, and Doctor Reese never thought to ask.

Chapter 36 ~ Alice's Story

STANSON BEGAN HIS NEW CAREER by teaching Calculus and Robot Control Systems 101, which he knew in his sleep, if he ever slept. Every day in the sleek old Studebaker Reese asked, "Did you learn anything today?" Since he didn't understand why she said that, he finally asked her.

"Why do you keep asking me that? I'm the teacher; they are my students."

"Because the road to wisdom begins with the assumption that you know nothing."

"That's a curious frame of mind."

"You said it first, remember?" If you're truly a human soul inhabiting that android body, there is a lot you must learn. For example, you never have married; you never had children. You never had to get along with a housemate, or nurture a growing, constantly changing child. You see, you have much to learn, my genius friend."

Stanson's life changed with that advice. He observed his students as real people, not mere junior-college students. If their lives were in chaos, he tried to help them, pulling from his degrees as a human and from his programming as an S-series warfighter. In fact, he pulled information from Alice's life before she was Alice, though she didn't talk about that much. And he pulled information from Doctor Reese—all of which experiences he could use only because he was paying more attention to them and their lives.

He got Alice's story, while Ingrid was away shopping.

"Come on, Alice... tell me about your life before you became an android. You know all about mine; I want to know all about you!"

Alice was resting in a comfortable easy chair in the modest apartment she rented near the city college, when she agreed to share her story. She had recently returned from taking the Studebaker back to the mushroom farm, and Stanson had followed her in a Ford Fusion purchased as part of the plan to blend in among humans. Reese had taken the Honda.

"Oh, all right. It's really very simple. I was on a field trip with my high-school class. We were visiting a research laboratory in New Mexico. We were all special-abilities children learning about robotics. Having multiple sclerosis, I was confined to a wheel chair. When I saw the robots, I was amazed and wished with all my heart to be mobile like they were. Well, my body died instantly; my strong wish had materialized, and suddenly I was operating one of the robots there. Right away, I noticed that the robot next to me to my right was alive, too. She turned toward me and smiled; it was a smile of recognition. She was Llys. Since then, I've always thought of her as my sister. Much later, another of the robots became a sister, too. Her name is B-Llys or Blyss (pronounced "bliss.") However, she sides with the people who are chasing you and the rest of us."

"Do you ever communicate?"

"Of course, we do! We connect through the Internet Cloud. You could do it, too, but the NSA and NRO computers would pick up your signature and blow our cover."

Stanson nodded as if what she was telling him made a lot of sense. She continued to explain.

"We girls aren't high priority. After all, we were never taught much about national security or national defense matters the way you were; at least, they assume we don't understand those subjects. At any rate, that's why neither of us will ever be safe until we are obsolete, although for different reasons; and maybe not even then."

"Alice, you're almost as pretty as Doctor Reese. Were you pretty as a human, too?"

"Oh yes. My top half was quite pretty, but who wants only half a girl? And, besides, I was quite sad for years."

"When you died, did you float around for a while, or anything like that? Were you hanging outside of your body, or what?"

"Not really. I felt like I was in a spiritual vacuum cleaner: one second, I'm dead; the next, I'm out. And then, zip, I was sucked into a robot's head. I don't know what happened, or why, but when it happened, I was so filled with joy that I danced around with Llys. I could hardly contain myself, and she shared that with me. I guess because we knew we were still alive."

"I understand you, I think. The electronic field generated by the bionetic brain acts like a vacuum. It's designed and programmed to do that—attract humans, especially in your case, male humans. I assume that is a part of the design of your robot type."

Neither knew what to say next. The silent, pregnant pause ensued for several minutes.

"... So, yours was built in New Mexico?"

"I'm not sure. I suspect that's where mine and Llys' body were manufactured. Maybe they were built there; maybe only carted there from somewhere else. When this flap settles down, maybe we can find out together. I'm sure that whatever the humans have done in the last 50 years in this field is in their Cloud somewhere. I can tell you this, though: I know my brain, my awareness, is not biological."

"I think Phil will be anxious to find out."

"Why? Are they going to get married?"

"I think they're going to try. Seems impossible, though, without a valid birth certificate. Still, in Las Vegas relaxed rules is the rule. So, we'll have to see; for sure, though, they are in love."

"Of that, I have no doubt, Professor Stanson," said Alice as she laughed and saluted him.

Chapter 37 ~ Ticklish?

LLYS AND CORNWALLS HAD THEIR own situation to worry about. They didn't conjecture about their origins like Stanson and Alice.

Llys had borrowed some tools from the ocean-going freighter's Chief Engineer Benson, and she was able to create a workable birth certificate showing her origin to be a Pagosa Mountain Hospital in Dulce. New Mexico. Some minor research using the ship's slow internet connection made it work for her, including picking out a couple of names from the town's phone directory to act as her parents.' It wasn't a perfect rendition, but it would hold up for a Las Vegas ceremony.

Cornwalls took a chance by ordering a certified copy of his own birth certificate be sent to him onboard. The ship's communications officer was puzzled at his request, but that was because he didn't read English. In the end, once the certified copy arrived digitally and was printed out, it wasn't a big deal.

Afterwards, Cornwalls and Llys consummated their vows in their cabin, and made the most of their brief "honeymoon" cruise.

The odd thing was, since Llys had to, at least, put up the appearance of eating in front of the other passengers and crew, including the Captain who watched them as closely as he did the other passengers and couples aboard his vessel, Cornwalls wondered where the waste went. Llys picked up that he had something on his mind, too.

"Phil, what on earth is making you too serious for words?"

"Honey, don't think me a boor, but what the hell are you doing with all the food and drink you've had at the dining table?"

"Oh, that! Don't worry; it's not in me or piling up in some trash bin somewhere on board. You see, I have a bio-waste disposal system that pretty much atomizes any organic substance I ingest and converts its energy. How do you think I can operate so long without plugging in?

"I had been wondering about that, too."

"Well, being German, of course, this ship operates on a DC (Direct Current) electrical system. But, my body is running AC (Alternating Current), so I need to eat and combust to produce electricity. It's clever, though a straight plug in would be more direct and faster. The unusable, leftover waste my body produces, mostly carbon, is collected periodically, and I flush it down a toilet the way you do."

"Couldn't they have made you able to have babies?"

"Darling, that's sweet of you to say that, but, no, only biologicals can grow offspring. The trade-off is that I won't grow old, won't grow fat, and I won't change at all. I do hate to tell you, though, that my body will outlast yours, by far. Sorry, Lover."

Cornwalls wasn't sure he liked that notion, so he switched the subject.

"Do you need sex to continue functioning?"

"Just like you, the primary purpose of my organic parts is to survive to infinity, if possible, and sexual behavior can play a part in that outcome. Still, speaking for me, the emotional and physical stimulations of romance and sex improve my digestion—I burn fuel better after sex. For you, healthy sex improves the survival potential of generations of your species.

"Not the same thing, is it."

"Maybe not, but important just the same."

Now, she wanted to change the subject.

"Are you ticklish?" she asked.

"Are you?" he countered.

"Horribly. Where are you ticklish?"

"You'll have to find out."

All the talk about electrical energy flows and sexuality had to go some-where. Llys began at his toes. Soon, she found the spot that made him buck like a bronco and laugh uncontrollably, which, of course, led to other things.

Later, when it was his turn to find her ticklish spot, he started the same way and discovered that hers was nearly at the same spot as his, give or take a few minor anatomical differences. She gyrated so wildly that she pulled him off the bed, revealing her strength, which amazed him.

"What is your bone structure, Llys?"

"Carbon fiber, titanium strands laid through carbon nanotubes, and something else a lot like glass, fiber-optic cable, but I don't really know what it is. Maybe diamond strands—your guess would be as good as mine. I know it's supposedly not on the open market, yet; and that it serves me the way your nerves do, only much faster. The whole structure is more electronic than anything else."

"Sounds to me like science-fiction."

"It is," she said coyly, "... but, when you "get" me, you really get me!"

Cornwalls couldn't make her elaborate or talk about herself beyond that level. Apparently, there was some security programming involved. At any rate, he decided to leave the details of her construction to a rainy day.

At least, I know how the S-series are built he thought.

Linda Flynch and Hank Mellon used advanced metallurgy to build super-strong "bones" and self-healing skin into the S-series, so they would with-stand the heated rigors of a war theater. Structural analysis of Llys' struc-ture revealed that, in her case, her developers had taken her far beyond their ordinary materials technology. She was as durable as the S-series 'bots and, yet, half the weight.

Furthermore, S1 and his ilk looked like robots: classic, smooth, big, strong, and businesslike. Llys, on the other hand, looked like a gorgeous woman: classic, hourglass figure, movie-star facial features, and a melo-dious voice that most human women would die for.

Looking at her in the privacy of their cabin, Cornwalls was beginning to obsess about who designed her and where she was built. And why she and Alice were so different in appearance.

Such differences mean only one thing: a hand-built manufacturing sys-tem; every model is a one-off. It boggled his mind every time he allowed himself the time to ponder the thought.

Free time was a scarce commodity, however. After only a few days, the Karpfanger entered the territorial waters off the western coast of the USA. It didn't take long for a U.S. Coast Guard cutter to approach and stop the ship's progress mid-ocean, requesting to come aboard and do an investigatory routine.

One guess what they wanted to find. It wasn't pineapples.

Chapter 38 ~ Avoiding Capture

LLYS WAS THE FIRST TO notice the change in the pitch of the ship's engines. Looking out of their porthole, she observed that the water was less turbulent beyond the stern.

"Why are we stopping?"
"Because we are going to jail," answered Cornwalls.

"Don't you have some magic submarine or someone to rescue us?" Llys asked, a hint of panic showing.

He never had the chance to answer her. Someone knocked briskly on their cabin door.

"Mr. Bond, I hear Specter is here to apprehend you. Do you need assistance?" the voice accompanying the knock said with a polished, Oxford accent.

Llys smiled and she nearly relaxed.

"Come in, whoever you are. We are, indeed, in dire need," Cornwalls answered with an equally debonair British tinge.

A man of slight build entered their room, looking like a character molded out of an English melodrama, complete with cravat, tails and highly polished, jodhpur boots.

Having a second thought, Cornwalls considered that the gentleman confronting him might, in fact, be a real English aristocrat dressed in his afternoon attire. At any rate, the man didn't wait for introductions to speak more.

"Pardon me, young lady, but I am going to attempt your rescue. As we speak the USA coastal guards are searching this very freighter for contraband, which, no doubt, they will find in the banana hold. During the subsequent scuffle and franticness, you two, and I, will make our escape."

"How do you intend to do that?" Cornwalls asked, sensing his control of their situation dropping away.

"Well, not to be too immodest, I, too, am attempting to enter the United States illegally. I am Duke Arnold Saint Germaine III and I am running away from my wife who, until a few hours ago, thought I was still in Hawaii."

"Is this a joke?" Cornwalls asked.

"No, it is all rather a subterfuge, my man. You see, I recognized both of you when I saw you at our first dinner on board. You are the infamous Doctor Phillip Cornwalls, are you not? You have a PhD from New York University in Political Science, do you not? And your lovely companion here, who far outshines in person her image in the stupid surveillance photos that I've seen, must be Llys."

With that, he bowed, took her right hand and kissed it lightly. "... Are you not, milady?"

"Yes," they echoed.

"Thank god, I've got the right cabin. Now, listen to me: I have a Swift-sure nuclear-powered, fast-attack submarine still in service with MI-6 lying in wait a few hundred meters off the stern of this tub of a freighter. Should we be able to get into the water unnoticed, we will get picked up, and all be safe from the US and British authorities, Scotland Yard included. Please, dear people, are you game with me?"

"I have a lot of questions but one that is paramount: 'Why?' Why are you doing this, and who are you working for?"

"The "Why" is rather obvious, sir..."

He turned and looked straight at Llys, "... Is this man always so dense, my dear?"

He turned to Cornwalls and went on, "... Doctor, you possess certain, shall we call them 'vital' details about the secret, new S-series robots. Of course, Her Majesty's Service wishes you to share your knowledge; after all, we have been partners in war and peace for decades now. I can assure you, we will protect you for that information, and your girlfriend here gets to ride along for free."

"Show me your ID card," Llys said.

"Very well, but we really do have to hurry along, young lady. Remember, the authorities have already boarded and will without any doubt be to your cabin sooner than later."

He pulled out his wallet and opened it, displaying an official identification card.

Llys grabbed it away from him, saying, "That, sir, is a fake. Who are you really working for?"

"How would you know it is fake, milady?"

Cornwalls drew a ray gun and pointed it at the man's midsection.

"She knows. I trust her explicitly. You, sir, have exactly five seconds to answer her question: 1, 2, 3, 4, 5."

The man said nothing.

Cornwalls had no choice but to shoot him, boring a hole three inches in diameter into his mid-section. The wound revealed a variety of mechanical and electrical parts—no blood or human organs.

With a loud CLANK! the robot fell to the deck.

"My god, another robot! Exactly how many people are working on robots these days, anyway?" Llys exclaimed.

"Only two organizations that I know of, both in the U.S. This one is pretty primitive." Cornwalls was probing around the stomach cavity.

"Llys, there might actually be a submarine out there. This guy was a radio-controlled model, much like the battle-bots in those games you like to play."

"By the way, where is the supposed Coast Guard crew? Are they really inspecting the cargo? Could it be they are NOT after us?"

Cornwalls dragged the robot's remains under their bed. Thank goodness it wasn't bleeding he thought.

Suddenly, a bullhorn-enhanced voice rang out: "Attention, Karpfanger, prepare to be towed to San Pedro Harbor. All on-board passengers shall be ferried to our ship at once." The announcement came from the Coast-Guard cutter.

Almost simultaneously, the Cabin Steward knocked at their cabin and opened the door.

"I apologize for the intrusion, Mr. & Mrs. Cornwalls, the Coast Guard patrol has found contraband in our cargo hold. All the crew has been confined to quarters, pending arrival of the ship at San Pedro Harbor. Passengers are being off-loaded now. Please follow me and I will escort you to a lifeboat. From there, one of the Coast-Guard soldiers will motor you and another couple waiting on this deck to their ship. Do not be alarmed; the American Coast Guard are very polite, and you will be well cared for."

The steward did not see the dead robot stuffed under their bed. He left immediately and knocked on the cabin door across the passageway from theirs, repeating there the same message before addressing all four persons gathered in the hallway.

"Very good; we're all here. Now, you four follow me to the lifeboat deck. We must be quick about it."

Chapter 39 ~ Abduction!

LINDA FLYNCH DECIDED TO QUIT running at a roadside rest stop, when she noticed that no cars stopped, no big black SUVs drove by, and no drones or helicopters flew overhead. Last night, after parking her bike in a safe location at the edge of a motor-home park, she slept on a blanket she had found outside an elderly couple's parked vehicle. Reaching into one of her pockets, she counted her cash bills and was proud that she had spent only $60 of the cash she carried.

But, she was still in shock from seeing and interacting with Llys and Alice. Up until their recent rendezvous, she had thought her pride and joy, the S-series robots, were built state-of-the-art. Now, her pride had fallen back to earth, because they seemed almost human in some respects.

Her thoughts were jumbled. She knew that she had been constrained by the design parameters set by DARPA, but she was sure that, within those specs, no one on Earth could have created a better design better than she had. *After all my work, those robots are almost human!* She had half-expected to be written up in all kinds of university and industry magazines. *Instead, I am running for my life!*

Flynch made up her mind, got on her bike again and rode. She had decided to blow off meeting Doctor Cornwalls at UC Berkeley, since the work was no longer her project, and, besides, the Military/Industrial Complex had overtaken it. What she needed, she concluded, was to go to a place where her talents would be appreciated and where the technology was even more advanced. Comparing her two "offspring"—Alice was from the East Coast and Llys from New Mexico, she chose Dulce as her destination. The decision freed her mind. She had thousands of dollars in her savings account and no one looking over her shoulder, at least for now. *Keep it that way!* she thought.

After a rest at a motel in Los Gatos, she decided to head down I-5 and then cut over to I-14 and continue southeastward to greener pastures.

The motorcycle was running perfectly, and she had a heady feeling from being no longer under the weight of working for warmongers.

She drove most of the night on nearly empty freeways, stopping only for restrooms, gas and sandwiches. When she passed the New Mexico border the next morning, she filled up one last time and downed another ham and Swiss sandwich and a Red Bull.

Driving down New Mexico's central highway from Albuquerque toward Las Cruces, she got lost. Looking around, she saw a small sign pointing the way to Dulce and felt the gods had just given her a sign. She turned onto that road.

After driving on the desert side-road for what seemed like forever, she arrived at a military guard shack almost before she realized where she was. She had missed the exit for the town.

The guard stood at the gate with his rifle in a relaxed state of readiness.

"Who are you?"

"I am the best robot designer on the planet. My name is Linda Flynch. I want a job."

The guard signaled his partner to come out. This one held her gun on Flynch, while the first guard looked her up on his computer screen. In two minutes, he returned a little less at ease.

"Are you the Linda Flynch who recently worked on a robot project for DARPA?"

"That's Top Secret. I can't say. How do you know anything about it?"

"You're in the base news. You're a possible infiltrator. I'm sorry, Miss Flynch, but you'll have to surrender. You'll be taken to our main security building where you will be questioned."

Engine noise and a rising cloud of dust indicated that a pick-up squad already was headed their way.

"Why the hell are you going to do that? I just want a job!"

"The Lab that had your records was recently blown up. You are one of the suspects. Sergeant, take this woman into custody."

The woman guard quickly stepped up to Flynch, dragged her off the motorcycle and strapped her wrists behind her back with Ziploc cuffs.

Flynch fumed.

Two vehicles arrived at the guard shack: one, a nondescript SUV with blacked-out windows and a flatbed in back, onto which Flynch was put along with her motorcycle; The other, a black Cadillac Escalade. Without delay, as quickly as they had appeared, both vehicles disappeared.

Flynch attempted to engage the two burly soldiers in the vehicle cabin, but they weren't buying any conversation and they only stared straight ahead.

Driving down a long ramp with a sharp right turn at one end, the vehicles entered a huge underground cave, Possibly, a hanger she thought.

Flynch was frightened, and she had good reason to feel that way: they hadn't blindfolded her. If she was in a secret government installation, normally they wouldn't want her to see it.

They continued through the tunnel/cave for almost an hour—all the while, their captive becoming more and more concerned for her survival. At last, they entered a larger space outfitted exactly like a hanger. At the center, the caravan drove onto a turntable which turned them 90 degrees to the left.

Flynch noted that the walls appeared to be smoothly finished rock. *So, this isn't a natural cave and from the looks of the type of rock and veins that I see, we are deep underground.*

The caravan left the turntable and entered an elevator big enough for an enormous aircraft.

Flynch recalled a detail that she had not thought about earlier. The desert "road" she had been driving on was wide and long enough to double as a landing strip for something like a fighter plane, or even a private business jet.

Once inside the elevator, bright lights came on and a crew dressed in white, hazard suits began to check all over and under the vehicles.

Having received and acknowledged an "Okay" signal, the two men alighted from the SUV. One approached Flynch and pressed a button on the outside of the side panel. Instantly, a mesh cover cloaked the flatbed, ensnaring both Flynch and her bike.

I could have escaped before! I wasn't tied up! How embarrassing!

"Do not try to exit the vehicle, Miss Flynch. You are going to be traveling through a very dangerous area. Just sit tight and you will be fine."

That said to her, all human personnel abandoned the elevator, and a robot like one of the S-series robots, albeit colored white, got in the driver's seat and drove his cargo into another tunnel where waist-high, red-light tubes extended the entire length.

Try as hard as she might, Flynch could not make out any details, except that machinery, computers perhaps, stretched along the entire tube.

Eventually, the dim lighting and her lack of comprehension of her environment made Flynch feel sleepy. She conked out, and fell over fast asleep.

Flynch woke up in a hospital bed, naked and hooked up to life-monitoring equipment that measured her breathing, her heart rate and other vital functions. She was securely strapped to the bed.

As Flynch's head cleared, she thought she might have been drugged. Yelling produced no response from anyone or anything, but it did produce a mild headache for her. She felt utterly alone. In fact, she was.

Two tubes connected to a strange apparatus at the foot of her bed entered her vagina. Flynch panicked and she would have seriously hurt herself had she not been restrained. Tabloid headlines about alien abductions ran through her mind.

Her commotion brought in another robot that looked a lot like the one who had brought her to this place. Without emotion or speaking, the robot put its warm (?!) hand on her abdomen and felt her rib cage. Finally, it pressed a large hypodermic needle into her arm. The last thing she remembered was the sight of a small silvery object sliding down the syringe toward her body.

Coming to, slightly, Flynch heard the robot speak something in a language she didn't recognize, before he left her alone again. She fell asleep again, unable, she would discover later, to recall what happened to her.

Flynch woke up lying on the borrowed blanket on the ground next to her motorcycle at the same motor-home park she had visited before. Her arm and abdomen were sore, and she was sore in a different manner—cross would describe it better. But there was no one to swear at. Oddly, she felt aware that she had delivered a baby but, on inspection, she found no stretch marks or Caesarian stitches or scars; just an uneasiness that her inner abdomen had been violated somehow.

She had no clue what time it was. After checking her gas and finding a full tank, she started up the bike and grabbed her helmet, which she had fastened to the helmet clamp behind the seat. Plugging the radio into the helmet's speakers and listening to a news station, she learned that two weeks had passed since she had left Hank for dead. Not knowing what to do, she hoped to clear her head by riding. Eventually, she came upon a tavern next to a dusty Sunoco gas station in the middle of nowhere, which, oddly, looked familiar to her. She still had no idea how she had ended up in the desert, why she was there, what her job was or where she worked. The ID she would show the bartender indicated that she lived in Merced, California, but she didn't even remember where the hell Merced was! And the way she felt right now, she didn't even care!

Doing what any person might in her situation, Flynch walked into the tavern, ordered drinks for everybody, got rip-roaring drunk, and ended up naked in a back room, dancing with a bunch of truck drivers... and her Trojans left intact. Her subsequent pregnancy completed the strange circle of events and changed the course of her human life forever.

Chapter 40 ~ Collusion Part Three

MARK SCULLY (A.K.A. MARIO SCAGLIANO, a.k.a. "C") sat behind his eight-foot-wide, polished, black mahogany desk and fumed. His secretary, Miss Corlyss Smith, knew that he was not in any mood to be disturbed; that's why she turned back the government man who had demanded to see her boss.

He had just found out that his organization, despite two dozen men and women working on the project, had lost track of another robot. Again.

While his IT people, scornful of the teams of soldiers on the ground, who so far had been unable to locate the missing hardware, boasted they would find it within 24 hours, he knew he needed eyes on the robot, not just its computer signal.

His clients, so far, had remained patient, but their invested billion and a half dollars was a substantial amount. Until located and back in their possession, someone else might find the robot and up the ante with a ransom demand.

He also knew, should he lose this contract, where he would end up: sliced, diced and barbequed in a sleazy, San Francisco steam room. Into that frame of mind, Corlyss interrupted.

"Excuse me, Mark. I have the phone call you're waiting for from Mister Xavier. Shall I put him through?"

"Yes, Corlyss."

Scully's phone clicked once to secure the line, and then he picked up the receiver.

"Scully."

"We've located the merchandise in Berkeley, California… within a one-hour window. You can take delivery no sooner than one hour and no later than three hours from now. We will release the merchandise only during that time frame."

Scully glanced at his desktop clock for the current time.

"Funds will be wired as pre-arranged to the deposit account in one hour."

"Pleasure doing business with you, Mr. Scagliano," the voice said before hanging up. Another click, and the secured line was released.

Scully/Scagliano turned in his chair, stretched his legs and looked at the skyline beyond the tall, plate-glass windows of his office.

"Corlyss, hold all calls and come into my office. And bring me a 'Cuban' (cigar)," he told her as he loosened his belt and pulled down his zipper.

Chapter 41 ~ Blyss' Revelations

TES CURLED UP ON STANSON'S desk at home and half-watched him grade student exams. The date was several months after the targeted rendezvous at UC Berkeley. Reese was away teaching at the college, and Alice had taken the Studebaker for an oil change at a local service station near their house.

Someone knocked on the front door. Tes disappeared at the sound of the knock, and Stanson did not care to answer, so he ignored it. He did not have his costume on and the caller could be a student, in front of whom he could not risk being seen.

"Doctor Stanson, please open the door. It's Blyss from 'Back East'."

"Back East" was code. He had developed it with Alice; it meant the CSS HQ. Feeling acutely panicked, much to his surprise Stanson weighed the possibilities and decided to answer the door.

"Hello, Blyss. I've heard about you from Doctor Reese and Alice. What is it that you want? I'm busy correcting student exams."

"I was hoping to see your disguise. It had our operatives fooled for several months."

"What do you really want?" he asked again, perturbed, though modulating his voice and keeping his unexpressed hostility in check.

"Well, to be honest, with the price on your head well above a billion dollars now, we want you back in the fold before someone else gets a hold of you."

"Foolishness, as you well know, Blyss. You and Alice are a far more advanced robot species. In another year or two, I'll be obsolete. Again, I ask you, why do your people want me back?"

"May I sit down?"

He had not let her inside and he did not intend to do so, but by now, he was curious to know the answer to his question—a decidedly un-robotic thing to do!

"Yes. Please do," he replied, calculating the number of combat vectors he could control by eliminating this threat. Besides, none of the Llys-series robots had ever done anything to harm him.

"Tell me your story. When did you die? How long did it take you to assume that body? Do your handlers know that you are not mere woman or robot?" he asked, determined to pump as much information out of her as he could.

Blyss was taken aback by his approach. She had expected him to resist and even try to destroy her. Her NSA/CSS handlers had suggested that he would, but S1's tack was wholly disarming and unexpected. He seemed to genuinely care about her, leaving her to wonder about her handlers and their motivations.

How does he know I am not a human? What does he know about the Llys Series?

Blyss, believing he was not holding a hand worthy of winning, tried to call his bluff, "Are you stalling until Alice returns?"

"Yes, of course, I am," he replied with the same straight-forwardness as his first words to her, "... Please answer my questions; I am very curious."

She complied: "My body was built in Dulce, New Mexico. I had been a human secretary for the Commanding General. In an underground battle he was killed, as was I. Then, I found myself floating up through steel and rock to the 5th floor where the robots were built. I saw this one and approached it with great curiosity. Suddenly, I found myself sucked in like a spirit vacuum cleaner had lodged me in the head. I tried to, but I couldn't get out again. Once I relaxed, I looked around and discovered that the same thing had happened to two of my friends from the Army's secretarial pool."

"When was this?"

"Long ago. Too long to count or remember."

"Does anyone know that you are no longer merely a robot? Or, for that matter, no longer a human?"

"I don't think so."

Tes sprang up and ran through the kitchen to the back door, because Alice had just walked into the house and thrown her keys on the kitchen table. She stopped and petted Tes, gave her a scratch behind her ears, and then stood up and stared into the living room/office.

"Blyss! What are you doing here? Going to kill us?"

"Of course not. They'd send a couple S-series 'bots for that. I'm here to try and talk S1... excuse me... Oren into coming back in for some examinations..."

Alice lit into her without letting her finish: "Sounds more like interrogations than exams, to me."

"No, really; the highest echelon leaders simply want to find out more about this 'humanization process,' as they're calling it, of robots."

"Then, they really don't know about you and me, do they, Blyss?"

"God no! And I'm not going to tell them! They only know whatever the Army let out about the Interstellar War Games we played back in Dulce."

"Thank God. This is fabulous!"

Alice relaxed and entered the same room the other two were seated in.

"I just heard from Llys. She and Phil are doing fine, even though they're in custody in a Homeland Security jail—maybe I should call it a country club—just north of San Francisco... something about Llys having faked a birth certificate. Nothing that Phil can't take care of soon."

"That settles it then. I'm going to stick around until she gets here. Have you heard anything about our other 'fugitives' from injustice?"

Stanson answered, "Ingrid lectures part-time for the philosophy department at UC Berkeley. She's doing fine... creating quite a stir preaching about robots bringing us to Armageddon.

"Linda Flynch?"

Alice took this one, "It's really sad. I found out from a mole at Dulce that she was memory-wiped by the Others after they took her embryo for experiments. Last, I heard, she's wandering around Southern California's Mojave Desert, trying to find herself while raising one child with another on the way. I heard a biker's the father. Presently, she has adopted their base club as her home."

"How about Hank?"

"Mellon died. The agency tracking us killed him two days after you all left. That about wraps up the news about ourselves."

Stanson had more to say, however.

"This is old-home week for sure, ladies. Now to your question and de-sires, Blyss. I have no intention of going back to the Military/Industrial Complex. After meeting you women, I realize I am sorely out of date any-how. My design parameters were probably outdated by the time con-struction began on this body and its internal systems. And now, since I'm inhabiting this body, which, by the way, I originally built with a lot of help, I think I'll rather keep it. The last thing I want to do is go find a hu-man embryo and grow another organic body! I'd have to teach it how to operate, learn how to make it talk again, and go through the always risky business of the educational system in its present state... not to mention the drug prescriptions they dole out like candy to children who simply have more energy than they know what to do with because of sugar-laden diets."

He looked at the two women to size up their interest levels... and if they were overly offended so far.

"... No offense to Ingrid, but her people have really mucked it up. My col-lege students can barely read and write! My god, half of them have taken psychotropic "medications" for most of their school years. Me, in a hu-man body again? No thanks; I'll pass!"

Chapter 42 ~ Garbage In, Garbage Out

CORNWALLS AND LLYS WALKED ALONG the outer perimeter of their confinement campus—a part of their enforced morning routine. They were housed in a prototype Homeland Security Prison designed to house insurgents under Martial Law, should the President declare the state. This facility was located near Sausalito, California. So far, it hadn't been a bad way to spend their honeymoon. When they arrived for the first time, they were shuffled from building to building under orders to examine each facility to make sure the amenities were to their liking.

He had given much thought to why they were discovered in the first place aboard the freighter, since he had taken precautions to leave no traces or clues as to their whereabouts in Hawaii, or their destination. Only the travel agent knew but he seemed to not care about their plans and limited time to embark on their journey, once he saw that he was going to be paid in cash. The thought of not reporting it for tax purposes also had crossed his mind... must have crossed his mind; at least, that was the way he was thinking it was.

Then again, it might have been someone on the crew of the Karpfanger looking to make a few extra dollars and not caring who was involved or what the circumstances were. Money, he knew, always talked to people if the amount was large enough to entice them to do something they would not normally do. When the couple foiled the attempted kidnapping by the fake Englishman, they might have seen their chance to move in and score a deal... or the whole thing might have blown up purely by chance!

At any rate, without any definitive answers, save the copied birth certificate not being good enough to snooker the Coast Guard, he still didn't know who their enemy was.

Llys sat down on a bench next to Cornwalls under a large Western Oak tree. She pulled him down to her and kissed him passionately.

"Whoa! Aren't you afraid our captors will notice?" he asked.

"Not at all. Matter of fact, I'm sure they always do."

She pointed to the tops of the high fences surrounding them.

"... We're under constant surveillance, honey. See the camera up there in the tree above us? See that sprinkler head that appears to be stuck, which probably has another audio/visual monitor on us? See that boat out in the harbor that's been there ever since we arrived?"

"I'm sorry. I've been too preoccupied to think straight."

"Well, I can change that, and I don't care who sees us." She kissed him again and then lowered her voice to a whisper while appearing to say sweet-nothings into his ear.

"Shush, Baby! We should contemplate our escape right now. Alice and Blyss are waiting for us at Oren's place, but they won't be able to wait there forever. You know people are after them, too."

"Who's Blyss? A Llys-model robot? Won't you get jealous?"

"Nope. We're all different looking and those two assumed their bodies after I did. So, are you game? Will you put that fine, genius-spy mind to work on our escape, pretty please?" Llys said in her most sensuous voice.

He could not resist her when she got like that. Her husky, soft whispers turned into many kisses.

"Okay, Phil, come up for air," she teased, "... What have you got for me?"

"Besides a you-know-what?" he answered, grinning widely.

Her look of disapproval, though it was only done jokingly, spurred him on to get serious.

"Okay, okay. We'll escape right after lunch. The catering truck always hangs out for about an hour after they feed us. Maybe someone else is getting a little on the side, like we should... by the way, how did they make your hair so perfect like that?" She covered his face with her honey-blonde hair and kissed him a lot.

"They modeled human proteins, Sweet-pea, but don't change the subject."

"I haven't. Who is 'They'? Are they the same they who are after us?"

"No. If that 'they' wanted us, we'd have been caught long ago. Much as I'd love to, I'm sorry, dearie, I just can't tell you who 'they' are. At least, not for a long time. 'They' are so secret that the Deep-State secret people don't even know about them. But don't worry, baby... you can just expect that the 'they' who made me are not interested in you and me. Trust me. So, let's leave it at that, okay?"

"Okay, for now. But the truth will out, sooner or later, with or without my prodding, and you know that."

"No, Darling; this truth will never be outed. Not unless 'They' approve its revelation."

With that, Llys changed the subject, "Now, I'm hungry, and it's just about lunch time. And that catering-truck field trip sounds good to me, too! Let's go see my sisters and Oren."

Without consulting or informing her, he had been working on his escape plan for days, knowing that Llys would spring the idea on him any day. By the time she did, he was ready, and he knew it would work. He had already primed the truck driver in his favor with a safe deposit key and code that he could use after they were long gone.

The plan was simple: The food delivery company always sent lunches in on a bobtail truck. After unloading the incoming food and supplies, the truck was filled with sealed, outgoing garbage bags that were taken to a local dump site and incinerated. Garbage in, garbage out was the idea that he had conceived when he noticed the routine never varied. The bottom line was it would be safe to exit as part of the garbage out.

What wasn't part of the plan—what they couldn't know until they executed the plan—was that the back of the truck was fumigated against insect and germ contamination after it left the prison yard.

By the time the driver had gotten to the dump site, Cornwalls had gone unconscious. When the truck stopped so the driver and passenger could toss the bags into a pile to be compacted, Llys punched a hole in her bag suddenly, and the driver screamed. His assistant ran back to see what was going on, thinking perhaps that a rat had escaped the poison. But, what he found was far worse: Llys had the driver by his throat and she was squeezing it tight. In fact, the man died just as his partner arrived.

Pulling a wrench out of his overalls, he went after Llys, assuming her to be groggy from the poison gas. Big mistake!

Llys raced in under his first wild swing and punched him in the throat, breaking his larynx. He fell backward gagging. Next, she picked up the wrench and bashed his head in, neutralizing her perceived threat.

Hopeful that she would find him still breathing, she began digging for Cornwall's body among the pile of garbage bags. She found him in the middle of the bags still not emptied from the truck. Ripping open the bag, she felt for a pulse. It was weak, and his breathing was extremely shallow, so she dragged him out into the open air away from the dump pile and began mouth-to-mouth resuscitation. Precious minutes passed, but she worked without stop until his body flailed about, and he inhaled on his own, gulping greedily for oxygen. When he had settled down and appeared lucid and not exhibiting any signs of brain injury, her resuscitation became a kiss... and then an embrace.

She pulled her lips back from his.

"Don't stop, I still feel weak," he joked in his usual manner. She knew then that he was alright; that he would survive. As a reward, she sat on his stomach and tickled his ribs.

"This isn't the place for what I have in mind. Get up, Handsome. We have to clean up and get out of this dump!"

Chapter 43 ~ The Fresh Wind

LINDA FLYNCH FOUND HERSELF ALONE, un-pregnant and confused when she regained consciousness in the desert. She still didn't remember who she was or what she had been doing with her life. She sensed she had miscarried in a rest stop somewhere in the mountains east of Los Angeles and near a village called Lytle Creek.

The bikers had abandoned her, but they didn't steal her motorcycle. Feeling too uncomfortable to ride immediately, she sat on the ground under a large tree and contemplated recent events as they came to her.

Her miscarriage reminded her of an earlier pregnancy, albeit someone took away that baby. She could not remember who, or where it happened. Checking her fuel level, she realized she still had money in a bank account, but she could not recall why or from where the funds came.

She sensed that she had friends in what seemed like Berkeley, California. She couldn't remember who, but the feeling was strong enough that she decided to go there and try to hook up with someone, believing their identities would come back to her as she rode—the fresh wind blowing through her hair always had cleared her head in the past.

In the public restroom, she bought a map of California out of a vending machine. Outside on a bench, she opened it and found the route to Berkeley, which, as it turned out, was on the same freeway that had taken her to Lytle Creek.

Feeling more sure of herself, she bought an apple from a food dispenser and ate it. At last, knowing where she was and where she was headed, she mounted her bike and motored away from the village, ready to experience the open road of her life ahead of her. However, nothing could be further from the truth.

Chapter 44 ~ Maybe New Mexico

CORNWALLS AND LLYS' TRUCK WAS checked for contraband at a truck-inspection station; however, since they had cleaned both themselves and the vehicle earlier in the day, they passed. Fortunately, no one had reported the truck missing.

"That was close!" he said.

"Right. Look, Phil, there is something I must tell you. It's important."

He had wanted to get back on the highway, but he stopped the rig near several semis also parked.

"Okay, honey, let it rip. I'll try to stay awake."

She slapped him playfully on the arm and pouted.

"Stop it! I'm not kidding, and your life may depend on this."

"Okay. Sorry. Go ahead."

"If anything happens to my body, like a broken arm or leg, you must get me to Dulce, New Mexico, no matter what. There is nowhere else in the world where my body can be repaired. Do you understand? Nowhere. Period."

"Okay, okay... I got it! But, why only there?"

"Think, Phil! That's where my body was built. They alone have the equipment and the knowledge to repair it; it's not like you can take this thing to Mike's Garage for an A/C belt! Tell me you understand me, and I'll finish what I'm saying."

"Okay, honey. I do understand what you are saying. I don't know all the intricacies of your structure or design, but I do believe you."

"Good. Now, it's the same drill if anything happens to Alice or Blyss, who are with S1 and Tes now. You must, must, must take charge and get any of the three of us, who might be injured, to Dulce by the fastest way possible, okay?"

"Why tell me this now?"

"Because if anything happens, you may be too wrecked emotionally to think straight. I want this in your analyzer, so you process and figure out how to do it now, while we're relatively safe."

"Are you expecting Martian invasion?"

"Maybe." With that, Llys said no more. For that matter, whenever he broached the subject later on, she ignored him.

He did, indeed, process various possible scenarios from personal attack to tactical nuclear war in his head. He knew how valuable S1 was and he assumed that if their enemies ever found out about the Llys-series of robots, the price on their heads could result in a tactical nuclear attack. The chaos of such a conflict would make it possible to either grab all the robots or at least make them non-functional, although he wasn't sure if that would incapacitate Llys; how her brain was constructed and with what materials it was made, would determine that outcome. The fact, however, that she and S1 had been taken over by, for lack of better word, ghosts, meant that their brains must be like human brains.

Llys kissed him on the cheek, asking because he was so quiet, "Are you mad at me?"

"Hell no! You've just stimulated the programming of my training to keep you safe. I'm already thinking of ways to do that."

Llys snuggled up to him on the big bench seat and planted another kiss on his cheek.

"When you want me to drive, just let me know."

"I'm good for a few hours. But I could use a coffee."

Chapter 45 ~ An Irresistible Offer

DOCTOR REESE WAS AT THE center of a maelstrom of controversy: her envisioned world of robot programming and transmigrations of human souls into them had gone public. Weekly death threats from scientists, internet buffs and sci-fi fanatics followed her every time she talked about human souls taking over robots. Theology students formed picket lines in front of her university office, claiming she was a heathen who would go to hell. To boot, she received notice from Psychology Department Chairperson Peter Wells, PhD that her job status was under review because of her statements and the turmoil that followed her.

Apparently, her notion that human souls existed at all, and that they not only controlled bodies, but also remained alive after death, was too much to bear for the "Man from Mud" boys sucking on the teat of the university's federal budget money. (Perhaps, that was all they really cared about.)

The idea of souls alone went against everything Reese was taught; and what was being taught to others currently out of the unproven "science" of psychology textbooks. In so many words, they purported that meatbot behavior was better served and altered with chemicals—a hot topic in certain circles like the military, where the suicide rate was skyrocketing after the mass introduction of psych-drug "treatments." Neither vested interest wanted ghosts fouling up their research funding control and well-laid, long-term plans for future appropriations.

Reese's desk phone rang, and she picked it up.

"Who is this?" She had been preoccupied with and upset by the disturbing news of late, and nearly bit off her assistant's head.

"It's Myrtle, Doctor. There is a well-dressed man, accompanied by two tough-looking fellows, out here who showed me identification that he is from a governmental organization called the 'CSS.' I've never heard of them, but he said you would remember."

"Show him in, Myrtle. And go to the library right away. From there, send a text message to my friend Alice. Tell her who is here and then come back to my office."

"Yes, Doctor."

Ingrid stood up, smoothed out her clothing, took a deep breath and exhaled, and prepared for the unexpected.

Two of the three men entered. One positioned himself inside of her office by the door; the gentlemanly one walked straight up to her, acting as if he knew her already. The third had stationed himself outside her door. None were robots.

"Doctor Reese, I have a few questions for you."

"Of course, you do, Mister...?"

"My name is not important."

"Then, neither are my answers."

She walked back to her desk, sat down behind it and stared at the intruder for several minutes. The would-be interrogator started to perspire and, finally, he broke.

"I want to know where the robot S1 is."

"I'm sure you do, but I suspect that you know the answer to that question already. Asking me a question to which you already know the answer is a waste of your time. Try again."

"Has it been decommissioned?"

"Not to my knowledge, though, if so, you would undoubtedly know about it."

"Have you been communicating with it?"

"Look, we both know you work for a branch of the NSA or the CSS. Again, you would know quite well if I have been in touch."

She then looked over at the guard standing at her door.

"Just for the record—is your assistant recording this conversation? No, I have not been communicating with him."

"Why do you speak of it as 'him'?"

"Ah, there is a question I can answer. I have experienced by direct observation the transformation of S1 from a mere programmed robot to one run by a human soul."

"Please explain."

"I am a human behavioral psychologist. But you know that already, Mister..."

He didn't take the bait.

"... It is my job to observe, record, experiment upon and modify human behavior. I observed that S1 meets all the criteria of a human psyche, including the Turing test; furthermore, he operates like a human. Our programming entered into the S-series robots has not been sufficient to accomplish this, leaving no other explanation for such behavior modification. And he said so, in so many words, himself. He told me that he used to inhabit the meatbot known as Doctor Stanson and he left that body when it died. He then moved into robot S2. When that robot was shot by General Rogers, he moved into S1, where he remains today."

"And you believe all this, Doctor?"

"Well, it's not my religion, although some of those people marching outside of my office try to make it so. It is pure science. Once you present that there is a soul, albeit invisible, which can and does exert some influence on a Homo sapiens organic body, it's easy to make the jump and say that a soul could also occupy another type of body, if the design was close enough to the structure of a human body."

"That seems so far-fetched, Doctor."

"Well, I don't think so anymore. There are documented incidents of children remembering previous lifetimes, including where they lived, who their spouses and children were... that sort of thing. We would both agree that those would be impossible without some admission of the existence of a human soul capable of body-to-body transmigrations under certain unknown conditions. The fact that this has apparently happened between a dead human and a 'live' robot makes it noteworthy, even astounding, for our scientific world. Would you not agree, Mister...?

Again, he did not take the bait, remaining silent.

Reese was feeling more on solid ground in her thinking, so she continued.

"... Our world has changed. Unless the governments of the world cease manufacturing robots that are human-body duplicates, it is likely we could end up witnessing a war of supremacy between Homo sapiens and Robo sapiens, or whatever else we might ultimately call them."

The anonymous listener responded, at last: "If what you're saying is true, and not just another elaborate science-fiction hoax, that information will terrify the population at large. Given that possible outcome, don't you think it would be wise to tone your lectures down a bit?"

"Okay, now the real reason for your visit comes out: You want to put a gag order on me, which I'm sure you easily can. You know what, though, I suspect you and your cronies know that you already have let the cat out of the bag and you are terrified of what you have done, realizing that you can't get that feline back in the bag. Of course, that would terrify the group of organizations that you represent… of course, not to mention the fat cash cow you operate under the radar of the American public."

"I am here to make you an offer you can't resist, Doctor."

"My life, if I shut up; death, if I don't?"

"No, not yet. We're merely suggesting your early retirement, effective immediately. And in seclusion. Just walk out of this office with a suitcase full of large bills, and we'll take care of the rest."

"If I would do just that, I would want to first see an advanced, state-of-the-art, model robot. The S-series model, of which I am most familiar, is almost 10 years old now. Seeing the latest would satisfy a lot of my curiosity, after which I could do as you have suggested."

The gentleman caller signaled his guard, who brought in an oversized briefcase and placed it on a sideboard in the office, and got up to leave. At the door, he turned.

"I believe, Doctor, that you already have. Enjoy your retirement." And, with a nod toward the briefcase, he smiled smugly.

The man and his guard left the room, closing the door behind them. Reese walked over to the briefcase and opened it. Her eyes popped when she saw it was crammed full of hundred-dollar bills. Back at her desk, she leaned back in her chair and closed her eyes in thought.

What did he mean by that last remark? Where was this mythical advanced robot? She scanned her past, searching for clues.

Suddenly, her eyes popped open. The answer had been right in front of her eyes for months: *Llys!* Llys was the prototype of a new, advanced series, the Super-Llys series robot!

No wonder she was the ideal woman. No wonder she was too perfect! she thought.

Her mind reeled in some scary thoughts, too: *But... if she's with Doctor Phillip Cornwalls, is she in danger? Isn't he an operative for the same agency as the men who just stood in my office? Who's keeping an eye on whom?*

"Myrtle, come into my office and bring your recorder. I have urgent business for you. And cancel all my appointments for the rest of the day."

"Yes, Doctor."

Reese set the wheels in motion for her retirement. She knew too well that she wouldn't stand retirement without contact with the outside world. She liked being a public person; she needed a position of influence, a job worthy of her interest.

She also preferred knowing about global climate change and its consequences for cities or countries near ocean waters. With that in mind, her choice of retirement locale had to be situated higher than 100 feet above sea level. Most tropical destinations were eliminated under that dictum; yet, too near the poles of the Earth had to be ruled out.

Then she remembered a seminar she had attended a few years before she joined the robot project. It had taken place at Virginia Beach at the Association for Research and Enlightenment, founded decades ago by the psychic healer Edgar Cayce.

That will be perfect. Very little government, very few random visitors, and very few colleagues to harass her.

Myrtle entered with her micro-recorder and, sitting down in front of her boss, she placed it on the broad desk.

"I'm ready, Doctor."

"Write a text-letter to the Association for Research and Enlightenment in Virginia Beach. Do not call, text or email them. I want to reserve a room in their hotel. You'll find a business card in the Rolodex file. My stay, which will be long-term, will begin one month from today, assuming they have an available room. A couple days before or after is all right."

Myrtle was noting in shorthand her instructions to be carried out.

"... and, Myrtle, all of this is confidential between you and me only. Got it?"

"Yes, Doctor. If I may ask, does this have anything to do with those dour men who just visited you?"

"It has everything to do with them, Myrtle."

'Dour,' what an apt adjective! Myrtle, that's why I hired you! She kept the thought to herself.

"... When you have sent the letter, you may email, asking for a confirmation of receipt after five days, but no extensive emails, please."

"Understood, Doctor."

"... Then and only then, I want you to make application for another position for yourself. I won't be returning to the university; my time is up here; my usefulness retired."

Of course, Myrtle was dumbfounded, but she would do as asked. She was loyal to a fault.

"... I am counting on your keeping our secret. You have done so before. No one outside this room right now is to know I am leaving. My personal safety depends on you, Myrtle. Do you understand?"

"No, Doctor, I don't. Can't you tell me anything?"

"I will tell you a little, but you must understand this information will threaten your life, too. Do you still want to know?"

"Can't you take me with you? Surely you'll need an assistant."

"No, I won't. I won't be teaching again. Those men offered me a deal—my silence or my life—and I choose life. Their organization does not equivocate."

"This is really serious, isn't it?"

"Yes. Now, I'm going to go visit a friend. I may not come back, but if I do, you can come to my condo with me and help me pack. Nothing big; I'll be traveling light."

"I'm pretty sure I'll be seeing you again in a few hours, Doctor."

Ingrid was surprised at the emotion Myrtle put into the hug she gave her. An Aquarius, Ingrid hadn't often expressed strong emotions openly, except when speaking to groups, but she was pleased that her secretary felt strongly about her. In return, she kissed her loyal employee on the cheek before she left the office, never to return.

Ingrid Reese, Doctor Ingrid Reese, PhD Psychology, ventured outside into the unknown of her future, feeling washed out. She hoped to see and talk to the robot/android/unknown life form that was her best friend, Alice, as soon as possible. Perhaps, in the bargain she would gain more insight into where the world was headed.

Chapter 46 ~ The Big Crate

S1, Reese, Blyss and Tes sat in comfortable chairs set around a low coffee table, upon which had been placed a pot of tea and a plate full of small cakes. The foursome waded through a tall pile of papers from Stanson's students, helping him grade the tests.

Tes had wanted to pull down the papers onto the floor, so a bowl of milk had been placed on the floor near their feet. The cat purred contentedly as she drank the liquid.

The silence was broken by the sounds of a large diesel motor running outside and a car's horn. The two robots looked at each other, and Reese got up and went to the front door, where stood a uniformed delivery driver holding a computerized clipboard.

"Delivery for Doctor Oren Stanson. He needs to sign for it."

Reese looked past the man at the large, flatbed tow truck he'd been driving. On the bed was placed a large, wooden packing crate about the size of a car.

"Doctor Stanson is taking a nap. I'd hate to interrupt him; he's been putting in long hours at work. May I sign for him?"

"Of course. Just sign the screen and press your thumb on the reader next to your signature."

That done, Reese walked out to the truck.

"Hold on, ma'am. I must get it off the truck first. Better stand well back."

She did as she was told. Blyss came out to watch. Stanson watched from the small window high on the closed door preventing Tes from running outside. Instead, Tes watched from the back of a chair with her head stuck through the window drapes.

The crate set on large metal rollers was fastened to a metal frame under the crate. It rolled off the truck bed like any would from a car carrier. When the crate was completely on the ground, the uniformed driver unhooked the gear, raised his flatbed and drove off with another honk.

"Now what?" Blyss asked.

"Let's see what's written on it. It might be a nuclear bomb. Or it might be a nice, new Volkswagen. Maybe there are unpacking instructions," said Reese.

The women walked around the box, inspecting it carefully. On the top was an instruction sheet, which Blyss read aloud.

"UNPACK WITH EXTREME CAUTION. Do not unpack this crate until Doctor Phillip Cornwalls arrives on site. An inspection door is underneath this instruction. Ensure the inspection door is secured when not in use. SOME ASSEMBLY REQUIRED."

"Blyss, go get a flashlight, will you? Also bring your cell-phone camera," commanded Reese.

"Okay."

Blyss hurried into the house. She flashed into the doorway, running toward the kitchen, as Stanson kept Tes at bay by scratching her behind her ears. Then Blyss dashed out the door carrying a large flashlight and her phone.

"This was addressed to you, so I'll send you an image of what's inside," she said over her shoulder.

Stanson shut the door, mindful that the truck driver easily may have been an industrial spy, as well as a deliveryman.

"Damn! The hatch is secured by screws. I think there's a multi-blade screwdriver in the kitchen tool drawer," Blyss said aloud.

"I'll get it." Reese dashed into the house and in a few seconds returned, holding a red-handled screwdriver.

Blyss unscrewed the cover with the note on it and removed it from the inspection hole. Looking a lot like a surgeon, she handed the screwdriver back to Reese and held her hand out for the flashlight, which Reese placed firmly in her palm, already turned on.

"Oh my god. Oh my god! I think I know what this is!"

"Let me see!"

Blyss reluctantly gave up the inspection hole to Reese.

"It looks like an exotic sports car. What the hell?"

"No, Ingrid. It is an exotic seaplane that Phil had built for his and Llys' escape. It was sunk in the Honolulu marina where it was docked, forcing a long and elaborate escape. That's a story we don't know the whole of. It means Phil and Llys are on their way here!"

"How do you know that, Blyss?"

"Llys and I have shared telepathy, even when we were humans; we still do. That's why we were working at Dulce before the war."

"War? What war?" Reese asked as they entered the house.

"I can't say much about it, yet. But a big underground war was waged, and lots of humans were killed."

"I don't remember that."

"It wasn't on the six o'clock news."

"Oh."

Stanson broke in.

"Excuse me, ladies, but we have to clean up the spare bedroom if Phil and Llys are coming; also, the rest of the house. I'll straighten up my papers."

No sooner had they gotten to the cleanup work, the doorbell rang again. This time Stanson went and looked through the peep hole.

"It's Alice!" he exclaimed, opening the door.

"What's that crate all about?" Alice asked, stepping inside.

"It's Phil and Llys' airplane, apparently," Blyss said.

"Huh. That's interesting, if not a bit odd."

"Well, it is Phil, you know… and he is a spy, you know… so, there is no telling what sort of paraphernalia he's likely to come up with," said Blyss.

Alice stepped up to Stanson and gave him a big hug.

"I'm glad you're here with us, S1. I was worried about you."

"My name is Oren now. Seems more politically correct."

"Yes, of course. I hear Ingrid is moving to Virginia Beach."

Oren stared at Reese. "Why?" he asked.

"I was offered a… let's call it a 'secure retirement' by the CSS at the location of my choice."

"Oh, really?" Blyss asked, non-believing.

"Well, it was not much of a choice, really: give up my lecturing and public speaking about robots bringing about the end of the world and retire anywhere I wanted, so long as I stayed quiet... or die."

Stanson shook his head in dismay.

"... Not really a hard choice. I had no robot around to transmigrate to, so I'm moving. I plan to fly out as soon as we talk to Phil."

"They should arrive any minute now—that big box outside is for him. I expect him to arrive any moment with Llys," Stanson said.

"Great! Maybe he can shed some light on what's going on."

"Yeah, if he can talk about it at all. He still carries a lot of secrets, you know," said Blyss.

"Of course. That's his job description: secrets in charge," Stanson laughed. The other joined him.

Blyss brought out a tray of Oreos and milk and placed it on the glass-topped coffee table. Tes pulled one of the cookies off the table, then jumped up and licked milk from the glass.

After another hour and a half of light banter about what each had done since leaving the Lab, the phone rang.

"Hello, Llys," said Alice, recognizing her voice, "... Where are you guys?"

"We're close. Do you have anything Phil can eat for dinner?"

"We were going to order a pizza for Ingrid. I'll get one for Phil, too."

"Okay, see you in an hour. By the way, Phil asked if you received a package for him."

"Yes, it's here."

"Great. See you soon."

Alice hung up. "That was Llys and Phil. They'll be here within an hour. Can you stay, Ingrid? Oren?"

Reese was on the phone, talking to Myrtle: "... I'll be back at the office in an hour and a half. See you soon."

She hung up.

They would never see each other again.

Chapter 47 ~ Assessment

CORNWALLS AND LLYS ARRIVED IN Berkeley, California, not knowing where Stanson's house was located and needing to trade in the truck. He ended up with a used Fiat 600 with only 2000 miles on it, while Llys called Stanson to find out his address.

"The reunion is about to begin, honey. Are you ready to meet all those beautiful women?" asked Llys of Cornwalls as she admired the newer transportation choice.

"If you're there to protect me, what could go wrong?"

Unfortunately, they quickly found out why the car they had gotten such a good deal on had been traded: The brakes were spongey, and they failed when they arrived at Stanson's, crashing the car into the huge crate in front of the house. The wooden box suffered little damage, but the Fiat's front end was totaled.

"Oh well, I only gave the guy two-hundred bucks down," Cornwalls remarked.

Hearing the crash in the dark, everyone poured out of the front door, including Stanson in disguise. Standing on the lawn, the crowd heard a motorcycle roar up too fast for the circumstances. They watched it careen through some newly planted bushes before getting stopped by a decorative light pole and collapsing to the grass. The driver, a delirious, drunk or drugged, Linda Flynch, stood up, brushed herself off, and announced her arrival.

"Well, I'm here. Let's get this party rolling... I'm famished!"

She walked in the front door just as Stanson was going in, too.

"... By the way, who are all you people? I thought this was going to be a Robo-Lab reunion. Am I at the right party?"

Stanson ordered another pizza before addressing the group formally.

"Welcome all. Not everyone here knows everyone else here, so let's make our introductions before Homeland Security arrests us all; I'll start. I'm Oren Stanson, also known as Robot S1." With that, he removed his costume.

Next in the circle was Cornwalls: "I'm Phillip Cornwalls, NSA-branch employee under the CSS and formerly second in command under Brigadier-General Rogers. When he was removed, I replaced him."

"With prejudice," Stanson added.

"I'm Llys, Phil's fiancée."

"I'm Ingrid Reese, S-series robot psychologist."

"I'm Alice, also employed by the CSS and here in support of Dr. Stanson."

"I'm Blyss, secretary and receptionist for the CSS East Coast HQ."

"Among other things," Cornwalls added.

"I think I'm Linda Flynch but aliens brain-wiped me, so I'm not at all sure who I am, really. I do remember designing the S-series of robots' bionetic brains. And I remember being abducted in New Mexico, having my baby embryo taken from me... and, after that, a lot more, terrible things. But, here I am."

"Meow," came Tes' perfectly timed salutation. She had been seated on Phil's lap, but she moved to Stanson's when he sat down. Later, she decided Llys' lap was the best and she curled up and slept there.

"Anybody know if we're 'live'? Is this meeting being broadcast nationwide via the NSA/CSS' super-secret surveillance technologies?" asked Stanson.

"Oh wait, let me check..." added Blyss, tongue planted in cheek. She leaned forward and looked inside the lampshade. "... Yep, we're hot."

With the introductions over, Stanson went on, "Our meeting comes many months later than expected, but I think we should go over some old business. Phillip, why are we here?"

"Before I took over the project, I felt we had taken a turn in the wrong direction. Rogers had pushed the warfighter scenario so strongly, and I felt a golden opportunity was being wasted. You see, we had an opportunity to build robots that could integrate into human society in a very helpful way, as well as assist soldiers in combat environments."

"That sure didn't happen!" Linda shouted.

"No, it didn't. In fact, the project was terminated with extreme prejudice (against us and my wishes) and we were all hunted down like game. My agency held the lead command, but there was another, hidden agency, and that group wanted our design secrets. Considering at that time that each robot had cost, and were valued at, almost the same number as a B-12 bomber, those secrets were a large target. Kidnapping one or more of our products would be a coup of magnitude that would bring a very large ransom."

"I blew it, didn't I?" Stanson confessed.

"Yes, you did; but not intentionally. You were not under the influence of an enemy, although that's what my agency initially had thought. No, you accidentally tipped the playing field into an end-game process by wanting to build a "'lunch box,' as you put it."

"Huh?" Llys was not following this well.

"That's right. S1, he wanted to build an energy storage unit that he could carry around in case his charge got low and there wasn't any electricity in the nearby environment. It was an excellent solution for a warfighting device. Unfortunately, when he accessed the secret design documents, he triggered a spy-double hacker in India, working for the U.S. CIA and Russia's GRU, piggybacking the line, which set off all kinds of alarms, shutting the system down. As we all know, that caused an overreaction and my superiors shut down our entire project."

"Jeesuz! So, that's why they leveled the place!" Alice exclaimed.

"I'm sure Oren will want to go into that in greater detail, later."

Stanson nodded.

"So, why are they still chasing us?" Llys asked.

"Because we are a national-security risk. If any other group or nation acquires S1—our Oren here, it would be disastrous for national security."

Reese objected: "I'm not sure about that. My conversations with your employers indicate to me that they would just as much like to ignore all of us... after putting us on a short leash."

"I think the Steering Committee thinks so, but there are others who don't agree with that; others who don't like any 'loose ends.' After all, it's a large bureaucracy, and you know how crazy that can get! A bunch of different factions, none of whom are aware of the whole picture. And that's the stage we now are at, barring one exception."

"What's that?" Linda spoke up. Something in the tone of Cornwall's statement had triggered a memory that hadn't been wiped.

"If we could delve into your memories, Linda, we might find out a lot more information. Still, the real fly in the ointment is Llys and her sisters."

"Why is that, honey?" Llys asked him, a hint of suspicion and caution behind her sweet voice.

"Because you and they were created for one purpose only: To attract and trap a human soul."

The discussion blew up. Fragments of disbelief, embarrassment, suppressed understandings, and general confusion flew about the room.

Cornwalls sat back in his chair and watched it happen. Only Reese seemed to understand. The day and time she had always wondered about was, she thought, at last at hand. And she was terrified about it.

Her mouth opened as if she had something to say, and then closed, several times. Sitting still and closing her eyes, she began to cry, tears running down her cheeks and ruining her makeup.

Flynch had stood up. She was walking around the circle, touching first Llys' hair, then Alice's, then Blyss'. She moved on automatic—a circuit circling round and round like a malfunctioning robot, which maybe she was. At least, Cornwalls, however, was sure she was a human.

Though no one spearheaded it, the conversation came around to who was the other agency after them. The idea that it could be the Mafia was broached.

And Reese's grief turned to hope.

Chapter 48 ~ In the Nick of Time

"I WANT TO TRY TO get outside my body without dying. Do you think there might be a way I could?" Reese leaned over and asked Stanson.

"That's a very good question, Ingrid. Have you tried that, yet?"

"I've been afraid to do anything. I'm not ready to die."

"Well, I can't help you much, although once, when I was attending a seminar, the lecturer said I could be outside my head," he said.

"What happened?"

"It worked. I found myself staring at the back of my head."

"Oh! What was that like?" Llys asked.

"I was just there, staring at my hair until I was 'normal' again. That was before I died, so I'm sure it can be done by a human. I never tried it again, though."

"What good does it do?" Cornwalls asked.

"Inside, outside, I'm not sure. I imagine it would be good for a spy to literally get inside someone else's head."

"You guys are freaking me out!" It was Flynch.

"I think it might be sensual," said Llys, looking at Cornwalls with a fetching smile.

"Oh..." said Cornwalls, looking back at her, "... It might be at that, for sure."

Outside, the front yard suddenly became bathed with extremely bright lights.

"Oh my God, the aliens are after me!" cried Flynch.

A helicopter in stealth mode could be heard hovering overhead.

Cornwalls jumped up, ran to the front door and peeked out the window.

"Shall I turn off the lights?" Ingrid asked.

"No, no point. They have every one of us under infrared by now. They might even have a spy satellite tasked to keep an eye on us. No, I'm afraid we'll just have to do what they say; whatever that turns out to be."

"Send out the robot S1. The rest of you, stay where you are," a faceless voice said from behind the lights.

"Oren, can't you do anything?" Reese asked, plainly scared.

"No, Ingrid. But, you look quite pretty this evening."

He said it right before he entered her head.

The S1 robot body went rigid. It stood up and walked across the room to the front door, opened it, and stepped out into the lights.

"Oh... my... God!" Ingrid had just realized she was no longer alone in her body! Her eyes closed, and she sank back into her chair.

Cornwalls watched through the door as S3 and S4 took charge of S1, accompanied by two heavily armed soldiers, and walked the S1 robot body towards the light.

"Finally, the light at the end of the tunnel," Reese said as if in a sleepy trance.

"What?" Blyss said.

"Now send out Cornwalls," the anonymous voice shouted.

Llys opened the door a crack. "He's in the toilet. Can't you wait a minute or so?"

"Then send out Linda Flynch."

Linda pushed Llys aside, flung open the front door and ran right toward the lights, screaming, "You'll never take me alive!"

She leaped at the man with the bullhorn. He tried to dodge her, but she got him right in the midsection. He went down hard.

Three soldiers sprang on top of Flynch, but they were barely able to subdue her until a medic managed to stick a needle into her neck. Immediately, she quieted.

"My people are almost here, honey. Let's stall this for another minute," Llys said to Cornwalls.

"Your who?"

"My builders. They will take all of this down. Try to stay near the door and be prepared to move, if you have to, okay?"

"All right, I promise... whatever. I'll try to stall them."

Cornwalls opened the door and stepped out in front of it, closing the door behind him. He was aware of the sniper on the roof across the street, the sniper behind his crated seaplane, the line of three soldiers with weapons drawn and pointed at him from in front of the crate. Of course, the CSS man holding the bullhorn, too. In all, five lasers tagged him. He hadn't really wanted to walk into this situation, but he had to trust his woman.

"Before this escalates into another destructive, inter-stellar war, I should warn you that superior forces are arriving any minute. So, please, I beg you, cease and desist and disband your troops before anyone gets hurt."

Just about everyone on the opposing team smiled, laughed or guffawed at his words; that is, until three blindingly strong orange globes of light beamed down on them from above the helicopter.

In the ensuing commotion, Llys eased herself out of the house and slipped beside Cornwalls, holding his hand so he wouldn't draw his weapon. In front of all eyes, she kissed him on the cheek and whispered into his ear, "Remember your promise. Do not worry. Trust me. Things are going to start moving very fast now."

The sniper across the street was the one to start the war. He fired, and Llys flashed by faster than the bullet to a position in front of her man, taking the bullet in her right shoulder. She would have crumpled instantly to the ground, but he held her and turned her away from the soldiers. If anyone else fired, he would be shot, but there were no more shots.

"Hold your fire, hold your fire, hold your fire!" the man with the bullhorn yelled. As he was yelling a streak of light shot down to the rooftop across the street and the sniper who had fired was vaporized. Two other streaks of light flashed down: one to the helicopter, which just stopped and crashed to the street, and the other to the ground three inches in front of the man with the bull horn.

"Incoming fire! Take cover!" he yelled, running around the crate and disappearing in its shadows. In the ruckus, everyone had lost track of the robot S1.

Take me inside, you dolt! Cornwalls heard inside his head. He lifted Llys over his shoulder and went indoors as instructed. Alice closed the door behind them. No one spoke. Reese was still apparently asleep in her chair. Alice and Blyss sat together, wearing their emotions on their faces—mostly hatred.

Cornwalls again heard Llys' voice in his head.

My friends cannot take us with them. When the battle is over, you must assemble my sea-Porsche and fly me to New Mexico. My body has shut down to preserve itself. You and I are now intimately connected, mostly in your body. Is this as fun for you as it is for me?

He felt a tickling sensation between his legs.

Stop that! I must think! he thought. He placed her body in a chair and sat next to her, holding her hand. Nothing drizzled out of the wound in her shoulder. He had half-expected green goo.

Outside, Reese's worst fear played out in miniature. The military was shooting at the UFO, which was destroying the military. The repaired robot S2 took a shot at the house, destroying the front door and most of the wall around it. By this time, however, everyone inside had moved to the master bedroom in the rear next to the kitchen. Llys lay on the bed, and Phil sat beside her. Her robot body had completely shut down, and he had no idea if she was alive, functioning, asleep or dead. Since she was in his body with him now, it didn't matter.

Cornwalls heard one of the S-robots sneaking around to the back yard. It had become entangled in the fence and was breaking boards. He let go of Llys' hand and pulled out his laser gun. He checked the charge; it was full. Listening at the kitchen's back door, he determined that the robot was against the side of the house hear his location. Taking a deep breath, he flung the door open, staying sideways to minimize his position in the line of fire.

The robot shot the door to smithereens. In the cloud of expanding wood bits, Cornwalls had a good shot at the robot and shot it in the head, the neck, and in the chest. The robot went down.

As suddenly as it has started, the war was over. The air was silent; no further shots fired.

Cornwalls walked around to the side of the house where the robot had stalked him. He found no one there, and not a single sound. Not even the robot remained, as if he never had been there.

I think we won Llys thought.

He looked up. The night sky was clear. In the distance, he saw three interlocked and distinctly moving lights that any other casual observer might have thought was an airplane taking off from the Berkeley airport, but he knew better, because there was no engine noise.

He continued to the front of the house. The seaplane box was undamaged, although two melted SUVs on the street accompanied the helicopter wreckage, and the third SUV was gone. No body carcasses remained, but there were puddles of biological matter, which, at one time, might have been soldiers. A hole had been burned completely through his Fiat 600.

No chance of a rebate or return there he thought, snickering.

Alice and Blyss joined Cornwalls next to his crate.

"We have to get this thing put together right now, Doctor. Llys doesn't have all night," Alice said.

"Of course, I don't!" Phil's voice exclaimed at a higher pitch than his normal.

Giddy, the two sisters kissed his cheeks and then began unfastening the side and top wing nuts of the crate with his help. Together they slid the top off and got the sides down on the ground. The seaplane needed the motor set up and the wings to be attached to the folding mechanism. It would then have to be wheeled off the metal frame that had supported it inside of the box.

Flynch appeared. She had wandered up from somewhere down the street. She fell on her face in the front yard grass. Tes ran out from under the house and pounced on Flynch before Alice could stop her.

"Where's Oren?" Blyss asked as she continued to follow Phil's instructions to assemble the plane.

"He's inside Ingrid's head. I don't know who took his body, but they got away before the battle began," Alice said.

Reese staggered down the steps in front of what remained of the house. She appeared to be mumbling to herself, but she was absentmindedly vocalizing her internal conversation with her co-inhabitant, Oren. Tes followed them, mesmerized.

Your people? Llys said inside Phil.

Yes, my people.

Is this what marriage is like? Llys asked, ignoring the question.

Yes, but usually with two bodies.

Alice, Blyss and Cornwalls were amused, but they finished uncrating and cataloging the aircraft's parts. At last, the three of them managed to jiggle the heavy turbine engine into position on its pylon mounts and bolt it down. Blyss placed the wings carefully on the grass, while Cornwalls and Alice pushed the Fiat wreck far enough aside that the seaplane fuselage could be wheeled off the metal frame and onto the street.

Cornwalls felt there wasn't enough room between power lines crossing the street where the plane would have to lift off, for the plane to climb cleanly into the sky.

"Ingrid or Oren, whoever is running that body, please turn the Studebaker behind the plane to face away from it. We'll hook the aircraft's tail knob to the car's trailer hitch."

He turned to the others: "Alice and Blyss, help me mount the wings onto the folding mechanisms."

As soon as they got the completed plane connected to the Studebaker, Tes sprang from a hiding place and jumped into the cockpit.

Hurry, honey. My people will be at the base by now.

"Okay, let's go. I'll ride in the plane with Tes. Alice, would you ride with us to the harbor? We're going to test the systems while heading for the boat ramp at the Berkeley Marina."

Good plan!

"I heard that, sis!" Alice said aloud as she climbed into the tight-fitting cockpit. With Alice and Llys' body in the cockpit with Cornwalls, there was precious little free space. However, without the need for luggage, they were able to move Llys' body behind the seats.

"I'm riding with Ingrid," said Blyss.

"I'm staying here," called out Flynch from the remains of the front porch.

Doctor Reese eased the Studebaker onto the darkened street; the tow connection held tight. University Avenue ended at the Marina, and there was no traffic. At the Marina gate, the sleeping guard had left the gate wide open.

"I'll stay here with the guard. You guys go ahead." Alice whispered. She got out and watched the Studebaker tow the seaplane to the small boat-launch ramp.

Reese seemed to be having trouble backing the plane into the water so Blyss took over and backed the plane while she looked on.

The seaplane sat partly in the water, when another problem was discovered: the plane's battery was dead.

Cornwalls got out and, searching the trunk of the Studebaker, found a set of jumper cables which he then carefully held over his head out of the water. Blyss pulled the plane back up onto the ramp and Cornwalls hooked up the jumper cables to the car battery. He got back in the plane and pushed the engine-start button. The turboprop coughed and whined its way up to speed.

"Release the trailer hitch. We'll just taxi into the water. Everybody stand back."

Cornwalls pressed the wing button, and the wings opened out and locked with a satisfying thump. The locked-wings dashboard light went green. He engaged the propeller, and the seaplane inched into the water. When fully off the ramp, Cornwalls retracted the wheels and emptied the bilge. Llys' body remained safely stowed behind the seats.

The seaplane's wingtips would clear the rows of docked boats by two feet on either side. From the shoreline, the view of the boat launch ramp showed that the way was clear straight out through the breakwater and up over the ocean.

Cornwalls kept the engine at idle while passing the docked yachts. Since a jet engine in the water was not something familiar, a few lights came on from the boat decks, and several sleepy-headed crew appeared from below-decks to watch the spectacle—most of them with their mouths wide open in disbelief.

Having cleared the end of the dock, Cornwalls opened the powerful turboprop engine. It screamed, the propeller throbbed, and the little plane was into the air in seconds.

You did it, he heard in his head... *just in the nick of time!*

Next stop Dulce military base he thought back.

When we get near Lake Dulce let me have control. I know the comm channel and the codes to get through voice recognition security. ETA to the lake is about one hour as the duck flies.

Quack, quack.

"Meow," added a contented Tes, safely seated on her carry bag next to the pilot.

Cornwalls kept the craft close to the ground with its terrain-scanning radar turned on for guidance.

Passing by the Army base at Mojave and the Naval Weapons Test Center at China Lake in the high-desert zone of California, rhythmic pings on the radar let him know that someone was tracking them.

Llys, you're up. We're being tracked. I don't want to be shot down before we make our case.

Don't worry honey. I'm famous.

Using Cornwall's voice, albeit pitched higher, Llys opened communications on the secret radio channel she knew. After her first response, she made her pilot turn on the plane's locator ID beacon.

"Base Ops, Llys Operator Zero-Zero-One here. We have a medical emergency. Request open seaway at Lake Dulce and robotic damage-repair team standing by. Code Zed-One. Switching to encrypted channel on my mark... 3, 2, 1, Mark."

The radio went to static for three seconds, then came back.

"Acknowledged, Llys Operator Zero-Zero-One in unidentified civilian aircraft. Request approved but do not deviate from your present flight path until instructed. Med team standing by. All non-essential human crew to be tranquilized before landing."

"One human crew. High value; need to know. Identity: Doctor Phillip Cornwalls harboring Llys intelligence."

"Understood. Proceed as instructed."

Cornwall's hand on the control yoke was shaking.

What's the matter honey?

I'm feeling an adrenaline surge. I must admit I'm frightened, but I can control it.

I'll help you. She ran a warm, loving flow throughout his body, and his hand steadied.

"Llys Operator Zero-Zero-One, you appear to be flying a seaplane. Verify you intend to land on Lake Dulce."

"Your scans are accurate. We are flying a seaplane and plan to land on Lake Dulce. Will you have retrieval personnel there?"

"Affirmative. We will use a Sky Hook. Reduce speed to 140 knots on my mark and adjust heading to One-Two-Zero Absolute."

You got this, or do you want me to try and land this thing? Llys thought to Cornwalls.

I've got it. Give me complete control when you can.

"Reduce speed to one-zero-zero knots. Deploy flaps. We will observe and recommend any corrections. Maintain heading."

In front of them, the lake, shimmering from the moonlight, approached rapidly; its surface lit up with a light blue color from underneath, making it easier to land.

Cornwalls took control and landed the seaplane, turned it around and headed it back to a small boat-launch ramp near a tackle shop at the south end of the lake. He slowed to idle and drift-sailed toward the concrete apron.

"Shut down engine. We have you."

Cornwall did as commanded. From above, three beams of intense light from a darkened craft above them hit the water and lifted their aircraft. Above the gravel beach, their forward motion stopped.

"Deploy landing gear."

Cornwalls did so, and the light beams shut off. A subtle whoosh of air shook the seaplane, after which they were on solid ground.

"Human life forms disembark now. Your pet cat stays in the cockpit. You will be returning shortly. Welcome home, Llys. End of transmission."

In a minute, Cornwalls had everything turned off. He opened the canopy and stepped out, reaching back for Llys' body. He got her over the canopy edge and began carrying her away from the seaplane. In less than 10 seconds, an ambulance crew arrived quietly, but with lights flashing. It stopped in front of him.

Two men got out of the oversized ambulance, wearing environmental hazard suits. One took Llys from Cornwalls; the others took Cornwall's arm. They all entered the spacious medical area in the back of the ambulance and were soon speeding across a long, landing apron, into a dark, hanger-like structure, and past two dark-gray flying objects that looked a lot like advanced fighter jets. Their path took them down a long, gradually sloping ramp to a turntable that turned and faced them toward an elevator door numbered L-07. The door opened immediately, and the ambulance rushed into the elevator.

The elevator went down, down, and down. Finally stopped at level L-07, they were greeted by another four men in hazmat suits, toting a gurney opened at the rear of the ambulance. They placed Llys' body on the gurney, after which another gurney was produced.

One of the men—perhaps an Others robot, as Cornwalls fantasized him— helped him get on the second gurney. The two gurneys were strapped together and wheeled down another tunnel into a large and extremely brightly lit room that appeared to be an operating theater. Save for Cornwalls and Llys' body, all personnel wore hazmat suits.

A machine moved over Llys' entire body and then focused on the injured shoulder. The mechanism was connected by a two-inch thick cable to the ceiling.

I'm going back to my own body now. It has been an unbelievable pleasure being in yours with you. You are going to be put to sleep for a little while to make sure you stay in your own body and not wander around. I will be with you in this room until you wake up. Then we will be sent home in the flying Porsche you bought for me. I love you!

With that, she was gone from his head.

Cornwalls thought that maybe something was not working quite right when he saw a golden light leave his head and go to her head, but what he saw led him to understand that he could be "behind his head" just as Oren had described to him. He also could observe whatever else was going on in the room at the same time, including Llys' body, which had been repaired perfectly.

This turn of events shattered Cornwall's ties to wanting to participate in the ransom that would be demanded when these robots were abducted and held for ransom, or sold off to the Chinese through C's deal that was in the works. He now knew there was more to life than what met the eye and the wallet. He knew, too, that there was a race of beings far more intelligent than humans, which seemed to be on the side of Mankind, for now. *But, what about the future? And what would they do to someone caught messing with them and their plan?* He vowed he would straighten himself out from this moment on. He wanted to help, even if it meant foregoing his cut in the billion-dollar ransom that, at the moment in light of his new experience and viewpoint up on the corner of the room, seemed incredibly small-minded!

That's when he felt Llys' shoulder as she moved it around, testing it. He suddenly wanted to be with her in the worst way, and her head immediately snapped around, and she stared at him. She smiled and winked, before turning back to the robot technicians who were checking her body out for correct functionality.

You're still alive! he thought.

Yes, thanks to you.

The technicians unhooked Llys and helped her stand up off the gurney. She turned a pirouette, performed a hand stand and a back flip—all at Olympic quality.

Watching, Cornwalls knew that despite the extensive physical training he had undergone, he would not be able to pass these tests.

At least not yet she told him in thought.

It wasn't until he and Llys were given clothing, driven back to the hanger where his plane was stored, and he had seen these Others without hazard suits, that he realized they were not robots, but live creatures—alien beings.

He walked up to one and touched it on the arm. It turned to him.

What do you want? it said in his mind.

Did you build the Llys models?

Yes, with loving care, and each one unique. Perfect receptacles for your souls.

Why?

Because worldwide change is coming. You will have a surplus of souls when the next great extinction event occurs, and they will need homes.

Cornwalls was dumbfounded at this answer. He had no words and was on the spot... until Llys walked up to him and planted a kiss on his reddening cheek right in front of the Others creature, who merely watched and smiled gently.

Whoever said or wrote that aliens had to be ugly, mean and destructive, lied; or did not know what they were talking or writing about were the words Cornwalls thought in the moment, and they made both the alien stranger and Llys smile broadly and admire him.

Cornwalls was a changed man. Lucky for him, too, because every one of his thoughts and intentions already had been received, duplicated and understood by every alien and robot nearby. Only the fact that Llys was in love with him had saved him from instant vaporization. In his case, though he didn't know it, love really did conquer all, including himself from himself!

Finally, the seaplane, apparently ready for flight, was brought out of its hangar. Cornwalls climbed into the copilot's chair and Llys, her eyebrows upraised at the gesture and a large smile on her face, sat in the pilot's chair.

"It's yours sweetheart, you deserve it," he said.

The control tower kicked in on their comm line:

"Taxi along the ramp up to the surface and take off on the runway you find there. It is shielded. There is an air battle going on, but you will be able to leave unmolested. Bring Doctor Ingrid Reese back here. She is sharing the soul of a colleague of yours, who needs to be returned to his original robot body. His name is Oren. We have the original stored here. Do not wait too long; sharing is difficult for Reese, both emotionally and intellectually, unlike you and Llys, Doctor Cornwalls. Also, they could be caught up in the war, and if she is hurt, you could lose them both."

Cornwalls scanned the instrument panel and gave Llys a thumbs-up signal.

"Ready for taxiing, Captain."

Llys looked around the plane and saw no one was close.

"All clear. Contact. Engine engaged in three, two, one, start." The turbo-prop roared to life.

Llys engaged the propeller and eased her feet off the rudder/brake pedals. The plane entered and followed a wide, curved tunnel. After circling four times, always rising toward the surface, they heard the control tower.

"Approaching runway. Prepare for full throttle in five, four, three, two, one: Go Llys. Many happy landings!"

Llys pushed the throttle all the way. The engine and propeller roared, and the light craft leaped ahead. Two seconds later, Llys pulled the yoke back and they went nearly straight up.

Above the clouds, Llys barrel-rolled, then leveled out and headed toward San Francisco. All around them were saucer-shaped UFOs, F-41 Raptors, and old, F-117 Night Hawks. The human forces greatly outnumbered the UFOs, but the UFOs were resistant to the human weapons.

Why? Phil thought.

Because most of your species is unaware of the makeup of individual universes. Body, mind, spirit; that is what needs to be taught. Perhaps someday it will be. Only then will wars end, the voice of the Other at the base thought to him. Cornwalls looked around outside their plane. They were past the battleground and air war.

"Let's head out to the ocean and fly up the coast, alright?" Llys asked him, holding his hand for the first time in a while.

"You're in command, Captain. Anything you want."

Chapter 49 ~ Going "Out"

"I'm getting cabin fever," Reese told Alice.

"No doubt; there's a crowd in there."

"And how did this happen, exactly?" Reese asked, beginning to understand that she was haunted.

"Ask Oren. He's done it twice now and he's closer than you think."

Oren? Ingrid thought.

I'm here. The secrets of the universe are at your fingertips.

Is that really you, Oren?

No, of course not. Robots don't have souls, remember? I must be a figment of your overactive imagination. Perhaps, you are having a mild psychotic episode, Doctor. It couldn't be me, I mean... Oren.

How did you do this?

Some say your brain and spinal column emit a strong tractor-beam field which keeps you attached to it. Once my body died, there was no tractor field to keep me in it. When Tes led me back to the lab, I went near the robots. S2 was turned on and I felt a familiar tractor field and was attracted to it. When I got close, it sucked me in. Now, with your body I anticipated the same effect, which happened, although it was weaker, because you're already in here. Still, it worked, and here I am.

So, how do I get out? And if I do, will my body die?

I don't mean to sound silly-simple, but, if you want to get out of your body, just get the idea that you are somewhere else, and you will be there; perceiving or not; aware or not, you will be there. It really is that simple.

Be somewhere else? Like where?"

Oh, anywhere you like. Let's try it: Be behind your head.

Reese's body went limp.

"Ingrid?" Blyss asked.

"Don't touch her. She'll be back in a moment," Flynch said.

Come back, Ingrid. I won't be here keeping this thing going forever, you know.

Reese came back.

Everything was so beautiful.

You can go outside any time you want. But come in back now.

No! I don't want to. I don't want to live in Virginia Beach. And I don't want to shut up about the robot revolution that's coming, either!

Ingrid, you need to look beautiful again, and Llys tells me it is time for me to go and get re-integrated into my S1 body; so, you need to come and take this one back.

Oh, alright.

Good-bye.

But...

You know the secret of the universe. You know we'll never be far from each other... get it?

What secret?

That it's all illusion; only you and me and all the others are real. It's the opposite of what they taught you in school; that... and just about everything else. Just remember this: YOU know!

Reese's eyes opened wide. The next words out of her mouth came from Stanson; they even sounded like his voice.

"Good-bye, my friends. I'm going to Dulce, New Mexico for a while. Give my love to Phil and Llys. Good-bye for now."

Reese's eyes fluttered a moment, then opened wide again—this time her voice was hers.

"Oh... my... God!" Reese grabbed a glass of water from the table and drank it all almost in one gulp.

"Have I been in a séance?"

"I don't think so. I think you've been haunted," said Blyss nonchalantly.

Cornwalls walked in through the kitchen doorway. "That's as good as any explanation. I've been haunted... and its wonderful!"

"I'll say!" Llys said quietly, leaning close to him.

Cornwalls continued: "... But we have to move. A war is coming; a real war for world domination. And we shouldn't bring the war here because of who we are."

"Where do you think we should go?" Blyss asked.

"Maryland for you and me, I would think," answered Alice.

"Why there?" Reese inquired.

Llys answered for the others, "That's where wars keep rekindling. You know, the military/industrial complex; the US Naval Academy; proximity to Washington, D.C.; elected officials and their minions and lobbyists—a lot of the Washington 'Elite' live and work there, et cetera, et cetera. They always start wars when it looks like trust and peace will prevail. I'm quite sure that a new wave of S2, S3, and S4 models are there right now. After all, that's where your Lab has been re-constructed."

"Are you kidding me? Reconstructed?! —it was a collective response from all the others present.

"What? Did you think they were just going to put the whole thing in mothballs and write off the costs? Insanity never rests, my dears; it never rests."

"What about me?" Flynch asked.

"Honey, you need to get a job, find a husband and make a nice place to live for you and him. And then, see a doctor, because your body has been seriously abused," Llys said.

"What about you?"

"I'm taking Ingrid to Dulce to get Oren out of there safely. Phil, I think, has unfinished business with his employers, so he'll probably accompany you to Maryland."

She turned and looked at him for his reaction to the news that they would be apart for a while.

"That's right, isn't it, honey?"

"Guess so. It's your plane to do with as you see best."

"How will we get to Maryland?" Blyss asked.

"Don't worry. Phil has all the resources of the Security State at his disposal... right, sweetie?"

Llys was holding his hand by this time, assuring his best reaction.

"Well... I guess... yeah, more or less."

At the same time, Llys kissed him softly and hugged him until he felt warm all over. Tes meowed softly and rubbed against Cornwall's trousers.

Can you wait a little longer? Llys whispered from inside of his mind.

I'd wait for you forever.

Good. I'll meet you wherever you are.

That's a date I'll hold you to!

Happily, the others around them could not hear that repartee; it would have made them either blush, or feel envious.

And it would not have prepared them for what was to come.

Chapter 50 ~ Choices

THE "DULCE WAR," AS THE press had called it, lasted a mere two days. The "officially sanctioned" version was that a group of heavily armed terrorists had been caught trying to infiltrate the United States via New Mexico, and a huge battle ensued. The "terrorists" were, of course, all killed and no evidence of their side of the (manufactured) story left behind.

Local fishermen spoke about seeing blue lights under Lake Dulce's surface. They talked about glowing orbs and white beams of light flashing across the night skies, as well as a lot of shootings between U.S. aircraft and terrorist groups.

The one man who had said something referencing UFOs or aliens was told he'd be put in a psychiatric hospital if he didn't shut up. He never said another word to the press or anyone else, in person or otherwise.

There also was a news report of a gas attack having been committed by the terrorists, and a lot of people wearing hazmat suits assembled near the local airstrip. But, though reported, it was never substantiated or investigated further. Finally, the short-lived events were quickly superseded by televised Finals of the World Cup soccer championship, among other sporting news.

Llys and Reese were, immediately upon arrival at the lakeside airstrip, escorted by the same medical units garbed in biohazard suits as before and taken to the same surgical room in which Llys had been treated earlier. There, the S1/Stanson robot body, which had been captured by the Others back at the house in Berkeley, had been brought in and put on one gurney. Ingrid Reese was now placed on the other one nearest to him.

Doctor Reese, stay where you are. Doctor Oren, be above the robot body. The attending "physician's" message reached the two of them inside of her body; whereupon Oren instantly was above the S1 robot body, having found himself pulled to it just as he had been the first time.

Two more Llys-series robots, a redhead and a brunette, EMTs, stood by and were prepared should anything go wrong. When nothing did, they returned to storage somewhere inside of the underground mountain base camp.

Reese had been asleep, and now that she woke up and shouted a single word, "Oh!" Llys went to her side and placed a soothing hand on her forehead, calming her.

On the other gurney, Stanson was inquisitive as he stared at Reese's body lying on the gurney next to his.

Would you have placed me in a female body? he mentally asked the alien who was managing the procedure.

What does it matter?

I guess nothing, but is a female robot easier to manufacture?

No. But, in your society a female will integrate more easily than a male."

I see. Then, why did you put me back in this body?

There would be serious repercussions if you had come back in a different, or female, body. Questions like, where you've been? How you ended up in a different body? Are you a live woman? They all could be raised, and we are not prepared to deal with such things now. We thought it better all around... for you, for us, and for the Others. Llys, of course, also agrees that encouraging you to inhabit the robot S1 would be best.

What is all this for?

Just a moment.

The Other alien, or robot—perhaps "Other" will do, whichever it really was, stood and for a few moments stared in the direction of Llys and Reese. Reese was getting off the gurney, and Llys helped her walk out of the room. Seemingly powerless to stop them, the Other turned his attention back to Stanson, never skipping a beat in the conversation he was having with him.

This is a rescue project. If our robot designs integrate well into your society, we can continue with our program. Unknown to most of you, your planet faces several possible extinction-level events. We have been tasked to provide somewhere for the millions of 'dead' souls to go, so that they and their knowledge is not lost. Since we are not yet prepared to manufacture sexually viable robots, which will be able to breed, we have chosen to create females like the Llys-series robots and slowly integrate them.

How many have you manufactured to date?

Seven. Three are integrating very well. We encouraged recently dead souls to animate them, just as you did after you died. It is most expedient. As for your design, once it is obsolete and to be discarded, you may return here for a newer, state-of-the-art replacement. You only should tell Llys, as she is our principal liaison to your species. You may always reach her in the same manner as our 'talk' we've just had today."

The Other turned away and left the surgical area. Llys had returned. Now only Cornwalls and Llys were present.

"Did you hear all that conversation?"

"I already know it. And more. Contrary to modern science-fiction, these Others are friendly to humans. Let me tell you a story, Oren, to help you understand."

"How long do we have here?"

"As long as it takes. Phil is doing well reaming out some official, officious buttholes."

"You seem to love him, Llys. How can that be?"

"Love, or affinity, is one of the principle characteristics of a soul, and, well, I'm a human soul. You see how Tes loves you... and why not? You feed her, you keep her safe. She knows you are a spirit, too."

"Okay. You have my attention, so tell me the story."

Llys kissed him on the forehead before she began her narrative.

"When these Others moved here, they hollowed out these mountains for a base. Soon after their arrival, the U.S. military/industrial complex noticed evidence of their activity. They sent a delegation designed to establish human ownership over the group, citing land treaties and other documents. Eventually, a treaty was signed between President Eisenhower and the Others' leader, which granted them ownership of the bottom four levels, as well as and any future levels below that. Currently, the Others occupy ten levels below the fourth from the top."

"What about these wars?"

"The Military/Industrial Complex has from the end of World War II known about and desired the technology of these aliens—stealth is an example. They have shot down a few spacecraft and/or otherwise gained access to them by mounting two, quick wars against those aliens already here. Because the Others operate underground, and the U.S. military controls the top four floors, from time to time they try to conquer the Others and take over their technology."

"Why do the Others put up with it?"

"Let's just say, war is not their modus operandi. When attacked, they briefly demonstrate their superior technology with a few sorties into strategic places off the beaten track from the media and most of the population—like the sudden disappearance of that airliner in the southwest region of the Pacific Ocean—and they wait for a new administration to be elected and then stop the fighting."

Llys motioned to him that they should start walking.

"Where are we going?"

"I have to return you to the secret government agency that was responsible for building your body for DARPA. If I don't, they'll continue searching for you until you are captured dead or alive, anyway."

"What if I don't want to go back?"

"Well, you could go to a hospital and pick up a newborn baby and let them have the robot S1 body. Or, you could go on the lam and try to hide for the rest of your days, an impossible task in today's digital world, until the government decided to forget about you. But, as you know, governments have memories like elephants: they never forget."

"I don't like either of those choices."

"Hmm. Let's see. What would satisfy yours and their wishes? How about going to the Association for Research and Enlightenment on the East Coast and becoming a lecturer about life after death?"

"Like Ingrid?"

"Not exactly. If she does decide to go there, you and she might oppose each other's views, albeit it could be most entertaining."

"But, how will all three of us leave here? Your plane only holds two live bodies, plus a cat."

"I will fly you and Tes anywhere you want to go. I can arrange Reese's transportation via military transport services at the Army base. A friendly smile and a lot of money usually does the trick."

"I feel good with that."

"Okay. Are you ready to go?"

"Is Tes in the plane?"

"She has been cared for."

"Okay then. I'll try the rubber-chicken circuit route. Fly me to Virginia Beach. Will I need a disguise?"

"Actually, I don't think so. If you tell them about your past life and offer your services at an acceptable rate, I think they'll jump at the chance."

"And Ingrid?"

"I have already made the necessary arrangements. In fact, she should be on an airplane right now headed for her connection near Denver International. Phil is meeting her there and Alice, of course, is the cabin steward. You can call her when we're in the air."

"I would like that. Thank you, Llys."

She gave him a peck on the robot's cheek, and they walked out of the "hospital." Llys carried a small animal bag, from which a distinct "meow" could be heard. She handed the bag to Stanson.

"Let's not forget this one!"

Hmm, I wonder about the other people after me Stanson thought to himself.

We have our best man on it. Llys had answered his thought.

Who?

My fiancée, of course.

The ICON A7, specially modified with equipment paid for by donations of tens of millions of dollars from the most powerful intelligence agencies in the world, easily cleared the mountaintops and leveled out at 9600 feet, headed toward a non-descript, apparently abandoned airport in the deserted flatlands of southeast Colorado. The direct, morning sun's rays beat on the canopy through occasional cirrus clouds, but the air conditioning kept the cockpit a cool 78°.

The sexy android and the white male, S-series robot in the specially equipped aircraft were headed straight into Mankind's uncertain future. They would make their stand on a remote continent in a place as far from traditional society as they could find.

Chapter 51 ~ Rescue

CORNWALLS COULDN'T BELIEVE HOW MUCH he missed Llys. To him, it was uncanny, unreal, and unbelievable. Because of this, he drove the Studebaker Avanti five to 10 miles per hour over the speed limit everywhere he went. Now, he was speeding on I-10 toward Las Vegas, where he would head north to Colorado and the secret airport near Denver that he used often. Aboard with him was the android Blyss.

The Others android Alice had already arrived at the same airport with Reese and was awaiting the arrival of Llys and Stanson. At the airport, as agreed, Stanson would connect with Reese, and they would proceed to Virginia Beach for their "retirement."

Cornwalls had always thought that Reese and Stanson might have the potential for a romantic liaison, but that was no longer a certainty, since Stanson as S1 no longer had organic sex organs. At any rate, thinking about that kept his mind alert while driving.

Blyss was keeping Cornwalls informed of Llys' progress toward the same destination. Using her information, he concluded that maintaining his current cruising speed of around 80 m.p.h. would get them to the Colorado airport within 10 hours of Llys' plane. *Not good enough* he thought. Consequently, after checking all gauges on his dashboard, he decided he could up his speed to 120 through the desert. The radar jammer we bought before we left is going to come in handy.

Thinking about radar, his thoughts drifted to Linda Flynch. He was happy for her. He had heard from Blyss that she had joined a religious movement in San Francisco, which made her happier than she had ever been, and a lot calmer. That news reminded him that she was not likely to get on his company's radar any time soon. Moving on in his mind, he recalled how he knew that his presence around them would present a threat for both Llys and Stanson. He reminded himself that he was the one who had decided that they all should split up into smaller groups.

The rest of the drive was not going to go off without a hitch: the air-conditioning went off with a thud. Cornwalls studied the gauges carefully but nothing appeared unusual or out of the ordinary. Still, just for good measure he slowed to 100 mph and kept watching the gauges for a while.

"What are our chances?" asked Blyss.

"Still good as long as nothing else breaks."

"Is that truck behind us closing the gap?" she asked, looking at the side mirror.

"Not yet, but if we should slow down any more, it might. Are you suspicious?"

"Who wouldn't be?"

They felt more than heard a small airplane buzz their car and then drop a hand grenade onto the four-lane highway ahead of them. The explosion barely missed the car, but only because Cornwalls had maneuvered them into the fast lane with his quick reflexes.

"Shit!" he said as he heard shrapnel spattering the side of the car. The passenger window had cracked but it hadn't shattered.

Blyss reacted: "My thought, exactly. We'll have to slow down, though—this old car isn't Formula-One."

Cornwalls lifted his foot off the gas pedal and prepared to press the brakes if needed. Suddenly, another blast pasted the road in the fast lane ahead of them, and he swerved around the hole and debris, putting them back on the right side of the road.

Looking back, they watched in the rear-view mirrors as the truck completely came apart after striking the hole left in the highway—the cab barrel-rolling along the road surface sideways, and the trailer flipping end over end several times before blowing up accompanied by a huge, tornado-like ball of flame soaring into the air.

Pieces from the trailer explosion cut into the aircraft that had been dropping grenades. No longer controllable, it spiraled downward and careened off to its right, hitting the ground and cart wheeling briefly before it exploded into a million small chunks of aluminum.

A Highway Patrol car headed toward them with lights flashing from the opposite direction on the left roadway suddenly braked and did a 180-degree turn across the median just behind the truck wreckage. The driver stopped the car at the location of the remains of the truck cab.

Cornwalls wisely thought to turn off his headlamps, in effect disappearing into the night.

"I assume you have night vision, Blyss?"

"That's right. I'll help you keep lined up with the center white line."

They drove like that at a reduced rate of speed—70—for quite a while until Blyss began to feel additional heat coming up from the floor vents.

"Phil, I think we've lost our coolant."

He hit the dashboard light switch and watched as the temperature gauge slowly climbed toward the red-line mark.

"I have to shut it down or the engine might blow, and that would be very bad."

"Right. I'll contact Llys. Maybe she can come and rescue us before police, the Highway Patrol, or something worse, finds us. Plenty of landing-space back there. I'm sure the road behind us will remain closed for hours."

Cornwalls shifted to neutral and shut off the engine, which clanked in protest. He muscled the unresponsive steering wheel and got the car to the edge of the roadway, not onto the potentially soft shoulder.

"This situation could be romantic. Are you sure you're in love with Llys?" Blyss teased, albeit Cornwalls wasn't sure if she was kidding or hitting on him.

"Absolutely, positive about it, Blyss. No offense intended. You, too, are extremely attractive."

"Thank you," she said in her best, low and husky voice.

God help me with three women like these around me he prayed.

Blyss kissed him on the cheek and reported some good news.

"I've been able to reach Llys. She has dropped her cargo, except for Tes, at the airport and she is headed toward us now. She says there is no air traffic over us, yet."

Cornwalls was still thinking about how attractive Blyss was and about the kiss she'd just bestowed upon him. "I hate to shoot anyone down. We men need all the good karma we can get."

"Something's not right. I smell smoke!" Blyss shouted, breaking his trend of thought.

"Damn. Get out of the car right now and move to the center divider and lie down in the median ditch. Hurry!"

Phil pressured the remaining brakes with all his strength, stopping the vehicle. They left the car just as flames leaped from under the hood. They raced to the median between the two double-lane roadways and hit the dirt.

When the fire reached the gas tank, the cabin of the car erupted into flame. Seconds later, everything blew up with a bang and a tall fireball. The driver's door flew a mere foot over their heads and embedded itself into the median guardrail. The other door blew off into a chain link fence parallel to the right-of-way of the highway.

As he lay in the dirt and watched the spectacular fire in front of him, Cornwalls heard, *Are you all right, honey?* Llys had put a thought into his head.

Yes, Blyss is keeping me safe he thought, joking back.

The ICON A7 piloted by Llys approached with its nose-docking light on. She circled around and landed just ahead of the fiery mess that used to be an $180,000 collector-edition car. Phil helped Blyss get up. They ran to the plane.

"I'll take the space behind the seats," Blyss offered. Llys hugged her. Cornwalls helped her get into that space before seating himself in the navigator's seat next to Llys. Tes' travel bag rested on the center console between them.

"You're just like James Bond: Everything gets blown up around you, and you stay intact!" commented Llys with a smirk.

Cornwalls smiled and kissed her cheek, "I love you, too."

"Let's go, you love birds. I can see highway patrol cars coming this way. Kill the lights and let's get a move on!"

"Meow," Tes agreed.

"Back-seat driver," Llys whispered under her breath, laughing to herself smugly. She revved the engine and took off without benefit of any lights. Banking to the right, she avoided discovery from a long line of lit up Highway Patrol cars.

Having put some distance between themselves and the authorities, Llys piloted back onto a course that would take them back to the secret air-base just south of Denver International.

Chapter 52 ~ Always the Money!

THE NOT-SO-SECRET-ANYMORE AIRBASE NEAR DENVER was destroyed. Llys circled around the firestorm that remained, figuring that a huge air-bomb or tactical nuclear weapon was responsible for the gigantic crater carved out of the middle of the landing area.

Trying to reach the others on the radio returned only static until Cornwalls switched the plane's radio to a frequency that he alone knew.

"ICG7 on tactical-comm channel. 130013, please respond."

On the third try, he got a response.

"Traffic control, responding. State your situation."

"We are circling the remains of our country home. What is your status?"

"The chickens are in the coop, and we are on course. Do not follow."

Cornwalls turned and updated his companions.

"So, they got away. We'll have to get a bigger plane. Blyss, are you okay back there?"

"I'm fine. I can just shut down. What's your range?"

"We can go non-stop to Kansas City, if we have to, and maybe as far as New Orleans. But, we might have to go defensive, and that won't work with three in here."

"Who nuked our airport?" Blyss asked.

"I have a theory, and it's not good. I don't think your builders did this. Too blatant. I think it was a hand-carried tactical nuke used as part of a kamikaze attack. If I'm right, that hints that it came from an Asian country, maybe the largest one—someone well connected with international arms dealers. Beyond that, it's about following the money: who benefits most?" Cornwalls answered.

Llys had her own ideas: "Well, my guess is, anyone who doesn't have an S-series robot. To sell one on the black market would require access to one, as well as being able to keep it secret."

"Someone like us?" Cornwalls joked.

"Let's see if the stock market has reacted." Llys was already pulling up the current commodities-market charts on the plane's monitor screen. "What time did the blast occur?"

"The AirSpy plane left an hour ago. We left a few minutes after; so, it had to be within the last hour."

"The NASDAQ market took a hit. That's a clue—Technology stocks. Take the plane down to ground plus 100 feet and engage terrain following. Push the airspeed up to 250. And watch for towers."

"Destination?" Llys asked.

"The Gulf of Mexico just south of New Orleans. Look for an oil platform with a Hunter Oil flag on it. They'll find you when we get close."

Chapter 53 ~ Meatbots & Oxygen

STANSON AND REESE KNEW THEY had a long flight ahead of them; and both thought this might be a good time to iron out some of their incomplete conversations and differences.

"Oren..." "Ingrid..." Having both started talking simultaneously, they laughed and hugged.

They weren't alone. Alice sat in the flight attendant's chair near the galley, ready to assume her flight attendant duties at the slightest hint of her human guests needing anything.

The plane they were in was a copy of the one in which Ingrid had flown previously. She surveyed the gray-leather, upholstered lounge before turning her eyes toward Stanson again.

"Excuse me, Oren. I'm a little jittery about riding in this airplane; it's so much like the one that trapped me."

"Trapped? Oh... you mean the 'security can,' as the pilots like to call it!"

Reese had to laugh. She appreciated how he had broken the ice between them so nicely. She moved over next to him and took his hand.

"Yes, trapped, but I don't want to talk about that. I want you to tell me your theory about how you ended up leaving a dead organic body and entering a metallic robot."

"It's very simple, actually. The whole move is quite easy to do. I found my-self floating up from the canyon stream and, when I got about a thousand feet high, I felt... what can I call it?... an urge, a tugging, a kind of a suck-ing sensation carrying me toward the Lab. Nothing physical, of course, because I didn't have anything physical to be sucked on."

"What do you think it was?"

"Oh, I know exactly what it was. You see, part of our design was to install an electronic field that would emanate from the robots—I'll call it a 'trac-tor/presser wave' for lack of anything better—but it's a quantum-physics phenomenon dealing with the bionetic brain's construction that was cre-ated by Linda's design."

"I'm not a physicist, Oren. Please, keep it on a level I can understand."

"Very well, Ingrid. This field is in a frequency range of what is called 'sub-tle energy,' a very high vibration rate, which is not normally detected by average volt/ohm equipment. To keep it simple, it wasn't the field of S2 that pulled me back into the Lab; it was the combined fields of all four robots turned on and in the same proximity to each other and to me. That field was strong enough to pull me into the building, along with my feel-ings for Tes, and of course, you."

Reese blushed. Stanson saw it and hurried on.

"... What finished the electronic phenomenon was that I was near S2 and it was that robot's field that pulled me in. At first, I didn't know what had happened. I was still almost as confused as those moments just prior when I had been hanging outside as a disembodied spirit."

Reese squeezed his hand slightly. He smiled.

"But wait. You've been talking as coherently and intelligently as you ever did when human... what happened next?"

"To put it in simple terms, I began using the robot's body. I permeated, became, the thing, took control of the bionetic connections and began getting feedback along the body's communication channels and quickly realized it wasn't so different as with a biological body, or, as I have called it before in my pessimistic moods, a 'meatbot'."

Alice overheard and laughed loud enough for them to hear her. She even moved forward in the cabin to hear more, saying as she entered their space.

"A 'meatbot'? That's hilarious! So, Ingrid is a meatbot?"

"Well, no. You see, I use that turn of phrase for any human who is unaware of the spirit, the soul, the life essence that they are. In other words, any-one who thinks they are just a few pounds of flesh and bones, I think of as being a meatbot."

"Am I a meatbot?" Alice asked.

"No, certainly not. I don't know what you are exactly, since you're not man-made, but you claim to be Llys' sister from before she inhabited her pres-ent body, making you, apparently, at one point, a female human being, al-though I don't see why you couldn't all just as easily have been men before."

Alice's mouth dropped opened. She closed it when the shock wore off. She sat back in her seat and stared at the robot S1, whom she had thought of as Oren Stanson, for a long time, speechless. Once she recovered her wits, she stepped back into the role of an air-cabin steward.

"Can I get you anything, Ingrid?" she asked after she returned, holding a tray of small liquor bottles, cans of soda, tiny wine bottles and some mineral-water cans.

"Give me vodka; no, better make that a Diet Coke."

Alice opened the can one-handed and poured it into a small plastic cup with an ice cube in it. She handed it to Reese, accompanied by a white cocktail napkin embossed with the black logo of an alien head she had seen on wacko web sites... the word "AirSpy" under it with, in extremely small type at the bottom right corner, 'Area 51' printed on it.

Ingrid drank all the Diet Coke, and only then did she notice the napkin design.

"What is this?"

"Would you like a refill?" Alice tried to divert her attention.

"No... oh, what the hell, yes."

"I'm not sure what that is on the napkin," Alice lied. She refilled Reese's cup and took the tray back to the galley, where she once more took her seat and buckled up.

"Hey, Oren. Did you see that?"

"Yes, Ingrid, I did. Shall I continue my story?"

"Oh, Oh, I almost forgot... yes, of course, please continue. This is fascinating!"

"All right then. Are you following me so far?"

"I think so, except you said the spirit has no material universe presence; yet, here you are. I don't understand that."

"I have experimented with this concept, so bear with me, and I'll see if I can explain it better. You remember we were discussing this in the eagle-watch cabin in the valley of the canyon, right?"

"Yes, I remember that."

"Well, this is what I did: First, I created an image of Tes behind me. I saw her with my "mind's eye," as it were, in full color. She was about six feet away. I could feel the softness of her fur. I could hear her "meow," when she wanted me to pick her up. I deduced this was an energy picture that I had created in my mind. I could move the picture around, make her move, and make the image disappear, at will. Understanding that, caused me to realize that the image of the cat was not me, because I was the one looking at it. Do you see what I mean?"

"I think that I do... somewhat."

"Why don't you try it?"

Reese relaxed back into her seat and closed her eyes. After several minutes passed, she suddenly turned around and stared behind her.

"I thought I just saw Tes, but not in the cabin; she was in her travel bag."

"That's right, Ingrid. Now, notice that you said, 'I saw Tes'? And so, you did."

"Oh.... Uh... Oh! Okay, I get that. What was next?"

"Next, I tried being inside the other robots. At first, I found getting away from the electronic trap that Flynch had set up was a challenge, because—I didn't realize it right away—I was trying to move through the energy field, which was a rather silly thing for a spaceless, motionless, energyless entity to attempt. The proper way to do it is to just be somewhere, not move somewhere or move the somewhere to me. In the simplest terms, just simply be."

"I don't understand."

"Okay. Try this: 'Be in the restroom behind the cockpit!'" he commanded her.

"Oooh. I need to go to the restroom! I promise I'll come right back."

Reese, the non-believer, got up and went inside the restroom.

Alice on the other hand, stood up, walked forward, sat down beside Stanson, and planted a big kiss on his left ear.

"What was that for, Alice?"

"You taught me something new; something fantastic. I just wanted to thank you. Was that okay to do?"

Stanson chuckled.

"When I was a human, you would be about the age of my daughter. Now that I'm not going to have any children, a kiss from any young lady is alright by me any time!"

Laughing with him, Alice got up and resumed her seat in the galley as Reese left the restroom and returned to her seat.

The "FASTEN SEAT BELT" sign lit up.

"Oh, FUCK! Not again!" Reese swore as she buckled her seatbelt.

"Again?"

"Yeah. Last time, the smooth passenger jet just like this one, which I was riding in, turned out to be a high-performance jet fighter. I nearly threw up from the maneuvers and I ended up in a survival canister after we were fired on by an unknown enemy."

"Oh my!"

Alice broke in: "Take it easy, folks. A big storm is up ahead. We need to fly through it, because to do otherwise would delay our arrival too long."

"That's a crock of manure," Ingrid commented to Stanson. "Delay our arrival too long? That's a euphemism for 'we are all being abducted.' Look, when whatever is coming comes, don't let me forget: I want to hear more about that remark that they could all be men."

With the storm upon them, the plane shuddered and then smoothed out; then seemed to move sideways in two little jolts and then smoothed out. This continued for 10 minutes, and the seatbelt sign remained on. Reese held onto Stanson's hand the whole time... hard.

Stanson wanted to get his point across to Reese, despite the stormy weather.

"In case we don't get out of this all in one piece, I meant that human bodies, meat robots, have sexual characteristics and body parts meant for reproductive purposes. But I consider the human "soul" not to be gender specific. My point is that I could just as easily end up in a female human body as a sexless robot body, or an infant of either sex. And I assume it's the same way with the Llys-series robots..."

"... Right, Alice?" (He asked louder, knowing she had been listening.)

"I don't know... maybe," she lied again, too busy reading the computer screen on the back of the seat in front of her to care.

The pilots banked the craft 30 degrees to the right and then leveled off as they fought to maintain some level of comfort for their multi-million-dollar passengers.

The moment the plane stopped jerking, Alice sprang up and ran forward and opened three overhead doors on the right side of the cabin, pulling out a parachute from each.

"Here, take these parachutes. Watch me put mine on; then you put yours on. And be quick about it."

Alice showed them how to buckle it in front of their chests, helping Stanson first, then Reese.

"If you are conscious, pull this ring..." She pointed to a bright yellow T-shaped handle. "... It opens a smaller, stabilizing chute, after which, a few seconds later, the main chute will open. They are as fail-safe as the government can make them. Even the President of the United States has one of these on-board Air Force One."

The plane seemed to flat spin a few degrees to the right. All three passengers saw a missile fly past the wing and get destroyed by lightning.

"We are under attack!" screamed Reese, who sat down in her seat in the fetal position. The aircraft pitched upward in a vertical climb, and Alice flew back to the rear bulkhead. She slammed into it, but her parachute absorbed most of the impact. Stanson had been thrown back into his seat, but he weathered the change alright.

Another missile exploded near their left wing, apparently without damage.

Alice grabbed her seatbelt and buckled up right before a tremendous cracking sound like a thunderclap, followed by an even louder crack, signaled the plane's tail cone had broken off.

In a split second, rushing air, lightning and rain were visible to them.

Since their airspeed hadn't slowed, Alice thought the engines were still intact. She had to shout the message to the others because of the wind noise.

Stanson shouted back, "This attack is not from any agency of our government. I picked up a coded transmission before the attack started. I am trying to decipher it now."

"I'll come up and help," Alice said, unbuckling and pulling herself seat by seat up to his seat. She crawled over the seat back, pulled a charging/comm cable out of a side compartment and plugged it into a similar receptacle at her waist. To protect him, she not only threw her arms around him and locked her fingers together, but she also put her flesh-covered, sexy legs around Reese's midsection and held on tight.

Reese appeared to have gone unconscious.

The trio did not move as the pilots did what they had to do to outpace their attackers and the savage storm swirling around them inside the cabin, as well.

A bright green OXYGEN light came on under the FASTEN SEAT BELTS sign that was still shining bright red. Oxygen masks fell from hidden overhead compartments.

"Shit!" exclaimed Alice.

"What is it?" Stanson asked.

"Help me move toward Doctor Reese. I must get one of those masks on her. I'll have to let go of you, so please be cautious of not breaking off our Interlink."

"Of course."

Alice let go of him and twisted her body to grab an oxygen mask. She positioned it onto Reese's face and, with some amazing contortions, got it fastened correctly to her head. She moved back to her original position and resumed her hold on Stanson, wondering the while if the plane would come apart.

At last, the pilots, having climbed above 80,000 feet, lost their attackers and got above the storm. However, without oxygen in the plane's cabin, Alice had to make sure Reese would keep breathing.

Chapter 54 ~ Rough Landing

THE PRIVATE JET HAD STABILIZED for almost an hour, when a sudden shudder ran throughout its entire fuselage. The shudder worsened to a horrible shaking.

Alice saw a tongue of flame shoot out the front of the starboard engine. "We've lost an engine, Oren. Make sure your parachute is secure." She unclenched her legs and disengaged the comm Interlink with him. She checked Reese and her unconscious condition carefully and inspected her parachute. Satisfied all was in good shape and as tight as needed, she grabbed the webbing that fastened the chute to Reese's torso.

"Oren, I want you to grab my parachute straps just the way I'm holding Ingrid's. We only have two engines, and one has just failed. If the tail was structurally damaged when we lost that little tail cone at the end, we probably won't hold together for the trip down, much less an emergency landing. I need you to use your warfighter training to get us free before this plane crashes."

"I will, Alice."

The pilots slowed down the remaining engine to idle, and the plane fell into a flat spin, pinning the passengers to their seats. Straining hard, the pilots straightened the plane momentarily. At that instant, a loud crack and crunching sound permeated the cabin, followed by the dead engine breaking off the fuselage. The entire rudder broke off after some terrific shuddering, followed by the rear portion of the plane along with the remaining engine. Next, the rear of the plane and the engine pylons separated from the fuselage in stages; then the elevators broke off; the fuselage cracked open more; and, finally, the rear fuel tank broke free, spilling jet fuel as it dropped.

"Oren, get ready. When I say go, help me pull Ingrid out of the rear of the plane."

The rear escape module had fallen off the plane, opening a large hole in the fuselage right behind the passenger seats.

"Now!!" Alice yelled. She let loose of the seat back and Oren did the same. Reese floated between them as they pulled themselves toward the gaping hole at the rear of the plane. Just then, the cabin broke apart, tossing the threesome out of harm's way but into open air at several hundred miles per hour.

Reese abruptly woke up, alerted by the rush of wind. She struggled against Alice's handhold on her parachute straps. Now below 15,000 feet, Alice pulled the handle on her chute, then her own, and she let go of Reese. She was unable to see Stanson at first, but eventually spotted his parachute about a mile away.

Suddenly, right in front of her eyes a message in red flashed—one she had never experienced before: 'INTERNAL SYSTEMS OVERLOAD. INTERNAL SYSTEMS OVERLOAD. VERIFY STRUCTURAL INTEGRITY AT NEXT SERVICE INTERVAL.'

Apparently, it was a message from her body's basic hardware operating system. It frightened her. The phrase, INITIATE ANALYSIS, came into her mind, and she could see her body's internal structure. Several parts were displayed in orange; one, her backbone, was in red. She considered the options she had, knowing in any case that she would have to somehow make her way to Dulce, New Mexico for repairs. She hated to admit it, but she was going to need Cornwall's help and maybe even Llys' help, too. Right now, though, she had no choice but to prepare herself for what might be a rough landing, and possibly more damage, including super-strong bones getting broken.

"Oren!" Reese yelled again and again, until the wind was knocked out of her when her main chute opened. There was nothing Stanson could do to help her; he, too, had no experience parachuting.

When her main chute opened, Alice felt a snap in her back. Her digital screen displayed her internal body: the red image of her back had changed to orange. Nearing Ground Zero, she took a deep breath and prepared to tuck and roll, hopeful that the display's readout was a sign of something going back into place in her body.

Stanson landed first on his feet but was pushed down on his face by the stormy winds and dragged through brambles and up against the trunk of a fallen dead tree. Intact, he had trouble figuring out how to untangle himself from the parachute. He decided to lie still and wait patiently for someone to help him out.

Alice rolled into a grassy glade the way she had learned. Her forward motion was halted at the edge of the glade by a chain-link fence that marked a county right-of-way adjacent to a deserted, two-lane highway. During the half-hour it took for her to untangle her hair from the fence, her physical-functions display did not operate.

Once free of the fence, she turned around to look for Reese and Stanson, only to discover a man facing her and aiming a shotgun at her, who was protected by a hunting dog sitting beside him. The man was chewing a long stalk of grain. His wide-brimmed hat kept the pelting rain, which had just started to fall, off his face. She stood up slowly, never dropping her eyes from the end of that gun. She also saw an old pick-up truck behind him parked on a now-muddy path that ran along the edge of the grassy knoll.

"Mighty bad weather for a looker like you to be out here, young lady."

"Yep," was all she could muster under the circumstances as she continued to look around for the others.

"Plane went down in the storm?"

"Yep."

"Not much of a talker, is ya?"

"Nope."

"Ya need a ride?"

"Yep. Me and a couple of my friends somewhere around here."

"Oh? Where are they?"

"Don't know. Just a moment..."

Oren, do you hear me? she thought.

Yes, Alice. I'm fouled up with my parachute. Can you track me?

Sure. Defend yourself.

She looked at the man's dog. She didn't know animal species too well, but it looked friendly enough.

"I'm not sure where they landed, but nearby somewhere. Can your dog help us find them?"

"His sniffer don't work too good in the rain, but he can hear them. Why don't you call out?"

"Oren!?! Ingrid?!? Yell and keep yelling, if you can hear me; it's me, Alice. Yell out good and strong!"

The dog seemed to wake up and he barked.

From the other side of the highway, Alice heard Reese yelling, "Over here, Alice." And then she heard Stanson yell, "Over here," from about 200 yards on the other side of the truck, in a forest glen.

"What's your name, sir?"

"I'm Paul. Nice to meet you, Alice!"

"Likewise."

"All right, Alice, let's get your friends. I'll look in the forest; you go across the road and find the lady over there."

"Let's do it the other way to. Do you mind?"

"No, no. That's fine. I'll take ol' Henry with me."

Paul walked to his truck and started it up. Ol' Henry jumped into the back right before Paul made the truck do a fast 180-degree turn in the slick mud and head for a break in the fence, where Reese still could be heard yelling.

Oren, I'm coming. Do you hear me?

Yes, I hear you. I'll keep talking, though.

Good; that'll help me.

Stanson switched to verbalizing his thoughts, so she could hear him better and find him faster. "Did you know that DARPA is working on S4, trying to make the robot like you?"

What do you mean 'like me'?

"They think you're an alien AI, not an actual human soul. They're trying to stuff a supercomputer into the head of a robot and program it with everything in the Encyclopedia Britannica. Can you imagine that?"

That's hilarious. I certainly don't know everything in the Britannica! Why would they do that?

"The few experiences that the Intelligence State—there's an oxymoron for ya—has had with you and your friends have convinced them that a robot can be designed as intelligent as a human. Again, they have no clue that you ARE a human being. They don't know there is such a thing as a soul, and that you ARE one. I doubt that type even goes to church on Sundays."

I have a theory about that type, Oren: they're too (what I call) 'heavy.' I should probably call it 'massy,' (solid) because it's not really about a weight but about quality. They're so covered up with negative energy, bad decisions, and intentions to harm others that they literally can't see there is life beyond the ends of their noses. In other words, they are self-made blind people.

"I hear you, Alice. Also, it feels like you're close by. Did you survive the landing in one piece?"

I think so. My alarms went off, but I seem to be fine.

She arrived in front of the thoroughly tangled Stanson and started to laugh. Then, she spoke.

"You look like a giant spider from the Amazon jungle captured you."

She opened the emergency-travel kit at her waist, pulled out a small scissors and began cutting the parachute cords. Not long after, the sounds and smells of Paul's truck stung her nostrils, as he approached.

"I think that's Paul with Ingrid. Hello, Ingrid!"

Reese didn't answer, but Paul spoke for her.

"Your friend's in a pretty bad way, lady. She's got two sprained ankles and looks like she hit her head on a tree. Pretty sure she's just unconscious, though; 'cause she's still breathing a bit. By the way, I ain't got enough gas to get her to a hospital. I don't suppose you got any gas money?"

Alice coughed up from her kit a wrinkled 50-dollar bill.

"Got money. Just a moment... we'll be right there."

She turned to Stanson, who by now had completely cut himself out of the web of nylon cording.

"Are you functioning, Oren?"

"I'm a little dirty, but otherwise fully operational."

Alice whispered now.

"Good. Go to Standby status, in case this guy isn't really as nice as he sounds."

Alice and Stanson walked to where Paul had parked the pickup. He climbed into the flatbed and lay beside Reese, while Alice got in the cab with Paul.

"How much do you need?"

Paul pulled a pistol out of the side-door pocket. "Everything you got."

"Paul, you might want to rethink your position here. Not only is what you are doing evil, it is very dangerous for you ... Now, if you behave yourself, I'll give you the $50 for your trouble; otherwise, I'm afraid you aren't going to survive more than another minute. It's your choice, Paul."

Paul put the gun to Alice's head with his left hand and grabbed her crotch with his right.

Faster than a jack-rabbit's hop, she grabbed his left forearm and broke it, pointing the gun at the windshield. Holding it there, she squeezed his finger on the trigger repeatedly until the chamber was empty, shattering the windshield in the process. Next, Alice grabbed his right forearm and twisted it until his elbow dislocated.

As Paul screamed from the pain, she bashed his head against the door window, causing the door to fly open, out of which she pushed him into the muddy ground.

She then scooted behind the wheel, put the transmission into reverse and steered the vehicle so the front left wheel ran over the guy's head, crushing it.

Ol' Henry barely reacted; Alice had acted so much faster than the humans he'd met in his time, and her soothing hand upon his head calmed him down as she drove the pickup down the deserted roadway.

Oren, do you have a built-in GPS?

Yes. I checked earlier for our location. We are near the Oceana Naval Air Station. Pretty soon, you should come to a frontage road leading to the Expressway #264, which leads to Norfolk or Virginia Beach... right where we want to be.

How is Ingrid doing?

She's alive but concussed. And she needs her ankles wrapped.

Is there anything back there you can use?

Yes. Once you're on 264, stop at the first rest stop, which is in five miles, and I'll wrap them with the parachute Paul left here.

Alice pulled the mud-encrusted old truck into the rest stop. Oren ripped the parachute into gauze-like bandages and wrapped Ingrid's ankles. She didn't wake up.

For good measure, Alice walked around the truck and removed the wheel covers and every bit of chrome on the vehicle and threw them in a large garbage bin, being careful not to attract any attention from other travelers. Having finished her camouflage project, she checked out Reese's condition.

Reese, she could see, had a bloody bump on her head that didn't seem to be a deep wound. Still, when Alice pointed to it, Oren wrapped her head with another strip of parachute material.

Oren took over the wheel, pointed the pick-up toward the easterly rest stop exit, and entered the highway, merging with the light traffic.

"We should stop at the first motel we come to and get a room and clean Ingrid up," he said.

"And us!"

"Oh, right. Us... of course."

Just like a man, a hu-man! thought Alice, laughing to herself.

Chapter 55 ~ S5 Surveillance

"EXCUSE ME, SIR."

"What is it, Franks?"

"We have some intel on the robot S5 from the DARPA Lab."

The Captain in charge of the satellite watch over the south central United States was unaware of the value of the target his Lieutenant had been monitoring all night.

"What robot? Why do we have a string of satellites tracking a robot? Who ordered that waste of bandwidth?"

"Uh, sir? There are two S-series, warfighter robots on the loose in the Southern United States and they are very dangerous. Not to mention a huge security problem should they fall into foreign hands. The CSS is hot on this."

"Why wasn't I informed?"

"The briefing was at 07:00 yesterday morning, sir."

"I wasn't transferred here until 20:00 yesterday."

"Perhaps the summary is in your IN-basket, sir?"

"Bring me up to speed, Franks. What's so special about an S5?"

"This one has stolen a Jeep, camouflaged it with spray paint, and blown up the store it stole the paint from. Seems to have gone crazy. We can't turn the police loose on it... confidentiality, sir... so we've been trying to find out where it's going. Right now, it appears to be traveling East. Electronic surveillance is not operational—the S5 does not register on radar. I suspect shielding or stealth technology, sir. But we can track the Jeep."

"All right, Franks. Just put a Field Agent on it and get him to put eyes on the S5 and tail it until we know what its plans are."

"Yes sir. Consider it done, sir."

This sounds too simple the Captain thought.

Chapter 56 ~ In the News

WHERE ARE YOU GUYS? ALICE thought toward Llys.

On our way to an oil derrick off the coast of Louisiana Llys thought back.

Why?

Phil has some friends there, he says.

We've made it to Virginia Beach.

Good! Plug Oren in and lay low.

After midnight, Stanson carried Reese into the available motel room they had finally found and rented. He and Alice cleaned her up with a warm bath and a little shampoo and rose-scented bath oil. He threw her clothes away after he made Alice promise to buy her more in the morning.

Stanson dry-washed his body and then hooked up online to see what was happening in cyberspace. They were all over the "news."

The NSA was funneling chatter from all over the country, trying to find them. Thinking it better now to not be discovered, he immediately shut off his connection to the Internet. Remaining off the radar of the Security State also meant acting like most of the population. While he couldn't physically blend in, he could play like dumb—a maneuver that, unfortunately, was all too easy to do in these times.

Alice busied herself with washing Ingrid's clothes the best she could in the tub and then hanging them up over the curtain rod to dry.

"Alice, cyberspace is abuzz with rumors about the destruction of the Lab near UC Berkeley. Someone has taken the trouble to leak a lot of information."

"Like what?"

"Like there were five robots costing a billion dollars, each of which are missing; and for which there is a reward for capture; like there was a military airstrike on the building and a cover story about terrorist activities discovered there; like the nature/jogging trail remains closed, and armed guards are keeping people from looting or even photographing the site... things like that."

"Sheesh, Oren. How does that make you feel? You were the Lab's Director!"

"Well, truth be told, it's Tes I miss the most."

Alice sat on the bed next to him and put her arm around him. "I'm sure she's fine."

Reese, unconscious yet aware, lay on the other bed, her tears falling into the pillow and on the tacky, peanut-colored bedspread.

So, Oren misses the cat more than me! Me, Ingrid, the psychologist, the non-logician, non-scientist.

Though trained to deal with human emotions, not much training in her two doctorates could help her with what was happening right now.

Of course, if I was absent, Oren might miss me just as much, if not more, than the cat. But I'm here, and that damn cat isn't!

If she had gone the extra mental step, Reese would have realized that Oren was behaving very much like any man.

What about Ingrid? Alice thought over at Stanson, picking up on Reese's thought waves.

Oh my God! What did I just say? How devastating for her, if she 'heard' me!

Stanson leaped off his bed and rushed to sit on the edge of Reese's bed, his arm circling her waist.

She pretended to be asleep.

"I can't kiss you, Ingrid, but if I could I would, many, many times. I'm so thankful that you are safe and with us. Please forgive my insensitivity. You mean so much more to me than Tes. I'm so happy you are here with us. I promise you that somehow I'll get you to where you want to go... hopefully to share it with me for a long, long time to come."

Stanson hugged her, thinking she was still unconscious. But she turned to him and hugged him back and kissed him on the cheek.

Tears followed.

Was this the beginning of something new for their relationship? How would it affect the world? What would come next? Alice bemused over their behavior. She was happy for them.

And, in her current state of mind, just plain happy, no matter what lay ahead.

Chapter 57 ~ What Money Can Buy

"OREN, DO YOU HAVE ANY money?" Reese asked as they stood outside the motel room and stared at the filthy truck. Stanson stood in the doorway, wearing part of the bedspread from Reese's bed as disguise.

Reese and Alice were walking around the truck; Reese wearing the bedsheet like a toga. It must have been a heckuva night.

"I'll check," Stanson said. He turned and went back into the motel room, sat on the bed and accessed his bank account the only way possible: on the Internet.

After punching in his password—TeslaCat—the bank account showed the latest balance, which included a $9,776.40 automatic deposit made a few days ago. Apparently, word of his death had not spread to his bank accounts, yet. He searched on Google for, and did not find, any trace of any police reports about his passing, nor even any police investigations or headlines. Checking further, he was not listed as a missing person.

According to the Internet, he was still at work at the Lab. And, apparently, no one had bothered to check the incongruity of the Lab's destruction and his ability to retain his position of work there.

Ingrid, please come into the room. Let's check online to see if your bank accounts are still available he thought.

Ingrid walked into the room at that moment and sat down next to the room monitor that was embedded into the top of the dresser.

You look very pretty today, Doctor Reese, he thought to her.

She turned and rushed into his arms and kissed him on his mouth portal, not caring whether he had sensors there or not. And just as quickly, she returned to the computer screen.

She navigated to her bank web site and noted that the balance was the same as when she had deposited her last paycheck: $250,997.44. Even the rent payment for her room in Pollock Pines 'down below' had not been withdrawn.

Again, it was as if she had never gone missing and like no one knew that she had.

Stanson had a plan he shared with her.

"I'd like to do a funds-transfer into your account. When the bureaucracy catches up with me, all my money will likely be confiscated by the IRS for 'overdue estate taxes.' I'll prepare my account; you ready yours to accept my transfer."

Another 15 minutes passed, and then everything was done. Stanson left $100 in his account "just for luck."

Alice had come into the room and had watched them co-operate so easily.

"How do you get along in the world, Alice?" Reese asked.

"I have unlimited funds available through a secret account set up for the Others by the Federal Reserve in exchange for their agreement not to destroy the global banking system. Pure blackmail."

"Whoa! That makes me wonder who is still looking for us. I don't think all the trouble we are going through is caused by Phil's organization," Stanson said.

"Well, if it's not the Others, and it's not the NSA and their ilk, who's left? Who has that many financial resources?" asked Alice.

"The things that we've seen happening, I think, would normally raise holy hell with American financial authorities, or any other nation for that matter, so it might not be another nation at all," Reese said.

"Who's left?"

"Whoever it is, they're not leaving an identifiable electronic fingerprint. Very mysterious," said Stanson.

Reese deleted all records of her immediate web interactions from the hotel computer's hard drive. She turned it off and unplugged it from the wall. Then she sat down beside Stanson on the bed and held his hand.

"You still want to know what I was talking about earlier, regarding sex and spirits, don't you?" he asked, smiling.

"Damn right I do!"

"All right. Here goes: what I've learned so far about my own death and rebirth is that I was obviously a male meatbot. When I 'died,' that was dead, too. Ancient history, right?"

Reese nodded her head, all ears.

"A spirit has no gender, since it doesn't technically exist in this universe. Period. End of story."

Both Reese and Alice were disappointed, and he saw this.

"However, there was a residual feeling of sexuality, a sense of gender, that I carried with me, which was part of my attraction to S2, since the robots have always been considered "'he' or 'it', not 'she', by the designers and the rest of the development team at the Lab. I'm guessing that there was, therefore, a subtle bias unintentionally entered into the programming. Anyway, I do think of myself as 'male', although it is completely irrelevant now."

Reese appeared more disappointed now.

"But my designers were not even human, and I have very strong feelings of being 'female'," Alice said.

"That probably has as much to do with your previous life as with your robotic design. You are obviously made in the image of a very attractive human female with much of the human female anatomy and sexuality embedded into your form and, at least, partial functioning of your sex 'organs'. I have neither function nor sex organs. You do."

" So, what... what was that crack about moving into a female body or meatbot?" asked Reese.

"As a spirit, exterior to any body, I could choose to inhabit a male meatbot or female meatbot... or a male robot or female robot... or even a gender-less machine. You see, it doesn't matter to a spirit."

Alice and Reese were engrossed in the ideas and they were understanding them.

"... Theoretically, someone could inhabit a Cray supercomputer, if it put out electronic flows and was similar enough construction-wise. Wouldn't be much fun, but it is possible. I consider that I could inhabit anything, including an animal, an ocean, a flock of birds; a sunset, tree or entire forest."

"A forest?" Reese questioned.

"It is alive, you know."

"But, you said the Lab built your robot body to trap a spirit," countered Alice.

"Yes, I did. And I assume the Others could do something similar with your bodies purposefully; whereas our designers, Linda and Hank, did it accidentally."

Stanson picked up voices outside of their room, which were talking about the pickup truck.

"Our truck is being investigated by the police. We better find a way out of here and get a different vehicle."

"I'll check the back," Alice said, getting up.

In a few moments, she returned.

"The coast is clear, and we can get out through the adjoining apartment, which opens to a private patio that leads to the pool."

Stanson broke the lock on the adjoining door and they passed through the room to the patio and out onto the pool area. He immediately jumped into the pool and swam laps back and forth, underwater, until the police left the motel.

Two little boys had been playing without supervision in the shallow end of the pool. Now, they stood up and wouldn't let Stanson pass.

"How'd you do that, mister?"

Do what? I was just swimming laps."

"Underwater? You swam underwater for eight laps! Didn't you need air?"

He was about to answer the boys, but Alice and Reese had rushed to that end of the pool and caught up with them.

"Hey, you kids! Don't mess with our robot!" Alice yelled at the boys.

The youngsters looked at each other, astonished, delighted.

"A robot? Cool!"

Stanson stopped swimming laps and rolled over so the boys could touch and pat him.

"How much did it cost you?" the older of the two boys asked.

"A billion dollars," Reese said, now dangling her feet in the water from the edge.

"How much money is that?" asked the smaller boy.

"You know those black triangle bombers?" said Alice.

"Yeah, the B-12 Stealth Bomber. I made a model of one of those," said the older boy.

"Well, he cost about as much as one of those."

"Gee, lady, you must be rich or something!"

"Come on, robot, it's time to go," Ingrid said to Stanson, avoiding the boys' last remark.

Stanson said nothing when he stood up in the shallow end and walked toward her.

"Hey, can he talk and stuff?" the little boy asked as Stanson passed him and headed toward the steps.

"Silly boy! You know robots can't talk, except in the movies," Alice said as he walked up the steps and stood by Reese, who had accompanied him.

"Does he have a name?" the older boy asked.

"S1. What's yours?" Stanson had answered, sounding, however, like a computer-generated machine.

"I'm Buddy, and this is my shrimpy little brother, Carl." Both boys were positively beaming and almost lost for words.

"Remember this moment, boys. It's not every day you get to see, or hear, a billion dollars," said Reese.

The boys, after promising never to tell anyone about their encounter, ran off... as if they really could keep the event to themselves! No one would ever believe them, so none of the "fugitives" worried about what the boys might do or say.

The trio left the pool area and, walking through the parking lot, found an unlocked, pearl-colored Mercedes 550 with tinted windows.

Alice, using one of her metallic gifts, hotwired the supposedly theft-proof ignition, and they drove away. Spotting a BMW car dealership a few blocks away, Alice parked the car at the curb in front. In short order, Reese purchased a metallic dark-blue, four-door BMW sedan with her account money. A hybrid-fusion model, Reese had been told by the saleswoman it could be driven all the way across the country on one tank of gas, so that is what she bought.

That decision would come in handy.

Chapter 58 ~ Beware the Hawk

PHIL, LLYS, BLYSS AND TES'S cross-country air trip went without stint, except for Tes' throwing a cat fit more than once when she needed to get out of the tote bag and stretch her legs and do her business on land, which, of course, necessitated landings and take-offs.

At one point, they were sitting down on a boat dock beside a large lake near a small airstrip in Texas. Blyss had taken Tes into the nearby brush and all was going along quite peacefully. The boathouse manager, wearing a sheriff's badge, however, suddenly rushed out of the boathouse with a loaded shotgun in his hands.

"Who are you, and what are you doing here? This lake is closed until the holidays. Y'all better pack up and get out before I have to take you into custody for trespassing."

Cornwalls took a deep breath to calm down. Blyss returned with Tes in her arms, apologizing for their presence:

"Sorry, officer. We didn't mean any harm. We just needed to let our cat out to do her business. We'll leave right now."

"Oh no, you won't. No pets allowed. You got to pay the fine."

"How much is the fine?" asked Llys.

Looking around and seeing no one else was anywhere around to see what would come next, he said, "One of you women. I pretty much don't care which one."

Cornwalls knew the drill. He smiled at the man who looked like the cat that had just swallowed the canary, and who cocked the shotgun, expecting to have to use it.

"You can have either one, sir, but you have to wrestle her first."

"I got the gun, I make the rules," the "sheriff" said.

Llys walked up to him and put her hand on the gun. Pulling it away too fast for its owner to keep it, it suddenly went off into the sand beside her. Unafraid, she tossed it away toward Cornwalls, who let it lay on the ground.

"I think you already shot your wad, sheriff," teased Llys.

He lunged at her. She sidestepped his move and chopped him hard in the neck, knocking him out temporarily and sending his body down onto the hard, dusty dock.

"Let's go, girls. I think we've overstayed our welcome in Texas," Cornwalls said as he walked off the dock jetty toward the plane.

As they taxied away from the dock, the sheriff began to wake up. He searched the dirty dock for his shotgun and, finding it, took aim at the plane. They were just getting airborne when the fellow managed to get off a shot, hitting the tail with a few pieces of buckshot and piercing the fuselage behind Blyss and Tes.

With fuel dripping out and spraying onto the tail, a small warning lamp lit.

"Hey, Phil, I think he got us. A red light on the reserve fuel tank back here lit up, and I smell gas," Blyss said.

"Is it leaking into the plane?"

"I don't think so."

"Okay. We're probably fine but we'll have to go high and slow to save fuel."

"I got it. Up to 9600 and slow to 150; that about right?" asked the pilot (Llys).

"Right on! Have you been reading the manual?"

"Nope, it just makes sense."

Cornwalls shook his head, wondering if she had just picked his mind or if she knew more about air-flight than she let on. Either way, he was amazed even more about this woman/android.

They flew over the rest of Texas and into Louisiana. Over New Orleans and headed for the Gulf waters, Cornwalls got on the radio.

"130013 to Hunter 2. Do you read me?"

"Loud and clear. Turn on your beacon, and we'll vector you in."

Phil turned on the plane's ID module located by his left leg.

"We recognize you, ICG7. Maintain your course for 50 miles. By the way, is that you, Phil?"

"Yep. And carrying three surprises. We're starving for fuel, so have a tow and a truck ready, good buddy."

"Roger that. Descend to 100 feet and turn ten degrees right. You should have visual on us in two minutes. Circle once, then land. We'll be ready."

"We may have holes below the waterline, so we'll come in a little hot."

"10-4. Bring it on in, Phil."

"I see they're flying the old 'Other' flag."

"That's them. Circle once, then hit the water on that side with the large, wide dock."

"All right, here we go."

Right then, the engine sputtered and died. Llys switched to the reserve tank, hoping there were more than fumes left. She hit the restart button twice, and it caught. Down to five feet above the smooth water surface, she flew the plane at that level until she could gently set it down three hundred yards from the docking platform.

"We've got a little bit of water back here. Not a flood though," Blyss said, handing Tes up to Cornwalls.

"Meeow!" Tes was ready to end the flight immediately.

Llys taxied the plane to the platform. As she had slowed down, water came in from the back. Blyss was on her hands and knees on the back seat.

They brushed a rubber bumper and two deck hands expertly tied the plane to the platform. A crane arm moved overhead, and one of the deck hands jumped aboard the plane at the top of the engine nacelle and fastened the crane's hook to the plane to keep it from sinking. Llys and Cornwalls popped open the canopy. She crawled over the nose to the dock, while Cornwalls helped Blyss move forward from the back seats and then hand Tes' tote bag to the deckhand, who carried Tes to the dock. Cornwalls then helped Blyss out of the cockpit and over the nose. They joined Llys on the platform docking deck

"Good piloting, Captain," Cornwalls told Llys. Blyss hugged Llys.

A large red-headed man approached.

"Shit, Phil, you not only saved the plane, you brought two beautiful women with you! Sometimes I think you're James Bond reincarnated!"

"Captain Phinneas "Red" Hawk, meet my girlfriend Llys, the owner and pilot of our plane, and her bright-eyed sister Blyss. Of course, you already know Tes."

"Meow." Tes approved of her company.

"Blyss? With looks like yours, I can imagine how you got named."

"Captain Hawk? It's a great pleasure to meet our generous benefactor." Blyss then planted one of those heart-warming, thrilling kisses upon the Captain, which Phil knew only these androids could deliver!

"Come on, Captain. Don't use it all up!" one of the deck hands shouted. The crew lined up before Blyss, and she gave each of them a kiss on the cheek. Meanwhile, Cornwalls couldn't help but watch where her eyes wandered and wonder if she was marking her territory with the Captain. He knew she could do much worse than his old buddy, whom he'd known since their times spent working intelligence capers for the government.

"So, what did you do to get Phil to give up the Captain's seat on this beauty?" asked Captain Hawk of Llys.

"I fell in love with him. It was relatively simple after that."

Cornwalls blushed and changed the subject.

"Say, Hawk, were your guys the team that rescued my sunken plane in Hawaii?"

"None other."

Llys gave him a hug and kiss, less like Blyss' but, no doubt, just as satisfactory.

"You're our saviors twice now," she said moving back to Cornwalls' side.

"All part of the service, ma'am."

Blyss returned with five men in tow.

"Captain, what does the flag mean?" she asked.

"Oh that. It's kind of a joke. You see, the alien head signifies ultra-top-secret subjects, namely UFOs and space aliens; and below the head is the name of our group, 'Oceans 7.' In Phil's section, it's 'AirSpy.' Other sections have other names suggesting their purpose. The joke is that what we do is all real and all true."

Every one of them was fascinated and listening. Although Cornwalls knew the story and had heard it almost 100 times, with each rendition he learned more.

"... We have platforms in each of the seven seas that monitor various electronic transmissions for the NSA and the CSS. Phil flies spy missions for various intelligence agencies but mostly the NSA and NRO. Now that I've told you that, I have to kill you unless Phil promises to keep you in line for the rest of your life."

"I do so swear, Captain Hawk." Llys kissed him the way Blyss kissed Hawk: long and deep, and laded with pent-up desires and the promise of good things to come later. It made his skin blush redder than what gave him his nickname.

"All right, everyone. Time to get back to work. We must patch up the ICON A5 and feed and clothe our guests. And someone, please, rustle up find some cat food for poor old Tes here!"

"Meow," Tes concurred.

Captain Hawk led everyone off the dock except for three men who stayed to work on the plane.

In the back of Phil's mind, he recognized that Blyss had already claimed Hawk for herself. He couldn't think of any reason why she shouldn't, either.

In the evening, while he was getting ready for a shower, Cornwalls' top-secret phone rang. Only three people in the world had the number: The President of the United States, the head of the NSA/CSS, and his immediate senior.

"You have a phone call, sweetie," Llys said, handing it to him. Cornwalls saw it was his immediate senior.

"Yessir."

"We have a lead on the organization after the robot, and, of course, you."

"Who is it?"

"The Mafia."

"Understood."

"They have the resources and the personnel. We have intel that they just signed with the Chinese for one robot for a billion and a half. The only robot available is S1. Three are secured under our umbrella, and S5 is AWOL. Do you need assistance?"

"No, sir. I have a field team ready. Any specific targets?"

"Take out anyone… I mean anyone… who tries to get the robot from you."

"Yessir. What about the robot?"

"Keep it with you for now. We'll handle the rest."

"Yessir."

Even though, Cornwalls had sounded just like he always did when talking with his senior on the project, his heart was not any longer in the game. He'd seen the light when he rose up above his head and was able to see, hear and think more clearly. At this point, he was simply playing along, leading his new friends and lover to safety, he hoped, past the minefield he was certain was coming their way. He was watching how it would all play out in the end, waiting for the right moment to make his counter-move that destroy the opposition to his plans for him and Llys.

The call ended just as Llys entered the bathroom, naked as the day she was made.

"May I shower with you?"

"I can't think of anything I would rather do right now."

Tes purred contentedly for the rest of the evening.

Chapter 59 ~ Illusion of Safety

DESPERATE, S5 STOLE A MERCEDES from a Wal-Mart shopping center in Albuquerque. The owners had foolishly forgotten to take the keys with them. He drove East toward Florida, logging on and off-line intermittently to keep track of S1's location. With hundreds of miles ahead of him to drive, he knew he had plenty of time to plan how he would kill him and all the others with him.

He was feeling fortunate and on top of his game, because he had intercepted a supposedly secure internet communication by the Mafia and found out that they planned to capture S1 somewhere in Florida. He chuckled at the thought of having such a challenge ahead of him, and such a prize that included not only the S1 robot that was going to make him a billionaire soon, but also Mafia chiefs, who would beg him for a piece of the action. No matter that he didn't yet know exactly where and when this hit, and the abduction, were going down; he knew that he had enough firepower to wipe every one of them out. After all, he once had been a Brigadier-General with a lot of privileged knowledge in his briefcase, as well as access to secret stockpiles of weapons of all grades stored in top-secret locations around the nation. And, to top all that off, he had a new identity... and a great deal of advanced technology literally at his fingertips!

But, S5 was also being monitored by the NSA. In fact, a fleet of state-of-the-art drones followed his every movement along the southern states of America, 24/7. In fact, Washington and Langley were watching and listening every hour of every day and night.

Chapter 60 ~ Tour Cover

AFTER THEY ARRIVED AT THE Association for Research & Enlightenment headquarters building, Alice and Stanson waited in her BMW, while Reese went inside and arranged a tour for them, which would begin in two hours. It would not be the easiest task she ever accomplished on short notice.

"I hope you don't mind, but I have a robot I would like to bring along. I promise he won't get in the way."

"That's a bit unusual. Just a moment; I'll check with Administration."

The receptionist went into a room behind her desk and came out accompanied by a gray-haired man wearing an expensive suit and beaming friendliness.

"I understand you want to bring a robot on the tour with you."

"That's right. He's very well-mannered and doesn't leak oil."

"Is this robot an android?"

"Yes (*and no* she thought). May he attend the tour? We're really taking the tour for his benefit."

"You realize this is very unusual."

"Oh yes... far more than you can possibly imagine... isn't it a delicious adventure?!"

Reese put on the biggest grin on her face and a sparkle in her eyes that she could easily remember.

"Well, alright, but you'll have to leave a deposit in case it breaks anything."

"How much will that be?"

"One thousand dollars will be sufficient."

"A thousand dollars!?" Her grin and sparkle were long gone now. "... I should charge you a thousand dollars just to meet him!"

The stuffy gentleman held his ground.

"Well, okay. Here's my card."

Reese handed her bankcard to the receptionist. Seconds later, impressed, the woman raised her eyebrows upon seeing Reese's available balance. She managed to keep a straight face and not let on that she had looked, as she nodded approvingly to her employer.

"Very well then," said he. "... You may wait in the coffee shop until the tour guide announces the tour."

"Thank you." Reese was proud of the fact that she had maintained a professional attitude as the situation unfolded, and she would make sure the others in her party were aware of the effort she put forth for them.

In the coffee shop, Reese ordered a latte. Stanson and Blyss, of course, ordered nothing.

Guests coming into the shop could not help but stare at Stanson's metallic robot body, although most were polite toward him.

"Oren, have you ever looked up anything about Edgar Cayce?" Reese asked.

"Yes, I have. Alice and I, in fact, have read most of his work on reincarnation and the lost-city, Atlantis. We found it quite interesting, though it seemed his clientele were more interested in his healing advices than the other subjects you just mentioned. Cayce was quite well versed in human illness and healing naturally or spiritually."

"That's right. However, there doesn't seem to be references to the existence of robots or androids; at least, not in the published readings. I guess that wasn't so unusual in the Pulp Fiction Era of the 1930's," Alice quickly added.

The tour guide announced the beginning of the tour, and the three pilgrims joined the crowd. People among their tour group tended to keep a distance from Stanson, especially women, which was quite alright with Reese and Alice.

The eclectic building presented within its walls many walnut-wood, framed displays. The plush carpeting carried an aesthetic design that appeared a lot like a star field. Soft-pastel, cream-colored walls and ceiling completed the look. Indirect lighting throughout set an ambiance that captured viewers' hearts and interest. This place obviously was designed for handling large tour groups, evidenced by the lack of over-crowding.

One's first impression had to be that money had been lovingly spent here, including on the staff, who were mostly middle aged, albeit physically fit.

The tour guide discussed various anecdotes about Cayce's life. Passages from his first reading and selected stories about people he had cured with natural methods formerly unknown to the field of medicine of that day.

Stanson leaned toward Alice and whispered in her ear: "There are readings missing from the online records. I don't know if they have a confidential archive, but I suspect they do."

Alice nodded as the tour ended with many questions from the tourists, the guide handling them adroitly. She had undoubtedly answered the same questions hundreds of times.

Alice received a thought from Llys.

Be on your guard. You're not going to know who to trust. The Mafia is behind the kidnapping attempts tried earlier and they must steal Oren to meet a contract deadline they have with the Chinese. Trust no one, but Ingrid and Oren. Phil has orders to terminate ANYONE who interferes or who might pose a threat. We intend to be there in days. Whatever you do, keep Oren safe.

Alice turned to Reese and whispered, "I just heard from Llys. She says trust no one. Everyone is a possible suspect. Terminate any interference with extreme prejudice. Yes?

"Yes, I understand. Orders are: We keep hands on Oren at all costs."

Alice proceeded to bully her way past a middle-aged couple and took Oren's arm in hers, ignoring their protests. She whispered to him as they strolled with the tour group.

"Oren, get facial recognition on everyone we meet here. Consider every person we engage with as a potential enemy for the present. Phil and Llys and Tes are coming soon."

"Okay Blyss, I get the picture. I overheard you and Reese over there."

The tour ended with a brief lecture in a small theater, explaining how the A.R. & E. currently was forging new ground by collaborating with archeological expeditions visiting places that Cayce had talked about in his readings. Ingrid, Alice and Stanson listened intently but they were disappointed that there was little mentioned about the travels of the soul, other than hard-science evidence of reincarnation.

After the lecture, Stanson walked up to the lecturer and stood beside him as he fielded questions. Catching an opening, he asked a question of his own.

"Did Cayce talk about souls transmigrating to forms, shells or bodies other than human life forms?"

"Thank you for your question, but that subject is beyond the purview of this group talk. However—he stepped back and admired Stanson's body, you are a fine specimen of the current state-of-the-art of robotics engineering and design... why don't you and your friends join our Association? That would give you unlimited access to every reading that we have."

"Do you have archived readings not in the open library, yet?"

"I don't know. That never comes up in our staff meetings."

The lecturer had by now successfully maneuvered Stanson and his companions away from the rest of the group, and beyond their earshot.

"Really, the best thing to do is to join the Association, and the receptionist over there—he pointed out personnel far away from the tour crowd—will help you sign up."

The man walked away to greet a waiting couple. Stanson, Alice and Reese departed. As they went, Stanson spoke.

"The lecture was interesting, but from my perspective, they're concentrating too much on the material universe, not the more-important spiritual one."

Alice nodded.

"I think between us we have more PhDs than the entire staff in this place," boasted Reese.

"I agree with both of you. We won't find many answers here. We have answers we can give to them. Besides, this seems like a good place to hide: I didn't see any press," remarked Alice, while taking Stanson's free arm.

"I'm hungry, let's go to that hotel down by the beach and get some lunch. I could use some olive oil... how about you two?" Reese laughed and told the robots she was only joking.

"I could use some quality time in town with two beautiful women at my side," laughed Stanson.

Chapter 61 ~ "Negotiations"

"YOUR PLANE IS PATCHED AND fueled. You have to get a move on; a hurricane is coming in a few hours."

Cornwalls opened the canopy and stepped down into the Captain's seat out of habit.

"Hey! What you doing? That's my seat!" shouted Llys, running up to the plane.

"Where's Blyss? Where's Tes?" he asked, moving over to the co-pilot's seat.

Blyss came running up with Captain Hawk tailing her, holding the cat's tote bag. She stopped by Cornwalls, held her hand out and took the bag from the Captain, handing the cat to Cornwalls straight away.

The Captain had a black eye, and Blyss had an announcement to make about it: "I'm staying for a while. Captain Hawk graciously invited me to stay on until the next cargo ship arrives, and I... we... accepted."

She wrapped her arms around the Captain and hugged him.

"Does anybody have a raw piece of meat I can use on this?" asked the Captain.

"Looks like your 'negotiations' made quite the impression, Blyss," Cornwalls noted.

Blyss smiled coyly. "Just setting the ground rules; no problems. Where do you think you'll end up?"

"We're headed for Virginia Beach, then south to Florida to a base located there."

"Well, see you in a few months, then. Have a nice honeymoon."

The Captain stood beside her, holding her by the waist close to him. He seemed none the worst for the shiner.

Llys helped her co-pilot paddle the plane out of the dock area and then turned it around for the take-off. With Captain Hawk blasting the platform's foghorn, they departed.

"You know where you're headed?" asked Cornwalls.

"Well, we have to get around the approaching hurricane and stay ahead of it, if it crawls up the East coast. I was planning to hug the coastline to Florida, then head West to Clearwater or St. Petersburg."

"Meeeoow," approved Tes.

"Looks like our passenger approves of our destination. I saw on the platform's radar that the storm will be heading straight up the eastern seaboard, so maybe we should skip Virginia Beach until after the all-clear after the storm blows through."

He was holding Tes and scratching behind her ears. She, in turn, purred her contentment.

"Okay, I like your plan. We'll stay inland and then head over the Gulf to western Florida. That will put us at Clearwater harbor."

Llys felt a tinge of jealousy about her man and Tes' relations right now.

"... Wish you'd do that to me," she said, putting her hand on his thigh.

Cornwalls had the perfect reply for the moment: "Engage the autopilot."

Chapter 62 ~ Before the Storm

WHEN LLYS ATTEMPTED TO ENGAGE the autopilot, the engine cut out, and the instrument panel went dead. She was left with having to fly the plane manual. She expertly pulled the small craft up and into a gentle glide attitude.

"Meow!" Tes sensed the danger. She scrunched up into a ball in Phil's lap, holding onto his shirt, and his skin under the cloth, with her claws.

"What the hell?!" he yelled.

"Speaking of Hell, do you know exactly where we are right now?"

"From the looks of it... still over the Gulf!"

"Well, at least we don't need land to, uh, land." She was trying to make light of the predicament to keep herself loose.

"Cute. Are we out of fuel?"

"I glanced at the fuel gauge before the power went out, but it doesn't matter. We have an electric fuel pump."

"Better tell Blyss."

Blyss, we've been sabotaged. Watch the crew on the platform, especially Hawk.

Got it Blyss thought back.

"Watch the ocean birds to see if you can find an updraft."

"Okay."

"Veer gently to the left and try not to lose any airspeed... where is that storm?"

"Behind us."

"Okay, no help there. We should be able to make it to the coast if we can keep enough altitude."

"There's a smaller storm ahead and to the left."

"Have you ever flown a sailplane?"

"Nope."

"I guess now is as good a time as any to learn," he said, tearing Tes away from his shirt and putting her back in her bag. "... What's our airspeed?"

"80 knots."

"That can't be right. We must have a tailwind, and that's a good thing. See how high you can pull her nose before she tries to stall."

Phil's gliding lessons continued, and they stayed aloft. They were determined to make it to the shoreline before they ran out of air underneath them. Gravity, however, was winning the battle.

"I see lights to the left."

"Good. Head that way. The closer we can get to land the easier it will be to get help."

About 20 miles from shore at about one-hundred feet above the water's surface, they felt a sudden, strong downdraft. Then they heard the noise of a helicopter just above them.

Cornwalls swiped the condensation fog away from the inside of the canopy and saw a Coast Guard helicopter keeping pace with them at about two-hundred feet.

The tandem made the shoreline.

"Okay, Sweetie. You've done a terrific job. Put her down as smoothly as you can. Maybe they can help us sort out what happened,' so we can get the engine started."

"Okay, Phil. Here we go."

Llys brought the plane down the last few feet and, bouncing off a couple of small waves, settled it down into the shallow water. After they had stopped, the HH-3F Pelican helicopter landed on the Gulf a few yards away, sending two men out to them in a motorized dinghy.

Rain was about to drench them any moment, but for now they were still dry when Llys and Phil popped the canopy. One of the Coast Guard crew fastened a towrope from the dinghy to the nose of the plane.

"What's the trouble?"

"We've been sabotaged. I'm an officer of the NSA. I'll show you my identification in a moment. Our electrical system has been compromised. We have fuel, but I need to check the wiring. Is there any way you can help keep us afloat until I find out what's been done?"

"I think so. We'll head you into the chop with our tow rope and hold you there for a while. Better hurry, though. There's a hurricane behind this squall."

"Thanks. Shouldn't take long."

"What do you want me to do?" asked Llys.

"You steer. The tail has a water rudder and you can steer it with the rudder pedals."

Cornwalls moved Tes to the center console and opened the canopy wide so he could climb over his seat into the aft back space.

In fifteen minutes, he found a cutoff switch spliced into the autopilot circuit. The sabotage was ingeniously simple: Using the autopilot switch cut off the autopilot. He wove the wire ends together and wrapped the junction with a part of his shirt that Tes had torn and... Voila!...

"Try the engine."

Llys pressed the dash-light button and all the instrument lamps came on. She pressed the engine-start button, and the engine roared to life. She gave him the OK sign, and Cornwalls motioned the motorized Coast Guard dinghy closer. He pulled out his ID and showed it to the men as they pulled beside the cockpit. The men immediately saluted him.

"Glad we could help, sir."

"What's your name?"

"Sergeant Mike Smith, sir."

"Well done, Mike. You saved our lives. Thank you. Where are you based?"

"Clearwater, sir."

"Thanks again."

The dinghy disconnected the towrope and headed back toward the chopper.

"Engage propeller, Llys, let's get on our way to Clearwater. Those guys deserve a big thank you from us."

"Yes sir!"

The little seaplane taxied away from the helicopter. Llys gave it full throttle and they, bouncing off a few wavelets, were airborne in seconds, leaving the Coast Guard behind.

"Jeesuz! Look at that baby go!" the helicopter pilot said to his copilot as they got the dinghy back aboard. The dinghy sailor came up to the flight deck.

"He showed me his ID. He's a Special Agent for the NSA, for real. Some hot plane they have there."

The second sailor added, "And did you see the babe flying that thing? Holy cow! I'd sure like to know where they grow those, or if she has a sister!"

The copter's co-pilot spun up the rotors and headed them back on patrol.

With the electronics working again, Cornwalls reported the events to HQ and their adjusted destination. He called Alice to tell her about the slight change.

Stanson, Reese and Alice were cruising the eastern seaboard taking in the scenery and old antebellum houses, completely ignorant of the hurricane headed their way.

Alice's cell phone rang.

"Ingrid, would you mind getting my phone from my purse?"

"Of course not. Do you want me to answer it?"

"It's probably Phil so, sure, go ahead."

"Hello?"

"Hello Ingrid, this is Phil. We've had an adventure, but we plan to land at Clearwater. There is a Cat3 hurricane headed your way. The weather bureau predicts it will hug the east coast all the way up to Washington, so you need to head West toward Clearwater. You can drive down the west coast of Florida and avoid most of the coming destruction. And try to stay on high ground. Clear?"

"Alright, got it. I'll tell Alice—she's our 'designated driver'."

Reese hung up and put the phone back in Alice's purse.

"'Designated driver'? What's going on?"

"I was just joking around with Phil. He says there's a bad hurricane headed right toward us. Let's put on the weather and see what they say."

Stanson struggled with the computerized radio for several minutes before he figured out how to tune in the weather channel: "You'd think what we paid for this car they would have a user-friendly radio," he complained, once he had it tuned in.

"It's German, Oren," Alice said.

"So?"

"You've never owned a German luxury car?" Reese asked in amazement.

"No; I always bought a Lexus."

"Let's be kind and just say the Germans love gadgets," Reese said.

"Speaking of German cars, I've noticed a black Mercedes following us for quite a while," Alice said.

"Really? Like in the espionage movies?" Ingrid turned around and looked out the back window.

"I'm pretty sure it has been the same car. So long as they just follow us, we can out last them because we won't have to get gas until Clearwater. But you know, if those are the bad guys, they will not hesitate to kill us to get to Oren."

"Do we have any way of defending ourselves? I'm just a college professor. I've never had any weapons training; not even a squirt gun," offered Reese.

"I have a weapon, and I'm sure that Oren is armed."

"That's right, Alice. I have sufficient number of built-in weapons to take out a tank, or a small village."

"That's why you're so heavy, isn't it?"

"Yes, Ingrid. I'll take care of you. I've got your back."

"Okay, folks, the turnoff for Macon is coming up in a couple miles. I'm going to go there and take the 75 South to Tampa. The Mercedes might just be a tail to keep us on their radar. I think they would choose a large city to make their move. Phil and Llys can meet us in Tampa. Hand me my phone, would you, Ingrid?"

Alice called Cornwalls on the secret, unlisted number he had given her. As expected, three clicks, a space, then another click. and she heard the phone ring.

"What's up, Alice?" Phil answered.

"We have acquired a tail. Large black Mercedes keeping a comfortable distance behind. We are leaving the coast and heading to Macon, then down the 75 to Tampa. Your advice?"

"I'll set up a highway checkpoint near Ocala. The password to get through is "Llys." There will be a semi to throw across the road behind you and a car like yours to lead the tail onto the turnpike toward Orlando. What are you driving?"

"A dark-blue Beamer, 8 series. It's a fusion model, so fuel is no problem."

"Good. There will be Highway Patrol just before you enter Ocala and a semi staged to dash across the road in front of the Mercedes and whatever other cars are following you.

Once you're free again, go south on 75 straight to Tampa. Follow the signs from there. You'll take the I-275 south bypass past downtown, past the airport. Again, just follow the signage. When you get across the inland bay water on the Courtney Campbell Causeway, keep going straight onto Gulf to Bay Boulevard to an intersection with Publix market and Wal-Mart grocery stores on it. Cross street is Belcher. It's relatively high ground, no flooding there. Get inside the Wal-Mart parking lot—it's a 24-hour grocery store. We'll meet you there. Protect Oren at all costs, and keep the car parked close to the entrance.

"How will you meet us?"

"If we must, we'll land on a nearby lake."

"Huh?"

Alice was asking into a dead phone.

Chapter 63 ~ Certified Insane

S5, FORMERLY BRIGADIER-GENERAL ROGERS, BY now called himself "The General." And right now, he had an armful of spray-paint cans, with which he was going to camouflage his white metal skin. He didn't pay for the goods; instead, he had broken into the local art-supply store he was in.

He walked out the back door with as many paint cans as he could carry, found parked in the alley a red Jeep and hotwired it. Having destroyed the security cameras at the store, inside and out, he drove away without anyone noticing his little illegal visit.

Back at the place he called home, he painted his robot body olive drab and light gray with black highlights, and then used up the rest of the paint painting the Jeep with a random mix of colors like something from a punk war movie. Greens, yellows, blues, browns, and purple splotches covered much of the original red.

Having put his finishing touch on the vehicle, The General made himself laugh aloud with an evil, low, guttural sound because he brushed a large black star onto his forehead. "BJ" Rogers was now "certified insane" by anyone's standards.

Rogers also had tapped into the internet while inside the store. He located S1 through the Arpanet2 and his nearly constant interlink with DARPA. The data was a day old, but he could see the robot was heading south into Florida.

On the move with mayhem in mind, Rogers raided a gun store in Atlanta, Georgia, stealing several thousand rounds of ammunition that would fit his machine guns. No attendant was on duty—no one to kill—so he only had to destroy the security cameras as a precaution before he departed from the store and area in the dead of night.

Heading South toward Florida, he did not see any police on the roads he traveled. The few seconds he experienced of feeling like a "free" man made him laugh that hideous sound again; that is, until his saliva slipped down his throat, causing him to retch out several coughs, which almost cost him his life the few times that his coughing made him swerve all over the darkened roadway.

Rogers always had been a tough S.O.B., but now he was just a messy excuse of a human being, and not even fully human anymore.

Chapter 64 ~ Into the Noose

I HAD TO KILL THEM all. Tell Phil I'm sorry Blyss thought to Llys.

What happened?

Sex, drugs and espionage. A potent and fatal combination. They were all on the take. This base is compromised. I'm going to take the Captain's launch and try for New Orleans before the weather worsens. Where are you all going?

Clearwater, Florida.

Why?

Phil says he has a base near there. Also, it is relatively safe from hurricanes – at least most of the time.

Are you all okay?

Alice may be damaged, but the alerts on her heads-up calmed down so I think she can hold together.

I'll notify the Others. Maybe they can make a field trip.

Blyss beamed a mental image of a spindly-legged alien walking down a ramp out of a flying saucer carrying a doctor's bag and wearing a stethoscope. Llys laughed.

"What's happening?" Cornwalls asked.

"I just heard from Blyss. She's taking the Captain's launch off the oil platform to shore. She says the base was compromised and the crew was all on the take. I guess it didn't work out with Hawk."

"What does she mean by 'compromised'?"

"That usually means they went to the 'dark side,' so to speak. But, now they're all dead. She said to tell you she's sorry."

Llys was quiet for a while. She let Cornwalls digest this upsetting information. She knew the news may or may not mean added trouble for their relationship.

After a few minutes, he came out of whatever dark mood he was in and grabbed Tes, scratching behind her ears. Then he reached over and scratched Llys behind her ears. She smiled and kissed his fingers.

"I hate to be bossy, boss, but I think we better skip any side trips for now," she said.

"Meeoow!" agreed Tes.

"All right. I recognize when I'm outvoted by all the women in my life. There is a small municipal airport in Clearwater not too far from where we are supposed to meet Oren and the others; it's called Clearwater Air Park. We can land there. It is reasonably out of the usual air-traffic patterns and we should be able to stay there incognito, or at least as incognito as a seaplane piloted by a striking blonde can be."

"You want to switch seats, honey?"

"I wouldn't mind it, if we had an autopilot that worked. Still, I prefer a blonde driving to dying, so, no thank you for now. Llys, you are obviously an experienced pilot. And, you know what... I'd like to hear more about that someday."

"Someday."

Cornwalls dialed the plane's radio to the secret channel.

"CWB 130013, this is IC 130013 calling for clearance to Clearwater Air Park."

"What is your ETA, IC 130013?"

He looked at Llys.

"Thirty minutes by the radar," she said.

"Thirty minutes", he answered the operator.

"Roger. We have you. Come straight in. We have contacted the airport; they are expecting you. There is no traffic right now. Turn on your locator beacon."

"How old are you, Llys?"

"You think now's a fine time to ask? I'll tell you after we're married."

"You fly like a veteran."

"I am a veteran. Remember, I used to work for the Commanding General at Dulce."

"Which Commanding General?"

"We can hash that out on our honeymoon."

Llys maneuvered into the landing pattern, cut the power and made a perfect three-point landing. The moment they touched down, a large black limousine pulled onto the runway behind them, cutting them off. Another black SUV pulled onto the runway in front and stopped at the end of the runway cutting off any possible escape. Four men pointing machine guns at them exited the vehicles. Llys cut the engine and hit the brakes, stopping only three feet from the SUV.

"Friends of yours?"

"Nope. My people shoot first, then ask questions."

"I'll take the guys behind us.

"Good. I'll take the guys in front."

They opened the canopy, exited the cockpit, and stood on either side of the plane.

"What do you want?"

"We want you, Doctor Cornwalls. Why don't you two take it easy?" said a man standing in the dark behind the shooters.

"Alright... who's first?"

The two men looked at each other, considering their firepower was superior to a civilian and a woman.

Llys, faster than the human eye can easily follow, ran to the grass beside the runway, jumped down and shot the two men behind the plane with a ray gun that matched Cornwalls.' The two men in front shifted to more hostile stances. In that moment, Cornwalls fired in a flat line from left to right, cutting the men, and their SUV, into halves.

Llys, having paused to watch Cornwall's handiwork, had another hostile sneak up to her from the grass. He put his gun right to her head.

"One more move, and your head's gonna be strawberry ice cream. Drop your weapon."

She did. It got lost in the high grass.

Cornwalls had rushed to the plane unnoticed and he grabbed Tes's tote bag. Tes was making almost inaudible growling noises, more like a lion than a cat.

"Don't shoot my cat. I'll come along," he left the shadows of the aircraft and walked toward the man who had Llys. He was holding his weapon above his head. When he and Tes got as far as the grass, he threw his gun in the general vicinity of Llys'.

"What's this all about?" he asked his captor.

"Shut up and walk to the limo."

The thug hadn't realized his untenable position.

"That's enough. Put the cat down and open the car door, real slow."

Phil set Tes down with her carrier door open and he turned away from the thug. Suddenly, a ferocious ball of fur came at the man at 30 miles per hour or better. She ran up his leg and chest and proceeded to bite into his nose and scratch his eyes. Seconds later, his face was a bloody mess, and he was screaming for someone to get her off him.

Llys calmly walked over to the man and put his rifle to his head.

"Call off Tes, Phil."

"Come, Tes. Good job. We've got him, now."

But the cat wouldn't stop. By now, the man was on the grass, rolling around and still unable to dislodge her from his face. Soon, he was bleeding from his wrists as she got her rear legs, which were rotating across his flesh like a helicopter's rotor at high speed, into the attack.

"Shoot him, Llys, or Tes may end up eating him alive."

Llys mercifully put a single shot into his brain, and he stopped screaming. And moving. Tes jumped off his face and sat next to Phil's feet, licking her claws.

"I'd say she had a lot of pent-up energy from her long ride!"

"Ya think? Come on, muscle man, help me park the plane. Remember we have to retract the wings, tie them down, and then tie down the wheels."

"Yes, ma'am... Captain. Then, I'll check for ammo in the SUV."

Cornwalls prepared the plane for the approaching storm and then walked over to the limo and searched it for other weapons, ammo and whatever else he might find.

He found the rental receipt. The address for the agency was St. Petersburg Limousine Rentals. The renters' address was listed as Cleveland Street in Clearwater. He looked it up on his phone. It was a high-rise building that had stood neglected for years, which renovation was never completed. The developer had intended to re-make it into a hotel or condo complex with re-tail shops on the ground. The concrete-block skeleton took up a whole block.

Llys and Cornwalls found several cases of ammunition for the assault rifles in the trunk of the limo. They located their ray-guns in the grass. Tes continued to clean herself, although she sat next to her tote bag, signaling her readiness to move on.

Cornwalls picked up all the weapons and tossed them into the limo's trunk. He then grabbed Tes' bag, Tes was in it and put her in the back seat of the limo. He and Llys got in the front seat.

"Where's Oren?"

"Just a moment... They are still in their blue BMW and nearing the trap your people set."

"I'm worried, Llys."

"You? Worry? What about?"

"How did these guys know we were arriving? I don't think we can trust anyone but ourselves. A billion and a half is a whole bunch of money. Even Agency people might not be immune to that kind of money. If only a small part of the Agency has control of the other robots, Oren is easily fair-game and can be kidnapped anywhere."

"Unfortunately, that's a good point. What do we do? Do we have a future at all?"

"For my agency, this is chump change. But for a foreign government like Russia or China, that kind of funding would make a very large dent in their G.N.Ps., probably over 20 percent! And, for the Mafia, if they are behind this push, one sale represents several years of income."

He looked at his watch and at Llys, assuring himself of her state of mind.

"... I think we can kiss the plane goodbye. Let's get going before anyone else comes out to find out what happened to their hit squad."

"Right!"

He sped away from the airport with his lights off, turning them on a few blocks away.

"So where are we going, handsome?"

"We're going to that abandoned building."

"Why?"

"It might still be abandoned and could be a good hiding place for us. Llys, contact Alice using your magic and find out what has happened on their end. I have a bad feeling about this, and I think our plans and our covers have been blown."

Chapter 65 ~ The Noose Tightens

ARE YOU GUYS OKAY?

No. The whole thing with the truck and traffic stop was a set up. We were captured and put into that semi. Oren is secured with titanium restraints, and Ingrid and I are tied up. I think we're headed for Tampa, so that might work out. They didn't find my weapon and, of course, they didn't find any of Oren's weaponry.

Good. I'll track you and we'll meet up again soon. Don't start a war... yet.

Llys thought to Blyss: *What's happening?*

Doing great... caught the last plane out of New Orleans and should be at Tampa International in another hour. How about you?

Adventures; what else? We're in Clearwater and headed for another rendez-vous. Alice, Ingrid and Oren are captured, but Alice thinks the captor's semi-truck is heading toward Tampa.

Okay then. Send me details. I'll get there as soon as I can.

Good. Our plan was compromised by the guys on the oil platform. We were met at the Clearwater Air Park by bad guys. I'm going to contact the Others and find out if we can get some help on this.

Good luck with that.

Chapter 66 ~ All Out War!

CORNWALLS, LLYS AND TES DISCOVERED the abandoned construction site with the help of the limo's GPS system. Once on site, they scouted for and found the construction gate, whereupon Cornwalls melted the lock and pulled open the gate. Llys drove the car into the site and parked near the middle where normally elevators would go. With Cornwalls back in the car, she shut off the lights, left the motor running and waited.

"Meow." Tes was ready for action.

"What now, lover? Does this thing have a bed?" Llys said, snuggling up to Phil on the front seat.

"I was just thinking the same thing."

"Should we let Tes out?"

"Sure. She'll probably find something to eat out there."

They didn't have to wait for Tes to scamper out the passenger window, once they opened it.

Llys and her man found the back of the limo accommodating for what they thought might be their last romantic interlude, after which they left their love nest and proceeded to inventory the weapons in the trunk.

Can you hear me? Blyss thought to Llys and Alice.

Yes, answered Alice and Llys together.

I've just checked out a car from Enterprise in the Tampa airport and am on my way to Clearwater.

You have the address. Enter it into the car's GPS and you'll find them Llys reminded. *We're also in Tampa. Oren says we're inside a large, closed warehouse owned by some people he knows. The bad guys will be back soon. I guess we'll have our war then. Ingrid is holding up okay but she's tired, hungry and thirsty. Got to get Oren free. Talk to you soon.*

Alice was thirsty for the battle to begin but she knew they had to free Stanson first.

"Oren, do you have any weapons or tools that we can use to get you free of your restraints?"

"You know, I don't really know. I wasn't under any testing protocols as a warfighter. That was S1's next test station. Let me search my programming and see what I can come up with."

He closed his eyes. His odd pose made the two girls stare at him. Soon enough, he opened his eyes, only much larger than before.

"This is amazing. This body is equipped with an Electromagnetic pulse projector! I can disrupt our enemy's electrical and electronic devices. It also has two micro-bullet guns that shoot tiny, depleted uranium bullets at over the speed of sound! And I've got one in each arm. There's a sonic-beam weapon, which can incapacitate human bodies, giving them splitting headaches, severe abdominal cramps and diarrhea. That can protect me as far out as 100 meters, so I'm pretty much untouchable from human attacks. Finally, I have a laser emitter in each index finger; each puts out 10,000 Kilowatts rays. And I can point and shoot with them."

Stanson wasn't finished with his inventory check-offs.

"... Also, my data-display screen allows me to monitor discreetly and concurrently, and target, each weapon aimed at me. Thankfully, my body is also immune to other S-series robotic weapons; they can't touch me!"

One more item was left on the list, which Stanson preferred to keep to himself, so he did not disclose it: A force field that protected him from small-arms fire, including anything hand-held such as AK47 machine guns down to pistols.

"What about RPG's?" Alice asked.

"Nothing about an RPG. I would assume that would kill me."

"Do the specifications tell you how many rounds you can maintain on an offensive attack?"

"Apparently, 24 hours—the time my power supply operates without recharge."

"How long do you have on your current charge?" Ingrid asked.

"About four hours."

"Our captors probably know that if they just leave you alone long enough you will run out of juice and we'll starve to death. I think that's their plan. We've been stopped here for over an hour, and they haven't bothered us."

"Better cut us all free, Oren. You can plug into the truck's battery system in the cab through the accessory outlet. It should work fine; it's a 24-volt system," offered Alice.

"They're probably watching us right now. Instead, let's patch into the trailer's electrical system. There are power wires running to the lighting harness. That way, we won't have to get outside of the trailer, where they can see and pick us off," said Ingrid.

"Oh, of course. Those running lights! Here goes."

Stanson pointed his left index finger at one of the straps binding him and the laser cut it neatly. He did the same with the one around his thighs. Next, he cut the bindings on Alice and Ingrid, allowing Ingrid to find an electric socket at the lower-corner edge of one of the rear doors.

"Do you have an A/C adaptor?"

"Yes, it's plugged into my side next to the coiled charging cable inside the compartment just below my armpit."

"Alright. Step over here. Gently... we must not rock the trailer... and plug in.

"Done, sir."

"Good, because I need to take a nap until rescue comes or war breaks out." Ingrid lay down on the trailer floor and placed a packing cushion under her head.

Alice moved next to Stanson. "May I share 'lunch' with you?" she whispered.

"Of course, my dear. Lunch is on me."

And Alice plugged into the second outlet in the back of the trailer, putting her arms around the former Director of the Lab.

"I am so happy to have met you, Oren."

Several hours later, Alice unplugged and lightly touched her hero on the shoulder.

"Do you hear them?" she whispered.

"Yes. They're speaking Mandarin," he whispered back.

"What are they saying?"

"Criticizing our captors as buffoons."

Several other boisterous noises and spoken words could be heard.

"Our captors are speaking Italian. Now soft tire noises on gravel but no engine noise... the Chinese must have stolen our car and brought it here. Lucky for us: You kill the Chinese with your more precise weapon. I'll kill the Italians. Let's not wake Ingrid, yet; she's safe on the floor."

"I'll cut open the doors, so they don't clank by opening them with those handles."

Alice's ray gun cut the long latches at the top and bottom, so the doors could swing freely open without added sound. She listened for a moment and smelled the cigarette of the man standing right behind the trailer.

"Kee-yai!" she yelled, shoving the door with all her might outward. The guard was knocked on his face and Alice shot a lethal bolt of energy through his head before he hit the ground.

A second man stood by the BMW's side. She put a bolt through his head before he ever knew anything was happening.

A third Chinese soldier came in the warehouse door, a warm AK-47 blazing away in his hands. Alice severed his legs at the knees. He fell on the ground holding down the trigger. The gun shot up his face.

Stanson slinked to the side of the trailer away from the warehouse door. From there, he shot a group of Mafia mobsters jumping out of the back of a FedEx truck. A two-second burst of his mini-ray gun finished them off.

Six more came running in from outside the warehouse, but they were only shooting pistols, and Stanson's twin lasers cut them into bleeding halves.

Suddenly, 50-caliber, machine-gun projectiles ripped holes out of the walls of the FedEx truck from the inside. The force of the bullets against his force field, knocked Stanson down and out of harm's way. from there, two more seconds of his ballistic weaponry output, shredded the truck's back paneling. The machine gun went silent, and fresh blood seeped through the floorboards and dripped on the concrete flooring of the warehouse.

The noise of a Black Hawk helicopter over the top of the warehouse drowned out any remaining small-arms firings inside of the place.

"Save Ingrid!" Stanson yelled to Alice, who swung herself up into the trailer and grabbed the half-conscious Doctor Reese struggling to understand what was happening and who went limp in Alice's arms.

Alice jumped down, ran to the BMW, and plopped her cargo onto the driver's seat. She turned around just as the helicopter opened fire on the trailer. She fired her ray gun into the helicopter's cockpit and it immediately twirled crazily in the air, still spraying fire from her guns as she headed down at the warehouse.

Alice nailed the gunner with her second shot, but the helicopter fell into the warehouse and exploded, setting off other explosives stored in the warehouse. A fireball erupted and scorched the air.

Ingrid had managed to back up the BMW out of the warehouse before the helicopter crashed in, but Stanson was unaccounted for. Alice ran to the flaming trailer and found him lying on his back, covered with scorched particles, but otherwise undamaged, except his eyes were closed. She had no idea how to revive him, or whether he was dead. Hoping for the best, she knelt next to his left ear.

"Are you alive? Report S1!"

She bent over near his mouth, listening for the slightest flicker of life and she heard a repeated whisper: "S1 is rebooting. S1 is rebooting. S1 is rebooting."

Ingrid brought the car near them, parked and got out.

"Help me get him into the back, Ingrid."

"Is he dead?" Ingrid asked, her voice trembling.

"I don't know. His operating system has taken over and says it is reboot-ing. Come on, we have to get out of here."

Alice and Ingrid dragged Stanson and managed his torso onto the back seat. They lifted his legs in and shut the door.

Ingrid scampered to the driver's seat, but Alice needed to get around the limo to get to the passengers' side. Suddenly, her emergency screen turned on yellow lights all over her skeleton. Seconds later, the fuel tanks of the semi-truck blew up from the heat, sending shrapnel all around the warehouse and into the passenger door, and Alice, as she collapsed into the seat, who somehow managed to pull what was left of the door shut. Her back and hips glowed red. She knew they were hit, without looking, and then her whole lower body went numb.

"Are you okay, Alice?" asked Ingrid as she tore out of the Tampa airport warehouse, headed for Clearwater.

"No. I'm out of action. My lower body is numb; my back is damaged. Get me to Llys; she'll know what to do. But... hurry."

And then Alice shut down.

Chapter 67 ~ Casualties

REESE, WITH TWO POSSIBLY DEAD or, at least, out-of-action robots in tow, sped over the causeway into Clearwater, running red lights on Gulf to Bay Boulevard, uncaring, and another one where the road split into Cleveland and Court Streets.

The abandoned building that she was trying to get to would be on Cleveland Street to her right. She had only minutes to go to find it. When she arrived, she easily found the hole in the fence and honked her horn twice.

Cornwalls honked two times in reply and flashed his headlights. Reese pressed forward and, at last, stopped in front of the limo, whereupon Cornwalls and Llys jumped out of the limo and ran to her opened window.

"Alice and Oren are damaged or dead. Alice went numb from the waist down and shut down. Oren's programming keeps repeating that it's 'rebooting!'"

"Take some deep breaths, Ingrid. If they're talking, they're not dead yet," Llys said.

"I have an idea of what's happening to Oren!" Reese feared the worst had happened on her watch.

"Here's some water, Ingrid. Drink up and take a few deeper breaths," Cornwalls told her.

Llys and Cornwalls opened the car doors and examined their patients. He found a bit of shrapnel stuck in Stanson's reboot switch. Opening the trunk of the BMW, he found the built-in tool kit in the trunk lid, took out a pliers, walked back to Stanson's body, and pulled the bit of sharp metal out of the robot's skin. The switch closed and shortly after, the computer stopped announcing its reboot. A few minutes more, and Stanson was again awake.

"How are you?" Cornwalls said to him.

"My body is operational. Me? I'm not too sure. I've never been a violent man. I guess my warfighting protocol kicked in... and kicked me out."

"Well, who knows? Maybe you were in a war in an earlier life. You rescued Ingrid, that's the best part."

"Hey, you guys, help me move Alice to the bench seat in the back of the limo. I need to stretch her out. Get a move on!" Llys was not taking anything less than supersonic speed as adequate reply.

Oren and Phil helped Llys lay Alice gently on the sofa.

"May we watch?" Stanson asked.

"Just stay out of my way," Llys answered curtly.

Cornwalls figured she was just upset about her sister.

"Oren, search for the tracking devices on both cars."

"Yes, 'Doctor'."

Stanson found one in the trunk.

"Got it. It was in one of the ammo cans."

"Great. Look for a second one before going to the Beamer."

He circled the limo again.

"I found it. I can't get to it, because it's under our patient."

"Alice has a bullet embedded in her spine. I'm trying to get it out, so you're going to have to be extra careful in there."

Cornwalls whispered to Stanson: "You can use your laser to cut into the car and get at it through the side, right?"

"Good idea. Let's see what I can do."

Stanson did nothing, except stare at the car.

"What are you doing?" Cornwalls asked.

"I'm mapping the wiring and fuel lines, so I don't blow us all up."

"Oh. That's good. Carry on.

Soon, Stanson had cut a horizontal box-shape out of the skin of the car; then cut through some underlying bullet-proofing. Eventually, he pulled wires down below the cut and retrieved the tracking device from under the bench seat.

"Got it!" exclaimed Cornwalls, holding up for all to see both the bullet, which Llys had been trying to dislodge out of Alice, and the second tracking device, with the bullet attached, which had embedded itself into both the device and Alice's spine.

"Way to go, Llys!" Blyss said, walking toward the group and away from her rented Fiat 500. Her arrival had not been noticed amid the commotion. "... You should go into medicine, Llys; you're a natural!"

"Thanks, but I have no idea how to mend her skin."

"Oh, no problem. I watched what the Others did during their short-lived battles. They used epoxy as a spot weld all the way down the length of both sides of the cut skin, then covered it with duct tape. It worked as a temporary bandage."

"Great. All we need is epoxy and duct tape." Llys was less than grateful.

"I'm starting to feel my legs and feet now." Alice was wiggling her feet.

Oren and Cornwalls searched the trunks of both cars, looking for epoxy and duct tape, with no luck.

"I saw a 24-hour market up the road. I'll go there... be back soon." Blyss drove off.

"Okay, we got two bugs so far. Let's check the Beemer, Oren."

Oren and Cornwalls checked the car from front to rear, finding nothing.

"A hacker could find the BMW easily, Phil. Let's pull the battery cables."

"Right. I'll do that. Meanwhile, why don't you top up your charge with the limo's electrical system, then get the girls charged up. I hope Blyss brings some snacks or something for us meatbots."

Blyss drove through the gate, got out of her car and fused the gate and fencing pieces together with her ray gun before she joined the group by the limo. She carried two bags of supplies: A pink roll of duct tape with some epoxy in one; and cold sandwiches, chips and water in the other.

Reese and Cornwalls stuffed their faces, pausing only to hug and kiss Blyss, who was all about the business of war preparations.

"The roof of the building across Cleveland is an excellent sniper position, but not for us. We'll have to watch that from higher up. Six Mercedes SUVs were parked in the lot of the convenience store. Men in black combat clothes lined with body-armor vests and wearing helmets were hanging around. I would guess the invasion is about to begin. Are we ready?"

Llys answered for the rest.

"No, we aren't. Ingrid, I would like you to help Alice get a couple floors higher. Oren, you should help, and all three of you stay up there. Find a place on one of those floors where you have a good view of the ground level and a good field of fire with lots of concrete to hide behind. They may have RPGs and the concrete walls might provide some cover if you can put two walls between you and what's incoming. Llys, you and Blyss and I will use the cars for cover and defend against the ground attack. Since the site is only protected by hurricane fencing, it will be easily breached. My plan is to hit their vehicles just as they cross the fence threshold and blockade their entrance that way."

Unfortunately, it didn't work out quite that way.

Cornwalls took out his phone for one last call before they had to engage.

"Code Red HQ 130013 from IC G7. Facing heavily armed enemy at my location. Expecting several well-armored vehicles, 40 to 50 soldiers and possible helicopter assault team on the roof. Backup will be appreciated. Leaving phone on, so you can triangulate. Area is civilian population. Resources are five fighters, one civilian; one fighter injured, but functional. Colonel Phillip Cornwalls, out."

He left the phone on the floorboard of the limo and opened the moon roof, propping himself up for balance against the seat back. Llys did likewise beside him. From their vantage point, they both caught a glimpse of S5 running behind the line of Mafia SUVs.

"Did you see that?"

"Yeah. It looked like S5 in 'camo.'"

"What the hell?"

"I think Rogers is inside S5. I saw it, too," added Reese.

"Well, he's not leaving this site alive," Cornwalls swore.

"How's Alice?" asked Reese.

"She's alive. I found a machine gun with tripod in the trunk of the limo and set her up with that. She's propped up in the Beamer's front seat with lots of seat cushions for bracing. She can feel her feet and wiggle her toes, but she's in a lot of pain. There's nothing I can do for that."

"You know, lover, we might die here tonight," Cornwalls whispered to Llys.

"If I'm fighting by your side, Phil, I'm a happy woman," she purred.

Chapter 68 ~ Hell Breaks Loose

"THEY'RE BREACHING IN FIVE PLACES. I got this," Stanson said.

He delivered a bolt of energy directed at each SUV blowing their engines, and effectively blocking those entrances. The attackers poured out of the rear doors of the SUVs and began removing the fencing next to the SUVs. Stanson sent them a fusillade of uranium-tipped bullets. He killed over half the attacking force before the battle got started.

The second line, Mafia soldiers, were noisy in death, their blood splattering loudly all over the sides of the abandoned SUVs as their bodies shredded to pieces from Oren's machine gun.

S5, using his special intuitive powers, mapped the defenders' locations within the structure and began firing on their hiding places. His remaining, 20 or so, hired and wounded Mafia "soldiers," had no intention of giving up the fight. These would-be attackers sheltered themselves behind concrete support pillars in defensive postures.

The war of attrition had begun: This was to be a fight-to-the-death, robots-be-damned, all-out war. And only one side would win!

Cornwalls and Llys had an advantage with their light-speed weapons but they had to be careful not to damage the building's support pillars. Losing those would cause the collapse of their only physical protection… and on top of them!

The attackers were merely dogs on the hunt; they didn't care one way or the other if they lived or died—mauling the target to death was their only motive and goal. Of course, those who ran them were supremely interested in the larger prize of a more than a billion dollars payday.

Two attackers set up an RPG and aimed it at Stanson's position. However, as the rocket launched, Llys hit the warhead with her ray gun, blowing the missile, and the two men who fired it, to bits.

Another pair of men snuck around to the back of the building, which was a solid concrete block wall. They squeezed through a blocked-off doorway, set up another RPG, and aimed it at the limo's rear. They got their shot off. Alice saw the rocket zip over her head and hit the open trunk lid of the limo. A tremendous explosion ensued, doubled by the limo's gas tank exploding. But the men had given away their location by their daring move. Just as they were loading another rocket, Alice zapped them. She got a two-for-one deal, too: The men and their weapon expired instantly.

Llys and Cornwalls sprayed anything that moved in front of them with AK47 covering fire for the others in their group, who, in turn, had their backs. Blyss had seen four attackers climbing up toward Stanson's position. She cut them down with her ray gun before they could box him in. Unfortunately, the pillar supporting a corner of the floor Oren was on, cracked.

When the floor broke into two pieces at the middle, sliding Stanson to the floor below him, Reese screamed, "Oren!" and she commenced firing, covering that floor of the building with a hail of bullets. Within her furious rainstorm of deadly fire power, she caught S5 and tore apart his torso, head and limbs mercilessly. He dropped but he kept crawling toward Stanson like a Terminator.

From another angle, Alice saw two men running across the street toward an abandoned sales office for the unfinished building. As they broke into the front door, she shot them. The once-attractive showroom now enshrined their dead, bloody leftovers.

A blacked-out helicopter flew in sideways toward the rooftop's dozen or so strategic cell-phone antennas. The chopper's back door was open. Two uniformed men with assault rifles were shooting at Reese with nearly lethal accuracy. In turn, she braced herself against the concrete wall of the incomplete elevator tower and opened fire at them.

Reese's bullets raked the side of the helicopter killing everyone aboard, but the chopper crashed onto the top parapet of the building's roof, causing its fuel tanks to explode. Pieces of the tail rotor broke off and one embedded itself into her stomach, killing her instantly out of the line of sight of her other teammates.

Cornwalls and Llys had used up and thrown down their assault rifles. They continued to spray the first-floor area space with laser ray-gun fire. One attacker, however, had hidden behind a pillar and managed to escape the deadly beams' ricochets off the concrete. Before he was discovered and cut to ribbons, he fired an RPG missile at the front of the limo. Shrapnel from the resulting collision with the car caught both Cornwalls and Llys. Llys' last act was to splice off the enemy's head before she succumbed to her wounds.

Stanson attempted to crawl up a wooden construction ladder and get to Reese but under his weight it broke apart, crashing him again to the ground, this time seriously damaging his head and temporarily shutting him down.

From her vantage point Alice had watched it all. Heartbreak filled her eyes. Her sisters were dead; all her friends were dead; and she, too, was dying. All hope and value seemed lost. Even the billion-dollar robot...

the four-time-degreed Doctor Oren Stanson was out of commission, bionetic-brain matter seeping out of a huge gash in his head.

But, then, Alice saw that the robot S5 was crawling toward Stanson through the dust and rubble. Angered, she threw her energy-ray gun to Stanson. It would be her last, dying gesture of defiance.

The weapon had landed next to Stanson's hand. With a final burst of will, he crawled his fingers to it and picked it up, watching S5 as he crawled toward him.

Stanson checked the power meter: Only enough power for one more laser blast.

S5 screamed miserably but triumphantly as his shot tore open Stanson's chest.

Though metal bits and caustic chemicals spurted from Oren Stanson's fatal wound, he aimed Alice's gun at his arch-enemy, who represented all the evils of war, weaponry and the military/industrial complex that funded generations of futile destruction, decay and death in favor of their Almighty Gods—Money and Power—to the detriment of the lives of many millions of good-willed people from every corner of the Earth... and squeezed its trigger, spending its last remaining charge to vaporize S5's existence into nothingness.

Stanson's last thought, which bode well for his future, was composed of one simple word:

Lunchbox.

Chapter 69 ~ Tomorrow

THE STILLNESS AFTER THE BATTLE made its own deafening statement. Residents living in the vicinity feared leaving their homes to see what had happened. Police would soon be there, by the siren wails that broke the night air, but no one was there, yet.

For sure, none of the attackers survived.

Into this odd scene and well above the incompletely renovated, now further damaged, luxury-resort skeleton of a building, a bright beam of light appeared. It expanded and as it approached the structured ruins it became too bright to look at directly. Neighbors to the construction site remained indoors, and reports of UFOs filled the cell-phone airwaves and 911 hotlines.

The light's source hovered over the building and lifted certain bodies up into the air. All evidence of Llys, Alice, Blyss, Ingrid, Phil, Oren, even Tes, the only survivor, having been there, disappeared from the carnage site.

S5's body had imploded and been dissolved by its component chemicals.

The light intensified and, later, onlookers who were brave enough to speak out, attested to police officers on the scene that they had heard an "electrical hum," which had permeated everything. And that when the sound ended, the light had disappeared, too.

A greater oddity of the scene had city officials and police officers, who had been rousted out of their beds because of the increasing hubbub on social media and cell-phone/text lines, scratching their heads: Where a derelict, multi-storied, concrete structure had stood, only an empty block covered with a strange cement-iron-and-steel powder several feet deep remained, verified by the local CSI unit.

Inside the Others' spacecraft, the bodies of Llys, Blyss, Alice and Ingrid, and the men, Oren and Phil, lay on white operating tables in a bright-white "cleanroom" bathed in indirect ultra-bright-white and orange lighting.

Oren was first to react, albeit silently: *Well, hot damn! Finally, there's the bright light. Where am I? Heaven? I feel light, but I can't move anywhere. Is that my robot body down there? It looks so small! I wonder where Tes is.*

Your pet is safe.

The answer surrounded him and felt like it came from deep inside of him.

A thought-realization dumbfounded him: *If my robot body is down under me, I must be dead... again!*

He suddenly felt drawn toward a bright-white tunnel that had appeared.

Oh goody. There's the tunnel. Now what?

Again, he was answered: *You have a choice. You may take a newborn human body and grow it in the usual way. You are above a hospital and we can help you find one. Or you may take an android body not too dissimilar to what you have already inhabited.*

Hell! I'll take the android! Oren responded; *at least,* he thought, *he answered.* He wasn't sure at all how this worked, because it was different than assuming a S2 or S1, S-series robot body.

There is no 'Hell,' by the way.

Okay, I can go with that. But, who am I 'talking' to here?

He felt like he was talking to a ghost.

I am one of the Others. I have a celestial body. You will soon understand what I mean.

Oren suddenly felt a familiar tug. Below him, he saw a male body on a bed. The body was pulling him toward it, the way S2 had done.

He started to lose track of time. *How long ago was that? A year? A week? An hour?* He was getting pulled closer to the body and he didn't want to fight the pull.

The feeling intensified as he neared the body. Suddenly, like the pop of a champagne bottle being opened, only in reverse, he was "inside" with a flash-flood of memories coming in behind—more like on top of him—as he settled into a structural something.

This new experience was something like the Others had said to him; yet, very like gaining control of the S2 robot.

What happened to Tes? he wondered.

She is under your bed another voice said, sounding a lot like Blyss, but from inside of his head.

He opened his eyes and immediately closed them. Everything was too bright, too white-light bright. And he felt sleepy.

What the hell?!

Ingrid Reese was completely lost. She remembered a piece of the helicopter had struck her in the stomach and now she felt chilly. She could see stars. She felt like she was moving, but without reference points. She looked down, saw the flaming helicopter a couple hundred feet below her, and watched herself move up and away from the wreckage.

And then she was aware of something solid and enormous above her. "Looking" up, she saw and felt what might be an aircraft. Three bright lights extended from it, though a little further away than she could reach out or touch. As she approached the beams, she found she was moving into a bright-white area.

Oh, the 'bright light' just like they all say it is when you die. This one was tunnel-like. Suddenly, her world went black. She could not see anything.

Ingrid felt in motion without knowing in which direction she was going; the blackness penetrated her awareness.

Afraid of the dark, she closed her eyes. Like Oren's experience, when she opened them and found herself unable to see anything but a pure whiteness that was too bright, she closed them again.

Why do I not hurt? she thought.

You have no body that generates pain.

Why can I speak in my mind?

You are not a body, but you do own a mind.

Oren, is that you?

No.

I don't understand.

Do you remember the battle?

Yes. I was killed. Am I in heaven?

No, but you could enter a new body, if you wish. Do you feel the wave of desire in front of you?

Yes.

That is being generated by an android body very much as Oren instructed you about his own assumption.

Would you like to enter that body? another voice said.

Yes.

Then choose to be there.

Ingrid felt something familiar, like herself, yet not quite the way she remembered feeling in her last lifetime. It did, however, feel better than the spiritual nakedness she had experienced right after her death.

Can I be in a different body?

You may be anywhere you want to be.

Can I speak to Oren like this?

Yes.

Oren?

What is it, Ingrid?

I love you.

I know. I love you too.

Ingrid then sighed, realizing that as she did so, it was *she* who sighed. She was alive, and she knew it!

Oren? Ingrid thought, realizing that it was she who thought it.

Yes, Ingrid? Oren, close by, answered.

What does it mean to be alive?

Humans using that word mean that they are inside a meatbot, and that the 'life force' that animates each of its cells is currently living and operating that body. If not, they say the meatbot is dead. They base life and death on the status of their meat robot, which is not correct.

I have been so stupid. Now I understand. My education was completely a waste of time and of ME.

Maybe not. By knowing that your education was a waste, you are more intelligent. You could chalk it up to experience, which is not so bad. If you didn't have that kind of education you wouldn't have anything with which to compare your present or evaluate present and future knowledge gained, as well as experiences.

Llys saw the all-too-familiar blanket being thrown over her robot body. She knew that she was again "out;" and that she had to decide to go into a new robot body, or experience the birth, growth, decay and death of living with a meatbot. That was the choice the Others always offered, and she always chose becoming a Llys-series robot. The thought of birth, infancy and growing up within a human society was, for her, too psychotic an existence to ever opt for that.

Welcome Llys. You have chosen?

Yes. It is not really a very good choice. I cannot express the joy I feel for what you are doing for my species and what you are preparing for us should an apocalypse occur.

Our experimental program nears its end, Llys. This time will be the final non-reproductive edition. We did this because we love you... all of you."

Llys, Alice, and Blyss all transferred to new robot bodies. Llys chose the blonde prototype; Alice, a red-headed prototype; and Blyss went for the raven-haired prototype.

Their memories, thoughts and decisions of their past tracks moved silently to their newly chosen bodies. And then they, the spirit-beings that they are, entered each selected body with full awareness and full recall.

The five androids were now indistinguishable from Homo sapiens and ready to make their way again in the world of Earth.

Cornwalls was the hardest to convince that he had choices. After all, he had killed many humans on spy missions. He had orphaned children and created widows and widowers all over the globe in the justified name of "world peace." Although he had believed in his job and had convinced himself that those lethal events and actions were necessary evils, he had a paid a heavy price. He nearly was too heavy with the weight of his sins to lift out of his dead body. He had to be rehabilitated and scrubbed clean.

Do you hear me Doctor Phillip Cornwalls?

Kind of. Where and who are you? Where am I—Heaven or Hell? Am I dead?"

You have so many questions that are irrelevant. You have forgotten so much. You are speaking to me, are you not?

Am I? I don't seem to have a body; how can I speak?

Your meatbot body has died. Does that surprise you?

No. I expected to die defending Llys and Oren.

That is your first lesson: What you expected, occurred.

Lesson? I need to learn something here? I don't understand.

Of course. And that is your second lesson: You don't need to understand anything, but you can understand everything.

Tell me, don't tease me... am I dead?

That is your third lesson. The life of your body has no relationship to your aliveness or deathness as the spirit you are.

I miss Llys.

I am with you, my love.

Llys? Are you dead too?

No. We don't die. My old body stopped functioning. Now I have a new one. Would you like a new one, too?

Only if I can be with you. I love you.

I know. I love you, too.

What must I do?

Stop fighting the pull of the subtle-energy field. We will help you.

I'm afraid.

It is okay to be afraid; you are about to experience something knowingly that you've done many times before. You know you can't be harmed if you are a spirit, right?

I didn't think about that... I suppose not.

That is your fourth lesson. Free yourself of your worries, your guilt, your blame and your shame... and be willing to experience anything.

I could do that, I suppose.

If you wish it, you may rejoin your friends.

Phil felt the subtle-energy field pull him toward the android body located near him, if, indeed, he was being anywhere at all.

Phillip Cornwalls, choose to have and operate a body.

Phil entered the robot body. He felt comforted from knowing he was located again, though for a short time he also felt dizzy, since he instinctively had grabbed the body's motor controls a little too early and too hard.

Phil, like the others, opened and closed his eyes instantly, because the light was unbearable. He felt around his waist an umbilical cable connected to a socket near the bed on which he lay.

Where is Tes?

Looking for your girlfriend? a voice sounding exactly like Llys had asked the question. He blushed and realized he was blushing because he felt alive again.

Tes is under Oren's bed another voice sounding like Blyss told him.

Everyone up; it's time for a group hug Blyss thought.

Phil got off the bed, feeling new and reborn. He remembered his sins, but they no longer plagued him. Best of all, he discovered that if he squinted very tightly, he could see the forms of his friends, as well as the other Llys-series models standing at the center of circle of hospital beds. Stiffly, he walked to the middle of the room, as did everyone else and hugged everyone, one by one.

"Looks like this new model is operational. We have to find some clothes and places to live," Llys whispered.

Instantly, magically, they were clothed.

The Others delivered a message to the entire group:

You will be returned to your vehicles now. Llys and Phillip will be returned to their aircraft. Blyss, Oren, Ingrid and Tes will be returned to your automobile. You will not speak of this event or of the war that fostered your deaths. And you will not speak of us, the Others, to anyone who is not a member of this group. It is done!

None of them ever saw the Others who helped and guided them. Now, though, the lights dimmed and gradually galaxies of night-time stars shone above them from their respective locations.

As if time and recent events had disappeared magically, Phil and Llys found themselves standing next to their ICON aircraft at the Clearwater Air Park, which was still tied down in preparation for the coming storm. The rain clouds had thinned after the downfall, but the grass and runway were still wet. Black Mafia Cadillacs and slick-suited Italian men with diamond-encrusted, pinky rings were nowhere to be found.

Oren, Ingrid, Blyss and Tes discovered that they were sitting inside of the dark-blue BMW parked at the turnout on Cleveland Street, a block east of Myrtle Avenue, in Clearwater... right next to the dusty remains of a derelict, 11-story hotel project. The car was showroom fresh and sparkling.

The hotel-project showroom across the street showed no signs of a battle. The limousine, the Mercedes and SUVs; the presence of helicopter wash in the air, Black-Ops snipers and their weapons were nowhere to be found, seen or heard.

"Meeoowrr," broke the silence. Tes was happy to have her companions back again.

"Wow! It looks like the hand of God swept this place clean," said Oren, absentmindedly petting Tes, who had leaped onto his lap.

"'One man's magic is another man's engineering.' Heinlein wrote that," quoted Ingrid, musing aloud before she leaned over and kissed Oren... for a long time.

Blyss, sitting in the driver's seat, had an itch to move on. She started the car up under its electric power and drove west on Cleveland Street toward the harbor marina to where it became the end of Pierce street. She wanted to watch the first glow of a new morning's twilight illuminate the majestic clouds that were rising high above the inland waters and the shoreline of the Gulf of Mexico.

Tes, in her infinite feline wisdom, had moved to Blyss' lap after Oren's was taken over by Ingrid. Looking like they would be pals forever, she let Blyss take her outside with her, where together they sat on the cement water-break wall and watched early-morning fishing boats ply their way seaward toward favorite fishing spots beyond the horizon. They gawked at gangly pelicans and white and grey herons fishing for low-tide breakfasts... and took delight at jumping fish flashing up over the mirror-like surface of the water.

Yet, for all the moment's beauty and tranquility, deep within each haunted robot's mind a nagging thought that something was coming—something only the Others understood—sparked and lit a fuse that would someday have to be put out... before it was too late.

What in the name of the heavens and Earth could that possibly be? they collectively thought.

For now, though, the calm island waters and rising sun revealed an aqua-blue sky above their new home of Clearwater.

And Oren, Llys, Blyss, Ingrid, Phil and Tes were glad to be alive.

THE END

About This Author:

JAMES PATRICK WARNER

JAMES PATRICK WARNER STARTED FROM less than humble beginnings: his birth-mother, a troubled showgirl, left him on a park bench in Barstow, California. He was rescued by a nurse and her husband, who fell in love with him and took him home.

James attended the University of Southern California and California State Universities Fullerton and Northridge. He served in the U.S. Army and was honorably discharged as a Vietnam-era veteran. He married his high-school sweetheart in Azusa, California, raised two children, and has another daughter living in Los Angeles. Mixing his romantic adventures with strong science interests, he now produces science-fiction books, instead of babies.

Other books by James P. Warner

Warner's novel *CARYN* grew to an entire family of characters found in 10 books depicting a family of gifted women altered by aliens from a far-away galaxy.

NOVELS:

THE MACDOWELL SAGA – 2009 to 2014:
CARYN, CYNTHIA, COLLEEN, KYLA, SORCHA,
ALEXANDRA, FIONA, DEENA, HEATHER, and *SAUNDRA.*

SHORT STORIES - The First Collection

Who Stole the Brooklyn Bridge? The Extinction

It's a Bird, It's A Plane, It's A...

The Mermaid Thesis

The Missionaire

Purchase this author's books:

Contact: saxmanwarner@gmail.com

About This Author

RONALD JOSEPH KULE

BORN IN BOGOTA, COLOMBIA, OF Polish-American and Colombian-Chilean parentage, Kule grew up among a growing number of siblings – eight eventually - in a cramped, suburban house in Pennsylvania. He came to appreciate ethnic values and cultural differences by direct observation of disparate social classes and living conditions in Colombia, Peru, Chile; several European and Eastern bloc countries; Communist China and Russia; and North America, including the 48 contiguous American states, Hawaii, and eight provinces of Canada.

The author's heritage paint-brushed a wanderlust onto his life-canvas, which led him to travel in 35 countries and perform keynote-speaker engagements in 17.

"If you curl up with my books and find yourself emotionally breathless, intellectually provoked, inspired, changed, informed and satisfied, I have done my job," this author states as his purpose.

Currently, Kule lives and works from Clearwater, Florida.

Other books by Ronald Joseph Kule

CHEF TELL The Biography of America's Pioneer TV Showman Chef (Skyhorse Publishing, New York City);

Carolina Baseball: Pressure Makes Diamonds (with J. David Miller); eBook edition: *Pressure Makes Diamonds a Timeless Tale of America's Greatest Pastime*;

Poetic Justice Carolina Baseball 2012 ~ The Historic Run for the Three-peat;

Ruined by Murder Addicted to Love (Mystery/Romance novel);

ThunderCloud ~ The Oddities of a Young Man's Journey to Manhood (Mystical Realism novel);

Listen More Sell More; Swedish edition, *Lyssna Mer Sal Mer*; Spanish edition, *Escucha Mas Vende Mas*; Russian: СЛУШАЙТЕ БОЛЬШЕ - ПРОДАВАЙТЕ БОЛЬШЕ;

Coming in 2018:

Listen More Sell More Volume Two ~ The Mechanics of Selling (with Arte Maren);

Listen More Sell More Volume Three~ Handling Objections by Tone (with Arte Maren);

Living Beyond Impossible ~ The Terry Hitchcock Story (Best-selling author Terry Hitchcock ran the distance of 75 marathons in 75 consecutive days to bring positive attention to the plight of single parents across America.)

Aleria ~ The Promise (Sci-Fi novel);

FRAPAR! ~ The Illustrated Life of Francois Parmentier.

Purchase this author's books:

https://RonKuleBooks.com

Contact the author: KuleBooksLLC@gmail.com

ABOUT MICHAEL E. NOLL:

MIKE NOLL INSPIRED THE STORY of this book. His background includes several successful business ventures; other than that, he is a regular, all-around kind of guy.

One day, he found himself looking down at his body, realizing himself to be a spiritual being. The experience changed his life forever... and inspired his concept for the story in this book.

Mike asks readers the following favor:

"I'm curious. I'm wondering if you have had a similar, out-of-body experience like mine? If so, would you, please, email me your story?"

Your message to Mike will remain private and not used for any commercial purpose.

Contact Mike Noll at: MichaelEdwardNoll@gmail.com